WOLVES

by
Cary J. Griffith

Adventure Publications, Inc.
Cambridge, Minnesota

DEDICATION

For Nick and Noah, keepers of the flame

Cover design by Lora Westberg
Book design by Jonathan Norberg
Edited by Brett Ortler

10 9 8 7 6 5 4 3 2 1

Published by Adventure Publications, Inc.
820 Cleveland Street South
Cambridge, MN 55008
1-800-678-7006
www.adventurepublications.net
Printed in the U.S.A.
ISBN: 978-1-59193-436-3

ACKNOWLEDGMENTS

Nearly three decades ago I sped home over lunch to enter into a brief 45-minute writing spell in the rare quiet of my nearby home. The awful pursuits of the Iron County Gun Club fell out on the page. Eventually that story morphed into *Wolves*, early versions of which were read by my sons, Nick and Noah, my wife Anna, Lois and Laurie Sauerbry, and Dorothy Molstad. All provided both encouragement and suggestions and held to the steadfast belief that this novel needed to see the light of day.

Thanks to Nancy Jo Tubbs, chair of the board of directors for the International Wolf Center, who also graciously read an early version of the manuscript and provided valuable feedback. Mary Logue pored over the first third of the book and provided insight, suggestions, guidance and encouragement. It was Mary who first heard about Adventure Publication's foray into publishing regional mysteries and recommended Wolves. Thanks to Pat Dennis for appreciating the book and passing it on.

Much of the wolf biology and related information in this book is based on information gleaned from discussions with wolf experts, and various officials from the Minnesota Department of Natural Resources and the U.S. Fish & Wildlife Service. Also indispensable were site visits to The International Wolf Center in Ely, Minnesota, and the Wildlife Science Center in Forest Lake, Minnesota (where you can learn about and view wolf-dog hybrids, rare red wolves, Mexican gray wolves, coyotes and more).

In Minnesota we are not only blessed with the largest population of wolves in the lower 48, but also a robust public discourse about how best to manage wolves, a conversation that involves hunters, trappers, environmentalists, outdoors enthusiasts, and everyone in between. Our media gives ample coverage to this discourse, and this book has been better informed because of it.

Finally, five percent of the author's proceeds will be divided equally and donated to the Wildlife Science Center and the International Wolf Center.

CHAPTER ONE

JANUARY 27TH, AFTER MIDNIGHT—THE WINTHROP FAMILY FARM
OUTSIDE DEFIANCE, MINNESOTA

The farmhouse lay 12 miles outside Defiance, at least as the common raven flew. The house was a compact two-story peaked square with peeling clapboard sides and a tar paper roof. Behind the house a stand of red pines marked a short ridge and the start of wilderness that stretched all the way to the Canadian border. To the right of the house was a barn where three feeder calves huddled, protected against stray wolves and the deep cold. The field beyond the barn lay blanketed in fresh snow. It was January 27th, one of the coldest nights of the year.

Sheriff Dean Goddard and Deputy Smith Garnes turned into Williston Winthrop's farmhouse drive. The house was lit up like a Chinese lantern. The drive was long and narrow and they pulled up and parked behind two trucks, an SUV and Bill Grebs's patrol car.

"Looks like a damn party," Garnes commented.

"That it does," the sheriff agreed.

When they got out of their cruiser, Bill Grebs opened the farmhouse door, stepping into the cold. He was dressed for the weather, which was well below zero. Thankfully, there was no wind and the nearly full moon was high and clear. While Grebs walked up the plowed path, the sheriff watched him zip up his policeman's jacket, then his down parka over the jacket. He flipped its hood over his short-cropped gray hair. The sheriff guessed Grebs was near retirement; he hoped so, anyway.

"Sheriff," Grebs nodded as he came forward.

"Grebs," the sheriff answered. "You know Smith Garnes?"

"Sure," Grebs said, nodding at Garnes who reached forward and took Bill Grebs's gloved hand.

The three men were tense in the cold. It wasn't just the weather, or the corpse beyond the house and barn. Grebs, Defiance's town cop, had long made an effort to keep Sheriff Dean Goddard out of Defiance's law enforcement affairs, which was fine by the sheriff, who kept the rest of the county to himself. The sheriff's office was ten miles east of Defiance, in Vermilion Falls. There had been times the pissing contest crossed borders, requiring the two men to work together, which neither did well or enjoyed.

From the sheriff's point of view, Bill Grebs had never quite passed the smell test, and that was one reason why small-town cops were best limited to the narrow confines of their own city limits, particularly when it was a Minnesota Iron Range town like Defiance. On more than one occasion the sheriff had received complaints about the graying lawman. But he had been forced to back off when Williston Winthrop interceded. Now that he thought about it, the only thing Sheriff Dean Goddard appreciated past midnight in cold like this was being rid of that son of a bitch Winthrop, if the reports were true. He would no longer have to worry about pulling his punches with Bill Grebs, providing Williston hadn't shared their little secret. What made the sheriff edgy was his doubt that the dead man had kept his word.

From up the road another pair of headlights opened over the rise. The three men watched a red Explorer approach and turn into the drive.

"Coroner," the sheriff observed.

"You have headgear?" Grebs asked Smith Garnes. "It's over a quarter mile to the site."

"I got it," Garnes said.

Sheriff Dean Goddard was much taller and younger than Bill Grebs. He was also a better politician, having just won his second four-year term in a landslide. Smith Garnes was near retirement. Garnes was long and wiry, lined in the face and lean in body. He still moved like a man half his age. He was the best investigative deputy on Goddard's staff, which is why he was the first person the sheriff contacted when the call stirred the sheriff out of bed.

"Sounds like a hunting accident at Williston Winthrop's place," the sheriff said, still coming awake. "Not sure I know how to get there. You remember the place?"

"I remember," Garnes said.

Didn't sound like he'd been sleeping. It was almost 11:00 p.m.

"How bad?" Garnes asked.

"Winthrop's dead," the sheriff managed. "I'll be over in ten minutes."

The second person he contacted was Dr. Susan Wallace, the Coroner.

"Dr. Wallace?" he started.

Belinda, Sheriff Goddard's wife, lay in the adjacent bedroom. Although it was late, she sometimes stayed up reading the Old Testament.

There was a pause. "Hi," Susan said, surprised, still sleepy.

"Business," he said, low. Then he told her about Winthrop's accident.

"You don't think," she started.

"No goddamn idea. Hard for me to believe a man like Winthrop would take his life. Even with the assistant DA breathing down his neck."

"I'll follow," she said.

He couldn't be sure, but he thought she sounded pleased.

Now the Coroner parked her Explorer behind the squad car. The three men waited while Dr. Wallace stepped into the cold and zipped up her heavy down coat, pulling the hood over her head.

"Who's in the house?" the sheriff asked.

"The Club," Grebs said.

"Card club?"

"Gun club, but mostly we play cards."

The sheriff nodded, remembering. "Remind me who's in it," he said.

"There's Hank Gunderson, Hal Young and Angus Moon. We were supposed to play cards tonight, over at Moon's place. Williston hasn't missed a game since I can't remember when. And no one heard squat. So after a couple hands of poker we decided we'd better come have a look. Found his trail in the snow, his shotgun missing. Followed the trail out to the slough," Grebs pointed. There was a well-trodden path turning around the barn, disappearing into dark.

Susan Wallace approached as the men looked toward the trail.

"Doctor," the sheriff nodded.

"Sheriff," she said. "It's a cold night." She looked at Grebs, then Garnes, nodding to each in greeting.

"Yes it is," Smith Garnes agreed. "You dressed for a hike?"

She nodded. "I guess."

"Let me take that," Garnes said, stepping forward to shoulder her bag.

"Thanks," she smiled.

Susan Wallace had been an Iron Range doctor her entire professional career. A year ago Sheriff Dean Goddard recruited her to be the county's coroner, an effort he came to appreciate more than he'd expected. What he saw, when she wasn't bundled up and looking like a marshmallow, was a fit blonde just past forty with a professional demeanor that had taken some time to crack.

Dean Goddard was still surprised by the absence of judgment that had, over the last six months, put him in the doctor's bed (or at least on numerous occasions a bed in the Vermilion Falls hotel), where they had finally decided they had something they could not live without.

The Club decided to remain in Williston's farmhouse. The sheriff asked them not to leave, he'd have some questions. Past midnight they hiked out to the narrow slough. Garnes brought along a sled they could use to return Williston to the doctor's Explorer, for transport to her makeshift morgue. First they would have to make a cursory examination of the scene and take some photographs.

Moonlight helped, though by the time they reached Winthrop's body Sheriff Goddard was ready for a rest. Smith Garnes was barely breathing. Susan was in the same shape as Garnes, proof you could work sixty hours a week and still have time for exercise, providing you had the doctor's energy. The sheriff was comforted by Grebs's heavy exhalations, much like his own. Dean Goddard wasn't Vermilion County's only out-of-shape law officer.

"Should have used the Cats," the sheriff remarked, thinking snow-mobiles would have made hauling the body back a hell of a lot easier.

"It'll be OK," Garnes assured.

The sheriff disagreed.

Grebs explained the scene. Williston was hunting snowshoe hares, approached the slough after last night's snowfall. There'd been a clear, solitary path to the heavy cover of this ravine, trampled over now by Grebs and the others. They'd followed it to the fallen birch, searching for their poker partner. Just this side of the birch Winthrop's body lay with his back in the snow. By now the front of his head was a grisly visage, frosted over and staring faceless into the night sky.

"That's a damn unfortunate accident," Smith Garnes observed.

"Awful," the sheriff agreed.

Susan Wallace, familiar with death, had never seen this kind of massive gunshot trauma. But she didn't look away.

The sheriff took a minute to examine the scene. There was a wide area of trampled snow. The shotgun lay on the ground near the fallen birch, in front of Williston Winthrop's body. Williston wore a heavy camo orange down coat with orange camo coveralls beneath them, both frosted over in the cold. The sheriff recognized the shotgun and coveralls. He'd seen both hanging in Winthrop's office last Sunday, when they'd had their meeting. Before Winthrop told him why he'd asked him to visit, the sheriff had asked about the shotgun, which was oversized. Winthrop told him there were two, nicknamed the Decimators: ten gauges handcrafted near the turn of the century, one of them missing, though the dead man claimed he knew who had it and swore he would get it back. Now the sheriff guessed it didn't matter.

The sheriff didn't like to remember their meeting, where he had to betray one friend to protect another. Now he might not be losing any more sleep over the dead man, providing Williston had kept his secret to himself. Sheriff Goddard had been robbed of revenge, but under the circumstances he was willing to accept it.

"Did you check the pockets?" the sheriff asked.

"We didn't touch anything," Grebs said. "Once we saw there was no point."

The sheriff patted down the pockets, felt the outline of four shotgun shells. He felt inside, pulled them out, put them back. He unzipped the heavy down coat and saw a billfold bulge in the top right coverall pocket. He unbuttoned the pocket, parted it and extracted the billfold. Deputy Garnes held out a plastic bag and the sheriff dropped it in. The rest of his pockets were empty.

The entire scene looked like they'd walked into some kind of deep freeze. It was laid out exactly the way Bill Grebs described it.

Sheriff Goddard used a pair of heavy tongs to lift the shotgun out of the snow. "Damn big gun," he said.

Smith Garnes helped him crack open the double barrel and look inside. One shell fired, one ready. He sniffed around the opening. An acrid burn. The safety was set to off.

"One hell of a gun for snowshoe," the sheriff observed.

"That gun's been in Williston's family for years," Grebs explained. "You get anywhere near a hare, it drops it. The spray's so big only a few pellets usually hit, but it's plenty, coming from a gun like that."

"It's a wonder anything's left of a hare after a shot from a gun like that," said Garnes.

They retrieved what was left of the orange-billed hat from behind Williston's body. Garnes took the necessary photos, the brilliant flash illuminating the carnage and the trampled snow.

"You could have been more careful," the sheriff said, turning to Bill Grebs.

"Sorry about that, sheriff. All of us came out to find him. We were practically on top of him before we saw it. Then we rushed to his side before we knew what happened," Grebs explained. He wasn't looking at Williston Winthrop. He was contrite and solemn, which Dean Goddard understood, given the presumed accidental death of one of Grebs's oldest and closest friends.

There was no reason for Sheriff Goddard to doubt the events, but it was hard not to feel they were peculiar, given what he knew. It wasn't only the hour, the cold and the accident. The sheriff wondered if his disclosure of the subpoena's contents might have precipitated Williston's demise. He wasn't sorry to see the man dead. He was sorry to see the man escape justice. Williston Winthrop, the sheriff guessed, had paid the ultimate price. But assistant DA Jeff Dunlap would be disappointed. Given the markings along the birch bark and Williston's bulk lying frozen in the snow, Dean Goddard wasn't going to push it. It was too damn cold, too late and he was too tired. And when he stared at the body, he could not help but feel some measure of reprieve.

The hat's bill had been torn clean off. Smith Garnes also examined the fallen birch, saw where the barrel slid across the waterproof bark and discharged. "Damn odd," he said.

"What?" the sheriff asked.

"Man like Williston sitting down a gun like that with the safety off."

"Probably saw a hare jump. Wanted to be ready," Grebs suggested, reasonable enough.

"I guess," the sheriff said.

"Can we turn him over?" Susan Wallace asked. "I should at least try and figure out when this happened."

Goddard and Garnes bent over the frozen body. It turned over stiff and awkward in the fallen snow, as though they were flipping a fallen log.

The dead man fell over with a heavy *whump.*

The sheriff checked the back pockets, found three of the dead man's business cards—Williston F. Winthrop, Attorney at Law, with his office address in Defiance. There was nothing else on them. No writing. Nothing. The sheriff added them to the bag with the wallet.

Susan Wallace worked a long thermometer needle out of her bag. She tried to insert it through his lower back, trying to probe an internal organ so she could get a temperature reading. She could use the dead man's internal body temperature to determine the approximate time of death. But the body was already frozen.

"Can't get it in," she said.

"Seem reasonable?" the sheriff asked.

"In this cold?" she said. "Sounds like the body's been here for more than five hours. It's like a deep freeze out here. That'd be enough time."

The sheriff looked back to the body. "Alright. Let's get him in that bag and put it on the sled."

The scene was clear enough. By the time they returned to the farmhouse it was just after 2:00 a.m. When they approached they noticed a Datsun pickup added to the covey of cars.

"The Gazette," Garnes said.

"That Diane's truck?"

"Looks like it," Garnes observed.

Diane Talbott, the *Vermilion Falls Gazette* reporter, was already inside the farmhouse interviewing the other members of the Club. She'd just about finished when the sheriff entered the house.

"Diane," he nodded.

"Hi, Dean."

"How'd you find out?"

"Couldn't sleep and I was out. Saw your patrol car. Then I saw Dr. Wallace's car. Looked official. Just a hunch," she said.

Over the last few months there had been too many hunches, the sheriff thought. He suspected Diane was monitoring their official radio channel. Scanning wasn't illegal, but if the office knew she was scanning they'd probably return to a stricter adherence to the use of codes, or start scrambling their signal. "You could get in trouble, following me around."

"Sorry, sheriff. Just couldn't sleep." She managed a weak smile that told Dean Goddard he'd have to keep an eye out for Diane.

Diane Talbott was one of those women Dean's father described as 'built like a brick icehouse,' which meant she was strong, attractive, had some style and a body that easily fired the imagination. For someone around 50 who had spent most of her adult life on the Range, she was still surprisingly unaffiliated, which was to say without a man. Not that there weren't plenty who had tried. Some said she'd been known to party when she was young. But now she spent most of her time at her job, either for the *Gazette* or writing freelance, mostly covering wilderness issues.

"OK if I take some notes?" she asked.

The sheriff thought about it. "Williston have a next of kin?" he asked Bill Grebs.

"No one," Grebs said. "There was a son, some years back. Disappeared. And you know Miriam died two years ago. Just us," he added, indicating the four Club members in the room.

"Alright," the sheriff said, turning toward Diane.

The sheriff spent the next ten minutes taking the Club members' statements. Hal Young was the local insurance agent. He was the same height as Angus Moon and Bill Grebs but very different in stature and temperament. Bill Grebs was mean, but savvy enough to hide it. Angus Moon was like a wolverine, wild as the woods he hunted, with a temper that could turn on a dime, the few times the sheriff had crossed him. Hal Young was a businessman, and other than the Iron County Gun Club, about as four-square as a white cardboard box. Hank Gunderson was the dead man's size, owned the Ford dealership in Defiance. The four Gun Club members filled in the details—solemn, maybe a little nervous, the sheriff figured, because their lifetime friend had just met his grisly end, maybe from a self-inflicted gunshot wound, though none of them betrayed that suspicion. Regardless, incidents like this one were sober reminders of one's own mortality.

They'd assembled for poker. When Williston didn't show, they came looking. And found him. They were quiet and grave in the poorly lit front room of Williston's farmhouse. They looked tired.

While the sheriff spoke with the men, Grebs and Smith Garnes loaded Winthrop's body into the doctor's Explorer. Once he was finished in the house, the sheriff gave Diane the details she'd need.

"Hunting accident," he said. "Massive head trauma. I'm sure you'll say it using more words, but that's the sum of it."

Diane nodded. "Thanks, sheriff."

He nodded and turned away.

Once outside, Dean Goddard approached the doctor's car.

"I can drive with you to the office; help you unload him and get him squared away, providing you can give me a lift home."

"No problem, sheriff."

He thought maybe she sounded a little too eager, if anyone was listening. "Smith," Goddard turned to his deputy. "Can you take the squad car and follow us over? You'll have to help me with this cargo, at least to unload it. Then you can take the cruiser home and the doctor'll give me a lift."

Garnes nodded. "See you there."

"Get your truck out of the road, Diane. Go home and get some sleep."

But she was already too preoccupied to think about sleep, contemplating the story she was about to write. The sheriff knew he'd be reading about Williston Winthrop's accident by morning.

They got into their cars and started their engines in the cold. Then they turned toward Vermilion Falls.

For the first mile the sheriff and coroner rode in silence, following Diane's truck. Deputy Garnes followed them in the squad car.

"That was a horrible accident," Susan Wallace finally observed, careful not to turn her head. "But it could uncomplicate things."

The sheriff exhaled as though trapped air were being let out of a bag. "Could," he said tersely, but clearly pleased.

"You think he mentioned it to anyone? Shared that video?"

"No way to know," he remarked, eyes careful on the narrow lane in front of him. They were traveling over back roads. Williston Winthrop's farmhouse was in one of the most remote areas of the county. On either side dense wilderness closed in on the narrow lane.

"What are we going to do, Dean?"

"You're not going to do anything. I'm going to find that video." He paused, thinking. "If I know Winthrop it's someplace safe. I'd bet his office or the farmhouse. But it's not going to be easy finding it."

"What about his house in Defiance? Miriam's old place?"

"Could be," Dean guessed. They drove another half mile in silence.

"I guess I'm going to have to sleep on it," he said, his hands intent on the wheel of the doctor's jeep.

The doctor stared ahead, peering to where the edge of headlights disappeared in darkness. Dean Goddard thought she was pondering the location of Winthrop's evidence when he felt her hand inch over and graze his right thigh.

He could feel the heat of it through his jeans.

"Maybe we should sleep on it together."

CHAPTER TWO

JANUARY 27TH—U.S. FISH & WILDLIFE, DENVER FEDERAL BUILDING

By the time Sam Rivers arrived at U.S. Fish & Wildlife, Judy Rutgers's message was being broadcast to a half dozen co-workers needing a Monday morning chuckle. Judy was a sheep rancher who lived over two hours southeast of Denver, Colorado.

"This is Judy Rutgers," she blurted. "Last night one of my ewes was taken. A wolf! I got all the proof you'll need. And I'm sitting here with my rifle, hoping the cocksucker shows its ugly head. When it does, I'll be blowing it off."

There was a pause, during which Maureen, the office assistant, said, "Wait. She's not finished."

Sam's co-workers paused over Maureen's speakerphone.

"I'll give you till sundown to get out here and look, Rivers. Then I'm settin' traps." The line went dead.

"Sundown!" Maureen repeated, parroting Judy's rasp. The office broke into mild laughter.

Sam Rivers's appearance caused his co-workers to fade back to their desks.

"Morning, Sam," Maureen nodded.

"Maureen," he nodded back.

His sallow-rimmed eyes told her all she needed to know about his weekend. She'd keep it to business, but like the rest of the staff she was waiting for an end to Rivers's depression. Or maybe for his transfer back to national field operations. "Judy Rutgers has issues again."

"I heard."

"What should I tell her?"

"Tell her I'll be out after noon. First I need to talk with Kay Magdalen, then finish some paperwork." He had received another troubling email he hoped Kay could help him track down.

"Should I see if Kay's in?"

"Her Outback's in the lot."

Maureen's ears tracked gossip like a pair of Doppler radar dishes, and she had a mouth like satellite radio, which is why Sam never shared anything with her. Maureen might have been the one to overhear his business about Sam's dog, Charlie.

"That's two Kay Magdalen visits in less than a week," she said. "You sure you feel OK?"

Maureen was fishing. He almost never visited his old supervisor. "Clarence is a Rockies fan and I have a lead on some tickets," he lied. When she didn't recognize the name he added, "Clarence is Kay's husband. He and I go way back."

Truth is he and Kay Magdalen had worked together for more than a decade—at least when he was a national field agent—and he had never met Clarence.

Maureen nodded. "Oh. OK. I'll let Judy know you'll be there this afternoon."

"Thanks, Maureen." Then he turned and disappeared into his cubicle.

Charged with protecting and managing the nation's wildlife, the USFW had taken Sam Rivers, one of its best national field agents, into places no sane person would want to go. That is until a year ago, when his failing marriage and then his failing best friend—his dog Charlie— prompted him to step down from the national spotlight to take a job in local investigations.

Five years earlier the *Denver Post* ran a Sunday feature on his work at the USFW, "Saving Endangered Species One Animal at a Time." The article recounted one of his most recent cases. Rare Florida deer were being annihilated from a section of the Florida Keys. Their total disappearance from an area they'd previously inhabited was suspicious. Rivers investigated, and after some digging and a few lucky breaks he discovered a small group of developers who believed concern for the Key deer, which the USFW estimated to number around 800 animals, was negatively impacting their development plans. They'd hired a south Florida hunter to rid the proposed development site of any trace of the small, endangered deer. And they would have succeeded, if the hunter hadn't begun selling Key deer skins, hooves, horns and venison on the black market.

The article called Sam Rivers 'the predator's predator,' a moniker that stuck, at least within his office and the USFW. There was a picture of his 6′ 2″ frame standing in front of the South Florida bulldozer he had singlehandedly idled. His square shoulders and 195 pounds looked small in front of the huge shovel blade. But his greasy black hair, disheveled undercover clothes, and four days' worth of facial hair made him look like the swamp rats he'd hunted. The article recounted how before it was all over, Sam had to fight his way out of a backwoods bar.

Maggie had been proud of the *Denver Post's* coverage. She cut out the photo and taped it to their fridge.

Kay Magdalen was as surprised to see him as he was to be there. "You're coming back," she opined.

"Not exactly. Still thinking about it."

Kay Magdalen was heading up the new Interagency Task Force, and she wanted Sam Rivers back on her team. Kay had the demeanor of a truck driver, the appearance of a fullback, and could bull her way through USFW law enforcement bureaucracy unlike anyone he had ever seen, which was a rare quality and just one of the reasons Sam liked her.

"It would do you nothing but good, Rivers."

"I suspect you're right. I just need a little more time."

He reached into his back pocket and pulled out a folded piece of paper, passed it across her desk. "Got another one of these last Friday."

Kay opened it. Another message from canislupustruth@yahoo.com. This one was short. "Soon," it said.

"Soon what?" she asked.

"Good question."

Sam had been receiving these messages for the last two years, spread out at least a month apart. They'd started after his mother died. The first he'd almost mistaken for junk mail. He still remembered it, because it was brief and personal. "Clayton?" it asked, in the subject line. The text of the message repeated the question using his full birth name: "Clayton Evan Winthrop?" That was all.

No one had called him Clayton Winthrop in years. He treated it the way he treated everything else from his childhood; he highlighted the message, and pressed Delete. But the email address was interesting. *Canis lupus*, the scientific name for the *gray wolf.*

And then a few days later he'd received a second message. This one contained a single phrase in the Subject line: "Seen this?" There was an attachment with the email. It was a PDF copy of his mother's will. It left everything to the old man. There was the house, car, the proceeds from a large life insurance policy, and the money Sam's mother had managed to save, a little over $179,000 and change. Sam was surprised, both by his absence from her will and the size of her estate, which he'd always assumed would be meager.

He'd spoken with his mother just weeks before her end. He was comfortable with their parting. Sam always remembered her as an old-school wife. For years she had been largely estranged from the old man, living in separate residences. But there had never been talk of divorce. There was logic to her leaving everything to Williston. But Sam was still surprised.

Over the last two decades he and his mother had only seen each other a handful of times. But the absence of visits hadn't diminished their connection, such as it was. Though she'd been unable to stand up to Williston Winthrop, Sam considered his mother a positive influence in his life. He assumed he would be a partial beneficiary in her will, though they'd never discussed it. He wondered who had sent the will, and why. He immediately considered the old man, but then excluded him. Coy wasn't the old man's way. There was no good reason for the old man to be secretive *or* to send him a copy of the will. Why invite trouble, should Sam want to contest it?

Twenty years earlier Sam had fled west, changed his name, and disappeared. It had taken more than a year to reach back to his mom. And even then it was only by phone. Eventually he shared his new name and whereabouts, but made it clear she should keep it in confidence.

He had not seen or spoken to Williston F. Winthrop since the day Sam had wreaked havoc in the heart of their farmhouse, letting the old man know how he felt about the Winthrop family heritage. Then he fled. But not before stealing one of the old man's precious Decimators.

There had been other cryptic messages. After wondering about it, he recovered the first email from his 'deleted' folder. Then, he'd created an electronic folder—named Defiance, the name of the closest town to his childhood home—and dragged the messages into it one by one over the intervening months, where they remained unanswered.

This message, like all the others, was typically cryptic. He printed off a copy to share with Kay. He wanted her to find out whatever she could about the sender. She had solid contacts in the USFW information technology group and he didn't want to draw a lot of attention to it. He just wanted to know about canislupustruth@yahoo.com. Where did he/she live? Where did the message come from?

"Sorry, Rivers," Kay said. "Another bizarre message isn't going to change anything. I'm sure it's annoying, but until something more specific happens, like maybe a threat, there's nothing IT can do about it."

She told him what he'd expected. Yahoo guarded the privacy of its members like Fort Knox gold. Truth was, given the ease with which Yahoo email accounts were set up, a person could easily register an email using a bogus name and address.

"IT tells me the only thing that they *might* be able to tell you," Kay added, "would be the identity of the computer from which it was sent. But that would take some work, backtracking through code, IP addresses, proxy servers and plenty of email traffic, whatever that means. Nothing they'd even think about without a warrant."

"I thought these people were your friends?"

"Colleagues, Rivers. We don't have friends. I know them well enough. And if I wanted to push it, I could probably get them to look into it without a warrant, see what they could find out. But this is personal," Kay said. "You know how the Service is about using resources for personal stuff."

Her answer was bullshit and they both knew it. The flash of a badge enabled an agent to cut to the head of a line or get some free donuts and coffee, and Sam had seen it used countless times, had occasionally used it himself. Kay Magdalen knew what he was thinking.

"The last time I checked," she said, "personal annoyance wasn't enough for a judge to grant a warrant."

She was using it. If he told her he was coming back to national field ops to be part of her Interagency Task Force, she might spend a little of her IT capital to help him. She was dangling a carrot.

"What's keeping you from coming back?" she asked.

"Not ready."

She considered him for a long few seconds. "You know what you need?"

"No idea."

"You need to take some time off. Maybe head over to Las Vegas. It's probably been a while since you've had your . . ." she paused, wondering how to say it. "Your pipes cleaned out. You should take some time. You've got plenty of vacation built up. I've seen your file. If you don't take it before the end of the year you'll lose some of it."

"Are you telling me I should buy a whore?"

She looked away, a little miffed by his crass characterization. "I think it's more of a rental fee. Personally, I find it morally repugnant. But men feel different about these things."

Truth was, his appetite for sex left with Maggie. He knew it would return. But hiring a hooker was about as far from his mind as vacationing in Cancun.

"I think I'll pass."

"Just saying," she said, but left it there. Then she handed the paper back.

Sam returned it to his back pocket and stood up. "If I came back on the team, would you use your IT contacts to find out what you could about canislupustruth?"

Kay looked at him, considering. "Who knows? Teams are funny things. If a team member is going through a rough spot and it impacts the organization, then from my perspective it makes sense to do whatever you can to help out."

Sam thought about pushing it, but he had his answer. She could get IT to look into it if she wanted, but until he decided to come back and work for her she wasn't going to expend the capital to get it done. He turned to leave, and then remembered.

"If you happen to run into Maureen down in local investigations and she asks, Clarence and I are old friends and I got him tickets to the Rockies game this coming Saturday," Sam said.

"Rockies? Clarence has never been to a baseball game in his life. You've never even met him."

"I know. And I'm not taking it personally."

She grinned. "Whatever, Rivers. I'll cover for you. Just get your head on straight. We can't wait forever."

Sam Rivers didn't get out of the Denver Federal Building until after 1:00. He contemplated skipping lunch, knowing Judy was waiting by her rear picture window with her finger on that trigger. Her ranch was one hundred fifty miles southeast, a two and a half hour drive. If he pushed it he could be there before 3:30 p.m. But it had been a very long night and his head still felt muddled from last night's wine. The remnants of four glasses of dry red were giving him heartburn and a headache. He didn't relish facing the big woman on an empty stomach.

There were two things that could fix a mild hangover.

Hair of the dog that bit ya', was a phrase that came to mind.

Sam Rivers had spent twenty years putting the old man behind him. Williston Winthrop's voice rising like a cork was, like Sam's drinking, a testament to the pain of recent days. It was becoming increasingly hard to remember any good days.

It had been less than two weeks since Kay Magdalen told him his ex-wife was dating Salazar, a USFW accountant Sam barely knew. And then, almost as though Providence *wanted* to increase Sam's suffering, Charlie's cancer finally took him. Sam Rivers suspected the end of this recent struggling chapter was up on Green Mountain, where in the middle of the night he had taken Charlie's body and buried it in their special place. It was in clear violation of Green Mountain's rules and regulations, but Sam Rivers knew it was the right thing to do. Besides, it was a minor transgression, and Charlie—who had always disregarded the Mountain's leash law, running pell-mell over its slopes— would have liked it.

Sam's weekend gave him a bad case of whiplash, but he felt pretty certain the worst of his recent past was just about over.

He aimed his jeep toward the Pepper Jack's truck stop in Erie. It was on the way and he could set his cruise control high enough to make time. The typical eastern Colorado sunshine didn't do much to ease his headache, but his dark glasses helped.

About the only thing that had changed in his twenty years was his life's direction. At least he no longer felt rudderless. Becoming a Special Agent for U.S. Fish & Wildlife was, now that he considered recent events, one of the most fortunate turns in a life that had been plagued with bizarre missteps and switchbacks.

After a half hour he pulled into Pepper Jack's and put his jeep in park. Though he had little taste for it, experience told him that black coffee and eggs smothered in ketchup and hot sauce and choked down with a piece of dry toast was a better antidote than the old man's whiskey. He walked in, ordered his potion and started to eat.

For a while he had considered his courtship and marriage to Maggie the single most positive event in his life. But she had tried to surface things he didn't want to think about. In the end, their relationship's demise left him feeling more alone than ever. Loneliness, when you are young and ignorant, is expected, part of the landscape. But after you have fallen in love and experienced a partner's companionship and then lost it, that kind of loneliness is on a different plateau altogether.

He ate just enough to assuage the dull throb in his head. Then he paid, walked out to his jeep, got in, and pulled back onto the interstate, setting his cruise control and trying to think about nothing.

CHAPTER THREE

JANUARY 27ᵀᴴ—THE CABIN IN SKINWALKER'S BOG

The dead man walked out of the cabin and paused, listening for Angus Moon's approach. In his right hand he held a .45 caliber pistol. The first thing he noticed was the cold, probably twenty below in the shadow of these trees. He listened carefully, but heard nothing. Maybe a little wind through the pine tops, but you could never tell, they were bunched so tightly here, the cabin hidden in their midst.

The man knew he would hear Angus Moon's approach along the swamp edge. Now he hustled down the path, searching for a place to hide.

Almost 24 hours earlier the man snowshoed across Skinwalker's Bog. It was a three-mile hike and unless you knew where you were going and how to get there, the trip would probably be your last, in this kind of cold. He had reached the cabin after dark, let himself in, shook out the cold and fired up the potbellied stove. Then he switched on the CB radio and scanner, but heard nothing until the call to dispatch around midnight, from the sheriff's cruiser. There had been two calls; one by the sheriff telling dispatch where he was headed and why, and one on the way back, from Smith Garnes, telling the office they were finished and returning. That was around 2:00 a.m. but the man only half heard it. By then he was dead drunk, celebrating with three-quarters of a fifth of rye.

Damn good thing Angus was bringing more supplies, he thought.

Now he stepped carefully over yesterday's tracks, weaving through the thick wood for a little more than a hundred feet until he stopped again to listen. Nothing. Just wind, definite at the tree edge. He could see the intense afternoon sunlight through the perimeter's boughs. He stepped forward, using the pistol's barrel to part the branches, and peered across the frozen swamp.

No sign of him . . . yet. He leaned back, concealing himself, and waited. It was a full minute before he remembered to cock his weapon. If he waited until Angus passed through the tree edge, the wary woodsman would hear it and be warned. He pulled back the trigger until it clicked and held. Then he listened again, but it was still quiet. Now he just tried to remain still.

The discovery of the vagrant James T. "Jimbo" Beauregard happened less than a week ago. Jimbo's entrance triggered a series of events that happened so quickly the dead man's head still spun. Since then, he'd been looking forward to spending some time alone at the Club's cabin.

The cabin was in the heart of a remote tract of wilderness the Ojibway had always avoided, probably because it was so covered over by swamp, bush and mosquitoes that it was no place to hunt. Even deer had trouble navigating the place. The Iron County Gun Club managed to build a secret, remote cabin in the center of it. And to keep it secret the Club members promoted the name Skinwalker's Bog, reporting that the natives stayed out of it because within its ten-mile-square tract of swamp, strange things occurred. Never mind that Skinwalker was actually a Navajo myth from the American Southwest. The Club thought 'Skinwalker' sounded a whole lot better than Wendigo, the Ojibway boogieman. So they appropriated the name for their own purposes, and it stuck.

In the summer it was impassable. In the winter, not much better.

But by the early afternoon the man started feeling stir-crazy. The morning hadn't been a complete waste. He'd spent some serious time contemplating future moves, and he'd come up with something so compelling and perfect it was an inspiration, in keeping with their latest spate of good fortune. No one had seen Jimbo coming. He'd stumbled into Defiance, broke, freezing and ready to do anything for a meal and a warm bed. Bill Grebs took one look at him and recognized the opportunity.

But no one would see this opportunity. It would take some work getting the others to recognize it. What he needed was to make one of them believe it was their idea. And he thought he had figured out how.

Now he stood hidden at the tree edge, his pistol raised and ready, waiting for Angus Moon. Finally he heard movement across the snow.

Angus Moon snowshoed through the brittle sunlight, skirting a rare stretch of open swamp, searching among the ancient stumps for the dark entrance where the path turned off into tree-covered shadows. Angus didn't like hiking into the Bog in the middle of daylight. He preferred coming late in the day, or under cover of darkness.

The Club members were careful about approaching the cabin in Skinwalker's Bog. Starting in the full light of a clear afternoon, even though the temperature had only climbed to a -15, was risky. Someone might see where Angus had turned off the highway onto an old logging road. If they followed the tracks they'd find his truck more than a quarter mile up the path, concealed in a stand of black spruce. But they'd have to hike it, Angus thought, since he was always careful about relocking the heavy gauge chain that stretched across the logging road entrance, padlocked at one end. Someone'd need a bolt cutter to take it down, Angus knew, which is why he wasn't too worried about it.

He was more irritated about Williston's goddamn calves. Now that Williston was gone, the chore of tending his livestock fell on Angus Moon. He had to check on them twice a day. This morning he'd fed them and made sure the propane tank heater was still on and operational. The arctic wind sometimes blew it out and froze the tank solid. He would have to check on it later, on his way back, and Angus Moon didn't much care for the extra labor. Tending to his own dogs was about as much work as the old woodsman wanted.

Few people knew it, but Angus Moon's most ambitious venture involved hybridized wolf-dogs. He'd brought a powerful Arctic wolf down from Canada. The wolf killed two malamute bitches before he took one for a mate.

In some states, breeding wolf-dog hybrids was illegal. But in Minnesota breeding and selling them was a legitimate business, though there were few who pursued it, because wolf-dog hybrids could be problematic pets, if not outright dangerous. Angus didn't care. He charged the out-of-state breeders $1,500 a mutt but made sure the transaction was confidential. He was careful about his work and happy for the supplement to his meager income. But he chafed against even the minimal work his breeding operation required. Now, for instance, he would have to drop off supplies, have a drink, and then gather himself for the hike out. Calves and dogs, they were pissing him off.

He was familiar enough with the cabin path to snowshoe without thinking. His short, bandy legs knew the way. Besides, he was damn close and getting thirsty. Whiskey'd take the edge off. Now he pushed through a swale of pine boughs, pausing just beyond its edge to let his eyes grow accustomed to the shadows.

When the waiting man heard Angus approaching, he positioned himself carefully amid the tree boughs. He raised the gun in both hands, holding it straight out in front of him, waiting and ready. Angus came through the tree edge and stopped.

The man adjusted the pistol's aim so that it focused on the center of Angus Moon's hood-covered head, less than three feet away. Then he pulled the trigger.

The hollow metal ping made Angus Moon jump like a snowshoe hare startled by a lynx. He jerked, grunting, and then turned so see Williston Winthrop aiming the pistol at his head.

"You're a dead man, Angus Moon," Williston said, and then laughed.

"You could get killed, pullin' a stunt like that!"

The pistol dropped to Williston's side. "I'm already dead," he said.

For half a second Angus Moon's eyes flashed.

Williston saw it, and added, "Take it easy, Angus. A dead man can't be too careful. Besides, I was getting bored and needed a little fun."

Moon looked away, still pissed.

"Let's go get a drink," Williston said.

Once inside the cabin Williston poured them both a full tumbler of cheap rye. They drank it off in one long swallow and Williston refilled their glasses.

"So how'd it go?" Williston asked. He could see the whiskey was working.

"The paper's out," Angus finally said. "Already got a story."

"The paper's already covered it?"

"That Talbott bitch was at the farmhouse last night, askin' questions."

"With the sheriff?"

"Came after, when the sheriff was out lookin' at the body."

"That's interesting."

"Talbott must've seen the patrol car," Angus guessed.

"Maybe. But that's good. We're ahead of schedule."

Angus pulled the *Vermilion Falls Gazette* out of his bedraggled pack, followed by three cans of chili and two more bottles of whiskey. Angus got settled and had another good long drink, feeling the pleasant burn.

"Who all checked on the body?"

"The sheriff, Grebs, Smith Garnes and Doc Wallace."

"Sounds like a goddamn convention."

"Grebs said everything went off like clockwork."

"Did they take the Decimator?"

"Took the shotgun back to the morgue with Jimbo's body."

Less than a week earlier Bill Grebs found Jimbo holed up in the abandoned rail station on the outskirts of Defiance. He was a bum, on his way north to work in his sister's café, somewhere up in Canada. Grebs liked rolling bums, but the first thing he noticed about Jimbo was his look; except for the face, he could have passed as Williston Winthrop's twin. The face was definitely different, but the Club finally figured out how to fix it, and they did. Angus Moon'd pulled the Decimator's trigger, removing the front of Jimbo's skull.

"You make sure and get the Decimator back," Williston said.

"Course," Angus said.

"Did they check the pockets?"

"Grebs said so. Took your wallet and some business cards from a back pocket."

"Perfect. I won't be needing that license anymore. Or the cards," Williston laughed. Then he picked up the paper. It was column 1, front-page news on the *Gazette*.

LOCAL ATTORNEY DIES IN HUNTING ACCIDENT
Diane Talbott
The Vermilion Falls Gazette, Jan. 27

VERMILION FALLS - Williston Francis Winthrop, 62, of Rural Route 3, died Monday evening of a single gunshot wound to the head, the victim of an apparent hunting accident. Winthrop was hunting alone on his rural acreage when he leaned his shotgun against a fallen tree. Straddling the tree to step over it, the shotgun slid down the log and discharged.

The shooting was reported to the Sheriff's office at approximately 11:00 p.m. Sunday by friends of the deceased. The friends, all members of Williston Winthrop's Gun Club, went searching for the late attorney when he failed to appear for their weekly card game.

Vermilion County Sheriff Dean Goddard and coroner Dr. Susan Wallace said the full coroner's report would be released pending further investigation and consultation with the County Attorney's office.

Winthrop was a well-known Iron Range attorney and hunting rights advocate. One of his recent high-profile efforts was ardent opposition to Minnesota's *Wolf Management Plan*. In several public comment hearings Winthrop argued that wolves had returned to the state in sufficient numbers to have them de-listed from the Endangered Species Act. He noted that wolf depredation of livestock and pets was on the rise, and he believed it was only a matter of time before wolves attacked a human. His most controversial recommendation was to re-instate wolf bounties, a population control method not used in the state since 1965. His suggestion was never seriously considered.

Williston Winthrop was preceded in death by his wife, Miriam Winthrop, also of Defiance. He is survived by a son. Funeral services 3:00 p.m., February 1, Defiance Lutheran Church. Interment 4:00 p.m., Defiance Cemetery.

He smiled when he reached the end. "Goddamn," Williston said. "I'd say she just about nailed it. Except for the part about my suggestion to return to wolf bounties."

Angus had read the article, but quickly, just to make sure there was nothing worrisome. "What?" he asked.

"She got the stuff about being opposed to that goddamn *Wolf Management Plan* about right. But she says here my 'suggestion to reinstate wolf bounties was never seriously considered.'" Williston scoffed, smacking the paper with his hand. "There are plenty who think it's a good idea. And if I'd lived long enough I would have seen it through."

"Damn straight," Angus agreed.

"I forgot Talbott knew the boy," Williston said.

"We wondered about it."

"Nothing to wonder about. The kid doesn't matter. He won't do anything. It's been 20 years. Even if he found out about it and returned, there wouldn't be a goddamn thing he could do. Grebs'd take care of it."

The two men sat for a while, sipping whiskey, talking about plans.

"We still have scores to settle," Williston finally said.

Angus Moon grunted, already thinking about his hike out. The afternoon light was starting to settle, and those goddamn calves would be waiting for more feed.

"You tend the calves?" Williston enquired, knowing the woodsman hated the job.

"Course," Moon said, displeased.

"They still fat 'n happy?"

"Big," Moon said. "Eat too much. Sooner we sell 'em the better."

"They're not quite ready."

In years past Williston sold off the animals and used the butchering proceeds to keep the Club in beef. But this year was going to be different.

"It'll be a while," he answered, reminding the woodsman his labors would not end soon. "Meanwhile you'll need to check on 'em. Twice a day."

"I know it," Angus snapped.

"Morning and night," Williston said. "This wind could blow out that propane tank heater. And now that they're just about ready, I don't want wolves coming in to take them."

"Wolves?" Angus didn't like the idea of two daily trips to Winthrop's farm. Given the drive and the added chores it was *too damn much*. But Angus Moon knew wolves, and they'd never enter a barn.

"Wolves," Williston mused. "Now that no one's around those vermin might take advantage. Might see opportunity."

"No wolves gettin' into a barn."

"Just because they haven't done it yet doesn't mean they won't. You sound like the DNR. Wolves don't give a rat's ass where their meal comes from. If it's easy and available and there's nothing to stop them, they'll take it. They're vile opportunists."

"You know damn well I'm no friend of the DNR. But Williston, wolves don't go into barns and take cows. Just don't happen."

"Yet," Winthrop returned. "If wolves came in and took 'em, one thing's for damn sure. It'd shake up the DNR. And U.S. Fish & Wildlife. Teach 'em these vermin are getting out of control."

"Like to see that."

Winthrop paused. "What if there was a way to lure some in and set 'em loose? We'd teach every tree-hugger in the state these wolves are hell-bent on one thing: destruction." He waited for the woodsman to catch on.

"Wolves don't lure. Not into a barn."

"It's only a matter of time."

Williston let Angus think about it. It didn't take long.

"We should let my dogs have at 'em," Angus said.

And *that* was Williston's plan, because it made sense on so many levels. Angus's hybrids looked and acted enough like wolves to be the real thing. And Williston had witnessed the wolf-dogs' work, tracking down wounded deer and keeping them penned until Angus gave the signal. They were accomplished killers.

He waited long enough to let Angus believe the inspiration was born of Angus's own tongue.

"What?" Winthrop asked.

"You want 'em dead? My dogs'd take care of 'em. Fifteen minutes." Angus was always bragging about his animals, and with good reason.

"Who knows about your hybrids?"

"Whaddya' mean?"

"Who knows you have them? Raise them? Sell them? Anybody local?"

"Out-of-state breeders. Nobody local. Could cause problems. I don't want anyone local bitching to the authorities, or returning one of the mutts."

"Angus. I think you're onto something." And then he explained the myriad reasons it made sense. For starters, it would eliminate Angus's need for twice-a-day tending. When they finally sold the three cattle they would have to truck them to market. Trucking three head was expensive. But in the event a wolf pack gained entrance to the barn and slaughtered his livestock, his beneficiaries were entitled to full market value. The slaughter would be paid for by the Minnesota Department of Agriculture. A DNR conservation officer would investigate, but Williston knew there would be none of the usual absence of evidence. The barn would keep the slaughter confined. The barn floor would be bloody with the remnants.

And having the government pay for the slaughter of Williston's livestock had a beautiful logic the Club members would understand. The DNR, the Department of Agriculture, and U.S. Fish & Wildlife Service were three governmental entities Williston had spent his life battling. Now they would unknowingly assist the Club in some recreation. The slaughter would support his assertion about the menace of the growing packs, and once the kill was verified, the state would pay for it. And for the Club, the slaughter of his calves would be a spectacle reminiscent of the Christians and the lions, a wagering opportunity that could not be denied.

"By God, Williston, I believe you're onto something."

"I'm onto something?! It was you who thought of it, my friend. God-damn it," he said, excited by the prospect. "What do you think is the next best step?"

Angus considered. "I know damn well what we gotta do," Angus said. He stood up and moved over to pull his coat off the nearby peg.

"What?" Williston said.

"I'm headin' back right now. First I'll make sure those fatlings are fed and watered. Then I'll get back to my place. And nail every one of those dogs into their houses. Give them nothin' but water for a couple days. Get them good and hungry."

"That's it!" Williston said.

"Goddamn right," Angus agreed. He finished suiting up.

"Radio forecasts a big storm, Wednesday night," Williston said.

"Poker night," Angus said.

"Maybe that's the night. We could crate them up from your place and take them over to the farm. Then let them loose . . . after poker. Wolves'd come in the middle of the night. And if it's coming down as hard as they predict, nobody'll be out in it."

"Two days with nothin' but water," Angus said. "They'll be ready."

"Damn right. Tell the others. I'll keep an eye on the weather. Pick me up night after next, after dusk, and we'll have ourselves a little party."

Angus grinned, opened the door and stepped down into the shadowy woods. The pot-bellied stove and the whiskey had warmed him. The more he thought about it the more he liked the idea of his dogs taking care of those calves. Night after next, they were going to have a party.

CHAPTER FOUR

JANUARY 27TH—JUDY RUTGERS'S SHEEP RANCH OUTSIDE DENVER

Just after 4:00 p.m. Sam pulled onto Judy's gravel drive. The sky was clear, with the sun starting to drop into the distant ridge of mountains. Sam recognized Judy's large silhouette in her living room window. He wondered how long she'd been waiting for him.

Sam and Judy were members of a citizen wolf management committee. The USFW created it to provide a platform for ranchers to air their opinions and be heard. Judy wasn't shy about sharing her perspectives. But she was disappointed that few of her arguments were sufficient to move anyone at the USFW, or change Service regulations.

Her front door swung open and the substantial Ms. Rutgers stepped out, cradling the Marlin 336. She wore a faded work shirt over an anemic red T-shirt. The work shirt hung blouse-like over her large, barrel-shaped middle. There was nothing fragile about Judy Rutgers. Her arms were stout as stove wood and her oversized legs disappeared into a pair of well-worn cowboy boots. Carrying the rifle, she looked menacing. But Sam knew it was more bluster than blow.

Sam turned to the back trunk space of his jeep and extracted his camera bag.

"Bout time, Rivers," she said, her voice like a distant chainsaw. "I called your office this morning."

"Judy," Sam nodded. "Came out as soon as I could. I was under the impression you had plenty of evidence. And we both know a wolf, if that's what it is, wouldn't return in daylight."

"*If* it was a wolf!" Her round face started to turn crimson. "Goddamnit Rivers, you know me. You *know* I wouldn't call if I wasn't one hundred percent certain it was a wolf."

Sam had his doubts, which would heat her blood to a fractious boil. "You've read the latest wolf population report. U.S. Fish and Wildlife made a careful census of Colorado."

"Don't tell me about that goddamn Report," she interrupted.

Sam paused, turning to look at the distant Front Range, hazy in the late afternoon. From here the mountains looked far off, inviting. Judy needed time to cool.

The *Report* was Fish and Wildlife's annual *Rocky Mountain Wolf Recovery Report*. Since Sam had relegated himself to remaining local, he'd spearheaded the effort to research and write the new report. It detailed Colorado's wolf population, which was practically non-existent. There were a few places on the western fringe of the state where wolves were starting to repopulate, but those were far from Judy Rutgers's ranch.

Like many livestock owners Judy, had an expert's eye for tracking and sorting through the remnants of a kill to determine what had done it. It was possible a wolf had come into her flock, one of those on a walk-about from a western pack, though its appearance this far east would be unusual. A lone wolf's range could carry it hundreds of miles in just a few days. If had read the report, she would have noticed that just last year a wolf was struck by a car thirty miles west of Denver. It had been collared, and the most recent tracking data indicated it had covered 446 miles in less than two weeks. Wolves were marathoners of the highest order.

"The Report's pretty specific," Sam finally said. Even though her tongue was as coarse as a truck driver's, he liked Judy Rutgers but didn't care for how she felt about his reportorial efforts.

"Goddammit," she said, this time a little softer. "Don't mess with me Rivers. I've got enough to deal with just runnin' this place."

True enough. A sentiment plenty in wildlife management were reluctant to admit.

Judy stepped around the corner of her house. "Let's go have a look, Rivers."

On their way past the barn she noticed the absence of his good-natured companion. On the few occasions he'd visited, Sam's dog Charlie, an Australian Shepherd mix, had loved Judy's ranch. Tending a flock was in his blood. "Where's the dog?" she asked.

Sam returned her question with a steady gaze, searching for the right words. "Gone," was all he managed.

Judy understood. "Damn shame," she said, turning into the bare field. "He was one hell of a dog."

"He was," Sam agreed.

They hiked out to the gulch. Sheep grazed in the waning sun, sticking close to the house, paddock and barn. At the ditch edge Judy pointed, then started down toward a small hollow rimmed with scrub oak.

They rounded a bend of head-high brush. They were still twenty yards above the hollow. The side of the hill was open and there were clear signs of struggle.

"Here's where he took her," Judy pointed to the dry ground.

There were few things that could focus Sam Rivers's attention like a prey site. The grass was broken and the earth torn up in two or three places. There was a dark splash of something that looked like axle grease. Sam stepped carefully to the stained ground and peered at it, suspecting it was blood. He dabbed two fingers onto the spot; it was dry, but sticky. He smelled it. Wet iron. Five feet downhill there was a scrub oak thicket, the perfect hiding place. Sam imagined the predator waiting in the brush until the ewe grazed close, then springing. A big wolf could finish the job in less than ten seconds. But so could a cougar. He looked for other signs, but found only dirt from the scuffle and blood. "Tell me there's more than this."

"Oh hell yes." Judy turned and started down the hill toward the bottom of the gulch. They bushwhacked through heavy scrub oak. When they pushed through the brush edge their racket startled three ravens that rose squawking in the dusk light.

"Ravens," Sam said, watching them rise into the afternoon light. He paused to watch their loping wing beats carry them over the ridgeline.

"Goddamn scavengers," Judy said.

The ravens were a good sign. Ravens were sometimes known to follow wolves. And it meant there was still evidence.

In the narrow opening they found what was left of the ewe. Her gaping throat had the look of a wolf kill, Sam thought. Something had fastened on and tore. Coyotes dart and nip, usually at the flanks or hindquarters. They seldom made frontal attacks, particularly on a full-grown ewe in a flock. Cougars dropped or leapt onto their prey, raking its back while trying to break its neck. This ewe had her underthroat torn away in one deep gash. Wolf. He was pretty sure. The hindquarters and entrails were largely missing. Last night's dinner, Sam guessed. Or a very early breakfast.

Judy made a wide sweep around the ewe, carefully picking over the ground. "I think you'll find some good prints over here," she said, pointing to the bush edge.

Sam looked down, pulling his camera out of the bag. He pulled off the lens cap and bent over the prints. There were two pairs, the front and hind paws. The pairs overlapped, as though each foot attempted to step inside the footprint made in front of it. Coyote prints were similar in position, but much smaller; two and a half inches in length, or less. Wolf prints were four and a half inches in length, or more. Certain large breeds of feral dog could approach the size of a wolf's print, but they were usually set much further apart. Sam had seen hybridized animals, wolves crossed with dog breeds that made them practically indistinguishable from full-blooded wolves. But these prints appeared to be the real thing.

Affixed to the camera was a 200-millimeter macro lens. He paused over each print, focusing the lens. He was almost certain it was a wolf. But he noticed the prints were a little small, and the observation caused his pulse to increase. He reached into his bag and pulled out an eight-inch measure. He placed the rule next to the print, then bent over, focused, and snapped. These prints were just over three inches in length, including their claws. He took a couple more shots and placed the ruler perpendicular to the print, repeating the action with the camera.

"That's interesting, Judy."

"What?" She didn't like his tone.

"Any hair?"

She turned around the carcass and pointed to where a tuft marked the sharp end of an oak branch. Sam closed the space between them, reaching into the satchel and extracting a plastic zip lock bag.

"Let's step careful. I think we want this one to return. Any other prints?" he asked.

"Just these. But they should be enough," she said, defensive. "We want him back so we can shoot the sucker," she added.

"Take it easy, Judy. I'll issue you a shoot-on-sight permit, no questions asked. And if it's a Rocky Mountain gray wolf, you have the government's blessing to take the animal down."

"It's a wolf, Rivers," she affirmed.

Sam paused, absorbed in his work. "Yeah," he finally said. "It's a wolf." But he was intent on the hair.

He bent down with the camera, focused the lens on the hair tuft, and took several shots in rapid succession. Then he placed the tuft into the bag, careful to keep it clean. "I have good news and bad news," he said. "Which would you like first?"

"The good news better be full reimbursement. The bad news is the bastard got away."

"That is the good news," he said. "You'll receive full compensation. The evidence is substantial. Prints too big for a coyote, and this hair," he said, holding up the bag in the fading sunlight, examining it. "Take a look at the color," he said, holding it so Judy could see it in the light.

Judy examined the follicles. "Hair," she said, bluntly. "Wolf hair."

"And the color?"

She took a closer look. "Black. Grey. It's got some red in it."

"And that's a subtle feature. That, and the prints over there," he said, pointing to the wolf prints.

"What about 'em?"

"A normal Rocky Mountain gray wolf, particularly a lone hunter on walkabout searching for a mate to start a pack, would have a paw length over four inches. Coyotes aren't even close to three inches. This one's right in-between. Could be a feral dog, but its prints are too close together. It has the gait of a wolf. Could be a coyote-wolf mix. There is a remote chance it could be a Mexican wolf, slightly smaller than the Rocky Mountain or Great Plains sub-species. A very rare Mexican Gray Wolf. And that's surprising," Sam said.

Judy was just happy it was a wolf. "So what's the bad news?"

"It may be a Mexican Gray Wolf."

"You said that."

He looked at her carefully. "There are around 150 of them throughout the Southwest, at least that we know of," he explained. "One this far north and east would be unusual, but not impossible." He continued, watching her. Clearly she didn't understand. "This subspecies isn't threatened," he said. "It's endangered."

There was a pause before recognition and outburst. "Oh for Christ's sake!"

"Judy," Sam started.

"I don't give a shit. If that wolf takes another ewe and I'm anywhere near it, it's a dead wolf. A dead *Mexican* wolf."

"That could be a problem, Jude."

"I don't give a rip, Rivers. And you know I'll do it." She was blistering, her fists clenched.

The most recent wolf recovery plan had eased rancher's concerns regarding the Rocky Mountain Gray Wolf and the Great Plains Gray Wolf. Populations of the subspecies had sprung back healthy enough in other parts of the country so they were downgraded from endangered to threatened. If ranchers found the common wolf skulking around their barns, or attacking their stock, they could apply to U.S. Fish & Wildlife for permission to trap or shoot them. The kill had to be reported, but it was legal, no questions asked.

But Mexican gray wolves were extremely rare. U.S. Fish and Wildlife was doing everything it could to cultivate the animal. Sam had never heard of one this far north and east. Never in Colorado. But given wolves' loping gaits, long legs, ultrathon capabilities, and drive to find a proper mate, it could happen. Judging from the animal's morphology it looked promising. But morphology, the art of discerning a species from its physical characteristics, was always dubious. He would have to send a hair sample to the U.S. Fish & Wildlife's Forensics lab in Ashland, Oregon, just to be sure. DNA tests would give him a definitive answer. But it would take time. And meanwhile Judy would be waiting with her Marlin 336.

Sam knew Judy could cross the line. She didn't give a damn about Mexican wolves, only that they were taking her stock. He liked Judy, but her perspective on wolves was shortsighted. "You shoot it, you pay," he said, evenly. "Might even do some time."

One good swing of Judy Rutgers's arm, with that mitt for a fist, and his face would be down in the dirt.

"We're gonna help you out," he added. "I'll come out tomorrow with tranquilizer traps and we'll catch him alive, if he ever comes back. Now that he's killed livestock he'll have to be taken in, made part of our captive breeding program."

"You mean he gets to live?" she asked, incredulous.

"If he's a Mexican wolf, he's too rare to kill, Judy. We've got to keep him alive. We can use him."

"To make more of these ewe-killing devils?"

Sam had no illusions about the animal. Wolves were merciless killers. But they were remarkable, tender, even loving parents, fiercely loyal to their packs. They could also be ruthless and deadly, killing the members of other packs to defend territory or maintain order. They were complicated social animals, like humans, which was just one of the reasons Sam appreciated them.

"I've got a claim form back in the jeep," Sam said. "No question about compensation," he added. But Judy wasn't mollified.

Before Sam left he completed the USDA's *Wolf Compensation Claim* form. She'd get a check in the mail in just a few days. It would probably be a few days after that before she calmed down enough to thank him. This time Judy needed a little extra time to cool.

One of Sam's favorite aspects of fieldwork, particularly when it involved a prey site, was how investigations engaged him. His absorption was instantaneous. His senses calmed and he focused, his blood coming alive. The act itself was one of forgetting, of putting the pain of his recent past behind him, of ignoring headache and heartache until the details of an investigation totally absorbed him.

But he had no illusions about the night. On the way home he pulled into Caldecott's Liquor. He always bought one bottle of medium-priced red. From experience Sam Rivers knew if wine were in his townhouse, he'd drink it. This way he could limit his intake to, at the very most, a bottle.

The cashier nodded. Sam nodded back and paid.

By the time Sam returned to Yellow Rock it was after dark. He walked into his unlit townhouse, tired and hungry. He flipped on the kitchen light, tossed his mail on the table and scrounged in his kitchen drawer for a corkscrew. He opened the bottle and poured the blood-red wine into a glass. He swirled the wine, sticking his nose in it. Then he took a slow sip and . . . damn . . . that tasted good.

He took the glass into his living room and over another sip fired up his laptop and started checking emails.

He read more than 30 messages, mostly office work to be addressed. Then he found two messages that focused his attention; an attachment from canislupustruth@yahoo.com and something from dianetalbott@gmail.com. He recognized the name of his mother's friend, but the subject line —Williston Winthrop is dead—sucked all the air out of the room. His chest and stomach lifted, as though he'd hit turbulence. The old man was dead?

"Sorry for the blunt message. In the event anything happened to your father your mom wanted me to tell you. She gave me your email address . . . hope it still works. I tried to dig up a phone number, but I couldn't find one.

It's been a long time, Sam. I'm sure you remember the times you and I paddled your mother into the Boundary Waters for some R&R and a good fish dinner. I have missed her these two years. She was a great friend with a heart the size of a kettle drum and kindness for the whole world and everything in it—even, inexplicably, your father.

Before she died she made me promise that if anything happened to Williston I was to let you know. She knew you wouldn't come home if he was still alive. She wanted me to remind you about the things you left in her house, things she wanted to make sure you recovered.

Sam remembered. His mother had told him as much before she died. And it was true. He would never return home as long as the old man was alive.

She said she'd added to them since you'd left, and you must come home and get them. I wish I could tell you more, but I think that was the sum of it.

For what it's worth, Williston was never able to sell her home and it's still sitting vacant. The way things are on the Range your father never put much effort into fixing it up and selling it. It's not exactly a seller's market.

Your mom told me some of the details of why you disappeared and changed your name. I didn't like your father before I learned about it. Afterward, I liked him even less.

Now you can come back for a visit, Sam Rivers. Now that Williston's dead everything has changed. So if you decide to return, please stop by. Here's a link to the business about your father.

All the best,

Diane Talbott

Sam remembered every detail about what he and his mother had hidden in her house, minutes before he fled. And she'd added to it? He couldn't imagine what, wasn't really sure it mattered, though he was definitely curious.

He clicked on the link and opened an article to the online version of the *Vermilion Falls Gazette.* He'd forgotten Diane was a reporter.

LOCAL ATTORNEY DIES IN HUNTING ACCIDENT
Diane Talbott
The Vermilion Falls Gazette, Jan. 27

Sam stared at the screen and re-read the article twice, in disbelief. The old man was dead. It was impossible to fathom. A hunting accident? There was a time Sam had spent a fair portion of his waking hours dreaming of Williston Winthrop's demise. But gradually the interests and pursuits of his own life absorbed him. And now the old man was gone?

He remembered his mother's friend. She was over ten years younger than his mother. When they canoed into the Boundary Waters Sam had been impressed by her ability to paddle and by her appearance. He was just a kid and Diane Talbott was probably in her late 20s, but at 15 Sam couldn't help admiring the woman, who had a compelling contour.

After his last battle with the old man, Sam stayed away from Defiance because you never knew when a man like Williston Winthrop would make good on his promise to charge him with attempted murder and make it stick. Sam didn't really have any other meaningful connections to his former home.

Sam returned to his email and opened the message from canislupus-truth. This time there was no note, only an attachment. He opened the PDF and read "Will & Testament" printed across its top. It was a copy of the old man's Will. The list of properties included the 300-acre farm, all of the farm's machinery, three feeder calves still in the barn, one truck, a car, his mother's house, apparently vacant, and her car. And money, lots of it.

The old man had over 2.3 million dollars in various Ameritrade accounts, and over 50,000 dollars distributed throughout money market, checking and savings accounts at the Vermilion Falls State Bank. An additional 2.5 million-dollar term life policy was listed in his father's name.

Everything else was tied up in personal property. Williston Winthrop's signature was dated almost two years earlier, not long after Sam's mother's death. At the line marked BENEFICIARY(IES) he had written "The members of the Iron County Gun Club, to be divided equally: Angus Moon, Bill Grebs, Hank Gunderson and Hal Young."

Sam was shocked by the size of the old man's estate. Maybe legal work on Minnesota's Iron Range was more lucrative than he'd imagined. More likely, the old man had figured out a scheme for bilking clients.

The absence of his own name on the list of beneficiaries was no surprise. Sam Rivers's miserable connection to the old man had ended with their last disagreement, the one that broke three of Sam's ribs and knocked him sprawling into North Dakota's emptiness.

Why would the old man carry a two and a half million-dollar policy on himself? For the benefit of his Club? They'd been that close? Sam remembered their weekly meetings, their out-of-season hunting excursions, even their talk of building a remote, isolated cabin in Skinwalker's Bog.

The man who'd suggested re-instating wolf bounties; *that* was the man Sam remembered. He could imagine the old man standing at a public hearing and arguing, vociferously, that wolves should be de-listed, hunted, even exterminated. Bring back the bounties.

Sam was familiar enough with wolf depredation figures to know such encounters were increasing as the wolf populations grew. Like most wildlife biologists, Sam believed the population would eventually reach a carefully managed balance. The depredating wolves, like Judy Rutgers's, would be captured or killed. There would always be livestock taken. If you were going to have wolves, it was unavoidable. Most farmers and ranchers appreciated the wild animals, were willing to work with the state to ensure their survival. Williston Winthrop's perspective was a minority opinion, but there were plenty who shared it.

The old man was right about one thing. There had been some well-documented encounters between humans and wolves. In 2005, in a mining operation in Saskatchewan, a man apparently walked into the woods and was stalked, attacked, killed and partially eaten by a pair of wolves. In 2010 a female jogger in Alaska was killed by wolves. These were two recent North American occurrences, and there were others elsewhere around the world. But compared to human depredation by other species (crocodile, shark, bear or cougar, for instance) wolf/human attacks were incredibly rare.

Sam leaned back from the screen. Canislupustruth again. And two days after the cryptic message: SOON. Soon what? *Soon* there was going to be a hunting accident? And why send him the goddamn messages? A will would only be public in Minnesota if it was probated. Sam assumed this will wasn't probated, so the only people who likely had copies were the beneficiaries. But why would they send him a copy? If it was probated there would be a copy filed in the Vermilion County Recorder's office, and he might be able to track down whoever pulled it, if he was willing to drive more than 1,000 miles to find out. Those were a lot of *ifs*.

Sam Rivers sat in his chair a long time, recalling scenes from his childhood. He remembered the way the old man cooked breakfast. He remembered his fixation on hunting, and the way he instilled in Sam, who did not have the heart for it, hunting's commandments.

"Surprise," the old man said, "is what you hunt. Not the animal. Look for the unexpected place they feel secure, where you can smell it in their blood."

"You've got to put it down," the old man told him, on one of the occasions he'd tried to teach him trapping. They were laying baits around foothold traps on the outside of a wolverine's den. The rancid meat smelled awful, and Sam turned up his nose and held it at arm's length.

"If you don't put it down they won't come around. The worse it smells, the better. Distracts them from the traps."

It was one of many things the old man tried to teach him. And though he was a capable student and learned the lessons easily, he chose not to use them, at least for the kind of trapping the old man pursued. But he was surprised by how easily he recalled the lessons.

After a while Sam got up, went to his freezer and pulled out a nearly full bottle of Grey Goose, a more fitting drink given the circumstances and the old man's end. Sam wasn't big on hard liquor, which was why it didn't bother him that it was sitting in his freezer. But there were times, like this one, when he needed something stronger. He took a clear glass out of the cupboard, filled it with cubes, and topped them off with the thickened liquid. He raised it in his empty kitchen air, trying to conjure some words . . . something.

His father's death was sudden and unexpected. It was amazing how a single afternoon could change life entirely. That's the way he felt, though he did not know where the new direction led.

"To the son of a bitch," he finally said, and drank off a long swallow. It burned down his throat, across his rib cage. Fitting.

He sipped the rest of the Grey Goose meditatively, the night deepening in his townhouse windows. Eventually he returned to Diane Talbott's message.

"Thanks for the information," he wrote, considering. He thought about what else to say. "I hope you're well," he concluded.

Then, "More, later."

"—Sam"

He dialed his Supervisor. At the voicemail's beep he said, "Something's come up. I need to leave town for a while. A week should be plenty. I'll get Becker or Barnes to set those traps at Judy's place tomorrow morning. But I suspect my hunch about that wolf not returning is correct. I'll call you tomorrow from the road."

The funeral wasn't for five more days. He thought he might like to be there when the old man was dropped into frozen ground. He'd enjoy seeing the look in the Club members' faces. If they were still the raw group of outdoorsmen he remembered he would relish making them squirm. They had been the kind of men who would harass anyone they thought might threaten their claim to the old man's estate. If his father had ever filed an attempted murder charge against Clayton Winthrop (Sam's childhood name), Bill Grebs would have reason enough to give him trouble. But Sam never heard about any charges and besides, the difference between Sam Rivers and Clayton Winthrop was twenty years and a lifetime.

Now that the old man was out of the picture, Sam felt ready to return. He needed to recover his things. He would have to be careful about getting back into his mother's house.

It was just after 9:00. He worked through the details in his head.

He was nagged by his mother's house and the contents of their secret basement recess. Her house was still vacant. He wondered what she'd placed there, in the bag next to the old man's precious heirloom.

He cleaned up, thinking about what he'd need to take with him.

Some tools. Couple sets of clothes. He remembered northern Minnesota. It could be blistering cold this time of year. He'd need some serious gear.

But how to get into his mother's without being seen . . .?

Gradually, the outline of a plan began to take shape. He worked out the timing in his head: the 20-plus-hour drive, the post-midnight hour of his arrival. If he left well before dawn he could probably make 15 hours tomorrow, which would put him in or near Minnesota. Close to northern Minnesota, if he retraced the Dakota journey he'd taken 20 years earlier. He could find a place; sleep in, rest up, and head out around dinner time on the 29th, which would land him in Defiance late that night or early the 30th. Better early the 30th, when everyone would be asleep.

If nothing much had changed in Defiance, it could work. For the first time in long while, Sam was looking forward to first light.

CHAPTER FIVE

JANUARY 29TH, JUST BEFORE MIDNIGHT—ANGUS MOON'S NORTHWOODS CABIN

The five men walked out of the cabin into the woods where the dogs' houses stood. Williston Winthrop held the lantern. Its mantles flared in the dark. The others followed him up the ice-covered path through the trees. When they reached the houses, Winthrop peered into the black sky. A few thick snowflakes filtered down through the lantern's light.

"It's starting," Winthrop said.

"Gonna be a hell of a storm," Angus Moon said.

"It just gets better and better," Hank Gunderson chuckled.

The others considered their words, peering into the dark. They'd spent the evening in Angus Moon's remote cabin, playing cards and being liberal with the juice, waiting for midnight and the forecast onset of storm. The wind-driven pines and the first light dust of white told them it was time. Now Williston carried the lantern into the wooded enclosure. He lifted it to show the first dog's house, then turned to look at Moon.

"You sure they're ready?"

Angus nodded. He stepped up to the side of the closest house. The five houses stood at different angles in the narrow enclosure. They were fashioned out of scrap lumber. Large pieces of plywood had been nailed over each door. A thin opening at the bottom allowed a shallow bowl of water to be shoved through. As they came closer the pungent odor of the dogs' confinement was nauseating.

"Christ," Bill Grebs muttered.

"Jesus, Angus. Sure ain't the Duluth Radisson," Hank said.

"That'd be for us, later," added Grebs, smiling.

Gunderson and Hal Young chuckled, but Winthrop knew there was work to be done.

A small wolf head peered out from behind the nearest house. The visage startled Young and Grebs.

"What the hell is that?" Grebs asked.

"What's left of the last litter," Moon said.

"Couldn't sell it?"

"Not yet. And gettin' a little old. Might have to keep it for breeding stock. But that one's got more dog than I ever seen come out of a match between the Arctic sire and Malamute bitch. Not sure the others'll accept it. Might just have to cut the little shit loose. Or use him for target practice." The youngling cowered behind the house.

"Git," Angus snarled, and the dog disappeared, its collar and chain jangling into the dark. "See what I mean?"

Just to give them the feel of a real hybrid, Angus brought back a steel-toed boot and kicked the nearest house. There was an explosive growl and the sound of teeth gnashing against the plywood wall. It captured Hal Young's attention like a slap in the face. He stepped back, afraid the boards might break.

Angus turned and smiled, watching Young's retreat.

There was nothing in Angus Moon's unshaven face, or the intent focus of his gray eyes, that betrayed his role in what happened that Sunday night on Williston Winthrop's farm, though all the Club members knew it was Angus who brought on the vagrant James T. Beauregard's doom. When the scheme was conceived, unanimous decision appointed Moon the executioner. Now he spit across the path, comfortable with his new stature, sending a spasm of brown saliva directly behind the tremulous Hal Young. "They'll keep," he said.

"How long they been in there?" Young asked, more to make conversation than out of curiosity.

"Two days," Angus said. His tongue moved to resettle his chew. When he smiled he revealed two rows of stunted yellow pegs.

The five hybrids now penned and starving had been kept for breeding and the Club's amusement. They could run down deer better than their wild brethren. And a hefty wooden club let them know Angus was their unchallenged leader. They touched no part of a downed animal until Angus Moon gave them the nod. Now the prolonged absence of food had caused their lupine instincts to surface like an ancient muscle group.

In the growing snowfall the first dog's howl triggered a chorus of low snarls. The other four houses vibrated with the noise.

"I think they're all just about ready for a little meat," Angus added.

He turned and stepped up to each house and kicked it, eliciting the same whipped fury of teeth and feral growls. Under the force of one of the dog's gnashing, a plywood board bowed out. Young stepped back. Winthrop heard his shuffle and raised the light to look at him.

"They won't get out until we let them out."

"No need to rile 'em, Angus," Grebs admonished. "They're ready."

Williston Winthrop raised his lantern. At the edge of the trees there was a black tarpaulin thrown carelessly over stacked metal cages. Angus threw off the tarp and hauled a cage to the nearest house.

"Come here, Young. Give me a hand."

Young hesitated. Then he stepped to the opposite side of Angus. Young was five foot ten, one hundred eighty pounds. He wore a heavy down coat that accentuated his flaccid pudginess. Over his right breast, stenciled yellow letters declared *Hal Young Independent Insurance.*

Standing across from Angus, he appeared to be the same height and build. But where Young had narrow shoulders and an upper body molded to the contours of his desk, Angus Moon, who spent most of his life outdoors, was weathered, compact and powerful.

"All of them part wolf?" Young asked, distractedly.

"Half wolf. Every one of 'em. But some of them act more wolf than others." He nodded toward the cages and said, "Grab a couple of those pine poles. We don't want our hands to get bit off."

The others watched Hal Young retrieve the poles and he and Angus inserted them into the cage's top metal squares.

Winthrop, Bill Grebs and Hank Gunderson looked on.

Winthrop knew his death was an unusual accident for a man with his hunting expertise. Unusual, but not unheard of. Once the estate was settled and the insurance claim paid, they'd divvy up the shares. Williston was taking half. Under the circumstances, he considered it generous, considering the money he'd managed to squirrel away into Belize banks—client trust money he knew he would eventually be at pains to explain.

Over the next five years the Club had planned two more deaths. Angus Moon would go missing in the wild. Angus was easy. They'd have to wait a year, settle with the insurance company for a lesser amount. But Williston knew they'd clear a million. Bill Grebs would be more difficult. But Williston Winthrop hadn't funded Club members' life insurance policies to assist insurance companies with their bottom lines. Only Hal Young and Hank Gunderson would be left to live out their natural lives. The Club needed contacts back on the Range. They couldn't lose complete touch, though on paper Winthrop, Moon and Grebs would be desiccating corpses.

Identifying his own corpse had been routine. The front half of Winthrop's head was entirely removed. Witnesses could only identify his clothes and the shape of his body. The Coroner knew Williston well enough to recognize what was left of his white hair and the orange hunting cap's torn away bill. The sheriff had his identification. Besides, Sheriff Dean Goddard had seen the corpse's outfit only two days before the accident. And he recognized the weapon. What was left of his grisly countenance was the worst hunting accident any of them had ever seen. And while everyone spoke of it as an accident, Williston assumed the sheriff told the Coroner about the sheriff's investigation into Williston's legal practice, and that Williston knew about it. Williston Winthrop would not be the first aging lawyer to choose death over a prison cell. And truth was, they were all anxious to cover over what was left of his grisly head. And they were all thankful to be rid of him.

Prior to staging his own death, Williston's brief meeting with the sheriff had been necessary to find out how close the county DA was to Winthrop's illegal activities. And he'd been damn close, closer than Williston dreamed. In his own way District Attorney Jeff Dunlap had sealed the vagrant James T. Beauregard's untimely end. And the sheriff had been the messenger. Everything about Williston's accident had happened perfectly. The sheriff's relief, the intense cold, a tough hike, the black middle of the night, and the grotesque wound that made Goddard's investigation perfunctory.

Come Saturday Williston Winthrop would be laid to rest in the grave next to his estranged wife.

Moon and Young placed the cage in front of the dog's house. When the plywood was pried loose and slid away the dog was expected to leap into the cage and the wire door slam shut. When everything was in place Angus pried the plywood open. There was a low snarl.

"Get ready to drop the door," Angus ordered.

Young slipped off the catch and pulled it open. In the dull light his face appeared tense and worried.

"Ready?" Angus asked.

Young nodded.

Angus slid back the board and the dog charged out. Young dropped the door. The dog reached the end of the cage, spun around, and gnashed out between a thin wire square, trying to get a piece of him. Young fell back, sitting down in the snow. Angus started laughing.

In the same way, they caged the other four dogs. They used the poles to carry them out of the woods, loading each of them onto Moon's pickup. As they worked, the snow came down more heavily. By the time they finished, the trail was disappearing beneath a thick film of white.

"You should go first," Winthrop told Grebs. "Stay on the radio. You see anyone going or coming, give us a couple clicks on the CB," Winthrop directed.

"Sounds like a plan." Grebs turned and started walking toward his car. He was as medium in stature as Young and Angus, but he moved with an authoritative air.

"Angus and I will be five minutes behind you. You others follow us, but give us some time. We don't want a caravan."

"We'll be careful," Hank Gunderson said. "Just don't start the show without us." He was a big man. The skin on his face and belly sagged in alcoholic puffiness. His face was clean shaven and his eyes were bloodshot. "I've got a hundred on the she-devil to draw first blood," he said.

"That's a wager I'll take," Williston said. "You always pick the bitch, Hank. That big Arctic will take the lead."

"I guess it'll take a hundred to see who's right."

"I guess," Williston agreed.

"It's turning into a pretty good night's work for a dead man and four stiffs." Hank smiled and turned away.

Winthrop laughed. He and Hank had known each other since they were kids. When things were tense, Hank had a way of making him grin.

Grebs had been gone over five minutes before Winthrop and Angus pulled out of the woodsmen's long, narrow drive. There was nothing on the CB. Winthrop sat up, watching the snow come down more heavily. Then he motioned and Angus turned onto a side road that disappeared in a rough diagonal through the trees.

"You checked this way out?" Winthrop asked. He peered ahead. Through the driving white they could see the snow banked high. On either side of the narrow lane their headlights flashed over a wall of winter bush and pine.

"This morning," Angus answered. He looked ahead and steered carefully over the ice-covered ruts. In spite of the whiskey, he drove soberly. The truck jostled and on occasion the cages in the back shifted and clanged, but the dogs were quiet now, sensing they would soon be free.

For the remainder of the crossing they drove in silence. Winthrop was careful to stay out of sight. There was little chance anyone would be out on roads like these at this hour in the middle of a building storm, but when it came to the law, Williston took no chances.

The days since Grebs had first found Jimbo were characterized by inspired design. The other members of the Club had quickly seen what could be done. Everyone except Young, who had reservations. But they needed Young's insurance angle to make it work so they bullied him.

Williston didn't like it. They bullied Young the same way Angus forced him to help cage the dogs. Angus was reacting on an instinctual dislike for cowardice, but it was the exact thing Young needed to force his participation. Still, Young was the weakest link and Williston worried about him.

In a few short days Williston would be buried. Into the ground with him would be laid all the unpleasantness from the investigations into his not exactly legal practice. There had been three investigations, none of which amounted to more than a mild wrist slap. The real crimes, of course, were right under their noses—three client trusts Williston had been bilking for years. That was the fourth investigation, recently begun. He needed Angus to clear up one last issue, an office fire engulfing every piece of wayward paper and incriminating computer file. All record of his clients' trusts would go up in flames. And without evidence?

It was a detail he had not shared with any of the Club members, because there was no need. Like the other reason for the slaughter of the calves in his barn.

In a matter of weeks the dead Williston Winthrop would resurrect himself, someplace warm to start, one of those countries south of Mexico, where the dollar ran on forever and no one enquired about your past. He would miss the Range, but he'd spent time south of the border and knew there were places a man with his particular talents could thrive.

As he looked back on it, it had been a satisfactory life. He regretted his dead wife, or perhaps more specifically the 179,000 dollars she drained from her account in the months preceding her death.

The day Miriam died, Williston went over to her house, let himself in, located her will, and altered it, forging her signature. She was going to leave everything to the boy. It was a simple matter, changing the will. Hal Young was a notary public. Hal notarized the revised document, and pre-dated it a month before her death.

After Miriam's death the will was probated. There had been two enquiries; one from the sheriff and one from that bitch Diane Talbott. Talbott claimed, so Goddard told him, that Miriam said she was leaving everything to the boy. But Miriam's notarized signature was legal proof they couldn't refute. And where was the goddamn boy? No one had heard from him in years. Williston hoped they might bring him forward. He had a score to settle. In the end the flap over Miriam's 11th-hour change of beneficiaries blew over like a northwestern squall.

When Williston finally enquired about her accounts, he found out about the missing cash. Williston knew people at the bank. They'd worried about her, about her state of mind. She was frail, and withdrawing that kind of money in hundred dollar bills over the last six months of her life was worrisome. But Miriam knew Bill Radcliffe, the bank President, and convinced him it was for a variety of worthy causes, including her estranged son. Bill agreed to keep it quiet. No one at the bank said anything to anyone until she died. When Williston found out, he exploded inside Bill Radcliffe's office like a detonated propane tank. But Radcliffe showed him the withdrawal records, everything was legal.

In the days following Miriam's death, he'd turned the old house inside out, searching for the cash. He assumed she'd somehow gotten it to the boy. But he'd checked with the post office, checked with all her friends. None of them remembered anything about a series of large stuffed envelopes or boxes that might be used to ship stacks of bills. Or they weren't talking. He thought about trying to track it from the other end, going after the boy, but finally decided it would be safer to let it alone. There was still the life insurance money. And he needed her house and share of the farm, no questions asked. He and the boy had accounts to settle. But he didn't want the insurance money or the farm to be part of them.

If the boy had another copy of the will there could be problems. But he suspected the kid would stay away rather than risk his arrest for attempted murder. It was doubtful Williston and Grebs could make the charge stick, but the boy wasn't stupid. A tree-hugging chickenshit, as Williston remembered; someone who wouldn't want to risk his luck, particularly in a Northern Minnesota court. The boy was more Miriam's son than his own. But that made it all the more likely the boy wouldn't show his face to enter into a contest with someone he knew, one way or another, would win.

After twenty minutes they turned onto the snow-covered ruts that took them down to Winthrop's house and barn. The buildings were dark and barely visible through the snow. The gray outline of Grebs's police car waited at the bottom of the drive.

"Go around to the side door," Winthrop ordered, pointing to where a pair of ruts disappeared behind the barn. "It's pretty well hidden. And if wolves came that's where they'd get in."

Angus backed the pickup to the side door. The intensity of the driving snow was starting to swirl around them. When they got out of the cab, Grebs appeared out of the white like an apparition.

"Startin' to come down pretty heavy," he shouted.

"Perfect," Williston shouted back.

A gust of snow whipped across them in a horizontal slant.

"Couldn't have asked for a better storm," Winthrop added. "An hour after we leave there won't be anything left to track."

The entry to the barn had a small holding pen where the dogs were corralled. The three men worked at the back of the truck. The cages were hoisted down to the side entrance, their openings set flush to the door. The cage lids were slid away. When the barn door opened the starving animals charged into the confined darkness.

While they worked, Gunderson, and then Young, came down the drive and made their way to the barn.

"Better get started," Winthrop yelled over the wind. "It's gettin' pretty wild."

Williston led them around the barn corner, up the rise to the loft door. He was the first through the small opening. He came out above the barn floor. The rest of them followed, leaving the storm outside, shaking off the snow and cold as their eyes grew accustomed to the dark. From the loft Williston turned on a small overhead light. They could hear the dogs beneath them. They watched the vague shapes of three feeder calves jostling at the other end of the barn. The three young fatlings made worried sounds in the dark, low and plaintive.

Williston looked down, excited by his front row seat at the timeless spectacle of predator and prey. The men stared over the edge, transfixed by the scene. Williston double checked everything, making certain there would be no doubt that the wolves forced their entry and slaughtered the animals while no one was there to prevent it. Hank Gunderson hauled up three hay bales, squaring them like park benches. "Come on, she-devil," he called, whooping for his chosen fiend.

The dogs were jostling in the narrow confines, anxious to be free. The five men listened to the young cattle, all less than a year old, ululating fear.

Outside, the winter storm increased. The snow buffeted the roof and the north-facing walls. The barn blustered and creaked.

Angus passed his tongue over his lips, contemplating the entire scene one last time. He sent a spasm of brown liquid over the loft's edge.

"Come on, Williston," Grebs said. "Let 'em out."

Williston reached down, opening the door less than a foot before the first dog exploded through the narrow gap. Then all the dogs were through it, roving in a pack of fast-moving whines toward the cattle stalls, recalling instinctively the methods by which wolves quarry and kill.

The Club members started yelling, cheering on the dogs they guessed would draw first blood, or deriding those who demonstrated weakness, cowering to nip and dart at bovine flanks.

It took less than fifteen minutes for the calves to be silenced. As usual, Hank chose the bitch and chose wrong. Money changed hands and Williston suggested the rest of them get back to town. He walked with them to their cars. It was late and the storm worsened.

As Young pushed through the howl, Hank Gunderson and Bill Grebs walked with Williston to their cars. Hank yelled above the wind. "When will they be found!?"

"Could be as early as tomorrow," Grebs answered, his head bowed. "If I know the sheriff he'll have to poke his head out here once or twice. If he does it in the morning he'll find plenty."

"If he doesn't make it," Williston yelled, "Angus can report it! He's supposed to be taking care of them!"

"Just make sure you make it out to the cabin," Grebs yelled. "We don't want the sheriff finding you."

"We'll get out," Winthrop assured. "We'll cage 'em as soon as they're done and get them back over to Moon's. Worst case, we can hole up at his place till morning."

Gunderson nodded and turned toward his car.

Grebs looked out to where Hank was already disappearing in the snow. They heard Young's engine grind and start in the cold. "What was today's price on feeder calves?" Grebs asked.

"I don't know what they closed at," Winthrop yelled, a smile in his tone. "Close to a grand an animal, I'd expect."

"Chicken feed, considering," Grebs smiled. "We'll be out night after next, for the party."

"Just remember about Miriam's house in Defiance," Williston reminded him.

"I remember," Grebs said. "I'll keep an eye out."

"I'm dead and these calves have been taken by wolves in a barn. It'll get reported. And once it does, others might decide to take advantage, now that no one's around to watch over our things."

"No one'll get into that house," Grebs assured. "At least not without me knowing it. Meantime, need anything?"

Winthrop thought for a moment. The snow whipped around their tiny huddle. "The check from Agriculture would be good. That, and some Cohibas," he added, talking cigars. "They have some of those knock-offs from the Dominican down at Websters! Good as Cuban!"

"Too early for the check!" Grebs said. "But the DNR investigation should be done. We've got time!" he smiled.

Williston nodded. "That we do." Then he looked up to consider the storm. "Better get going!"

Grebs turned, bent into the wind, and started toward his cruiser. "The Cohibas you can count on," he yelled behind him.

CHAPTER SIX

JANUARY 30TH, PAST MIDNIGHT—ON THE ROADS OUTSIDE DEFIANCE

Sam Rivers stopped at the snowy crossroads, trying to remember the way. The radio was playing Sheryl Crow's "My Favorite Mistake." His dashboard clock read 12:41.

The previous day he had driven 17 hours, three of them white knuckled, steering slowly through two Dakota snow squalls. He'd reached Grand Forks around 9 and took another hour to find, check-in and get settled into a Super 8. Then he crossed the street to a local café for a late night dinner. He was comatose by midnight.

Around 4 p.m. the sound of wind rattling his windows brought him awake. It wasn't a good sign; blows like this one usually presaged storms.

He rolled over, fell into a deep sleep, and dreamed of wolves hurtling through Northern Minnesota woods, closing in, blood in their eyes.

Sam awoke late and spent the day at the Grand Forks public library, where he used Google Earth to take a bird's-eye flight over his planned route. It had been 20 years since he'd returned to Defiance, and he worried the roads had changed. But from what he could tell—the images were from summer—they appeared to be the same.

He'd also checked the weather maps. He'd been right about that wind. There was a major winter storm blowing out of the northwest, which could be a good thing, given his plans.

Sam ate an early dinner, not much. He crossed into Minnesota around 7:00 p.m. Just after he crossed, the first heavy snowflakes drifted down through his headlights. Over the next five hours, traveling first down Highway 2 and then up 71, toward Minnesota's Iron Range, the weather worsened.

By the time Sam neared Defiance, he'd been driving for more than five hours. Now he had to find some place to pull over.

Heavy snow gusted over his jeep and covered the highway in broad patches of white. The radio DJ warned listeners about the first bad winter storm of the new year.

"We have four inches," he barked, "but I'm here to tell ya', that's just the start! We're going to see plenty more. Isn't winterland wonderful?"

Sam flicked off the jocular DJ. He recognized the crossroads. In the tight interior of his car, the heat was turned on full blast, but the icy gusts whipped at his windshield and doors. When he was a boy he'd loved these storms. The weather canceled school and everything but the most necessary chores. The typical follow-up was a temperature plunge so deep it broke plastic and froze skin, if you were stupid enough to expose it.

Now he stared into the storm. He peered ahead, replaying his planned entrance into town, imagining his jeep's tires speeding and banking over the snow. As he hit the deeper patches of white, he imagined the car making solid whumps in the dark. Given his post-midnight stealth and the reason for his return, he couldn't have planned better weather.

He paused at the intersection, considering how little had changed. Even through the driving snow he could see the crossroads still crowded with black spruce and popple. He looked to his right, down the dark tunnel of highway disappearing into blowing snow. No vehicles. At this hour, in this storm, he didn't expect to see anyone, hadn't for the last twenty miles. Perfect.

When he glanced left, peering up the northern stretch of highway, he thought he saw headlights. Then they disappeared. He waited, hoping he was mistaken or they'd turned off. Then they crested a far off rise and opened like a pair of carnivore's eyes. They were a quarter mile off, driving slowly over the snow-choked blacktop.

He accelerated across the intersection. It would be better if no one saw his jeep. He tried to remember some place to turn off. He searched along the tree-lined road and saw a mailbox marking a drive opening. Peterson's field!

Well beyond the drive a gap in the tree line revealed the narrow entrance to a pasture lane. Twenty years ago old man Peterson hired him to help cut a narrow road next to the highway. Between the road and blacktop stood a solid stand of black spruce. If that car turned onto the road into Defiance, the spruce wall would provide all the cover and privacy he needed.

Sam turned into the narrow lane, steered left and parked behind the stand of trees, cutting the jeep's engine. His headlights darkened.

He flung open the door, stepped into the snowy tree branches, snapped off a five-foot section of branch and carried it, running, back to the lane opening. He found the place where his tracks left the road and used the tree branch to sweep them clear. By the time he was nearly finished he saw the muffled glimmer of oncoming headlights, nosing slowly around the bend.

Sam tossed the tree branch behind him and ducked into the wall of black spruce.

The car crawled along the highway, looking for something. Suddenly high beams flashed along the wall. Sam remained motionless, well concealed. As the car approached he peered through the branches and glimpsed a small outline of overhead lights and a passenger door that read *Defiance Police*.

Sam remembered Bill Grebs, wondered if it was him. He watched the car pass the lane's entrance. It traveled another ten yards and then pulled onto the shoulder and stopped. He couldn't imagine the cop had seen him, but why stop?

After fifteen seconds a second pair of headlights rounded the bend. The police car waited while a new blue pickup crept up beside it.

The two drivers rolled down their windows and yelled over the wind gusts. "Thought I saw something," the policeman said. "You see anything?"

"Like what?"

"Thought I saw a car cross that intersection?"

"At one o'clock in the morning? In the middle of a storm like this?"

Their voices sounded familiar, but Sam wasn't sure.

"Could have sworn I saw something."

"It's your nerves, Grebs. Maybe you need a little more remedy."

There was a pause, a stretch and rustle, and then a sharp exhalation followed by Grebs's harsh voice. "Let's wait a minute," he managed. "If I did see someone, we'll give him plenty of time to get home."

"Suits me."

"It's one hell of a storm."

"Nothing like back at the farm."

There was a sharp flick and a yellow flare as the outline of the patrolmen's face lit up. Bill Grebs started a cigarette. "We couldn't have hoped for a better snowfall."

"Could have been a little lighter."

"Harder the better. Sock everything in for a while. We could use a little break."

"Just so they don't get caught in it."

"With Angus's truck? They're back at his place by now."

"Hope so," the pickup commented, nervous.

"It's not like you to worry, Hank."

Hank Gunderson. Sam heard a light cough, after what he assumed was another long swallow of remedy.

"I'm not worried," Hank said. "Just concerned for the well-being of our friends." There was levity in his voice.

Grebs finished his cigarette and flicked it out his window. He put the patrol car in gear. "Let's just keep our eyes open," Grebs said. "If you see anything, flash your lights."

"Will do."

Then they both started off down the road. Sam remained concealed in the snow-covered bush until their taillights disappeared.

He stood up and shook the snow off his coat. He wondered what he'd overheard. Angus . . . he assumed Moon . . . and someone else? Hal Young? At the farm? The old man's farm?

Sam pushed through the branches and stepped up to the highway, searching for the glowing butt. He saw a dark spot, reached down and plucked it out of the snow, held it close. The fine print above the filter read "Old Gold." Good to know some things hadn't changed, he thought, remembering Grebs's brand.

Sam returned to his jeep. From the glove compartment he pulled out a black-handled flashlight. The butt of the flashlight was solid steel, heavy enough to break a window, if it came to that. Or Bill Grebs's head. He switched the light on to make sure it worked. Then he flicked it off and tucked it into the belly panel of his coat.

When Sam was young, Angus Moon's gaze was enough to make him avert his eyes. Moon noticed the boy's furtive turning away. Sometimes he stared at him just to watch him squirm. Unless it involved cards, hunting or fishing, Angus Moon had an instinctual distrust for anything civilized. Sam hoped he'd have another opportunity to stare into the rugged man's face. This time he wouldn't look away.

Hank Gunderson owned the local Ford dealership. Or at least used to. He was a big man who 20 years ago drank whiskey like water. Gunderson had a reputation for hunting women the way the old man hunted deer. Only for Gunderson the season never ended. And instead of a deer head mounted on his wall, he'd pull an undergarment out of his coat pocket, grin with boyish pride, and tell the story of how he'd acquired his trophy with so much lewd embellishment even the crudest bar patrons turned aside.

Hal Young's independent insurance agency was attached to his house, not far from Sam's mother's place. Sam had often enough walked in front of it, when he was staying at his mother's. He'd even nodded to the man on occasion, who at least nodded back, more cordial than the others.

Grebs, Moon, Gunderson and Young. They were the only friends the old man ever had, if you could call them friends. Now the four of them shared almost five million dollars and what was left of his parents' property. "But who's counting?" Sam wondered aloud. It was a lot of money, but he didn't care about the cash. He'd come to recover his things.

He stared into the snowy darkness of the road. He would give Grebs and Gunderson time to settle into their beds.

He reached into the back of the jeep and pulled open his gray metal toolbox. He felt for his crescent wrench and a plastic case of small screwdrivers. He didn't believe he would need them, but he wanted to be prepared. He folded the wrench in a thin wool scarf. He pulled a stiff chamois from his glove compartment, wrapping it around the plastic case of screwdrivers. Then he slid them both into the belly panel of his coat, arranging them so they would not rub or clank.

He would have to be careful. He didn't know what Moon was doing, or with whom. But this storm would give them cover. Sam appreciated it for the same reasons. After he was finished he'd blow out of town before anyone knew he'd arrived. He'd plow south to Brainerd, establish his alibi, and then—after the storm blew itself out—revisit Defiance, the closest place to a childhood home he'd ever known.

The weather was taking on a life of its own. If he wanted to avoid getting stuck he would have to move quickly. After a couple more minutes he put the jeep in gear, backed down the narrow pasture road and edged up to the highway. Then he turned toward town.

CHAPTER SEVEN

JANUARY 30TH, PAST MIDNIGHT—WILLISTON WINTHROP'S FARM

Outside the barn there were occasional gusts of straight-line winds. The truck's headlights illuminated a wall of white. The windward side of the truck was already drifting with a high bank of snow. After another half hour watching the storm rise and seeing no abatement in the fury, Winthrop started to worry.

He turned off the truck and cut the lights. He opened the door and fought his way into a semi-upright position.

"Angus!" he yelled. The wind tore the words out of his mouth. There was no way Angus would hear him through this howl. If they hoped to make it out to the cabin before dawn, he would have to climb up to the loft and fetch Moon.

He pitched forward, feeling along the barn wall. He worked around carefully to the back upper side. He went in through the loft door. A dim light glowed from the rafters.

"Angus!" he yelled. There was no immediate answer. "Angus!" he repeated.

"What?" Angus finally snapped, startled from his observations of the dogs.

Except for occasional struggles the hybrids were quiet, their dark shapes shadowy in the poorly lit barn. The interior was heavy with the smell of carnage.

"It's getting worse," Williston said.

Angus stared down into his feeding animals.

"They finished?" Winthrop asked.

"Not yet."

"Can we get them out?"

Angus kept staring. He called to one of the hybrids, but there was no response. He picked up a wood chip and tossed it into the center of the feeding dogs. There was an immediate snarl.

"Not now," Angus said.

The wind blustered against the barn.

"When?"

"When they finish eating."

"How much longer?"

"Don't know."

"When do you think?"

Angus considered. "Hard to say. They've been two days without anything but water. They'll have to satisfy their appetites."

Williston peered down at the dogs. From this vantage they looked a whole lot more wolf than dog. For the first time his careful sequence of events was taking an unexpected turn. The storm was perfectly timed, but it was growing too violent. And he had underestimated the hybrids' reaction to two days of confinement and starvation. He began to realize the animals might have to be left behind.

"Goddammit! You think they'll run when they're finished?"

"Leave them?"

"You want to be stuck here with them?"

For the first time since the dogs began, Angus tuned in to the storm.

"What do you think they'll do?" Winthrop asked.

"Hard telling. Probably stay here until the storm ends. There's plenty of food."

"You think you can catch them?"

"They're my dogs. They'll come."

"Not that we have a choice," Winthrop muttered. "We're going to have to leave them."

He resigned himself to their departure. He didn't think the sheriff would come out tomorrow, given the storm and how busy the sheriff would be with emergencies in and around Vermilion Falls. But Williston couldn't risk being found here with Angus Moon's animals. With luck, leaving the dogs would only cause a slight alteration of plans. They could hike out to the cabin, and tomorrow Angus would return to the farm, cage the dogs and hustle them back to his place before anyone discovered them. Once they were safely stowed, Angus could return to the farm as if to feed the cattle, discover the carnage and report it.

"Let's get the hell out," Winthrop said.

He turned and Angus followed. They fought their way down along the edge of the outside wall. At the bottom Angus noticed the door slightly open. He tried to pull it shut but the storm had whipped snow into the hinges, widening the six-inch crack to a foot, freezing it there.

"Come on," Winthrop yelled, getting into the cab. "They'll stay put!"

Angus wasn't so sure. He kicked the door, but it was solid. He hunched against the howl and kicked twice more, trying to clear it, but the hinges were frozen.

"Motherfuck!" He hit it a third time before Williston laid on the horn and startled him. He turned to see Winthrop mouth the words "leave it," motioning him into the cab. Angus turned and fought against the wind, leaving the door ajar.

CHAPTER EIGHT

JANUARY 30TH, PAST MIDNIGHT—INTO DEFIANCE

Sam skittered over the highway, approaching the edge of town. He caromed through a half dozen blocks to the corner of Beacon and Elm. He watched for any sign of Gunderson or Grebs, but saw no one. He turned north on Beacon, accelerating up the long incline. As he crested the rise he cut the jeep's engine. His headlights faded and for a moment there was only the velocity of his car going forty through the blackness of the Defiance town street.

He could barely discern where the street turned and there was a solid thump as his wheels broke through a snowdrift, hardly slowing his progress. He banked the car and the wheels broke through another snowdrift. His eyes grew accustomed to the streetlights. He could see the snow-covered pavement flash in and out of sight as the pace of the car accelerated. Sam hit the bottom of the hill going forty and the jeep started its long gradual ascent. Near the road's end the street made a short rise. Sam peered to see the end of the street unchanged with the snow-covered ruts rising into the trees. He dropped off the pavement and the jeep jolted through two large banks before it plowed up the narrow path into a black spruce tunnel and he braked.

He breathed in the darkness. He'd expected at least some of the roads to be different. He had worried the dirt road might be overgrown, or that someone had placed reflector posts to mark the dead end of the street. But the streets were unchanged and the weather and early morning hour were keeping everyone indoors.

On his way to his mother's house he crossed in front of Hal Young's independent insurance office. There were fresh tire tracks up the driveway, just beginning to drift over. He looked up at the old house-office complex, but its windows were dark. Sam wondered about it, remembering Grebs's and Gunderson's comments. Maybe Mrs. Young had returned late? Or it was someone else out at Angus Moon's place? He hurried over the fading tracks.

He approached his mother's house in the dark. Her bushes were rounded over with high banks of snow. The driveway was an unbroken plane. The drive and the walk hadn't been plowed all winter. The front of the house faced northwest. The force of several winter storms had almost buried the porch. The snow had drifted to the middle of the front door, and the bedroom windows to the right of the door were drifted high up with snow.

Looks like a goddamn igloo, Sam thought. Perfect.

He was unprepared for how his mother's house made him feel. He was suddenly nostalgic for the decent part of his childhood, the part of it that redeemed him: Miriam Samuelson. When he was young she showed him the kind of unconditional love he had come, finally, to appreciate. Time away helped him see it. He had been too young and there had been too much collateral damage to make him appreciate what had been good about his childhood.

A sting of arctic wind and snow reminded him why he had come.

He rounded the garage and came up to the snow-covered back steps. Even if the house had been occupied, Sam knew its occupants would never find the articles he and his mother had hidden. A vacant house simplified matters, though he still had to find a way in.

He peered out at the neighborhood homes, obscured by driving snow. The rear entry was covered over like the front. He reached up, found the doorknob at the top of a drift and turned it. Locked.

He remembered a cellar window to the right of the back door. There was no sign of it now, buried under a high bank of snow. He remembered its approximate location and tunneled into the drift. Near the base of the hard-packed powder there was a hollow where a small cave had formed. Sam reached in and realized the deep window well hadn't filled in with snow. He felt for the window, moved down the pane to its bottom, grabbed the single-handled latch and tried it. Locked.

The wind buffeted the roof and house sides. There was more snow blowing into what had been the backyard, alley and nearby yards. It was enough to obscure even the closest house. Sam huddled against the worst of the blow.

He felt inside the belly panel of his coat and pulled out the steel handled flashlight. He reached down, extended the butt of the flashlight through the window and the frosted glass shattered.

He placed one arm through the broken pane, the other against the front. In one heavy effort he pushed and pulled and with a sudden jolt the window broke open. Glass sprinkled onto the basement floor and Sam's wrist passed over a shard edge. He jerked his hand back. He could feel the laceration, knew it would bleed, but it was a slight wound. He returned to the window, pushed it open and locked it upright.

He turned around and backed into the wide window well feet first, lowering himself through the tight enclosure. It was plenty wide enough for him to fit, even with his bulky winter wear. He let himself down and dropped to the floor.

It was quiet in the basement, out of the storm. Quiet and warm. His flashlight pierced the darkness. Against the far wall he saw a lamp, a sofa and a table covered in plastic. He turned the beam on his wrist. Drops of blood beaded along a narrow line, but it was just a scratch. He walked over and opened the preserve room door. His light danced off dozens of stacked jars, everything covered by a heavy patina of dust. Seeing all the jars put up by his mother's hands was like stepping into a mausoleum. He had not eaten since dinner. He hadn't thought of food. But when he saw the jars of pickles, jams, beans, corn, and every other kind of vegetable and fruit, his hunger surfaced like a cork.

He took down a jar of pickles. A piece of masking tape read "DILL" in his mother's awkward script. Sam set the jar aside and kneeled in front of the bottom shelf. He took a minute to remove the contents from the shelf and set it on the floor beside him. Then he tapped under the front lip and the shelf loosened. He lifted and slid it out from its mooring, setting it aside. He flashed the light into the floor-wall cornice and could barely see the heavy wires. He reached in and teased them out, making them taut. They were steel wires, and though they looked tarnished and dirty from 20 years against a basement wall, they still felt solid. He pulled on them, carefully, and a pair of foundation bricks nudged forward. Once loosened, he brought them all the way out.

He flashed his beam into the dark opening. Tucked into the cave there was a large bag. He reached into the black space and dragged it out. It was heavy and covered in dust. He kneeled in the basement storage room, lifted the heavy canvas bag and shook it. The air filled with a light cloud and he coughed. He hoisted the bag to his shoulder, picked up the jar of pickles, and stood, stepping out of the storage room and turning to the basement stairs. At the top of the stairs he flicked off his flashlight and let his eyes grow accustomed to the close darkness. A muted back alley light filtered through the kitchen window. It was enough to find his way down the near hallway. He examined the dining room, living room, bathroom, laundry and bedrooms. He entered his old bedroom. He could see the windows were covered over with snow.

He closed the door and the room went dark. He flicked on his flashlight and set it on the pillow so it faced down his childhood bed, illuminating the room. The bed was still covered in familiar white chenille. Beside the bed stood the old wooden spindle and faux birch bark lampshade, the white bark faded to yellow. His rectangular pine dresser was still in the corner. There was a pair of closet doors that opened into a recessed wall space.

After his mom moved to town, the old man refused to let Sam stay here more than a few nights every month. But his mother had made it nice for him and they had both endured the old man's control. All those years and she'd kept his room exactly as it had been when he was a boy.

He wondered what she felt as she passed it, after he had left for good, maybe waiting for him to return, suspecting and then knowing he would not. He wished things had been different and he'd been able to breach the chasm between them, to let her know that on occasions her remembered kindness reached out of the past. He recalled her hands preparing a meal, washing clothes, cleaning the house, canning preserves. His mother's heart was simple. She'd loved him without measure, abatement or conditions, done what she could to make him right. She'd lived with a kind of purity, and he wished now that she was here and he could tell her how he felt.

He turned to the duffel, loosened the drawstring and peered inside. Near the top was a thick envelope addressed to him. He set the envelope aside, returning to the bag. He found the ten gauge shotgun, one of his father's precious Decimators, the one with the fang-scarred stock. The old man once told him it would be his, but Sam had never lived up to the shotgun's promise. So the old man hadn't kept his word. Sam felt happy now to see it.

The bag also contained the army issue camo parka, pants, and boot coverings Sam had used for stalking in snow. And there was a full box of shells, also dusty and old. Sam guessed they were still operational. If powder remained dry it could hold its charge for decades.

Under it all was a wrapped plastic square, about the size of a shoebox, taped tight so it had the shape and heft of a brick. When he peered through the plastic he saw the blurry face of Benjamin Franklin. There were four of them, set side by side on what appeared to be thick stacks of bills.

If the entire brick was $100 bills it was a considerable sum. The unexpected treasure made his pulse spike.

He set it aside, opening his mother's envelope. There were several handwritten pages and another legal document. The legal document was a copy of her will. It was a long letter, dated just days before she died. He angled it to pick up the flashlight's beam and skimmed it in the half light.

She talked about her health. She didn't know how long she would live. She was starting to feel her age and she didn't think the end was far off. She had spent the last few months converting her retirement accounts to cash, gradually withdrawing the savings from her account, over $179,000. If she had drawn a cashier's check and mailed it, and then passed on, she was afraid Williston would have found Sam and figured out a way to recover the money. If she mailed it she would have to insure it, and Williston might find out where it went and why. "Your father knows a lot of people," she explained. "People who owe him favors."

Neither did she trust Williston about the will. She expected he would alter it, since everything had been left to Sam. So she'd taken the money and hid it in the bag believing, knowing, someday Sam must return. And she knew Williston would never find it, not in their secret place. She'd made sure to leave a second copy of the will, this one dated to be her last, "and notarized in Brainerd so if the older copy is altered you'll have proof."

She reminisced about Sam, when he was a boy, their lives together, about everything that happened to them. And she warned about confronting Williston, if he was still alive.

"Get your things, but be careful about it."

She told him to share nothing with Williston Winthrop, advice he didn't need.

She ended the letter with an apology: "I am so sorry for everything," she said. Then, "When you read this I hope everything finds you well. And please remember that I always loved you—more than you can possibly imagine—and always will."

As Sam grew older he wondered why his mother never told the old man to fuck off. The first time Williston raised a fist she should have drawn up legal papers and taken him for every dime he was worth. There was no excuse for accepting the years of belittlement and abuse. But it was his mother. He recognized her optimism in the face of despair, how she refused to let the old man's wickedness tarnish her perspective. And it was true; his father knew people. It would have been difficult to find justice on the Range.

When he was twelve his mother left the farm and moved into this house, to get away from the old man, not her son. But Sam recognized Williston Winthrop held the power. Sam was a boy and wasn't expected to live outside his father's rule. When he re-read the last lines of her letter, he knew she had lived her life according to her convictions. They weren't his convictions. Never had been, never would be. In the childhood room she'd prepared for him, he regretted not fighting harder against the old man's rule. But he had been a boy and the old man was his father and a powerful son of a bitch.

He picked up the brick of money and felt its heft; $179,000 and change, a considerable sum, particularly by weight. It must have pissed off the old man. Sam smiled to think about it. He knew his mother smiled too.

Outside, the storm was still howling. He would have to leave soon, or risk getting stuck, maybe even discovered. He carried the jar of pickles into the kitchen. He placed the jar in the bottom of the sink and twisted the lid open. He heard the vacuum seal pop and the fragrance of dill was released. The odor of dill and vinegar and his mother's special blend was overpowering. He pulled a pickle out of the jar and tasted it, remembering in a sudden rush the pickles he loved as a boy. It had been a long time since he'd had hunger for anything. The pickle tasted salty, pungent and remarkable.

He recapped the jar and returned to the basement. He extracted three more jars from the preserve room and slid them with the pickles into his bag. He replaced the bottom shelf and moved the contents on the floor back onto it. Then he crawled out the window, leaving the basement as he'd found it. He carried the bag on his shoulder, struggling back over the Defiance streets, returning to his jeep. He started the cold engine and in the early morning darkness managed to back out and plow past the dead end of the street. Then he spun the jeep's heavy treads through the thickening snow and returned the way he'd arrived, with stealth through the widening winter storm.

Eventually the town cop would discover his break-in. But by then the snow would cover his tracks. Weather reports indicated the heavy blow would drop a few more inches before it was done. That would mean it might be awhile before Grebs discovered the broken cellar pane.

He thought about his mother's letter and the money. Her hope and heart strength were her best epitaphs. And his mother's will had been altered. The proof rested in his breast pocket, where at the right time he would enjoy making it known. He wondered what the statute of limitations was on probating an estate? He'd have to find some legal counsel. But he would have to be careful about it. How he had acquired the will and when to make it known would require some planning. For the moment it was enough to have the old man's precious Decimator in the back of his jeep, nestled beside his mother's pickles, her $179,000 and three jars of her excellent preserves.

Part II

Behold, I send you forth as sheep in the midst of wolves: be ye therefore wise as serpents, and harmless as doves.

MATTHEW 10:16

CHAPTER NINE

JANUARY 30TH—THE CABIN IN SKINWALKER'S BOG

"Are you getting anything?"

"Nothing," Angus answered. "Not a goddamned thing."

Angus sat in front of the cabin's citizens' band radio console, trying to call out. "This is Woods Weasel calling the Defiance Star. Are you reading? Over."

Around them the dawn was just starting to break, bright and frozen. The snow banked to their windows, covering the front door. It lay in piles in the woods, along the few hidden trails leading to the cabin and the remote, abandoned logging roads leading to the trails. The pathways were impassable and both of them feared it would be more than a day before Angus could snowshoe the three miles back to the truck, and then dig himself out and return to the farm. Which meant the dogs would be alone in the barn for another day. With the goddamn door open.

"Just keep trying," Winthrop said. "We need to get word to Grebs."

Angus peered out of bloodshot eyes. "I know." He was growing weary of Williston's repeated demand.

"He has to go over and tend them," Williston continued, ignoring Angus. "Grebs has to find the kill and report it. And get your dogs," he added.

"I know," Angus agreed. When Williston was edgy, it was best to go along.

Williston hadn't stopped mulling plans since they'd been forced to leave the farm. Now he was trying to work through all the alternatives, tracking consequences, considering steps. He didn't like where his options led, but he didn't have much choice. The dogs unsettled him. Before anyone could be notified they'd have to be caged. And what if someone else found them? What if they ran? The goddamn wolf-dogs were a nasty loose end, difficult to explain and threatening to unravel his plan. He reminded himself that it was unlikely anyone would visit the farm, particularly after a storm like this one, especially given the roads. But he'd feel a whole lot better if they got word to Grebs.

"There's only one answer to this," Williston finally blurted.

Angus looked at him, waiting for the next directive.

"Remedy," he smiled. "A little remedy in our morning coffee."

It was an unexpected remark. "Now you're talkin'," Angus agreed. "Hair of the dog that bit ya'," he grinned.

As Williston walked across the room he heard Angus place another call into the ether: "Woods Weasel to the Defiance Star. Come in, Star. Is anyone out there? Anyone listening? Come in. Over?"

Winthrop was still stunned by the night's random misfortunes. They had been forced to leave the dogs. They had driven at a crawl through howling winds and blinding snow and were damn lucky to find the entrance to the abandoned logging road. When Angus went to unlock the heavy chain, he'd disappeared in a slantwise fury of snow. It reminded Williston of farmers getting lost in blizzards only yards from their front door.

In the dark, the truck's headlights illuminated a sideways howl of white, obliterating his view. At the point where Winthrop was certain Angus had been gone too long, was possibly lost, he saw fingers reach out of the blizzard. Angus's gnarled, weathered hand, accustomed to storms, groped and pulled himself through the blow. He struggled forward in a stumbling lurch. He fought his way into the cab.

"Did you find it?" Williston asked, inquiring about the lock and chain.

"Jesus Christ," Angus heaved. "Almost got lost out there."

"Where are your gloves?"

"I had to find the chain by feel, then the lock. Then the wind tore the gloves from under my arm. Had to let 'em go." He was heaving, clearly shaken by the storm.

"Did you get it open?"

Angus nodded. When he caught his breath he said, "but I'm not sure we want to drive into it."

After Angus dropped the chain they had no other choice but to inch forward. Normally Angus would have gone back and re-affixed the chain and lock, but after almost getting lost he refused to try.

They'd spent well over an hour edging toward the trail point. Fortunately, the abandoned logging trail was narrow and overgrown. In most places a healthy canopy overgrew it and afforded some protection against the storm. It provided them with enough visibility to find the trailhead. And once into the bog the trees helped lessen the blow. Still, they took an extra hour struggling along the narrow trail to make it to the cabin. Almost immediately they'd started calling out on the CB.

Now the radio crackled and sparked.

"It's the atmosphere," Williston observed, returning with the whiskey. "That goddamn storm choked the roads, the country, the whole fuckin' Range. Now it's whipping around the air waves, sucking every particle into a black hole."

"Must be right over us," Angus agreed. "I can't get a goddamn thing."

Winthrop topped Angus's coffee with whiskey. After Angus picked up his cup Winthrop raised his own. "Here's to making mayhem pay."

Angus raised his cup and sipped, still peering at the knobs and dials. He flipped a receiver switch and started moving the volume dial. As he did, a crackle faded into someone's voice. Words. They were barely discernible articulations, vowel sounds and consonants. They couldn't pickup anything clear, but it was a man's voice.

"There's something," Williston observed.

Angus tweaked the dials. He edged it left and the voice disappeared. He tried the microphone. "Hello," he said. "This is the Woods Weasel," he began, giving his call sign. "Just trying to find somebody. Anybody there? Over."

The voice came back, still muffled.

"Things are starting to clear," Williston said.

Angus barely touched the dial and out jumped a man's voice.

"This storm is not the work of Satan, but the Hand of God! If anyone believes for one moment that God is unaware of the devil's pernicious habits, his unyielding effort to turn men's minds to evil, then it is *he* who does not know God. For God knows all things. He is all-powerful, able to see into your heart, and mine. And yes, He can even peer into the black depths of Satan's puny muscle."

It was some religious nut, Williston guessed. Using the airwaves to preach his own personal sermon. And judging from the reference to the storm it had to be somewhere on the Range, someplace near. "Turn that asshole off," Winthrop snapped, which was just fine by Angus Moon.

CHAPTER TEN

JANUARY 30TH, DAWN—DIANE TALBOTT'S CABIN

Somewhere far out in the woods, the dawn's orange patina began to glow. Last night's storm left a high bank of snow against Diane Talbott's northwest walls. Snow covered her driveway in alternating drifts. Snow buried her old Datsun pickup so only the hood and wheels on one side were visible. Snow banked high on her front porch all the way to her bedroom window that was only now beginning to show the morning's first crimson light.

Diane had just fallen back into a deep slumber.

She had gone to bed early because there was nothing to be done about the storm. She was 47 and her sleep patterns had begun to alter with the first glimpses of menopause. In addition to temperature modulation and mood swings that swept across her like siroccos, she sometimes awoke in the middle of the night. She had friends who had been through it, so she knew what to expect. She'd had two checkups with Dr. Susan Wallace, who told her she could soften the effects with hormone therapy. Diane Talbott hated the idea of using a drug to ease what was a natural aging process. But she was tired of a poor night's rest, histrionic mood swings and hot flashes. She decided to give it a try. And it had worked. At least for sleep and temperature modifications. But a side effect had been slightly swelled breasts and an uptick in libido, neither of which did Diane, who except for an occasional fling had been single and unattached for more than five years, much good. It made her smile and was further proof of one of her core beliefs; we were little more than dullards when tinkering with Mother Nature.

When she shared her symptoms with Dr. Wallace, Susan told her whatever she was doing, keep doing it, because all her vital signs were excellent. "You must have inherited some very good genes."

Diane started laughing. Longevity ran on both sides of her family. But so did tipplers. "It's good to know eating like a chipmunk and this exercise regimen is having a positive effect. Now all I need is a loaner."

"Loner?"

"A man."

"You want a man who's a loner?"

"L-O-A-N-E-R," she spelled it out. "A borrow boy. Someone I can spend date night with. The whole night. He can leave in the morning."

Dr. Wallace smiled. "I don't know any loaners. But like I said, whatever you're doing, keep it up. You look great. And your blood work is perfect."

"I feel pretty good, too."

"So you just have to be aware of the symptoms and know what to expect and that they're normal."

And that's the way they left it.

So last night, when the skies around her small cabin were howling and the snow was shrieking like a banshee, she had to pee, regular as clockwork. Afterward, she had a hard time returning to sleep. But the inside of her small bedroom was like a cocoon and she enjoyed just lying in the dark, listening to the storm and thinking.

Finally, she'd drifted off. And now, with the light filling her windows, she had returned to deep sleep. That was sometimes the way it happened. Up for more than an hour in the middle of the night, just thinking. And then drifting off before dawn into peaceful oblivion, so deep she did not stir until well past her 6:30 a.m. wakeup. And that's where she was right now, like a black bear curled up in a den. Finally she warily cracked open her eyes.

She rolled out of bed still groggy and managed to get herself robed and in the kitchen. She flipped on her scanners and started filling a coffee pot, checking grounds, listening. The two scanners were a recent addition to her professional life. After speaking with a colleague in the Cities, she'd acquired two of the devices. One she kept tuned into the local law enforcement frequencies. The other she used to rove on CB band. The police scanner alerted her to Winthrop's accident, so it had already paid for itself. She was also enjoying the periodic conversation she overheard on the CB band, one of which started as she readied her coffee.

"Woods Weasel to the Defiance Star. Come in, Star. Is anyone out there? Anyone listening? Come in. Over?"

Who the hell was Woods Weasel and Defiance Star? She couldn't transmit, only receive. The law enforcement channel was silent.

When she looked outside she was startled by the snowfall. It was warm in the cabin but she could see orange sunlight rising on a frozen world of snow and ice. Her outside thermometer was set up so she could see it from the kitchen window. Minus seven degrees Fahrenheit.

"That was one hell of a storm," she said.

She waited for the coffee to brew. She doubled its strength, because she still felt the effects of deep sleep, almost like she had drunk too much wine the night before. Deep languor settled into her bones. But there was something else. An old desire: The need to stare into a blank screen and fill it with words. Coffee, she thought. I need coffee.

She kept on the scanners, heard Woods Weasel make one more unanswered entreaty, and then both scanners fell silent.

That's the other thing she believed about staying young, given her age. Diet and exercise helped. But there was nothing like having a purpose and rising to it every morning, anxious to begin anew.

She drank her first cup of coffee. She let the caffeine work. Today, she decided, she would begin by finishing her article. Then dig herself out. Today was one of those surprises given to you when you were both thankful and knew what to do with it. It was like being a kid on a snow day.

After high school Diane attended the University of Minnesota down in the Cities. She had the feeling she would like to write, but she was a poor hand at it. She tried one writing class and then another, but only managed average work. Then in her sophomore year she took an Introduction to Literature class. The TA, at 6' 2" with a full beard and looking more like a lumberjack than a budding English professor, assigned them an Ernest Hemingway short story called *Big Two-Hearted River*. It broke her open like an egg. It was about Nick Adams returning from the war and using the wild country of Northern Michigan to reclaim himself and heal. None of that was in the story, but the TA, over coffee, then drinks, and eventually pillow talk, explained it to her.

Diane was an attractive young woman, but without much experience with men. She had enough sense to know the TA was scratching an itch and their sex reflected his selfishness. But she was appreciative for what he'd explained about Hemingway. The encounter was short lived, but her interest in literature, writing and men remained.

Nothing else moved her like writing. And at the University she was exposed to everything, finally settling on Journalism as a more practical degree than creative writing or literature. She also began to enjoy the occasional party with friends, the periodic surfeit of wine, the pleasant afterglow of a good joint. And that's when she moved back to the Range.

After finishing her degree in Journalism she worked odd jobs, mostly with newspapers doing photography and layout, occasionally penning a story. There was a time she spent two or three years in a party blur, working just enough to scrape by, familiarizing herself with most of the region's northwoods bars. And people liked her, particularly men. She was almost five foot nine inches with curves in the right places and an engaging smile. And after a couple of sloe gin fizzes her laugh was, according to one of her friends at the time, "as seductive as a leopard's." She got on well with the Range men, careful about her occasional companions. In spite of her reputation, taking a partner happened less frequently than the bar men believed. But the last time one of those occasions took, at least biologically. Her partner had been a fun, capable lover. But to Diane it was clear as a deepwater lake that he would never be a father. Her miscarriage was painful, but fortunate. She lost the baby and was never forced to decide between a loveless marriage and the rest of her life. The stark choice made her reconsider her participation in the Range bar scene and occasionally what happened after they closed.

Not long after Diane's miscarriage, her aunt died. She'd owned a cabin outside Defiance, which she left to the struggling writer. Diane was ready to put her former Range life behind her. For six months she did nothing but write, coveting her savings like a miser. She dispensed it a few crumbs at a time, making it last. She read, heavily, which is where she first met Miriam Winthrop. Over 20 years ago Miriam befriended her and introduced her to a local women's book group, every one of them rabid readers.

The group gave her a social outlet. And the reading improved her writing. She finally took a job reporting with the *Vermilion Falls Gazette*.

When she peered out her kitchen window she realized it would be a while before she dug herself out. She phoned her boss. It was still early. The office would be empty.

"I'm working from home today," she said. "I'm finishing up that long obit on Winthrop, and if I'm reading your mind properly, I bet you want seven column inches about this storm, which you'll have by this afternoon."

She hung up. She'd wait for the thermometer to climb to zero before breaking out her snowblower. Meanwhile, she needed to finish that obit.

She'd barely known Williston Winthrop. But her research had turned up plenty. Jeff Dunlap, the assistant DA, alluded to an investigation, but she couldn't get corroboration or any sense of what it was about. And regardless, the *Gazette* wouldn't have run it in an obit. The *Gazette* believed you should never speak ill of the dead—even though Williston Winthrop deserved every ill word she could conjure. The only people she could get to go on record with a positive remark were the members of that Club. And they were the beneficiaries of the man's estate, something that prick Hank Gunderson was quick to point out, when she'd spoken with him at the farm. He was coming into some money. Diane still couldn't believe how the son of a bitch stared straight at her breasts the night of Williston's accident. There had been times he'd more or less propositioned her, but so had a score of men across the Range.

She needed a few more details to finish her obit. She'd try Hal Young first. If Hal couldn't help, she could always turn to Hank, who was clearly willing. She didn't like the idea of calling Hank Gunderson, but her other alternatives—Bill Grebs and Angus Moon—made her skin crawl. At least she had been able to joke with Hank, because Hank was a player. Hank was a 'good ol' boy.' She was hoping she'd have better luck with Hal.

She finished her coffee and poured herself another cup. Then she went into her bedroom where her computer sat on a small corner desk. She turned on her PC, brought up the obit, and started working. When she glanced over the piece she realized it would be afternoon or later before she finished. She just hoped she got lucky, and Hal came through with the information she needed.

CHAPTER ELEVEN

JANUARY 30TH—DEFIANCE, MINNESOTA

By 8:00 a.m. Sam was returning to Defiance from the east side of town. He had driven all the way south to Brainerd and made sure he bought gas and had something to eat at a local restaurant, keeping the dated receipts in his car, just in case. He'd come in behind the storm, not in the middle of it. The receipt would support his alibi.

The steeple of the Lutheran Church rose above frozen birch and pine, its pinnacled cross encrusted with a thick layer of ice. Sam imagined the view from the cross. He remembered a handful of stores, the lumberyard, the school, Gunderson's Ford, the Winthrop Building, the Naked Loon Bar, Opel Grady's Cafe, and more churches than God had any right to expect in a town with these dimensions.

Defiance was settled when northern Minnesota was the Northwest Territory and people came here in search of timber, fur, gold and the absence of any laws but their own. They cut down the original pine forest, and the fur lasted as long as the animals slaughtered to provide them. Instead of gold they discovered iron, much more costly and laborious to extract. But as long as anyone could remember, iron sustained the string of northern Minnesota mining towns across the Range. Until recent history.

For the last two decades Sam had read about the decline of the iron mines. Chinese and foreign imports had gutted the American steel industry, drying up the need for local ore. In the wake of foreign competition the old pit mines were abandoned, replaced by an effort to eke out a living in the tourist trade during the warmer months, at least for those who stayed. The winters charted the coldest temperatures in the continental U.S.

More recently some of the mining companies had begun to restart their iron mining efforts, while others had begun to develop non-ferrous metal deposits. The region was starting to come back, but slowly, and not here in Defiance.

He didn't need gas, but he did need information. At the edge of town Peterson's Standard had been transformed into a Holiday. He pulled into the station and topped off his tank. The clear sky wasn't helping with the cold; the station thermometer read -7. He'd blown in with a cold front.

Behind the counter a high school kid looked up from his textbook, waiting for Sam to pay. He had green eyes, a compact frame and square shoulders. Under the boy's insulated shirt Sam noticed broad shoulders and plenty of muscle. His hands were deft and capable, and his face could have graced a box of Wheaties.

Sam imagined the kid gliding over ice, smashing a hockey puck in northern Minnesota's greatest pastime. It was the eyes that suggested he might be a Peterson, one of the progeny of the clan he worked for as a kid.

"Your name Peterson?"

The boy looked friendly enough. "Yeah."

"That your dad who owns the spread outside of town?"

"My Uncle Paul," he said. He took Sam's card and sliced it through the register's reader.

"Do you know a Diane Talbott?"

The boy placed Sam's receipt on the table, waiting for his signature. Sam watched him glance at the cardholder's name.

"Sam Rivers," he said, referencing the name on the card. "My mother was a friend of Diane's."

"Uh-huh," the boy nodded.

"Sometimes Diane would take my mom and me fishing."

The kid nodded again, guarded.

"If I remember right, Diane loved catching snakes, just for the fun of it." *Snakes* was the local term for the long, aggressive northern pike, one of Minnesota's hardest-fighting fish, but also slimy and difficult to fillet.

"Sounds like Diane," the boy smiled. "She likes a good fight. Lives outside of town, on the Old Road."

The boy gave him directions while Sam returned the card to his wallet. When he looked out the window he saw that the Ben Franklin had closed. The old painted ads were peeling from its windows. The sidewalks in front of the store were choked with snow. Further down the street he saw a tavern closed and a church with its windows boarded up. The doors to the old Defiance Library were chained. Beyond it, peaking from around the corner, he caught the edge of the Winthrop Building.

"Defiance Hotel still open?"

The boy nodded.

"It's a wonder anybody's still here."

"I'm gettin' out. Soon as I'm done with school."

Sam noticed the kid's sincerity. He thought about telling him a story, about growing up and getting out. But Sam wasn't ready. Not yet.

He thanked the boy and left.

On the edge of town the Hotel Defiance stood like a sturdy brick fort before the abandoned Iron Rail depot and the woods that went on forever beyond it. The depot had been used to haul timber and ore when Defiance was still a boomtown. Now its windows stood broken and empty. The old depot door was padlocked. The ground around the dilapidated structure was thigh high with new snow. Until Defiance High School had closed down and consolidated with Vermilion Falls, its graduating classes had tagged the depot's brick sides with graffiti.

The hotel was still there. Its sign was faded and almost unintelligible, but its walks were plowed clean. A faded yellow VACANCY was taped to the window. Sam pushed through the door.

Behind the desk a television blared from a back room. Sam slapped the old-fashioned desk bell. He heard a chair creak, and in a moment an old man stood in the door's threshold.

"Yeah?" he said, eyeing Sam with suspicion.

"Have you got a room?"

The old man's head looked like a cue ball, its most prominent feature a pair of antiquated black plastic rimmed glasses. He wore a work shirt and gray khaki work pants with black suspenders. His clothes were threadbare, but clean and well pressed. His belly pushed over his belt like a distended watermelon, bulging his shirt buttons and parting the suspenders. Judging from the hotel's quietude, he had plenty of time for meals.

"Got 16 of them," the man finally answered.

"Good."

"I taped that VACANCY sign up over ten years ago. The only times I come close to bringing it down are hunting season and fishing opener."

Sam smiled. "I'm looking for something with a view," he said.

"You can have whatever room you want, but don't expect a view."

"How about a room that overlooks those train tracks, facing the woods?"

"That'll be seven. Right over my place."

Sam signed his name and completed the registration form with his Yellow Rock address and phone while the proprietor reached down and pulled a key off an inside cupboard. From the keys on the inside of the cupboard Sam could see he was the only guest.

"Business slow?"

"Depends on how you look at it." The old man considered Sam with a wry gaze. "This ain't Fitger's in Duluth, but you're my second person this week, and that's two more than last week." He glanced down at Sam's name. "Rivers?" he squinted.

"Sam Rivers."

"Elwyn Baxter," the man said, reaching over and shaking Sam's hand. "From around here?"

"A long time ago," he said. "It's been a while. I left quite a few years back."

"Any kin?"

"All dead."

"Seems like all the young ones leave," the proprietor mused. "Can't say I blame them. Nothing for them around here. Everything closing up. I don't remember any Rivers."

"None of them live here anymore."

"Figures."

"Does seem like a ghost town."

The old man laughed. "It's a ghost town alright. Plenty of old ghosts like me still hanging around." The old man leaned on the counter, settling in, and added, "If you don't want much it's a nice place to live. A person couldn't want for better fishing or hunting, or more beautiful scenery than our lakes and rivers."

Sam nodded.

"I'm not much of a hunter myself. Give me my 16-foot Alumacraft and my nine-horse Merc and there's nothing better than an evening throwing Red Devils along a rocky shoreline." He tilted his head and sighed.

Outside, a car came down the icy street. They turned to watch Bill Grebs's police car slow in front of the hotel, then pass by.

"Wonder what he wants?" the old man asked with unguarded derision. "Not in any trouble, are ya'?"

"Nothing that anybody knows about," Sam smiled.

Elwyn smiled back. "That's Bill Grebs, Defiance's police force. Not sure what a town this size needs with a police force, but he's it. Had the job for years. He likes harassing strangers and rolling bums. Saw him just last week. He was out back." Through his rear office window he motioned to the abandoned building by the tracks. "Picked up some bum. Big fat old man. Now don't get me wrong, no way I'm for vagrants filling our streets. But if you're down on your luck the only free shelter in town is that abandoned depot, and Grebs is out at dusk harassing him, trying to make a vagrant believe Bill Grebs is important."

Clearly there was no love lost between Bill Grebs and Elwyn Baxter.

"Made him get into his squad car and crated him off. Probably scared the shit out of him and ran him out of town." The old man looked at Sam. "What's a dying town like this need with a cop?" he repeated. "I expect Defiance is keeping Bill Grebs around for forty grand a year when everyone else is out of work. But it's not likely to last," the old man smiled. "What's he gonna' do when there's nothing left in the Defiance treasury? And from what I hear that day isn't far off."

The old man continued for a while: mostly talking about Grebs's uselessness, though his derision wasn't limited to the town cop.

Sam imagined Grebs harassing the homeless. From what he remembered Grebs would appreciate a vagrant's vulnerability. Grebs had a predator's instinct for finding the weakest animal in the herd. He probably whacked him a few times and drove him to the outskirts of Vermilion Falls before kicking him into the cold.

From the look in the old man's eyes Sam knew he was ready to speak at length about any subject Sam cared to discuss. But Sam was long overdue for a warm bed and rest. A long drive, larceny, and then another long drive were exhausting work.

He thanked Elwyn Baxter, excusing himself with an apology, and went out to his jeep to recover his bag and the duffel. As a source of information the proprietor might be useful, Sam thought. But he recognized a small town gossip, and knew whatever Sam told him would be fodder for the hotel's next guest.

Room seven was austere as a hermitage. The bed was narrow and flat. When Sam sat on it, the mattress absorbed nothing. He felt beneath the mattress and touched a seven-by-four-foot plywood board. For support, he guessed, and to give the mattress five more years of wear. Every mattress in the place probably felt like slate. But he was too tired to care.

A nicked up dresser stood to the side of the window. On the opposite wall there was an old picture in a natural birch wood frame—a northwoods trapper checking his trap line, the setting not much different from what Sam could see out his window. The bathroom, sink and shower were behind a door at the end of the hall. Sam set down his bags, took out his Dopp kit and went down to brush his teeth, more tired than he could remember.

The simplicity of the place was fine by Sam. He planned on resting here, nothing more. And truth is, he preferred his mattresses firm. Sam lay down on the unyielding spread. His watch said 9:30 a.m. He lay flat on his back with his clothes still on. He lifted his wrist, setting his watch alarm for 4:00 p.m. Then he closed his eyes and instantly fell asleep.

CHAPTER TWELVE

JANUARY 30TH—VERMILION COUNTY COURTHOUSE

In the Vermilion County Courthouse Sheriff Dean Goddard stepped into Jeff Dunlap's office.

Dunlap looked up and said, "Hey, just a second," and then returned to his papers.

Dunlap's office was a ten-by-fifteen rectangle with a window overlooking the parking lot. The long wall was lined with file cabinets. The cabinets were topped with archive boxes. His table was covered with several neat piles of paper, each pile an open case. He had one of those green glass desk lamps Dean figured was standard issue for everyone passing the bar. Other than the desk lamp and files, nothing about Dunlap's demeanor or appearance would have indicated he was one of the best prosecutors in the state.

Next to the 5′ 9″ county attorney, Dean Goddard felt big and rangy. Jeff Dunlap had feather-short brown hair parted on the side. His mustache looked like the frayed end of a worn toothbrush. He wore round, wire-rimmed glasses with tortoise shell enamel. The Sheriff had known him for almost a decade, but the man's appearance never changed.

The assistant county attorney and the Sheriff had been friends since their first days in local government. Dean Goddard was born and raised on a small farm outside Worthington, Minnesota, a rural community in the southwest corner of the state, about as far from Vermilion Falls as you could get and still call yourself a Minnesotan.

Dunlap was raised on a small acreage outside Defiance. His parents hunted, fished, guided, subcontracted lumber with the County and local sawmills, and cleared over four acres on which they planted Christmas trees. The tree farm was a long-term investment the elder Dunlap called his ten-year tax strategy, since the acreage wouldn't show a profit until the trees matured. Dunlap had grown up with a cabin roof over his head, and plenty to eat, much of it wild. But it was a season-to-season existence. They survived. He loved his parents, but when he was young, he swore he was going to have more than a pot to piss in, and so he did.

He'd spent four years as an undergraduate at the University of Minnesota–Duluth, on an academic scholarship. He got help to attend law school at the University of Minnesota. And then he got the county job, a good one. He was one of the office's top attorneys, and was considered the heir apparent to take over when Percy Lange, the current county attorney, strode into the sunset. There weren't many observers of county politics, but those in the know suspected Percy Lange's departure wasn't far off.

"For Christ's sake," Dunlap moaned, looking up from his pen. "I believe if Jedd Connors has one more DWI I can put him away for six months *and* force him to go through treatment for the second time this year."

"County would be better off," the Sheriff observed.

"Think it'll help?"

The Sheriff shook his head. "But we can hope."

"I guess." The two men were in agreement on most county law enforcement matters. Dunlap closed the folder, leaned back, and put his feet on the only open corner of his desk. "And I suppose the county's better off without that old crook Will Winthrop, though damned if I'm feeling good about it." Dunlap had been mulling Winthrop's death.

When Dean entered, he'd noticed a familiar yellow file in the middle of Dunlap's desk. It was the folder containing the draft subpoena he was going to serve Winthrop with until his untimely accident. He'd wondered about it.

As far as Dean Goddard knew, the only person aware of his relationship with Susan Wallace had been Williston Winthrop. There was a time he'd considered turning to Jeff Dunlap for advice, just to have someone with whom he could confide and help him figure out how he could clean up the awful mess he'd gotten himself into. But instinct told him his good friend would give him advice he wasn't willing to follow: end the affair. Given Williston's demise he was thankful he'd kept his mouth shut.

"What's his death mean for your investigation?" Dean asked.

"Our investigation," Dunlap corrected.

Dean was glad to hear it. The best way to search Winthrop's properties was to have the investigation remain open. He needed that video. He needed to send every second into the unmagnetized ether. The ongoing investigation would give him legal cover.

"It preempts justice," Dunlap quipped. "I wanted to make that old man swing by his thumbs. Gallows would have been too good for him, from what I can figure. I know Minnesota is no longer a hanging state, but there are times I wish it was a simpler day, when we could provide people like Winthrop with swift, certain and absolute justice. From what I can figure, that guy wasn't only a crook. He was a cruel S.O.B. capable of just about anything a criminal mind can conjure."

It was a familiar subject, though they only broached it with each other. Rigorous in their pursuit of criminals, they were just, above all else. And that made the Sheriff's infidelity all the more painful.

"I guess he got what was coming," Dean observed.

"Goddamn right," Dunlap said, staring off at the filing cabinets lining his wall. "But that doesn't mean his beneficiaries should enjoy the fruits of his labors."

The file in the middle of Dunlap's desk contained much more information than the names the Sheriff had shared with Williston Winthrop, well ahead of actually serving him the paper. The fourth investigation into Winthrop's law practice involved three widowed pensioners; Betty Jo Kalumet, Mary Slavenoh and Gertie Wendell. The three had been housed in an assisted living foster care facility called Pine Grove Estates, just outside Hibbing. Betty Jo died two years ago. Mary Slavenoh had been dead less than a year. Gertie was still alive, but had extreme dementia.

The three women shared several characteristics. The first and perhaps most important was their mental status: impaired. They slipped in and out of history with the ease of time travelers, rarely visiting the present. And they were a little fuzzy about particulars. Their own names, for instance, had been as elusive as everyone else's. They had no living next of kin. And in the sense that a pensioner is someone who lives on a small stipend, generally from a qualified benefit plan, these three only *appeared* to be financially stressed senior citizens in need of a safe home.

Beneath the corporate veil of Pine Grove Estates was a Minnesota Corporation with one Limited Partner and one General Partner. The limited partners were Bill and Matty Harris. They were paid by Iron County Care, the general partner. It was a Minnesota corporation with a P.O. Box address in Virginia, Minnesota. Beneath Iron County Care there were some additional limited and general partners that made the entire structure holding up Pine Grove Estates one of the most sophisticated and Byzantine corporate shell games Jeff Dunlap had ever seen. He'd retained a friend in corporate law down in the Cities to help him sort it all out.

Over the years the spinsters not only managed to accumulate considerable estates, but once they entered the comfortable foster care and assisted living provided by Pine Grove Estates, their stipends, and eventually their entire estates, had cascaded down through several corporate entities until they had finally been signed over to attorney Williston Winthrop, General Counsel. It was similar to the mortgage-backed securities crisis, when homeowners searching for the corporate entity that actually held their mortgage found pieces of it with different companies all over the world. In the case of Williston Winthrop, it appeared as though he'd managed to gain the necessary assistance from a local district court judge to make the scheme work, but Jeff was still trying to figure out all the angles of the complicated scheme.

In the end, Williston Winthrop was clearly the attorney identified as the individual who cared for the specific needs of the three women. And judging from their considerable medical requirements (at least on paper), their care was extensive and costly. Automated wheelchairs, intensive drug regimens, 24/7 attention by private nurse practitioners, special meal preparations, dietary supplements, and so on. The care, of course, was difficult to track, with the Medicare reimbursements managed by their executor (the attorney referenced by title).

Iron County Care managed the schoolteachers' last days. If they lived beyond their estates, stipends and insurance benefits, Pine Grove Estates agreed to continue their care *ad infinitum*. It was a safe wager. Actuarial tables opined the women would need to live well into their twelfth decade before their estates ran dry. Since no one in Minnesota history had reached the age of 120, the care facility (and those behind it) figured to make a substantial profit.

"Goddamn crooks" was how Dunlap described them. So far, the Corporation had been fortunate, and the deaths of the first two pensioners had left the Company with a significant largesse.

Everything had continued to operate well below the radar, until less than a year ago. Gertie Wendell had a brief bout with pneumonia and her regular physician was unavailable. Doctor Susan Wallace examined her. What Wallace saw made her wonder if Pine Grove Estates' care was adequate. She mentioned it to the Sheriff, who drove over to have a look.

He found the place clean, filled with plenty of sunlight, the air smelling of antiseptic. And Gertie looked as reasonable as one could expect, considering she seldom got out of bed and was recovering from a nasty respiratory infection. Still, the Sheriff wondered about it, mentioning the place to his friend Jeff Dunlap, who had a peek into the care facility's operations. He started digging. After almost three months of to and fro with the Minnesota Secretary of State's office, and the assistance of his corporate law expert in the Cities, Jeff Dunlap had finally figured it all out. Now he smiled.

"So this doesn't end it?" the Sheriff finally asked.

"No way. But it complicates how we proceed. God knows we're not going to get any answers to our subpoena."

"Dead men don't talk," the Sheriff agreed.

"Not in so many words. But we might yet hear something from his grave." Dunlap considered it. "For starters, I obtained a copy of Winthrop's will. It's a large estate, considering how he lived. He kept his net worth well under the radar. There's plenty, and those buddies of his are going to make out like bandits."

"Bill Grebs?"

"He's one of them. Along with that mongrel Angus Moon. And Hank Gunderson and Hal Young. You know them?"

"Moon's an outdoorsman. Lives pretty far out. Off the grid, far as I can tell."

"That's the guy. A hunter, trapper, not particularly pleasant. Tell you the truth, it surprises me Williston Winthrop had anything to do with him. But a lot of things about Winthrop surprise me. Did you know he had a son?"

"Where?"

"Nobody knows. He was ahead of me in school a couple years. He was a quiet kid, kept to himself. Then one day he just disappeared."

"Anybody look into it?"

"Nope. No reason to. He was old enough. Apparently the mother knew where he was. Rumor had it that old prick beat him up pretty bad and Clayton—that was his name—bolted. Didn't come back, and I don't blame him."

"What about Gunderson and Young?"

"Respectable enough. But it's a curious thing about Winthrop's estate. Over two million comes from a term life insurance policy. Who in the hell keeps that kind of insurance for a bunch of his buddies?"

Dean shrugged, but agreed that so much life insurance was surprising. Particularly considering his beneficiaries.

"I've learned a little about that business," Dunlap added. "Life insurance companies do a lot of research to make sure they understand a client's total life insurance picture; the companies, policies, amounts, dates of ownership, beneficiaries, that kind of thing. When consumers buy life insurance they're entered into databases. If some guy takes out ten $50,000 policies on his wife, making himself the beneficiary, they want to know about it."

The Sheriff wasn't surprised. Insurance companies were hesitant to part with money, so they took precautions.

"And any policies less than a year old are subject to pretty intense scrutiny," continued Dunlap. "For obvious reasons."

"So how old was Winthrop's?"

"You can be Winthrop's age and get a 2.5-million-dollar term life insurance policy for a little more than $3,000 a year, providing you took out the paper almost ten years ago."

"He's been paying on it for ten years?"

"Just about eight. Not cheap, but for a man like Winthrop, benefiting the way he did from these lady's estates, it would have been chicken feed."

"But he wouldn't gain anything. Just his beneficiaries. What's the point?"

"That part bugged me," Dunlap agreed. "The policy's beneficiaries are the four men mentioned in this will. I double-checked on who paid the annual premiums. It was Will Winthrop, out of an account setup for Gun Club expenses."

"Maybe they had something on him? Or he was a better friend than we give him credit."

"I don't for a second believe he was a good buddy. And here's the real kicker. That Club has been paying premiums on the same policies for every one of its members!"

The Sheriff didn't get it. "You mean every Club member has a 2.5-million-dollar term life insurance policy?"

"Every one of them. And they list all the other members as beneficiaries."

"That's a little bizarre."

"That's a lot bizarre. For almost eight years Will Winthrop, through that Club, has held paper on every member. The listed beneficiaries for each policy are the same, the members of the Gun Club. It looks like Winthrop, through the Club, has paid the premiums all along. That's over fifteen thousand a year."

Goddard was surprised. "That's a load of money. You think he was just gambling?"

"First of all, the cost was minimal, if I'm right about how much he bilked out of those pensioners. Second, it could have been an incredible gamble, if any of them died before him."

"Maybe he was thinking about offing one of them? Maybe a couple?"

"Maybe the whole damn group," Dunlap agreed. "Though it'd be tough to get away with it."

"Car accident," the Sheriff suggested. "House fire during an all-night poker game. Boating accident." He thought about it. From what he knew of Winthrop, anything was possible. "Maybe they got him first?"

"Maybe."

"Maybe it was just something the Club decided to do for its members? The more I think about it, the more I think it was just a gamble. From what I hear they were all players. Maybe Winthrop and the other Club members were figuring one of them would knock off before the end of the life insurance term. Didn't Percy tell you he'd seen Winthrop down at the Black Bear Casino on more than one occasion?"

Dunlap nodded.

"Well I guess his old buddies hit pay dirt."

"Two point five mil," Dunlap mused.

"Damn. That's a lotta jack."

After a few moments of silence, during which both of them briefly wondered what they would do with that kind of money, Jeff Dunlap said, "I'm not sure there's a whole lot we can do about that insurance payment. But we might be able to pry recompense out of Winthrop's estate, providing we can find paperwork that details his legal maneuvers with those pensioners. Tell you the truth, I'm not even sure we can do that. Our best bet is to prove fraud, which might be possible considering I never saw any high-tech wheelchairs. And some of those drug regimens are suspect, according to Doc Wallace. We could also try to turn that district court judge into a state's witness. Since he's in line for some overdue justice, we'd at least have a bargaining chip."

The Sheriff waited before he spoke, long enough so he didn't betray his eagerness to assist. He didn't like hiding it from his old friend, but he had no other choice. "Maybe I should poke around a little," he suggested.

"I was thinking the same thing. Maybe take a look at his office and that Defiance house, for starters. Then his farmhouse. It'd be within your purview to enter the place and nose around. I suspect we'll have to wait for a search warrant, but I can work those details, if one becomes necessary."

"What about Grebs?"

"What about him? There's no reason to bring Grebs into this. I don't give a shit if he's the town cop. Since he's a beneficiary, there's a clear conflict of interest. If Grebs catches you at Winthrop's office or his Defiance home, just tell him the county attorney wanted to make sure an old colleague's property was safe."

"Old colleague?"

"Percy's a lawyer. Winthrop was a lawyer. Colleagues. Call it professional courtesy."

"Percy's office investigated that prick three times in the last ten years."

"Then call it attorney collegiality," Dunlap quipped, vaguely.

Dean grinned. Finally, he stood up.

"We're going to follow that crooked bastard into his grave, dig around a little and see if he can throw us a bone."

"Maybe we'll get lucky," Dean said, turning and starting out of Dunlap's office.

"Let's hope so."

The Sheriff laughed, nodded and said goodbye. He was already contemplating a schedule that would allow for an early evening visit to the vacant Defiance home, definitely after dark.

CHAPTER THIRTEEN

JANUARY 30TH, LATE AFTERNOON—THE DEFIANCE HOTEL

The alarm awakened him. Sam's mouth tasted bitter and dry. He grabbed his Dopp kit and made his way down the hall to the bathroom, where he brushed his teeth, showered and washed away two days on the road. He decided to leave his three-day beard growth. Maggie had never liked his beard. It gave him a rough look. Maybe it was time to grow one. He wrapped a towel around him, carrying his dirty clothes back to his room. He changed into a fresh multicolored Western shirt and a pair of jeans and tried to make himself presentable.

When he looked out the window he could see the abandoned depot, the railroad tracks and the woods beginning to darken. He checked his watch and it was almost 5:00. He remembered how darkness came on quickly in northern Minnesota. Frozen woods at midnight could be a sanctuary, when entered at the right time, with the right equipment and the proper frame of mind. When he was young he liked hiking in pale moonlight, particularly in extreme cold, when he knew he would be alone. If he could walk into the woods after a heavy snowfall, so much the better. When the snow was fine and powdery you could walk through the forest with little more than the hush of your snowshoes. But his midnight excursions taught him to be careful about darkness, that sometimes it was better left alone.

Eventually Grebs would discover the break-in at his mother's house. And it was only a matter of time before Sam would be recognized. The burial was the day after tomorrow, when he would witness the old man's final interment. Then they'd know him. Once they discovered the break-in and knew he was in town, the obvious step would be some kind of search. That's what Sam would do. He considered seeing Grebs's cruising in his patrol car in front of the Hotel a warning. It was time to hide the duffel.

Diane Talbott was one of his mother's more unlikely companions. For starters she was over a decade younger than his mom. Sam had heard stories about Diane Talbott's wild youth, when she was in college and through her 20s. Truth is, during their day-long canoe expeditions into the BWCA or hiking some of the trails around Defiance, Sam recalled his mother's friend as a square-shouldered Amazon. Back then he guessed she was around 30. She was an up-north outdoorsy kind of woman. Long dark hair, strong legs that curved up to rounded, perfect glutes, and she had well-defined muscles on her arms, probably from all that time she spent paddling. And her chest was proportioned well enough to kindle a 15-year-old's imagination (though at 15 it didn't take much).

Before he left, he reached into his bag and pulled out his cell phone. It wasn't unusual for him to be out of contact for more than 24 hours. He was often in places cell phone signals didn't reach. But it had been an unusual two days, particularly since he'd turned off his official phone. He thought he'd better check his messages.

He wondered about service in Defiance, but when the phone finally came up, needing juice, it connected. Almost as soon as it connected, his message light came on. He dialed in and listened. Two messages.

First he heard his supervisor. Forensics in Ashland had finally finished running the tests on that fur. Judy Rutgers's sheep killer was a hybrid—part Mexican Gray Wolf and part coyote. They would have loved to have caught the animal just to see it. It had everyone stumped, since it implied there was part of at least one Mexican wolf in Colorado, or at least one within 500 miles. Unfortunately, it never returned. The traps were going back to storage. "Just thought you'd like to know," he said.

A hybrid, Sam thought, deleting the message and waiting for the next. That was a surprise.

Kay Magdalen's voice came onto the line. "The plot thickens, Rivers. You apparently decided to take my advice and cash in some vacation time? Good thing, since you'd be losing it at the end of the year. You aren't in Las Vegas, are you?" she asked, chuckling behind the comment. "Here's the deal," she continued. "You'll never guess who applied for your job."

Kay was already referring to it as Sam's job. Typical of Kay Magdalen, who usually got what she wanted.

"I'll save you the suspense. Carmine Salazar," she said. And then she let the news soak in a little. "That's right. Can you believe it? His name is Carmine. Like the color. Like a bruise." She snickered at her own wit.

Sam just listened.

"No wonder he goes by Sal," she added. "When you get a chance, give me a call. Let me know what you're thinking. The spot is yours. National

Field Agent on the Interagency Task Force. I want you to have it, Rivers. It's perfect for you. We both know it. But I can only hold off Salazar so long." She paused, and then said. "So I hope you're having fun in Las Vegas," and then hung up.

Salazar. Sam was surprised to hear he'd applied for the job. The new head of USFW was the kind of inside administrator, a USFW blueblood, that might appreciate Salazar's business and accounting acumen. But a field agent? Salazar? From what Sam remembered, Salazar was a pretty boy, someone he couldn't imagine wading through mud, both the real and metaphorical.

For a minute it pissed him off. Then he remembered the last 48 hours. He couldn't recall more than a couple seconds of thought devoted to Carmine Salazar or Maggie. Charlie had come to him a few times on the long drive to the Iron Range. Charlie would have liked crossing the South Dakota prairie. And Sam would have appreciated his friend's companionship. But beyond Charlie, Sam hadn't thought about his ex-wife, her lover, or anything else about the USFW or his Yellow Rock home. And that's because he still had work to do.

Kay Magdalen would have to wait. And he knew she would.

A few miles west of Defiance, Diane Talbott's mailbox marked a driveway that disappeared into the trees. 'D. TALBOTT' was written on its side. The lane curved up into a thick stand of black spruce. There was a pair of fresh tracks in the newly plowed driveway. He wondered if she had company.

Fifty yards beyond Diane's driveway, Sam turned onto a freshly plowed gravel road. He followed it until it bent around a copse of trees. Then he pulled to the shoulder, cut the engine and stepped into the frosty dusk.

His jeep was out of view of the highway. He'd just as soon check out Diane's place (and Diane) before assuming it was the best place to hide his duffel. He trusted not much had changed, but given the contents of his bag and what he was going to ask of her, it was wise to be cautious.

He peered into the back and made sure the bag was concealed and his jeep secure. The western horizon still held a distant faint glow of dull orange. In a few more minutes it would bleed into night. Occasional remnants of last night's storm blew out of the northwest, ticking the branches of leafless trees. It was cold, and getting colder.

He walked back along the road's shoulder, turned at the Old Road and walked another fifty yards to Diane's drive. It twisted up a slight rise through a thick stand of black spruce. You couldn't see the cabin through the trees. Sam bent to examine the tire tracks. Thick new treads, probably a pickup. There was only one set of them. She had either left and not returned, or she had company. If she had company he would just slide out the way he'd come, no one the wiser.

He climbed farther up the drive and saw the edge of the cabin through the trees, then the tail section of a new blue pickup protruding from the corner of the house. He couldn't be certain, but it looked like the same truck he'd seen on the highway last night, before entering Defiance. The truck was a polished powder blue. When he came closer he saw dealer plates.

Hank Gunderson's truck in Diane's drive? Maybe Mrs. Gunderson, if she was still around. Maybe Hank's wife borrowed his truck and was visiting? But from the times Sam had met Hank's wife he remembered her as a quiet, submissive, slightly rotund woman whose lips only opened to acquiesce to her husband.

He stepped quietly up the drive, closing the distance to the cabin's back corner. His breath clouded in the early dark. He stepped along the drive's shoulder, where the fresh, powdery snow muffled his footfalls. He walked up along the pickup and peered through the frosted passenger side window. On the pickup's front seat there was a half-finished pint of whiskey. Parked on the other side of the truck was an old Datsun pickup, its northwest side banked high with snow. Diane's car, Sam guessed. If he was right about the new truck, he was surprised Hank Gunderson was paying Diane a visit. But it had been a very long time and things change. He thought about turning around and leaving. And then he heard a woman's voice. Unless he was mistaken, it was a few decibels louder than pleasant conversation. He edged to the outside cabin wall. He moved within five feet of the front door, listening. When Diane's voice broke off, he thought he heard Gunderson's deep bass answer, low and measured, vibrating across the porch. He was pretty sure it was the same voice he'd heard last night. When Gunderson was done speaking, Diane's voice retorted: sharp, focused, angry. But he couldn't make out the words.

Sam edged further along the front porch, peering through the kitchen window. Wooden cupboards. Some dishes in the sink. A steak knife lay on the countertop, surrounded by a quartered lime. Sam ducked below the kitchen window and edged toward the door. Their voices grew louder. He stopped and pressed his back against the wall. From this angle he could peer around the corner and see a closet inside the front door. He was contemplating his departure when their voices sharpened. Sam flattened, turning his ear against the outside wall, listening.

". . . arrange a Ford Escape?" the man asked.

"Hank," Diane said, loud enough to make her point. "You need to leave."

"A new Escape could get you around a whole lot better than that Datsun socked in by the storm."

There was a long pause before Diane seemed to turn and face the door. "Get out of my house," she finally managed, cold and direct, louder than any of her previous words.

"What is it with you?" Gunderson blurted, ignoring her.

Sam heard him rise. His voice moved as he walked across the room. "I know people in Eveleth. They told me you were a party girl. That you lived for a good time. And that's all I'm saying now. I'll show you an excellent time."

"I haven't been to Eveleth in 20 years. And what I did when I lived there is none of your goddamn business. Now get the hell out of my house, or I'll call the Sheriff!"

Sam heard her move as she spoke. Their voices were louder, tense. He edged to the side of the front door and stepped back so he could see through the front door window. His face was obscured in the dusk light.

"This here is Bill Grebs's turf," Gunderson said. "You're still in Defiance."

A tattered sofa and easy chair were positioned in front of a fireplace. Some logs were smoldering in the grate, nearly ash. There was a throw rug in the center of the room. Gunderson stood in front of the chair. Diane was behind the sofa. Sam saw the back of her head, a thick salt and pepper braid trailing down its center. Her square shoulders were tense and alert. She looked stronger than he remembered, more formidable. A little wider in the hips and up through her torso, but he recognized the same backside he'd hiked and paddled behind.

"Go home to your wife, Hank," she said, trying to reason with him. Gunderson stared. "I told you about the money," he said, continuing to bargain. "A fair piece of change." There was a pause. "How much would you want?"

Gunderson wasn't begging. It was a business proposal: an exchange of commerce. He wanted to know her price.

Diane didn't answer.

"What would you do with five hundred bucks?" Gunderson asked. He started to smile. "How about a grand?"

She ignored him.

Emboldened by her silence, Hank stepped forward.

And then she exploded. "Get the fuck out of my house!" she growled, pointing to the door.

The color of Gunderson's face had been a healthy pink (which Sam guessed was the whiskey). Now it was crimson. In the yellow cabin light he looked old. He'd made his final offer. Diane was steadfast, shocked by the proposal. There was a little fear in her fury. And with good reason. Unless he was mistaken, it looked like rage building behind the big man's eyes.

Suddenly Gunderson turned, head down, starting around the couch toward the door. Sam jerked away from the wall. He hustled out of sight, then broke into a dead run, leaping over a snowdrift, trying to conceal himself before Gunderson stepped through that door. But in mid-air he heard the door's bolt lock snap shut. Gunderson never intended to leave.

Halfway back to his observation point he heard Diane scream. As Sam came up to the door he heard another scream and then Diane's "Get the hell out of my house!" accompanied by a heavy crash.

Gunderson crouched low to the ground, his big arms outstretched, moving like an upright bear. Diane was in a corner, wielding a pine-based lamp like a baseball bat.

"Come on, Diane." He was smiling.

The big man must be a whole lot drunker than he appeared.

"Get out!" she repeated.

"It's been a while." He took a cautious step forward.

Diane blurted something unintelligible and swung. Gunderson leaped back and the arc of the lamp brushed his shirt.

He started laughing, ignited by the gesture, as though it was some kind of perverted foreplay. He moved closer and Diane stepped back, boxing herself further into the corner.

"You son of a bitch!" She swung and Gunderson leaped back, then quickly reestablished his ground. Diane cocked to swing again.

"I'll pay," Gunderson offered. "You wouldn't have called me tonight unless some part of you wanted to consider my offer."

"Get the fuck away!" She swung again and he lurched back, stepping forward as the arc of her swing passed. For a drunk past 60 he was quick enough.

"If you touch me it'll be assault."

"Your word against mine," Gunderson said. Diane swung, again enraged. Gunderson pivoted, stepped in behind her. His huge arms closed around her and the lamp fell to the floor. "And Bill Grebs is a friend of mine," he said, tense, through gritted teeth.

Sam stepped back, made a solid kick and there was a loud thwack as the wood splintered and the door swung open.

The bunched pair turned to face him, Gunderson holding Diane tight in front of him like a shield. Sam stared, trying to measure the big man's resolve. And then something in the agent shifted. He could feel it build. He'd felt it before, in similar tight quarters. An adrenaline rush that if left unchecked made him feel as though he was capable of beating the aging car salesman until he was unconscious. Or dead. Only this time it was personal. This time he would have to be extra careful.

"Who the hell are you?" Gunderson finally coughed.

Sam glanced at Diane, thought he saw recognition, then disbelief.

"An old friend of Diane's." He stared at Hank Gunderson.

"Get the fuck out of here," Gunderson blustered. "This is no concern of yours."

Sam doffed his stocking cap, loosened his scarf and unzipped his coat. He took a second to shed the coat and drop it with his scarf over the back of the sofa. Now he was unencumbered. He turned back to close the door. Then he turned back around and ran his fingers through his hair, never taking his eyes off Gunderson. *Beat the shit out of him*, he told himself. *What he deserves.* But all he said was, "I think you should let her go, Hank." Sam's use of the big man's name unnerved him.

If Gunderson ever loosened that steel-clasp grasp, Diane was set to uncoil.

"This is none of your goddamn business," Gunderson repeated.

But Sam could feel a sudden shift in the battle.

"Rape?"

"I wouldn't have raped her. We were just having fun."

"Fuck you," Diane spit.

Sam held the big man's gaze long enough to convey reckoning. "Yeah," he said. "Fuck you." Then he smiled, but without humor. "Chances are, if we all got into it, you might land a couple of good blows. But to do it you'll have to let Diane go, and when you come after me something tells me she's going to be behind you, ready to finish the job she started with that lamp."

Sam watched Gunderson working through the problem, recognizing the change in numbers, how it worked against him. "Who the fuck are you?" he repeated.

"The name is Sam," he said. "Sam Rivers. Like I said, an old friend of Diane's. I was in town and decided to say hello . . ." When he was young, the old man made Sam address everyone as mister. It had been Mr. Gunderson. "Hank," Sam finished.

There was another long moment as Gunderson pondered his options. Then recognition. "Clayton?" he asked.

"Rivers," he said. "Sam Rivers."

Gunderson considered, startled by the realization. One of his overgrown legs moved away from his body and kicked the lamp across the room. His arms relaxed and Diane slipped away. She turned as she left. Her fist came up like a prizefighter's, cutting across Gunderson's jaw as she backed away. From the meaty sound of it she landed a pretty good blow. Gunderson's head shot back and she backed out of reach.

"You son of a bitch!" She started shaking. "Next time I'll have a gun," she managed, her eyes blurred with rage.

Gunderson stared at her, enraged by her parting shot. His hand rubbed his jaw and his middle finger reached into his mouth, coming out red. His left fist lowered and clenched. He appeared ready to charge.

"Go ahead," Sam said. "Maybe you'll get lucky."

Sam's voice was even, measured, calm. Gradually the blood ebbed out of the big man's face. The danger passed. He managed to turn and pick up his coat, made a wide arc around Sam Rivers. At the door's threshold Hank turned.

Sam could see he'd regained some composure. He looked at Diane. "Maybe I got a little out of hand," he observed. Then his eyes narrowed. "But next time I won't be so nice about asking." He turned to Sam. "My advice to you is get out. There's nothing for you here." Then he turned and disappeared into the cold.

CHAPTER FOURTEEN

JANUARY 30TH, DUSK—BILL GREBS SNOWSHOES INTO SKINWALKER'S BOG

It was not the first time Bill Grebs considered himself an outlaw. It was nine below, practically mild by Defiance standards but cold enough to make Grebs's elevated breath rise in columns through the trees. He wore a black ski mask, black mittens, and a midnight-blue snowmobile suit. If you were an owl, perched overhead and watching for movement across the snow, Grebs's dark shadow was as clear as a passing moose. But if you were anyone else, casting a sidelong glance through the darkening wood, he was an invisible burglar.

All morning he'd sat in his office, monitoring the Sheriff's radio chatter, waiting to hear news of the call regarding the wolf kill at Winthrop's farm. Even if Angus had only contacted the DNR, news would have filtered through the sheriff's office. Steve Svegman, the local DNR conservation officer, would have relayed the information to Goddard. There would be another investigation, this one by Svegman. And then they could file their claim with the Minnesota Department of Agriculture.

But word never came.

It was Thursday. He wasn't due at the cabin until Friday, to celebrate Williston's wake. Everything coming in from official channels was business about the storm, power outages and downed lines, a few stranded vehicles. A plow breakdown out of Vermilion Falls. Finally, late afternoon and unable to contact Angus by phone at either his place or the farmhouse, or the cabin by CB, Grebs knew something was wrong. He had to find out what.

One hundred yards short of the cabin he slowed his approach. There were five overgrown paths leading into the hidden cabin, little more than game trails, all from different angles, as though the cabin was the center of a huge wheel and each of the trails were twisted spokes. The Club members were careful to vary their approach, though at dusk Grebs took the shortest and most traveled path. The drifts were particularly deep in this part of the country, and he occasionally looked behind him to see his snowshoe tracks cut the fine dry powder. He didn't like leaving such a wide swath, but it couldn't be helped.

Ever since they'd built the cabin, Winthrop had involved the men in a game designed to hone their stalking skills. The game's goal was to approach the cabin without being seen or heard. Grebs knew it worked best after dark, but Angus Moon's wolf ears always heard his companions' approach. The walls were nine-inch timbers. The windows were double paned. But Moon had a preternatural ability to sense movement and sound in the wilderness.

The others thought Moon's keen observational ability was a trick. Those near him would watch the way Moon's head cocked to one side. He'd raise a hand for silence. And then they would all hear the snap of a twig or a leaf rustle. If it were dark, they'd douse the lights and grow still. If it were light, they would conceal themselves just outside the cabin, behind the outhouse, or in one or two hidden nooks inside the cabin.

In the near dark Grebs stepped carefully through the snow. From the overhanging boughs, twenty yards from the cabin's windows, the place looked deserted. Two pairs of snowshoes were stuck upright in drifts beside the front door. The kitchen table, just the other side of the front window—their primary sitting, drinking and gaming table—was empty. Given the rest of the day, he thought it was a bad sign.

Grebs shushed to the front door. He removed his snowshoes, deposited them in the snowbank next to the others, and stepped into the cleared-out space in front of the door. Not a sound. The door creaked on its rusty hinges. Still no movement. Then he heard it. A startled grunt, followed by a deep, sonorous snore.

"For Christ's sake," he muttered, entering the cabin, shaking himself off. He hung his coat and stamped his feet. It was enough to make the snoring stop.

The cabin was warm and smelled of wood smoke, bacon and cigars. It was a simple construction, but large for a hideout carved out of Skinwalker's Bog. They'd had plenty of timber to work with, and they'd used it. There was a great front room, open across a long plywood floor with a couple of dingy woven rag rugs, faded ovals across the scarred boards. Along one wall was a small bunk and along the back there were three small bedrooms—two with single beds lining each wall, a small dresser, a propane gas lantern, and a narrow walkway to allow a person to walk into the bedrooms with enough space to turn and sit. The third bedroom was furnished with a queen bed, a narrow walkway along one side. There was a large kitchen table in front of a wide pair of windows, frosted over in the cold. There was also a counter with a sink, a gas stove, a gas refrigerator, and along the right front wall some open cupboards with dented pots and dishware. It was a sparsely furnished place, but just fine for gaming, hunting and scheming. All in all it was a comfortable den. But Grebs wasn't feeling comfortable.

On the kitchen table were two coffee cups and an empty whiskey bottle. Grebs guessed the rest.

From the room with the queen bed Williston stirred. "What?" he seemed to mumble. There was a long pause before Grebs heard him mutter, "Oh, fuck."

Grebs walked over to the room's entryway and said, "Yeah. I'd say. Oh, fuck."

Winthrop lay across the bed face down. He'd been in deep slumber. "Goddammit," he managed, starting to come awake. He turned and saw Grebs standing in the bedroom's threshold. "We almost died last night," he muttered.

Grebs was in no mood. "You died Sunday."

"Gettin' out here was a nightmare," Winthrop said, managing to roll over. "We tried all night and into this morning to raise you on the radio. Couldn't get a thing." From the next room they heard Angus resume his snoring. "Guess Angus didn't hear you."

"Guess not."

"He almost lost it in that goddamn storm."

"Why in the hell didn't anybody check on the stock?"

Williston thought for a minute, trying to come awake. "What time is it?"

"After five."

"Christ," he managed, turning on an elbow. "When Angus and I couldn't reach anyone we decided to have a little something to raise our spirits." He could see Grebs wasn't mollified. "Don't worry," Williston added, waving an arm to ward off the lawman's concern.

Grebs backed up and let him come into the front room. There was a large potbellied stove near the center back wall. Williston limped over, still waking up, and threw another log into the stove. A wisp of smoke curled out the iron door. Then he turned to a shelf over the sink, took down some aspirin, shook some pills into his palm and downed them with a cup of water.

"Those calves'll keep," Williston finally said. "At least what's left of 'em."

"I know the calves'll keep. It's the DNR and Agriculture I'm worried about. We need to file that claim."

Williston paused for a minute, stretching in front of the stove. He stopped, then said, "You don't know the half of it."

"Half of what?"

"We had to leave them."

"You had to leave who?"

"Those dogs."

"You left them in the barn?"

"Yup."

"For Christ's sake!" Grebs exhaled. "Suppose someone goes out there and finds them?"

"Who?"

Grebs considered it. "How in the fuck should I know? Maybe somebody who thinks they can steal something out of a dead man's farmhouse."

"So how would they explain they were there, providing they went out to the barn, found the wolves, and decided to report it?"

Williston had a point. "Did you consider the Sheriff? Goddard's been poking around. Maybe he'd go back out to have another look at the scene."

"Goddard's the least of our worries. And if anyone pokes around, they'll find *wolves*. So what?"

"Did people get a lot more stupid in the last 24 hours? Why would wolves be corralled in a closed up barn?"

Williston paused, turning. "We left the door open. Couldn't get it shut."

"What?"

"The door froze open. The storm clogged the runner with snow and ice while those hybrids were killing and feeding. We couldn't shut it. But now that I think of it, that's the way they'd enter. Wolves. When Angus has to explain it."

"What if they ran?"

"Could have. I doubt it, given that storm. And the barn's full of food.

And they were damn hungry. We couldn't cage them because they were still eating. And we had to get the hell out of there, or get stranded. Did you want them to find *me*?" He scratched his head and yawned. "But think about it. Say they run and someone shoots them. They're wolves, aren't they?"

Grebs thought for a minute, not happy about it. But the hybrids definitely looked more wolf than whatever else Angus had bred into them. "More or less." But Grebs could tell Winthrop was talking himself into this new perspective, given the turn of events. "So what now?"

"We rouse Angus."

As if in answer, Moon snored from the middle bedroom.

"He needs to get back to town. There's something I need him to do at the office."

"What?"

"Loose ends," was all Winthrop said. "I don't want anyone to find any incriminating files. Goddard or Dunlap. I might have forgotten something." He paused for effect. "I want Angus to burn it," he said, knowing Grebs wouldn't appreciate a major Defiance blaze.

"A fire?"

Williston nodded. "A big fire."

"How big?"

"The Winthrop Building."

"A goddamn building fire?! It'll draw too much attention," he said, shaking his head.

"You think I wouldn't do it unless it was absolutely necessary?"

Grebs turned away. "I don't like it," he said.

"Neither do I. That's why Angus is going to be extra careful about how it's set, and when."

"Williston," Grebs exhaled. "Goddamn it. How's it going to look with your office going up in flames less than a week after your death?"

"Shit happens," Williston shrugged. "It's an old building. Old buildings burn every day. There's a bad socket with a bad fixture plugged into it, directly behind my desk. That and a little dust should make the place go up like a tinderbox. Besides, it's insured," he smiled.

"When's the last time we had a fire in Defiance?"

"It'll happen after midnight. You'll be home in bed, along with everyone else. There'll be an electrical spark from a faulty socket. And you know the place is full of paper. Dry paper, just waiting to burn. And the Fire Marshall practically condemned the place the last time he went through."

Grebs exhaled again, looking away. "I need a goddamn drink," he said.

"Hair of the dog that bit ya'," Williston smiled. He turned toward the other bedroom. "Angus!" he yelled. "Wake up! Angus!"

Angus stopped snoring.

"What about those dogs?" Grebs asked.

"You and Angus can get them in the morning. Angus! Goddamn it. Get the fuck out of bed!"

Angus moaned.

"What if the dogs aren't around?" Grebs asked.

"Would you leave in the middle of a storm when there was food and shelter right under your nose? They aren't going anywhere. Even if they do, they're wolves. It would appear to be a wolf pack returning to the woods. That might be better," he said, winking one sleepy eye.

"They'll want to trap them."

"Good."

"They're not exactly wolves."

"They look like it, more or less. Angus!"

"For Christ's sake," Angus moaned.

Grebs continued warming himself by the stove, not exactly calmed by his first heavy draught of amber liquid. He felt unsettled by the development, and the ease with which Winthrop discounted it. Whiskey, he thought. While he contemplated the next morning's efforts, trying to work out the timing, a lone howl pierced the nine-inch walls. It was far off, not loud, but they all heard it. The wail from the deep woods raised hairs on the back of Grebs's neck, even though he was used to wolf howls.

"That's the first time I've heard them in Skinwalker's Bog."

Angus creaked across the bed, managed to sit upright. "Maybe it's my dogs," he mumbled.

"Just what we fuckin' need," Grebs said.

"Maybe they decided to run." Angus wasn't serious, but he could feel Grebs's worry.

"You don't think they'll stay?" Grebs called into the bedroom.

"You just never know about wolves," Angus said, slowly, getting the words out one at a time. "You saw them take after those feeders," he added, bending over and starting to rise, stepping out of the room. "I didn't know they had it in 'em."

"They were starving," Williston observed.

"I know," Angus said. "Smart to keep them hungry so long. They remembered they were wolves."

"Part wolves," Grebs corrected. "They still have some dog in 'em."

"Last night they tore into that stock like full wolves," Angus said. "Maybe even something better," he mused, coming out of the room, heading to where the whiskey sat on the kitchen table. "But I know my dogs."

"I hope you're right," Grebs said. "Because if you're not, we're going to have one hell of a time catching them."

"Don't worry," Williston reassured. "Angus'll get 'em."

"Yeah," he said, agreeing with Williston. "I'll get 'em in the morning." Then he considered. "It's good a pack's come into the Bog. Just shows how much the vermin are spreading. Helps explain our kill."

As if on cue a chorus of low howls sounded through the cabin's timbers, far off but distinct. The men listened to their eerie wails.

Angus didn't expect his dogs to run. If they did he had no idea how he might lure and then cage five dogs that had finally recollected their ancestry.

"Angus," Williston said, after the woodsmen had a chance to drink. "I've got a little job for you."

CHAPTER FIFTEEN

JANUARY 30TH, EARLY EVENING—MIRIAM WINTHROP'S HOUSE, DEFIANCE

After dusk Sheriff Goddard nosed his cruiser into the alley behind Miriam Winthrop's vacant Defiance home. The temperature began dropping with the sun. It was already twelve below, heading deeper.

Good and cold, thought the Sheriff, happy about the arctic air mass. It would keep most folks indoors.

He pulled the cruiser to the side of the plowed alley directly in front of Winthrop's garage. Lights were on in the neighborhood homes. The sky was clear, but the moonrise was still a couple hours off. If anyone looked out their windows they might see the shadowy outline of his patrol car. Might, over the plowed drifts. Then again, this kind of cold frosted over glass. And it was dinnertime. Most families were gathered around their kitchen tables, taking in the warmth and a little chow.

Just to be safe, he'd driven by the town cop's home. It was a small, nondescript square house with no trees and a white expanse of fresh snow. The drive was newly plowed and either side was drifted high up with snow. The home's windows were dark, front and back, and Grebs's patrol car was missing. A subsequent drive through Defiance neighborhoods yielded nothing. Goddard turned the radio channel to the local police band, but there was only static. On the drive around town the static crackled over the speaker. Nothing. Grebs was gone.

Perfect, Dean thought, as he turned off the engine. He pulled down his hat, donned his mittens and got out of his car. He had thick down mittens with an opening for the thumb and trigger finger, so he could whip his gun from its belt holster, should the need arise. Or grab his can of mace. Or the shiny handcuffs, though he wouldn't need any of them tonight. He struggled through deep snow to the back of the house.

He'd already considered a couple different means of entry, but knew there'd have to be good reason. He squinted through the dark. In his side pocket he had a small black flashlight. He flicked its beam on the back door. He didn't expect to find anything, was surprised when it appeared as though someone had been there. He trailed the light down and saw old depressions in the snow, what looked like footprints buried over by last night's blow. They were barely visible, but still traceable.

Goddard followed the faint tracks around the side of the house, not thirty feet from the neighbor's outside wall. He flashed the light across the snow and saw a pair of boot prints almost covered over. Someone came and went, he guessed. From the looks of it he couldn't be sure, but it appeared as though someone had come from the front to the back, turned around the corner to the door, and then started back.

He returned to the rear of the house, had another look. Near the corner, to the right of the back stairs, Goddard saw a small depression in the snow. It looked like a deer had lain down in the snow, curled up in a ball to ride out the storm. He stepped over to it, flicked his boot over the surface, and the space opened. He stepped further into the hole, and his boot pushed down through the surface of the snow, well beyond ground level.

A window well, he thought. He kneeled in the snow, clearing a place. He reached his arm down and suddenly, surprisingly, the snow fell away and a wisp of warm air rose out of darkness. He cleared more space, flicked on his flashlight, flashed its beam into the hole, and saw the jagged edges of broken glass. A break-in, he wondered?

He cleared the snow away from the window, piling it around the hole. He could see where the pane had been broken, where the window had been pulled up. He reached in, felt for the latch, turned it, and pushed. The window was frozen. He leaned into the hole, extending his arm through the broken pane, pulling as he brought his other hand down and pushed.

Suddenly the window came unstuck. He lost his balance and his wrist flicked across the broken glass edge. "Goddammit," he muttered. He brought his arm out and looked at the broken skin. There'd be some bleeding, but not much.

The Sheriff reentered the hole. He locked the window upright. Then he leaned in further, flashing his light onto the basement floor. There were glitters on the floor where glass shards from the broken pane had fallen and scattered. He flashed around the room, but it was empty. He stowed the light and carefully let himself down, feet first, catching himself on the window ledge, dropping until he could step onto the floor. It was an acrobatic act for a big man with some extra pounds, but the window was wide enough. The strain of it left his heart pumping but his head clear.

He paused, listening. The furnace kicked on and startled him. He waited a while longer in the basement darkness, listening. But nothing stirred from the corners and there was no other sound in the house. The place was empty. He reached back up and dropped the window shut, latching it from the inside. Then he turned and surveyed the rest of the room. There was a sofa covered in plastic near the far wall, with some miscellaneous furniture beside it. There was a door to the left of the furnace, probably some sort of storage. A stairwell rose to the main level. The Sheriff stepped carefully over the floor, avoiding the glass. He moved to the door, paused before reaching down. He opened his coat, flicked it back, and lifted the trigger guard off his holster. Then he reached down from the side of the entryway, and turned the knob. The door swung open with a slow creak. The sound filled the old basement and Dean waited and listened, but there was nothing. No movement from upstairs. Nothing from outside. No sound at all from the rest of the house . . . except the furnace fan still blowing.

The dark room was filled with jars. Dusty preserves covered a series of wooden shelves. Down near the bottom it looked like some of the jars had been recently moved. He kneeled to have a look and saw rings in the dust where four jars were missing.

Goddamn thieves, he thought. Stealing preserves. The idea of it made him smile, taking the edge off his adrenaline surge.

He moved over to the stairs and started to climb. At the top of the stairs he listened at the door, and then opened it. There was a brief creak, but nothing else.

He was sure the place was empty, but wasn't in the mood for taking chances. He stepped silently down the hallway, treading carefully over the worn carpet. There were two doors down its length. He opened the closest one and it appeared to be an old bedroom. A white chenille bedspread lay across the bed. When Dean flashed his light across the spread, it was bunched near the floor, as though someone had recently sat on it. The burglar, he wondered?

He left the door open and moved to the next room. A bathroom, quiet, small, rectangular and tiled, with a sink, toilet and shower. He walked down to the kitchen and the light from the street illuminated the old linoleum. There was something in the air. Something familiar. Food? Pickles? He walked over to the sink and he thought the smell intensified. Goddard searched through the rest of the rooms. Other than in the bedroom, kitchen and basement there was no sign anyone had been in the house for a long time. He opened the cupboards, cabinets, storage closets, anyplace he thought Williston might have hidden some sort of digital storage device. He scoured the old bedroom, but found nothing. He sat on the edge of the bed and tried to think. Why in the hell would someone break in, steal four jars of preserves, and nothing else? Particularly when there was plenty of other stuff worth taking. In the living room there was a hutch. Two of its drawers contained silver. There was a television in the corner, old but probably serviceable. At least it would bring a few dollars at a Duluth pawnshop. Dean guessed there were a few hundred bucks worth of pawnshop pickings. Kids on some kind of lark? Williston hadn't been dead that long. Less than five days. High school kids ripping off the old man? Goddard could ask around, see if anyone over at Vermilion High knew anything. But it didn't make sense. Anyone going to that much trouble would have stolen something. At least something worth more than preserves.

He made another cursory examination of the entire house, searching for any cranny Winthrop might have used to store something. Anything he didn't want people to find. He looked through the linens, bedroom closets, under the kitchen sink, peered with his flashlight behind the fridge. The freezer was self-defrosting, empty. The fridge contained four bottles of Pfeiffer's beer. That did it. High school kids would have taken the beers for sure.

The Sheriff sat down at the kitchen table and squinted at his wristwatch in the dim light. It was already after 7:00 p.m. He'd found nothing in the vacant house. He guessed Williston could have taken the preserves, eaten some of his dead wife's pickles. But it was all too fresh. And the basement window was broken by someone who appeared to have entered the place last night, in the middle of that storm, judging from the tracks. None of it made sense.

Finally, he let himself out the back door, unlocking and pushing on the frozen door until it snapped open. It left a small drift of snow to the side, where the door opened. He locked the door behind him, looked around. Still no one. He shuffled the snow back over the door and did the same to the drift over the window well. Truth was, he didn't have a warrant. He knew the break-in would eventually be found. It would be simplest if he could get out of the place without being seen.

Back at his car he examined the neighborhood homes. It was cold and the frosty weather had covered every window with a thick glaze. No one could see anything, even if they had peered out at the plowed drifts.

He wasn't sure what he'd seen, but he knew what he hadn't found. He replayed the scratchy video in his head, wondering where Williston hid it. The two other most likely places were his office and the old farmhouse. He might be able to get into the office later tonight, but thought maybe he should wait. Wait for Dunlap to get that search warrant. He could easily check out that farmhouse, but Angus might be out there, tending to Williston's feeder calves. Better to wait on that, too. Let those remote roads get plowed.

For now, Dean thought, as he started his cruiser quietly and eased it down the back alley, it would be best to stay frosty.

CHAPTER SIXTEEN

JANUARY 30TH, EVENING—DIANE TALBOTT'S CABIN

In the wake of Gunderson's departure, Diane rushed to the door and slammed it, but it wouldn't catch. She turned, keeping the door closed with her back, as if some part of her thought Gunderson might return. Her hand went up to her face. Her knuckles were red from striking him. They both heard his engine start. Diane's head turned, listening. Her face was flushed and her eyes flashed with rage. If she'd had a gun, Sam guessed, Hank Gunderson would have been leaving on a gurney, probably with a sheet pulled over his head.

The truck started down the drive, its engine growing fainter through the trees. Sam listened long enough to make sure Gunderson didn't turn on the side road where Sam's jeep was parked. He heard the new blue pickup accelerate down the highway and disappear.

Diane's breathing became more measured. Sam wanted to say something, but until she calmed down it would be like offering solace to a puma. She stepped away from the door. She walked across the living room into the kitchen. Sam heard the freezer door open. She took down an ice tray and a dark green bottle with a red cap. Akvavit. She cracked the tray and cubes spilled into the sink. She reached in, grabbed several cubes and dropped them into her glass, focusing to get hold of herself. She twisted the cap and poured. There was a sharp pop as the thick, clear liquid washed over the ice.

She raised the glass and Sam watched her take a long swallow, punctuated by a sharp exhalation. She managed to return the glass to the countertop before reaching a trembling hand to her forehead. Her eyes closed and she turned her head, trying to gather herself. She reached down and emptied her glass of akvavit. Then she took the bottle and refilled her glass.

"That asshole," she finally managed, her hands a little shaky. She took another long pull from the glass. It didn't appear Diane Talbott was the type to choke out a sob, though it would have been warranted. Sam guessed it would take a few moments for her rage to subside. Then Hank Gunderson had better start watching his back.

Finally, she turned and Sam looked at her face, still reddened but fading to normal. "Clayton?" she asked. Then remembered. "Sam?" Sam nodded. "I figured it was time for a visit." He paused. He was still a little surprised by what he'd witnessed. Before he could say anything else she looked away, continuing to regain control. Gray streaks splintered her black hair. Now that all the excitement was over he noticed a trace in the air. Like dried flowers and witch hazel. The Defiance woods in late September. And maybe there was a little fear in the room, a pungent odor, like sweat with an underlying remnant of Gunderson's whiskey.

"Goddamnit," she managed. She turned to the sink. With her damaged hand she found the glass, raised it to her lips. She finished the restorative akvavit. Then turned and said, "You've grown up." She stared at him, then seemed to remember something. "How about a drink?"

"I could use one."

Diane took down a glass and filled it with ice and akvavit, then handed it to him.

"You OK?" he asked.

She looked at him, briefly. "Getting there," she said, and then poured herself one more tumbler.

"You should press charges."

She paused, then took another sip. "Probably should. But you've been away too long. Out here I'm still within Defiance city limits. And that means the investigating officer would be Bill Grebs. Do you remember him?"

Sam nodded. "I remember Grebs."

"One of your father's friends. And one of Hank Gunderson's buddies."

"You have a witness."

Diane stared at him. "Truth is, if I had a gun handy, Hank Gunderson's blood would be staining my throw rug." She looked away, considering. "And that would be the kind of kneejerk justice Bill Grebs and his Iron Range buddies might understand." She took another sip of akvavit. "But to press charges means eventually we could appear before a judge and jury and that means a fatass talker like Hank Gunderson would dredge up every nasty detail he could find about me. Nothing much recent, but there was a day I could party. It might cast enough doubt, in spite of my eyewitness. And remember, up here men are men, and women are their wives, mothers, sisters and whores."

"I think it's changed," Sam argued. "I think you'd have a pretty good chance."

She looked down at her hand and rubbed the cold glass over her red knuckles. "Don't worry," she said. "I'm not going to let that son of a bitch get away with it. For now I'll have to think on it. I drew a little blood with that fist to his face." She managed a tough grin. "You can bet if I get another chance I'll draw more. But not in a stand-up fight. It'll have to be ladylike." She turned to Sam, but didn't smile. "Hank Gunderson is long overdue for some Range justice."

Sam took a drink of the biting liquid and could feel the smooth, pleasant burn.

"Do you remember akvavit?" she asked.

"I remember. The 'water of life,'" he translated.

"Those Swedes know their drinks."

Sam drank the rest of it straight away and set the glass on the counter. He could feel the warmth in his throat.

"Have another?"

"One more might be nice."

Sam walked over to examine the door while Diane filled his glass. He bent to look at the broken lock. He fingered the splinters where the bolt tore away from the frame. He turned to look at her and she appeared to be much better. "Sorry about your door," he said.

She shook her head. "Your entry was as perfect as your timing."

Sam nodded. That it had been, he thought. Part of him was sorry they hadn't convinced Hank to take a chance with his fists.

Diane examined the place where the bolt lock broke away. He watched her fingers play over the wood, rub over two vacant screw holes. She picked up the piece from the floor and fit it back into its ragged slot.

"It can be fixed," she said.

That's what Sam remembered about Diane Talbott. Competence. The ability to live on her own on the edge of wilderness. He guessed it was one of the reasons his mother liked her so much. That and her willingness to put her whole body into a right fist to Hank Gunderson's jaw. He watched her piece in the splintered latch. Then she turned and looked at him. Sam followed the focus of her sharp green eyes. She was still a beautiful woman. She wasn't the 30-year-old he'd paddled and hiked behind, but he could see why Hank Gunderson would be interested. What he didn't understand was why the son of a bitch thought he had a chance. Sam retrieved his glass, raised it in front of him and said, "To timing." Diane nodded. Then Sam drained half of it in one gulp and the liquid burn diffused across his rib cage. He had forgotten about the drink. Akvavit was similar to vodka. And if it wasn't exactly the water of life, it was a damn good substitute.

"I don't think I've tasted the water of life since I left the Range."

She walked across the room, picking up the lamp from where it had fallen, replacing it on the end table. Then she turned and said, "it's been . . . what? Nineteen, twenty years?"

She wore a pair of blue jeans that were almost as tight around her hips as they had been 20 years ago. Her jeans were contoured around legs that Sam still remembered. A gray fisherman's sweater had a top-heavy sway beneath it. Clearly she had been expecting no one, given her comfortable attire.

"Twenty," he answered. He wondered what she remembered about the times they'd paddled with his mother, or hiked into the Boundary Waters.

She looked away, calculating in her head. "Yeah," she said, wistful. "Your mother's death was a sore loss for the Range."

"I should have come back."

"You should have." She paused. "But your mom seemed to understand, though she never quite got over the fact you had to run. She told me what happened, the day you left. Or at least what she knew about it." She walked over to the fire and placed two logs onto it. She still had a little nervous energy from the fight. She stepped over to the front of her couch and tried to sit down, but she was edgy. She leaned over to watch the logs, but Sam didn't think she was seeing them.

He came around and sat down in the chair across from her. He could hear the pine logs pop. He still held his drink. He watched her for a moment; thought he'd give her a chance to breathe.

Finally, she turned and looked at him.

"It doesn't seem like 20 years," he said, picking up the conversation.

"I agree. You look," she paused, searching for the right words, "grown up. Nice beard."

Sam reached up and rubbed his stubble. "I haven't had a chance to shave in a few days."

"You're a man," she observed, eyeing him. "You look fit."

"Unintended weight loss. It's deceiving."

She looked thoughtful about the comment. Then she glanced down at his hand, noticing the absence of a ring. "Your mom said you'd married."

"My marriage ended six months ago." For the first time he thought it seemed a lot longer than six months. He thought that was a good thing. "It just took me a while to figure it out."

"Sorry to hear that."

"She's already moved on," he shrugged. He thought it would take a little more time for his heart to catch up to his head, but he felt clear about it.

"Marriage can be tough. I don't know a lot of happy ones."

"Glad it didn't happen when mom was alive. She liked Maggie."

If his mother had been alive Sam knew she'd stand with her son. A mother's duty. But Miriam was the kind who always forgave, particularly if it was about a woman's relationship with a man.

"They got along," Sam added, "the few times mom came out to visit. Things just . . . didn't work out the way Maggie wanted, I guess."

"No accounting for a woman's perspective."

Sam didn't smile, but he appreciated the gesture. All he would get. All he deserved, he guessed. Though he still considered Carmine Salazar an interloper and his wife (ex-wife, he corrected) . . . he wasn't sure what he thought about Maggie anymore. "I guess," Sam said. "The same could be said for a man's."

"No disagreement there. A man like Hank Gunderson gets liquored up, with some spare change in one pocket and his dick in the other, and he thinks he's God's gift to women."

Sam smiled. Her comment and the akvavit lightened the atmosphere in the room. "If you ever need any assistance with that Range justice, count me in."

"Like I said, I'll have to think on it. But I appreciate your offer. It's not only about getting even." Diane set her glass down in front of her. "That'd do for starters. But I'd really like to arrange it so he won't, or can't, think with his dick ever again."

Sam thought that sounded dangerous. "You might have to settle for getting even."

She turned back to the fire. "You're probably right," she reluctantly agreed. "I had to call the guy on some background for an obit I'm writing about your father. He said he'd get back to me, he was in the middle of something. Before I knew it he was knocking on my door. Said he was on his way to Vermilion Falls and he decided to swing by and give me everything I needed."

She stared at the logs, which were picking up a good flame. "Not that I was surprised. The man hasn't had eye contact with a woman since puberty. He's too busy staring at their chests."

True enough, Sam smiled. And not just for Hank Gunderson.

Diane looked at him and said, "You're here to recover your things," as though she'd just remembered.

Normally, Sam would have been more reticent about his life, particularly since it had recently involved breaking and entering and theft. But spending a few moments in Diane's presence, and sitting down on her couch, seeing her cabin and remembering how she felt about Bill Grebs and Hank Gunderson and his father, Sam was reminded of everything his mother liked about her. It wasn't only her perspective, but the sense you had she was in control. Diane Talbott conveyed fearlessness. He hadn't known a lot of women like her. Certainly not his mother. Maggie was partly like her, but not entirely. The idea Hank Gunderson believed, even for a millisecond, he could sleep with Diane Talbott was a testament to the car salesman's ignorance or drunkenness or dick logic or all three.

"Already did," Sam finally said.

Diane smiled, a little surprised. "Your mother would be pleased. In the weeks leading up to her passing she worried about you. She was happy you'd done well, creating a new life, putting yourself through school, becoming a big deal in the USFW."

The idea that his mother shared her sense of pride pleased him, but also made him wonder if she had shared too much information with too many. *Someone* besides Diane Talbott had his contact information. He could almost hear his mother recounting every one of his small successes: to the postman, the grocer, Diane, to the entire crowd at Opel's Café. "I'm not a big deal," he corrected. "A field agent."

"You're a wildlife biologist and a wolf expert," Diane said. "Your mother had a big heart and the ability to see the best in everything, even your father. And she had blinders for the uglier parts in all of us. And she knew it. So the fact is when she'd give me updates about your career I took it as a mother's zeal. But then I saw a write-up about your wolf repopulation efforts in Colorado, in that magazine from the International Wolf Center in Ely."

Sam remembered it.

"You've done well, considering what you had to endure as a kid. A USFW field agent and wildlife biologist. Specializing in wolves, but if I remember right you've done work on all the American predators. It was the wolves part that made your mom the happiest, considering the Winthrop family heritage."

Sam smiled. "Someone from the clan had to atone for three generations of annihilation."

"Your mother was happy it was you. She didn't have what was required to spit in her husband's eye, but she was glad you chose a different path than Williston's. And hers."

"Did she ever let him know where I was, what I was doing, my new name?"

"Never. At least that I know of. But she would have known your efforts would have pissed him off. She might have said something, just to get in a dig. A woman's right and an estranged wife's duty."

True enough, Sam thought. He could only imagine what his old man, if he'd learned about Sam's efforts, felt about it. Now that he was back on the Range and seeing it through the eyes of a different time, a different life, he felt again the regret over not returning earlier and facing the old man. When he'd seen Gunderson, seen how he'd put on weight, grayed, had a throat wattle, Sam realized that Gunderson, the old man, all of them, were 20 years older. They'd aged and he suspected some of the bite had gone out of their teeth.

He should have come back.

Now that Gunderson knew about him, the others would soon find out. It would only be a matter of time before he'd have a chance to face them. He guessed Grebs, to start. He was looking forward to it. But even Sam knew he would have to pick his battles.

"About my things," he started. "Now that I've got them, I need to store them someplace safe. My jeep and my room at the Defiance Hotel don't give me a lot of options. Even Grebs might be able to find them."

"How much is there?"

He paused. "A duffel bag about the size of a dismantled 10 gauge shotgun, a shoebox full of money, and four jars of my mother's preserves."

Diane was surprised, then smiled. "Some of us guessed about some money. Your mom never said anything, but after she died, Marlene, over at the Vermilion Falls State Bank, overheard Williston in a heated exchange with the bank's president. Something about lost money and getting sued, though we never heard any more about it. Glad to know Miriam put it someplace safe. You can keep that duffel here," she offered.

"I can put it where no one will ever find it."

"I appreciate that." He set down his glass and stood up from the couch. "It's so damn cold out there I'd better go fetch it before those preserves freeze and the jars burst."

"Where'd you park?" she asked, for the first time realizing she hadn't heard his car come up her drive.

"Down off that side road."

"If you've got a four-wheel drive and can get up my hill there's plenty of room next to my Datsun."

"Sounds good." He put on his coat, hat, gloves, and wrapped the scarf around his neck. He paused for a moment, thinking. "There was also a note with my things. And a copy of mom's will," he said.

Diane looked at him. "And the will left everything to you?" she guessed.

"Everything."

"I knew it! Your mom told me that's what she was going to do. But there was another will in which she left everything to Williston."

"I know. Someone—no idea who—sent me a copy of that will. In a PDF file. But it pre-dates this version."

"I asked the Sheriff to look into it, but at the time everything appeared to be in order."

"I know. She left a letter with the will; worried the old man would change it. I guess she knew him pretty well."

"I guess," Diane agreed.

"Was the Sheriff a friend of Williston's?"

"Hardly. At least not that I know of. Dean Goddard, our Sheriff, is around your age. And from everything I can tell he's a straight shooter. If Dean Goddard had found anything he'd have brought it out. Williston had been practicing law on the Range for the last 40 years. He'd seen his share of last wills and testaments. If anyone would have known how to change a will, make it look legitimate, it would have been Williston. He had the ability and he had the motive and Miriam knew he'd do it."

"Know any lawyers? I don't know if, after a will's been probated, it can be reconsidered." He also wanted to know about Williston Winthrop's will. Who would have an electronic copy of the will within a day of the old man's death? If he could identify them, he might discover the identity of canislupustruth.

Diane thought about it. "Didn't you go to school with Jeff Dunlap?"

Sam remembered the name. Then he vaguely recollected the kid, a year or two behind him in school. Defiance was small enough so everyone knew everyone. "Little Jeff Dunlap?" he asked.

"Assistant County Attorney Jeff Dunlap," Diane smiled. "Like you, Little Jeff has grown up."

Sam nodded. "I remember him," he said. Then he turned. "I'll get my jeep."

Diane let him out. The idea Sam might be able to wrest Miriam's estate from the Club members' hands, particularly Hank Gunderson's, pleased her. It wasn't the kind of Range justice she had in mind, but it was a start. And the idea of getting even with Hank a whole lot sooner than she'd expected made Diane smile.

Sam walked back to his jeep, warmed by Diane's fire and the akvavit. Breathing in the 10-below air felt like the Swedish drink over ice. He started the jeep, turned around and headed back to Diane's cabin. He was taking a risk, trusting a woman he hadn't seen in 20 years. Yesterday he didn't have a whole lot to lose. Now he had a shoebox full of money and his mother's rightful will.

He pulled up her drive and parked.

He decided to take a chance. But he resolved to keep at least one eye open. Considering his subject, it wasn't an unpleasant proposition.

Part III

The caribou feeds the wolf, but it is the wolf who keeps the caribou strong.

KEEWATIN (INUIT) PROVERB

CHAPTER SEVENTEEN

JANUARY 31ST, AFTER MIDNIGHT—THE WINTHROP BUILDING

Dean and Belinda Goddard's phone rang. Startled awake, Dean wasn't sure where he was, what it was. He rolled over, rising out of deep sleep and the phone made another jangle. He reached over and picked it up.

"Yeah?"

"Dean?" Smith Garnes.

"Yeah," he managed. Belinda's bed creaked in the next room.

"Sorry to wake you. Thought you might like to know. There's a fire in Defiance."

"Yeah?"

"The Winthrop building is going up like a Roman Candle."

Goddard's eyes opened. "No shit?"

"Came into 911 about ten minutes ago. I was just making sure the volunteers were called up, but I doubt it'll do any good. Happened after midnight and it's an old wooden building."

Dean remembered. "Who called it in?"

"Old lady Cummins. She lives down off Main Street, above the closed Ben Franklin store. She'd just finished the *Tonight Show* and was in bed having trouble sleeping when she saw a yellow flicker through her window. When she got up and looked, the place was already covered in flames."

"I bet," was all Goddard could think to say. "I better drive over and have a look. Grebs been called?"

"Yeah. He's on the scene, or should be in a few minutes."

He thanked Smith and hung up.

On the corner of Main and Second the volunteer fire truck was plugged into a nearby hydrant. Grebs's patrol car stood parked across the street, at an angle that prevented traffic from getting through. But there wasn't much traffic, given the early morning hour and the deep cold. The fire was burning like a blast furnace. There were almost a dozen volunteer firefighters, all dressed in heavy gear. The water that wasn't affected by the heat had frozen solid. The adjacent buildings were covered with sparkling icicles, and clouds of smoke and steam rose into the frosty night air.

Grebs got out of his patrol car as Goddard parked and approached. "We caught it in time," he said. "They've got it under control. At least it's contained. The building's gutted, though. Not much left." Grebs was excited, like an athlete after a big game.

"Anybody know what happened?"

"Martha Cummins saw it first. It was late. Fire Marshall's been called. He's on his way. But I don't think there's much to see. By the time Martha saw it, it was pretty much ablaze."

"Anybody else see it?"

"Nobody."

"Wasn't Will Winthrop's office in that building?"

Grebs nodded.

"Anybody get anything out?"

"I got here right after they did. There was no way you could go near it. They started spraying down the fire and the adjacent buildings, trying to keep them wet."

"Or frozen."

"Either way. They didn't want 'em to burn. I think they contained it. But Williston's office is ashes."

As Goddard walked a little closer he could feel the heat on his face. The firefighters milled around the edges, spraying down the buildings, staying in that narrow zone between the blistering heat and the deep freeze. It was well below zero, terrible for fighting a fire, but it had to be contained. As they watched, the Fire Marshall's car came up Main and parked behind the Sheriff's cruiser. Walt Gibbons stepped out of his car, walked over to where Grebs and Goddard stood. Walt was a roly-poly man just past sixty, with a cherub face and a bushy gray mustache. Nothing put Walt Gibbons in a more jovial mood than a big fire.

"Gentleman," he said.

"How ya' doin', Walt?" Sheriff Goddard said, extending his hand.

"Couldn't be better," he said, staring at the fiery ruin.

Grebs greeted him with a nod. "Walt."

"Looks like a goddamn wood flambé with silver icing," Walt observed.

The three men stared at the fire. The Fire Marshall paced to the left, considered the smoldering blaze from a different angle. He walked to the other side and then came back to center. Around and in front of him the volunteers were doing what they could to both contain the blaze and stay warm and dry.

"Looks like they have it under control. It'll just be keeping it corralled from here on out. Anybody see anything?"

"Not until it was stoked up like a goddamn bonfire," Grebs said.

The Sheriff was peering into what remained of the caved-in structure. The timbers were still firing, blackened and charred beneath the yellow flames. There was no way anything, particularly anything combustible, could have survived that blaze. He didn't know if it was a good thing. Could be, if the only place Williston kept that video was on his office computer, where Dean had viewed it. If, on the other hand, he'd kept copies elsewhere, they'd still need to be found and destroyed. He glanced sideways at the two men, watching Grebs observe the smoldering hulk. If Grebs knew about the video he was damn quiet about it. And if Goddard knew Grebs, if he knew about it he would have already leveraged it. Either that, or he would have been a whole lot more circumspect about watching it go up in flames.

"I'll have to wait until well past morning to get in there," Walt said.

"What do you think?" the Sheriff asked.

"No way to tell. That building was inspected last summer. As I recall, it needed some serious wiring repair. A sprinkler install. Don't know if Winthrop made those improvements, but probably not," he said, looking at the Sheriff.

"Probably not," the Sheriff agreed.

Grebs was silent, watching the last of the building burn.

"The wife believes bad luck comes in threes," Walt observed, staring into the blaze. He turned and with a wry smile added, "I guess that means we haven't seen the last of Williston Winthrop's misfortune."

Grebs considered it. "Good thing dead men don't worry about luck."

CHAPTER EIGHTEEN

JANUARY 31ST, EARLY MORNING—WILLISTON WINTHROP'S FARM

Hank Gunderson could see Moon's truck and Grebs's police car in front of the farmhouse garage. He turned into the drive and sidled down two deep tire tracks that cut through the heavy snow. A bulging blue tarp covered the back of Moon's truck. The wind lifted the corner of the tarp, revealing a row of empty cages.

"Shit," he said, as if Clayton's return and the Winthrop Building blaze weren't complication enough.

Gunderson got out of his cab and examined the empty cages. Grebs and Moon came out of the barn. Hank zipped his coat, pulled on his hunting cap and thick, fur-lined mittens and started across the yard. It was bright and cold.

Bill Grebs and Angus Moon stood in front of the doorway and waited. The snow was deep and their tracks cut a clear line from their vehicles to the barn door. The rest of the yard was buried under a sparkling, deep alabaster.

"Having fun yet?" Hank managed to put on a smile.

"Looks like the dogs had all the fun," Grebs said, indicating with a gesture the inside of the barn. "What're you doing here?" Grebs wasn't happy to see Gunderson. Coming out to the farm and not finding the dogs was worrisome enough. Now Hank.

"Where are the dogs?" Hank asked.

"They ran," Angus said, looking away.

"What the hell happened?" Gunderson wanted to know. Missing dogs was troublesome news, though Hank wasn't one to worry about details.

"Into the woods." Angus indicated a broken trail through the snow that ran from the barn's entrance across Winthrop's side yard over the field to the line of trees. The blowing snow obscured their tracks, but they were still visible in the early morning light.

"Oh, for Christ's sake," Hank muttered. "How'd they get out?"

"Too much storm," Angus explained. "Me and Williston had to leave."

"You left 'em?"

Angus didn't appreciate Gunderson's tone. After a day of drinking, a short afternoon sleeping it off, and his late night arson in Defiance, his head felt pickled. He stared at Hank for one long second, conveying his mood. "If we hadn't left when we did we would have been stuck here with 'em."

Hank looked away, wondering about it. But he couldn't let it go. "Better to have been stuck here with 'em instead of letting them loose in those woods."

"And if they'd gotten stuck?" Grebs interceded. "How do you think they'd explain Williston's presence, just in case someone happened by?"

Hank chewed on the question, but didn't answer.

"Angus is coming out and finding the kill," Grebs said, setting up the scene. "Now we're seeing where wolves got in and what they did. Came in the storm." This conversation was a waste of time. "What're *you* doing here?" he asked.

Gunderson paused, looking at Angus, then back at Grebs. "I assume you know about the Winthrop Building?"

Grebs stared at him. "We know. That was Williston's business and it's done."

Bill Grebs was shutting Hank down. The car salesman was getting pissed. "And did you know Clayton Winthrop's back?"

It had been a long time since either of them had heard the name.

"Clayton Winthrop," Grebs said, recalling the jeep with Colorado plates. "I bet that was his jeep at the hotel?"

"He's got a beard? And he's a lot bigger than I remember," Hank started. "He's changed his name. Goes by Sam. Sam Rivers."

"No shit. When did you figure all this out?"

"Ran into him," Hank said, not wanting to explain the circumstances.

They all paused for a moment, letting the information ripple across the frozen yard, wondering about it. What'd he have to say?" Grebs asked.

Hank thought about it. "Not much. I got the impression he's grown up some. What's it been? Fifteen years?"

"More like 20. Though I doubt any length of time would be enough to shake the boy out of that skin," Grebs said.

"Horseshit as a hunter," Angus remembered. "I expect he wants money. Come around like crow on roadkill."

"What makes you think he's different?" Grebs wanted to know.

"He's not a kid," Hank offered. "We had a few words. I told him there was nothing for him here and he more or less told me to fuck off."

Grebs laughed into the wintry air. "You didn't need to do that, Hank. He may be Williston's kid, but he has no claims on the estate. We're all legal and proper. The will's pretty specific." Then Grebs thought for a moment. Something was missing. "Why did he tell you to fuck off?"

Gunderson looked away, considering. Then he turned back to Grebs and said, "I was visiting Diane Talbott."

"Talbott?" Grebs asked. He was trying to see it. Bill Grebs knew Diane Talbott. The idea Hank was hoping to get lucky with Talbott was absurd. But if Hank had been drinking, anything was possible, at least in the old car salesman's mind. "Get lucky?"

"Might have." Hank smiled, seeing where he could go with it. "But that goddamn kid interrupted us."

A shade fell across the town cop's face, the kind of shadow Hank had been hoping to avoid. "You just can't lay off, can ya', Hank?" Grebs started, carefully, so Hank would feel the pressure. Hank was Hank, and Diane Talbott, some affirmed, had a past. Only her past had been over 20 years ago and it was in Eveleth, across the Range, miles from Defiance and in Diane's case from a different lifetime. He admitted she still had appeal. But from what Grebs heard, she'd never partied for money, and never with an aging son of a bitch like Hank Gunderson.

"She called me wanting background on Williston's obituary. So I stopped by. No harm in trying. Once a party girl, always a party girl. It's a matter of timing." Hank held onto the smile, but it was unconvincing.

This time, Bill Grebs thought, Hank Gunderson's reliance on his professed pussy knowledge was not only wrongheaded, but stupid. "It's a matter of intelligence. You think with your dick."

Hank considered a response, but thought better of it. "Maybe it was a mistake. I just mention it because it was surprising to see him. Clayton Winthrop. Sam Rivers. And he wasn't running scared like he used to."

"We can deal with him," Grebs reassured. "The best approach is courtesy. If we have to, we can show him a firm hand."

Angus smiled at the prospect.

"As I recall, it didn't take much to get Clayton packing," added Grebs.

Hank looked away. "He's not a kid anymore."

"Aw shit, Hank. It's just what you put behind it. I'm not worried.

Williston will be interested to know he's come around."

"You think he's after the money?" Gunderson wondered.

"Of course," Grebs affirmed. "I don't know how he heard about Williston's death. I know Williston hasn't heard from him in years. Yeah," he concluded. "He's after the money."

"Fuckin' good luck," Angus said.

Grebs agreed. "His presence is a minor distraction. Once he reads the will and listens to probate, he'll hear reason."

"I don't think Diane Talbott was expecting him."

"Was she expecting you?"

Hank smiled. "Come to think of it, I don't think she was," he answered. "Seems to me we got bigger problems than Clayton. What about the dogs?"

"We'll get 'em back," Angus said. "They won't run far. It's goddamn cold and there's still a barn full of food. Not to mention a place out of the wind. What would you do?"

"I suppose." Hank looked away to where the dogs' trails disappeared into the trees. "I don't like it. If someone finds those dogs there'll be questions."

"Nobody's gonna find 'em," Angus reassured. "'Cept us. Besides, anyone see 'em would see wolves."

"Truth is, it doesn't matter a rat's ass what happened out here," Grebs said. "So far we still have a livestock kill to report, still have the evidence. And wolves would have run. They wouldn't have stuck around. Those tracks are fortunate, if you ask me. They're too drifted over to get any good prints, but you can see there were about five of them, and they disappeared into those woods."

"I'll get 'em," Angus said, looking up into the wall of trees. "Then I'll teach 'em a lesson."

"Maybe they got a taste of freedom," Gunderson suggested.

"They won't be gone long. Too damn cold and they'll get hungry in a hurry."

"I heard wolves can go a week without food," Gunderson observed. "And winter doesn't seem to get into their bones like it does us."

"Wolves." Angus nodded. He squinted in the sunlight, still peering toward the tree line. "Not my dogs."

"Maybe they've gotten a taste of their heritage," Grebs suggested.
"Right now they're out there trying to figure it out." He looked up and
recalled how those woods were the start of wilderness that stretched all
the way into Canada.

"Right now," Angus argued, "they're probably just inside those trees,
couple hundred yards in, sleeping off the gorge. Come night they'll be
back. They're good at tracking and killing, but they've never done it on
their own."

"Did the other night," Gunderson observed.

The three of them finally went into the farmhouse to get out of the
cold. After they shed their coats they began mulling their options. Angus
could stay at the farm and wait for his dogs. He could secure them in the
cages and return them to their houses, then call in the kill. Or they could,
according to the plan (or at least most of it), report the kill to the DNR.

"I told Williston we'd be out by 4:00," Grebs recollected. "The DNR
should be able to get somebody out before then."

"It's Friday," Hank commented.

"Slow day for a conservation officer. And I checked. Steve Svegman's
on duty."

"That's good," Angus said. "He's young, and he don't know shit, specially about me." He smiled. "I should call it in?"

Grebs nodded. "Call 'em," he said. "The timing's right. It's early. With
luck Svegman'll be out before 2:00. Just be sure and tell them you've got
a wake to attend. Arrange it. We don't want them coming out here when
no one's around. And get that truck into the garage. We don't want him
asking questions about those cages."

Angus agreed. Svegman's early arrival would be good. If he came out
anytime during the day, Angus knew, his dogs would stay put, sleeping
off their feed.

"This kill's going to set off some alarm bells in St. Paul," Grebs observed. "It's big and different. And I don't recall any others like it being
reported, at least in our county."

"It was only a matter of time," Angus argued. "Wolves're comin' back.
Some are takin' dogs off porches. Somethin' like this was bound to happen."

"I didn't say it was totally unbelievable," Grebs said. "Seems to me I've
heard about kills bigger than this out west. Idaho or Montana. Outright

slaughters. It's just going to take some care, is all I'm sayin'. We've got to be patient. This is definitely the work of wolves," he said. "Svegman'll see that. They just might bring in someone else for a second opinion."

"Let 'em," Angus said. "Wolves took 'em, damn straight."

"Just give him the essentials," Grebs advised. "You came out to feed them after the storm, and found this."

Moon nodded.

Williston Winthrop was to be buried tomorrow afternoon. They'd all attend. Tonight they'd each make their way to the cabin in Skinwalker's Bog. There would be a party, an unusual celebration. A wake, at which the dead man would play both host and guest of honor.

"What about Clayton?" Gunderson asked.

"What about him?"

"You think he's going to contest it?"

"How could he? We've got the will. It's all notarized and legal. And the fact is, Clayton's been gone for years. And everyone knew there was no love lost between him and Williston." He looked up toward the woods, as if thinking after the dogs. "Clayton's timing is interesting. I thought he'd disappeared. Maybe there's somebody still in touch? Maybe Talbott?"

"I don't think so," Gunderson answered. "She didn't seem to recognize him, at least at first."

"Well that's one big fuckin' coincidence," Grebs observed. "Clayton showing up a couple days before Williston gets planted?"

The three men considered it, but there wasn't much more to say. Grebs knew it was time to check Miriam's house.

Angus made the call to Vermilion Falls, since he'd discovered it. The DNR was surprisingly sympathetic. There were increasing kills across the Range, in tandem with a rising wolf population. Cattleman were angry about it, and the DNR and Agriculture had gotten word to give everyone the benefit of the doubt. They'd get a conservation officer over at Winthrop's place by 2:00, the dispatcher assured him.

"That'd be good," Angus said, feigning irritation. "I'll be waitin'."

After Angus hung up, Grebs said, "Just make sure those damn dogs are far enough in to stay hid. We don't want them coming back before dark. We'll come out in the morning and see if they've returned."

Angus nodded.

"After you meet with the DNR, we'll see you at the cabin?"

"Course," Angus nodded.

"Good. There'll be a full glass waiting for you."

"Keep my seat warm," Angus said. "It's gonna' be blisterin' cold tonight."

Gunderson and Grebs started out of the house. At the door Grebs turned and said, "Don't take any chances with those dogs."

"They're my dogs," Angus reminded him. "They'll do what I say."

Gunderson and Grebs hoped it was true.

CHAPTER NINETEEN

JANUARY 31ST, MID-MORNING—VERMILION FALLS

Sam and Diane sat in the Ranger's Café. Their breakfast had just arrived and they spent a few quiet moments focusing on their food.

The previous evening Sam had finally decided it would be prudent to bed down on Diane's couch. Diane didn't want to admit it, but she'd been shaken by her encounter with Hank Gunderson. She didn't think the man would return, but you didn't know about Hank Gunderson. Once he grew tired of yanking on his solitary dick, Sam thought, or once he'd had some time to chew on what went down or drink a little more remedy to stir things up, he might rekindle his interest in Diane. Sam could tell Diane felt better with him on her couch. And Sam Rivers felt fine, making sure his duffel was secure and for the time being safe. Though he shared his mother's instincts about Diane Talbott. She was a good human being. And something he suspected his mother didn't notice: she wasn't hard on the eyes.

As they finished their breakfast they talked about how best to explain the sudden appearance of his mother's will, post-dating the version that had been probated. After considering a few different options, they finally settled on using Diane as an excuse. Diane had been holding the will in a sealed envelope, with instructions from Miriam she was to give it to her son when he returned home.

"And Miriam was explicit," Diane said, rounding out their story. "Under no circumstances was I to mail it to you."

"Why not?"

"For the same reasons Miriam never mailed you the money. She was afraid, given Williston's wide-ranging contacts, he would somehow discover it. And she wanted to make sure you received what she'd left you."

"But the money's not part of the story. And you didn't know the envelope held a copy of her will?"

"I didn't know *what* was in the envelope. And I won't mention the money."

"Or the note."

"No note. The contents of the will was Miriam's final testament."

"The story's a little thin," Sam said, thinking about it. "Why wouldn't she have at least told me about it? Or why wouldn't she have told you it was a copy of her will?"

"You said she told you to come home. The truth was, Sam, your mom was a little paranoid about Williston. There are any number of reasons why she may not have explicitly told you about the will. It could have been forgetfulness in the last days of her life. But it was more likely fear Williston would find out and put a stop to it, to this second, proper will."

"And you never opened the envelope?"

"Miriam was my friend. It was her dying wish. Of course I wouldn't open it." The more she thought about it, the more she thought Sam had a reasonable shot at wresting Miriam's estate from Hank Gunderson and his friends. Bending the truth to obtain the right result was not ideal Range justice, but it was a start.

Sam thought it might work, but he didn't know if an estate that has been probated could be reopened, two years later. It was a question for Jeff Dunlap, and he wondered how well the story would hold up under scrutiny.

Diane appreciated Sam's perspective. The man was nothing like his father.

Diane's cell phone went off. It was another reporter. There was a quick exchange, then surprise. "The Winthrop Building? That's damn interesting. I finished his obit this morning. Should be in production."

The person on the other end of the line spoke.

"That's right," Diane answered. "I didn't mention it in the story because I couldn't confirm it, but I think he was being investigated. About what, I don't know."

Pause.

"Yup," Diane said. "Couldn't confirm it."

The reporter thanked her and then hung up.

"The Winthrop Building in Defiance," Diane said. "Burned down after midnight. Burnt to the ground."

"That's curious," Sam said, surprised.

"Started sometime after midnight. Went up like a dried-out Christmas tree. The place was mostly timber. At least that's what Walt Gibbons said. Apparently he'd warned Will Winthrop about the place a few months ago. Wasn't up to code and needed some retrofitting." She glanced at Sam, curious about his reaction.

"Any idea how it started?"

"Not yet. Walt said it would take a while, sifting through the rubble. But his preliminary guess was electrical. He remembered a lot of bad wiring. His recommendation was to upgrade it and install a sprinkler system, which would have brought it up to code."

They fell silent for a minute, mulling the news.

It was an odd development, Sam thought. A damn peculiar coincidence. Maybe someone did it out of spite, he wondered? A disgruntled former client? Someone on the other side of the bench who the old man had eviscerated in a legal battle? But what value would there be in setting the place ablaze, given the old man's death and, he suspected, the insurance money that would flow to the estate once the claim was settled? It all made Sam think arson was unlikely. And remembering the building, even if someone had set it off . . . if they'd been careful, it would be hard evidence to uncover. Inconclusive, at best.

"You heard me mention that investigation?" Diane said.

"The old man was being investigated?"

"I think so, but I couldn't get anyone to confirm it. I found out when I was researching that piece I wrote. So I called down to the Lawyers Professional Responsibility Board. They have a database. I'd heard he'd been investigated before. Over the last 20 years there were three investigations, none resulting in more than a warning. If I wanted to know more they told me I'd have to come and review the files myself. But then the clerk let something slip about another investigation, recently opened."

"I'm not surprised," Sam shrugged, "given the old man's temperament."

"When I followed up on the clerk's comment, he said he misspoke. I took that to mean there was no current investigation, but just to double check I asked Jeff Dunlap and he said they couldn't talk about ongoing investigations. So I think the clerk meant he couldn't say anything and Dunlap was telling me an investigation was ongoing."

They thought about it.

"What good is a burned down office building to a dead man?" Diane wondered.

"There's the paper trail, if the old man was foolish enough to leave one," Sam suggested.

"But about what?"

"About whatever he was being investigated about?"

"I guess," Diane said doubtfully. "But what difference does it make to a dead man?"

"If the old man was alive, it could have been cause."

"But he isn't."

The only thing that surprised Sam Rivers was that he wasn't surprised. He had a letter written in his Mother's hand, containing a will that was executed and notarized several days later than the date of the will on file. Her comments in the letter indicated she was leaving Sam everything, that she was suspicious of what her husband would do, which was why she was also leaving Sam the cash in the duffel in the hiding place only Sam and she knew about. But the letter was two years old, and now Williston Winthrop was dead. Sam wished the old man was still alive. He'd like to face him in front of a judge, reverse the finding of the probate court, and recover his mother's things. And if he could prove the old man doctored the will, so much the better. For now he'd settle for pulling his mother's estate from the dead man's hands, and away from the rest of his larcenous friends.

There was still the question of the statute of limitations on contesting estates. For now he would have to keep the letter out of it. Her words were important, but his later version of the will should suffice.

"Maybe it's time to pay Jeff Dunlap a visit."

"Maybe it's time to see if our story has legs."

CHAPTER TWENTY

JANUARY 31ST, MID-DAY—DEAN GODDARD'S HOUSE

Dean Goddard was finally snowblowing his drive when Belinda stuck her head out the front door. She waved for Dean to stop. When he did she said, "Jeff's on the phone. Wants to speak with you. Says it's important."

Dean looked up, nodded. He parked the blower so he could walk around it. The snow was deep. Eight inches in Vermilion Falls. He knew it was deeper around Defiance, and even deeper out by Winthrop's farm and the surrounding area.

"Guess what," Dunlap started.

"I'm in the middle of digging out. Give it to me quick."

"Guess who's back in town?"

"Rudy Perpich."

"Very funny." Rudy Perpich was a dentist turned three-term governor, one of few who came from the Range. He was popular, but dead. "I happened to have liked Rudy."

"I did, too. With everything else that's going on these days, I just thought we might get lucky."

"Clayton Winthrop."

"Clayton Winthrop? Who the hell is Clayton Winthrop?"

"Will Winthrop's estranged son. Remember me telling you he had a son?"

Dean remembered. "What's he after? A piece of the estate?"

"Sort of. Turns out he's been in Colorado all these years. Changed his name to Sam Rivers."

"Is he a nut case?"

"Not at all, from what I remember. He was two years ahead of me, kind of a loner, but a pretty good guy. Not sure why he changed his name, but he's nothing like his old man. He's a special agent for U.S. Fish & Wildlife. A wildlife biologist. Specializes in wolves. And here's where it gets interesting."

"Yeah?"

"He comes over here with Diane Talbott."

"Nice looking company." Dean looked over his shoulder to make sure Belinda was out of earshot.

"Not bad. I was waiting for her to do more than unzip that down coat. Hard to hide a body like that."

Dean Goddard smiled. "What did they want?"

"Diane's an old friend of Clayton's mother. I mean she was an old friend."

"Yeah?"

"Yeah. Clayton's mother left a copy of her will with Diane. Said if Clayton . . . Sam Rivers ever returned she should give it to him."

"What?"

"I know. It's a little strange."

"Why did Talbott wait?"

"She didn't know it was a will. Just a sealed envelope."

"And she never opened it?"

"Said it was Miriam's dying wish."

"Uh-huh," Dean said doubtfully. "And I've got a feeling I know what the will says."

"You guessed it. This one's a little different than the one probated two years ago."

"What a surprise."

"It's notarized. And it's dated several days after the will used by Probate Court to settle Miriam Winthrop's estate."

"Let me guess. In the probated will everything went to the old man. The new one leaves everything to the kid."

"You got it. Only he isn't much of a kid anymore. He's grown up. Serious. Pleasant enough. But he doesn't give me the feeling he's a pushover or a crook. They also had a copy of the probated will. Guess who notarized the one leaving Miriam Winthrop's estate to Williston?"

"Hal Young?"

"You're a hundred percent. You been taking Ginkgo Biloba supplements?"

"Just naturally intelligent. Is the probated version legit?"

"Appears to be. Miriam Winthrop's signature looks a little fruity, but that could have been her illness. On the other hand, it could also mean that scumbag Williston Winthrop forged his dead wife's signature and cheated his son out of his mother's inheritance."

"How's the signature on the new will?"

"Pretty damn good. Better than the probated version."

Goddard thought about the break-in at Miriam Winthrop's house.

"When did Sam Rivers get into town?"

"Yesterday morning."

The timing wasn't right. Goddard wondered about it. Maybe Sam Rivers was lying. "Why didn't Diane Talbott mail the letter to Rivers?"

"Miriam made Diane promise to hold it for him, not to mail it. Diane says she was worried about Williston finding out about it. Even if she mailed it from Brainerd."

"That's a little paranoid."

"A lot of people owed Williston. He might have gotten wind of it. But I agree, a little paranoid. Could have been a little dementia, too, on Miriam's part, given her deteriorating health."

"So he waits until the old man dies before returning home. I guess there was no love lost."

"None, from what Sam said. And he has absolutely no intention of contesting his father's will. But he wanted to pursue getting probate to change his mother's estate, because he believed it was his mother's wish."

"Can he do that?"

"Not sure. I'm not that familiar with estate law."

"It'd be interesting to see him take something from that Club."

"That's what I was thinking."

"So what's he like?"

Jeff paused. "If you met this guy you'd pick up a different vibe from him. He seems . . ." Jeff thought about it, "genuine, no nonsense. The kind of guy you'd like to spend time with in a fishing boat, casting a line and drinking a couple beers."

"So he's absolutely nothing like his old man," Dean said.

"Sitting in a boat and having a couple of beers with Williston Winthrop wouldn't be my idea of a pleasant afternoon. Sam Rivers is different."

The Sheriff still thought Sam's presence, the break-in at his mother's house and the appearance of a new version of the will were all incredibly coincidental. Though Dean had to admit, Sam Rivers kept good company—Diane Talbott was smart, capable and good looking. Maybe Sam

Rivers was a carpetbagger charmer? Dean knew some USFW people. They were nature people, not carpetbaggers. He would have to meet Sam Rivers and get his own feel for the prodigal son that had blown in from out west. "What are you going to do?" he finally asked.

"I'm going to call a probate judge. Friend of mine. See what's involved. Sam Rivers might be able to reopen the estate, if this new will turns out to be legitimate. On the other hand he might have to sue in civil court."

"I'd love to see him prevail." Dean thought of Bill Grebs. The cop, and the rest of them, wouldn't like it.

"That's what I was thinking. Anyway, Sam Rivers seems like a pretty decent guy. You know what field agents do for U.S. Fish?"

"All sorts of stuff. They police the species list. Take care of the animals," Dean said, grinning a little. "Paul Williams over in Grand Rapids is a fresh-water biologist and USFW special agent. He does a lot of work in wetland habitat, but in fairness he does plenty of investigations too. You heard about that walleye poaching ring he broke up last year, up by Leech Lake?"

"That was the USFW?"

"That was Paul Williams. There was a wetland reclamation project a couple years back that was illegal but plenty complicated. Williams surfaced it. U.S. Fish & Wildlife is a little more sophisticated than our local DNR conservation officers," the Sheriff said. "But their turf is the wild, not towns. And they only take notice if animals are involved, not people. Still, I should meet Sam Rivers."

"You should. I'll try to think of something. Thought you'd want to know."

"Thanks."

The Sheriff rang off and returned to his snowblower. He was at it fifteen minutes before Belinda stuck her head out the front door and motioned to him again.

"Yeah?"

"It's Smith Garnes," she said, holding up his cell phone.

The Sheriff parked the blower to the side and re-entered the house, taking the phone.

"What's up?"

"I guess Walt Gibbons was right," he started. "Bad luck comes in threes. You remember the feeder stock Williston had at his farmhouse?"

The Sheriff thought about it. He remembered walking by the barn. He remembered the smell of cattle, and someone mentioned it. "Yeah," he said. "Calves?"

"Yeah. Pretty big calves. Three of them. Wolves got in last night and killed them."

"I'll be damned," he said, matter of fact. When he glanced over the phone Belinda was scowling. He mouthed 'sorry,' and turned away. "Wolves went into the barn?"

"Sounds like it. Angus Moon called the DNR. They're sending Steve Svegman out. Svegman remembered about Williston's accident and thought we should know."

"That was good of him," the Sheriff said, thinking of the young conversation officer. "You ever heard of wolves getting into a barn?"

"Nope," said Garnes. "But I suppose it's possible."

"Maybe I should join our young CO. Just to have a look."

"Thought you might want to."

The Sheriff thanked the Deputy and rang off.

Dean returned to his snowblower. Sometimes clearing off long rows of white powder was meditative. He thought about Sam Rivers. He wondered about the will. He considered Rivers's occupation. Special agent with the USFW, a wolf biologist. Maybe Dean could kill two birds with one stone? When the Sheriff finished blowing he came into the house, stayed in his warm wear, and called Jeff Dunlap's office.

"Dunlap," Jeff answered.

"Hey Jeff. Dean. I'm taking a ride out to Williston Winthrop's farmhouse. Wolves got into his barn and killed some feeder calves."

"No shit?" Dunlap said.

Dean turned around to be sure Belinda had left the room. "Shit," Dean affirmed. "Apparently got in last night and killed them."

"In a barn?"

"That larcenous old man can't seem to catch a break."

"Not that it matters to him."

"I was thinking it might be an opportunity to poke around."

"Good idea. Does the DNR know about it?"

"Yeah. Steve Svegman's the one who called us. He's headed out later. I'll try and intercept him."

"Maybe Sam Rivers the wolf expert would be interested."

"Exactly what I was thinking. The more the merrier. Know where I can reach him?"

CHAPTER TWENTY-ONE

JANUARY 31ST, MIDDAY—DEFIANCE

Out at the cabin the CB crackled and popped, said something unintelligible, but with a familiar enough tone to make Williston sit up and listen. He came out of the bedroom, walked across the cabin floor, flipped a switch and managed a voice entirely unlike his own. "Come again?" said a gravelly monotone. "Over."

After the last remnants of the storm whipped out of the atmosphere, the radio gradually returned to order. Apparently the wake of this storm contained unusual atmospheric pressure, uncharacteristic for the region but a good explanation for the temperature drop and the radio's unreliability.

"Static," was how Angus had explained it. "Things still wild out there."

Now Williston was alone in the cabin and waited for a response out of the calming ether.

"You wouldn't believe . . ." started to come in, broken, but unless Williston's ear had grown rusty, the voice was Grebs. There was a long blank space, a couple of crackling sparks, and then, "over?"

"Come again? Defiance Star? Over."

"Defiance Star comin' across the Range at ya', Range Wolf? Over?" Grebs asked.

"Range Wolf picking you up now, Defiance Star. Over." Williston lifted the talk button and cleared his throat. This wasn't a popular channel, but thanks to the quirks of the upper atmosphere you never knew when you'd accidentally pick up a message from Anchorage or St. Paul. The beauty of working with a CB radio was that fewer people were using the technology. These days it was generally only truckers and police who used the radios, and less of both as time went on. Cell phones had taken over the airwaves, much easier to use and with much greater ranges. But cell phones were useless in Skinwalker's Bog.

The emergency channel was 9. It was quiet now, but you just never knew who might be listening. And having someone else hear his voice—a supposedly dead man, however remote the possibility—was something Williston needed to avoid. It would be wise to keep the messages short and enigmatic. Williston knew Grebs was smart enough to take care.

There was a long pause, then "Heir apparent has returned. Repeat . . . surprising heir in the wind. Checking the weather but wanted to know how you might check it if you were in town? Curious. Over."

Definitely Grebs. He appreciated the obscurity, but wasn't sure he followed. Air? "Repeat in different key," he said. "Over."

There was another long pause. Williston was just about ready to repeat his request, when the radio barked "Prince." Pause. "Music now being heard all over our little town on the Range. Haven't heard him in what seems like 19, 20 years? Thought the king should know. Over."

Air . . . Prince . . . King? Heir! It came to him like a cattle prod. The *prince's* return. Not entirely unexpected. But it was still surprising. He wanted to make sure. "Maybe they listen at the Pit." he said. "Heard they're hitting clay. Tons of it. Clay-tons. Over."

Another long pause. "Heard the same thing. Clay-ton of it. Can't believe I heard Prince in our small town. Particularly when it's so cold out. The weather here is clear, but cold. Haven't begun checking yet. Not sure where to begin. Thought maybe I should check around, see if the weather's the same all over town. Try to figure if there's any bad weather brewing? Over."

Williston thought, then depressed the call button. "Weather checks wise. Pinehaven a must . . . Hotel . . . Starters. Over."

There was another long pause. "Will do. All good ideas. Over and out."

Williston didn't risk goodbye.

Clayton had returned. He was surprised it made his pulse rise. The kid was a little late, but still in time to see his old man buried, provided he showed up at the grave. Williston looked off through the cabin window. Through the frost-rimmed glass the thickets of Skinwalker's Bog were bleary and opaque. There was no telling where this was going to lead, but he smiled, appreciating the development.

If anyone could lead him to his $179,000 and stolen Decimator, it was the kid.

Over the next couple hours Grebs made his rounds. First he drove over to Pinehaven. He pulled into Miriam Winthrop's drive, parking in snowdrifts near the bottom, wading through heavy snow to the front porch. Everything was covered. He circled the house. The snow along the side of the house was broken. Someone had tracked it since the storm. The wind had blown over the tracks, but Grebs saw they were fresh. He turned the corner and saw tracks leading up the back yard to the door, and then away from it. There was also the shuffle in the snow beside the door. The area was covered over with white powder, as though someone had kicked snow against the house to build a drift.

He looked around the neighborhood, but the homes appeared empty. It was just after lunch. He knew almost everyone in this neighborhood and knew at this hour they'd be working.

He took out his key chain and fumbled through the options, finally extracting one and gripping it in his gloved hands. Someone had already loosened the ice around the hinges. He'd have to ask Hank and Hal. He used his key to let himself in.

The house was dark, stale, tomb-like. He walked across the kitchen floor. He walked down the hallway, but everything was in order. He examined the rooms on the main floor. He opened the basement door, throwing the light switch. He walked down into the old basement and was pleased to smell its dank normalcy. But it was cold. He could see his breath in the basement air. He looked around and saw sparkles beneath the basement window. He walked over and found the broken glass, looked up to see one of the windowpanes broken out. There was a mat of frozen crusted snow over the spot, with some frozen lips of meltwater seeping down the wall.

"Goddamn it."

Grebs examined the rest of the floor, but everything else looked untouched. He walked into the preserve room and flicked on the overhead light. He looked at the shelves full of preserves. He considered taking one, and then noticed the undusted circles where four jars had been removed. He looked for others missing from their two-year hibernation, but there were only the four. He looked around for the missing jars, but didn't find them.

"Break into a house for four jars of preserves?" He wondered. Didn't make much sense, unless you were feeling nostalgic. Clayton. He'd check the boy's jeep, or his hotel room. It made Grebs smile.

At the Hotel Defiance Grebs waited while Elwyn Baxter came out of the back room. As Elwyn approached, Grebs nodded cordially. The smile was returned, but the two men had never liked each other.

"Need a room?" Elwyn asked. He had a strong suspicion why Grebs was here. Sam Rivers hadn't returned last night. Elwyn hadn't seen him all day. But last night when Sam was checking in, Elwyn remembered Grebs's slow cruise in front of the Hotel.

Grebs laughed at Elwyn's question. "Not tonight, Elwyn," he said. "Just some information."

"We got plenty of that."

"Excellent. Has Clayton Winthrop checked into your hotel?"

"No."

"Didn't I see his jeep out front yesterday?"

Elwyn and Grebs had known each other most of their lives, and to Elwyn there were plenty of things about Grebs that didn't measure up, the most prominent his salary, paid for out of waning tax revenues.

Elwyn looked down at the hotel registry. He flipped it open to the current page and read the name. "Sam Rivers."

Grebs smiled. "That's the name he's going by now. That's Williston Winthrop's boy. Left about 20 years back. Got into some trouble and ran. Now he's returned with a different name. But it's the same kid."

Elwyn thought about it. There wasn't much to say. It was an interesting development, and Elwyn didn't like Rivers's deception, but he'd kind of liked Sam Rivers, which is a sentiment he'd never felt for Bill Grebs.

"Is he checked into your hotel?" Grebs repeated.

"Yep."

"Which room?"

"Does it matter?"

Grebs sighed. He suspected it might come to this. There was a time he could have forced his way into someone's room without the proper papers, but he and Elwyn were too old and familiar. "I have reason to believe he broke into someone's house. I think he's in possession of stolen goods. I'd like to check his room."

Elwyn just looked at him. "Got the paper?"

Grebs's eyes darkened.

Elwyn liked what he saw. It was enough to make him smile, though he didn't.

"I don't have a warrant, if that's what you mean."

"You aren't talking about doing something illegal, are you?"

"Look, Elwyn," Grebs smiled, trying to adopt a conspiratorial tone. "This can just be between you and me. I need to have a quick look. He's not around. Shouldn't hurt anyone. We would be in and out in less than a minute. It would help with an investigation."

Elwyn returned Grebs's smile with a grin of his own. "But that would be breaking the law. I don't think I could live with myself. You better get some paper."

Out in the cold Grebs contemplated ways to get even. He'd get back at Elwyn Baxter, when the proper moment presented itself. Any questioning of Grebs authority pissed him off, especially when it was a little bug like Elwyn Baxter. Grebs would have to teach him a lesson. But for now there was enough money in the balance to buy out the hotel proprietor and several other Defiance storefronts. For now it would be better to keep his cards to himself.

Grebs decided to cruise, keeping an eye out for Sam's jeep. It wouldn't be difficult to find some pretense for pulling him over. Not much had changed in 20 years. In the meantime it might be useful to head back to the office and start in on the paperwork for a search warrant, though he still wasn't certain it was the best approach, or that he would be able to convince a judge. That might be something best decided by Williston, later tonight, when they convened at the Club Cabin for the dead man's wake.

Grebs turned the patrol car toward the other side of town. He'd need to change vehicles. It was a hike to the cabin. Tonight he'd make it easier and use the Cat. He was already starting to feel thirsty.

CHAPTER TWENTY-TWO

JANUARY 31ST, EARLY AFTERNOON—ON THE ROAD NEAR DEFIANCE

After their meeting with Jeff Dunlap, Sam Rivers was driving Diane back to her place when his cell phone rang. Kay Magdalen, he suspected. As he reached for his phone he wondered about it. It was Friday and until recently Kay didn't work Friday afternoons. She claimed they were a dead zone, work-wise, and a waste of her time. For her to be calling now must mean fresh news about the position. But he hadn't thought about the position since learning Carmine Salazar had applied for it. Truth is, in the last 24 hours he hadn't thought much about Salazar, Maggie, Yellow Rock or the new job.

With one hand on the wheel of his jeep, he finally managed to reach into an inside pocket and pull out his phone, still ringing. He glanced at the display. A 218 area code. It was a local call.

He flipped it open. "Rivers."

"Sam Rivers?"

The only person who had his cell number was Jeff Dunlap, whose office they had recently left. But it didn't sound like Dunlap. "Yeah?"

"This is Sheriff Dean Goddard."

"Sheriff," Sam answered. He glanced over at Diane with a question in his eyes, but she shook her head.

In the last 24 hours Sam was guilty of breaking and entering, burglary, and had come as close to assault and battery as that altercation in the Florida Keys. And technically he was driving away from fraud: he and Diane Talbott had lied about how they'd come across his mother's will. Dunlap must have given his number to the Sheriff, which meant Dunlap called the Sheriff moments after they'd left his office. Interesting. Sam Rivers wanted to know why.

"Jeff Dunlap gave me your number," the Sheriff confirmed. "He says you were old classmates."

"That's right. Truth is, Jeff was behind me in school. A couple years. But I knew him."

"I believe Jeff also mentioned you were a special agent with the USFW?"

"That's right. Currently stationed out of the Denver office."

"Nice city."

"Yes it is."

"I'll come right to the point. Seems there was a wolf kill out at Williston Winthrop's farm. Jeff mentioned you know something about wolves and wolf kills?"

"I've seen a few," Sam said. Judy Rutgers came to mind. "What kind of kill?"

"Your dad had three feeder calves. Sounds like wolves got into the barn and killed them. Last night. Were you in town?"

"Came in yesterday morning," Sam said, surprised by the question, which had nothing to do with wolves. "I was down in Brainerd when it finally blew itself out, but I've seen enough to know you got hit pretty hard."

"We did. Especially out at your dad's place."

Sam Rivers had never called the old man 'dad.' Son of a bitch, when he was trying to be accurate. But something else the Sheriff said was much more interesting. "Wolves got into the barn?"

"That's what I heard. Got in, killed and fed."

"That would be," Sam said, surprised as hell but trying to be measured, "unusual." What he was thinking was *extraordinary*. Wolves didn't enter barns. Wolves didn't usually take down calves. Cattle were large enough to fend off a wolf attack. Not that wolves didn't occasionally try. Sam had seen flesh wounds, gashes and tears along bovine flanks that looked like the work of wolves, but he'd never seen them take down an adult animal. He'd heard of newborn calves being taken, but they were small and on the edge of a herd and unprotected, at least long enough for an opportunistic wolf or a pack to take advantage. And they were always outside, usually on remote grazing land.

"Angus Moon called it in. You know Moon?"

"I remember him," Sam said. "One of Williston's hunting friends."

"That's it. Apparently he's watching the place. Came out after the storm to feed them and found them all," he paused, searching for the right word. "Dead."

"And they were in the barn?"

"That's what they're saying. I'm getting this secondhand. Moon called the DNR about it. A DNR conservation officer needs to investigate.

Once it's verified our Minnesota Department of Agriculture reimburses ranchers for confirmed wolf kills."

"Same out west."

"This CO, Steve Svegman, knows one of my deputies and knows about the accident at your father's place and thought we'd be interested."

When Sam met Jeff Dunlap he liked him. But he'd never met the Sheriff and for all he knew Dunlap had called the Sheriff out of suspicion. Considering his activities over the last 24 hours, the suspicion was warranted. Sam would have to be careful.

"Given what happened at your dad's place. I mean . . . his accident. I guess I better go have a look. That farm is in my jurisdiction."

There was another pause. "Makes sense," Sam said.

"And given your experience with wolf kills I was wondering if you'd like to come along?"

The offer surprised him. Sam's experience with local law enforcement wasn't often positive. During official investigations he'd rankled local sheriffs. It was a matter of turf. "Sure, Sheriff."

"Just one thing. Jeff mentioned you had no interest in contesting your father's will. To make trouble. That accurate?"

"I have no interest in Williston Winthrop's will or the dispensation of his property. But I assume he told you about my Mother's will?"

"He did. That's your business. I was more concerned about any issues you might have with Angus Moon, who's meeting us at the farm."

Sam thought about it. "In terms of trouble you never know what might set some people off. I've come back to visit. It's been 20 years and I was curious to see how the place has changed."

"Fair enough," the Sheriff smiled. "I can swing by and pick you up, say, in an hour?" the Sheriff suggested. "Where are you staying?"

Sam had always known he would visit the farm. But he would have preferred visiting alone. "I've got a few errands to run," he lied. "How about if I meet you there? I remember the way."

I suspect you do, Dean Goddard thought. "That'll work. Why don't we make it . . ." he paused. "Come to think of it I think my deputy said Svegman was going to be out there around 2:00? That give you enough time?"

"Plenty," Sam said.

"See you at the farm around 2:00."

Sam couldn't have hoped for a more legitimate excuse to have a second look at his boyhood compound, though he would have to step carefully. If what the Sheriff said was true, wolves had done something extraordinary. Puzzling. Interesting. And that's when he thought a little diversion might help.

"What was that about?" Diane asked.

"You know the Sheriff," Sam said. "What's he like?"

"A good guy."

"Think you might like to visit the old man's farm, see a wolf kill?"

"Wolves killed livestock at Williston Winthrop's farm?"

Sam explained what happened at the old man's place.

Diane was surprised.

"Wolf predation of livestock is normal enough. But I've never heard of wolves entering a barn to kill cattle."

"Sounds awful, but in a morbid kind of way, I'd like to see it. And the paper should damn well cover it. But I'm not sure the Sheriff would appreciate it."

"I'd like to look around out there. If we both went it might be," he paused, "easier." With Diane out there asking questions he might have an opportunity to at least look into corners he wouldn't otherwise see.

"I'd love to," she said, managing a small grin.

The old farmhouse had ghosts. Sam wanted to greet each and every one of them. It was the place where the late Williston Winthrop tried to tutor him, though Sam had never been a very apt pupil. Long after he left the Range, Sam's inability to measure up was the subject of hours of introspection, up to a point. He'd reached that point years ago, the one in which he finally understood the old man had been an unusually brutal father, an angry man and a son of a bitch. And those were the descriptions that easily came to mind. He was cruel, and in retrospect Sam was glad he had never accepted the old man's perspective on the world, or his way of living in it. Most of all he was glad he had run. But now it was time. He felt ready to meet those ghosts and send them back from whence they'd come.

CHAPTER TWENTY-THREE

JANUARY 31ST, AFTERNOON—THE WINTHROP FAMILY FARM

At 2:00 p.m. sharp Sam turned into the farmhouse drive. To either side of the pair of narrow ruts, high drifts reached the center of Sam's jeep. Tire tracks were grooved into several inches of crusted white powder. He was glad for the jeep. The clapboard house looked older, more dilapidated. Its sides were weathered, paint peeling like flaking skin. A thin trail of smoke wafted out of a stovepipe into a cold blue sky. The tarpaper roof looked more tattered and worn. Sam felt a whirl in the center of his chest, as though some remote spark was starting to burn. The farmhouse was rundown and beat up. If this is what 20 years had done to the homestead, or what the old man had let happen to it, he wondered what the years had done to Williston Winthrop.

"You OK?" Diane asked.

"Sure. Why?"

"You look . . . tense."

Sam could feel Diane's attention. "It's been a while," he said. "There's a lot of . . ." he paused, thinking about it. "There's a lot here. Plenty I'd rather not remember."

Diane reached over and placed her hand on his shoulder, an unexpected gesture. He was surprised by how it felt. It'd been a while since he'd been touched.

"I'll be OK," he said.

"I figured."

At the bottom of the drive there was a dark green DNR Conservation truck. The Sheriff's cruiser was parked behind it.

The Sheriff and Steve Svegman were on the front landing. Sam watched the door open and Angus Moon step onto the cement block, threading a wiry arm into his down coat. Sam saw Angus shake hands and then peer toward the jeep coming down the drive, wondering who else had arrived, unhappy about it.

Sam guessed Hank Gunderson had already alerted the others to his return. But Angus would be surprised to see him now, with Diane.

"Showtime."

"That guy creeps me out."

"Me, too. Always has," Sam said. "Or did. This time I'm looking forward to our reunion."

Sam parked and they stepped out of the jeep, zipping up their coats as they walked to the front steps where the three men were gathered in the cold, watching their approach. The Sheriff turned and said, "Sam Rivers?" extending his hand.

Sam nodded and took it. "Sheriff," Sam said. If the Sheriff was pissed about Diane he didn't show it.

The Sheriff was the same height as Sam, with a little pudginess beneath his down coat and ear-flap cap. He looked a little country-ish, Sam thought. But he thought he noticed something intense in the Sheriff's eyes.

"Diane," the Sheriff nodded.

"Sheriff," she greeted in return.

"This is Steve Svegman," the Sheriff introduced. "One of our local conservation officers."

Svegman shook hands, greeting them, and then said, "U.S. Fish & Wildlife?"

"Out of Denver," Sam answered.

Steve Svegman was a rookie. Sam guessed he had a military style buzz cut beneath his DNR hat. He was a little awkward on the front step.

"You're a special agent?" Svegman asked.

"That's right."

"A wolf specialist?"

Sam nodded. "I grew up with them," he said, glancing toward Angus Moon.

"And you remember Angus Moon," the Sheriff said.

Sam peered at the aging woodsman and offered him a hand, for appearances. He was glad Angus didn't take it.

The Sheriff sensed Moon's uneasiness. "Turns out we're fortunate to have Sam Rivers around, Angus," he started. "Sam's a wildlife biologist who happens to know quite a bit about wolves and wolf kills." He smiled, but Moon wasn't reflecting his good humor. And apparently he hadn't been told there would be another guest to their party.

Angus appeared smaller than he remembered. He looked older and tougher, but not in a good way.

Their breathing clouded the afternoon air.

Moon considered Rivers with a dark stare, then said, "This here is Clayton Winthrop."

Sam held Moon's watery brown eyes, happy for the opportunity to engage, even if it was just a look. He could see there was still plenty of fight in the compact hunter. But the years, and he guessed whiskey through plenty of cold winters, had rounded the man's shoulders and thinned him out a little. He looked older and meaner.

"Williston wouldn't like it," Moon added, turning to the Sheriff.

"Williston's in no place to worry about it," the Sheriff said. "Besides, I think we could use his help."

The Sheriff turned to Diane and said, "Diane, we've got a little situation here. If I'd have known you were coming along, I might have mentioned something to Sam. The DNR and Agriculture don't want news of this kill getting out. At least not until we finish our investigation."

Diane thought about it. She'd come along for two reasons. Sam Rivers, because it had been a while since she'd found any men interesting. But once she discovered what happened, and that it was significant, she was also interested in the story.

"Sheriff," Diane started. "I want to be a good citizen. But this might be the kind of story people need to know about."

"I agree. It's just nothing we need getting out until we're absolutely certain what we've got here. Don't your stories need to be accurate?"

"It's a wolf kill, alright," Moon said.

"Then people need to know," Diane reiterated.

"Diane," Sam started. "Now that the Sheriff mentions it, I'm tracking with him. Wolf kills are sensitive. *If* this one is real, and it's in a barn, there could be considerable fallout among ranchers in the state. And plenty of heat for the DNR. But first we have to know for certain what it is we've got here."

"That's right," the Sheriff agreed.

"What we got is goddamn wolves," Angus said. "Come into a barn and slaughtered three calves."

Diane paused, glancing at Angus before turning to the Sheriff. "I appreciate that. All I'm saying is people have a right to know. What if they kill again?"

"Damn right," Angus added.

"That's not how normal wolves operate," Sam said.

"Wolves kill anything."

"Wolves kill to feed. And for the record, they don't go into barns."

"Bullshit! Done it right here."

"That's why we're here, Angus," he smiled, but without humor. "To have a look at something that's never before been recorded in the annals of wolf livestock predation."

"Wolves kill every day," Angus growled.

"Not in barns." Sam watched a vein swell the side of Angus Moon's neck, a good sign. Before Angus could speak Sam said, "How about this, Sheriff? We make a thorough investigation of this kill. I can help officer Svegman sort through the details. If that's OK, Steve," Sam said, turning to Svegman.

"Sure."

"Once officer Svegman finishes writing his report and files it with the DNR, we give Diane *exclusive* rights to the story."

Diane frowned. She didn't like negotiating access to a story, particularly when it was in front of her and she wasn't one of the primary negotiators. She was suddenly a little pissed at Sam Rivers. He'd invited her on a charade. And now he'd turned paternalistic.

"We can't be exclusive," the Sheriff said. "But I suspect we could give her a good headstart on viewing the document. That sound fair, Diane?"

"I'm well within my rights to write any damn thing I want."

Before she gathered a full head of steam Sam cut her off, turning back to Sheriff Goddard. "I guess she has a point, Sheriff. But if I'm not mistaken, this is a crime scene, isn't it?"

Dean knew immediately where Sam was headed, and he liked the tack. "That's right," he agreed.

"And the Sheriff has the right to restrict access to the crime scene?"

"That's correct," the Sheriff said.

"Bullshit," Diane barked. Sam Rivers had bushwhacked her. "This isn't St. Paul. This is the Iron Range."

"Diane, your friend here has a point."

"You can't shut me out."

"Yes he can," Sam said.

She turned a withering eye on Sam Rivers. But Sam was ready for it. "On the other hand, Diane, I suspect the Sheriff would be willing to allow the press to accompany us, providing you held your story until you received the exclusive final report."

The Sheriff thought about it. "That's right," he finally said.

Diane didn't much care for where this was heading. But she wasn't sure, just yet, what she could do about it. Except play along. And when she got the chance, give Sam Rivers a piece of her mind. He had bailed her out of a tough situation with Hank Gunderson. He'd gained some credit with her. Now he was using some up.

"I don't like it," Diane finally said. "But I'll play along, providing the report doesn't take two weeks to write."

"Clayton Winthrop got no business here," Angus said.

The Sheriff turned to the woodsman. "Steve Svegman and the DNR are heading up the investigation of this wolf kill. But if I'm not mistaken, he can invite assistance from any party he chooses," Dean added, looking to Steve Svegman, already knowing the young CO would play along. "Isn't that right, Steve?"

Steve blushed a little. "That's right."

"Particularly from a USFW specialist," the Sheriff added.

"Uh-huh," Svegman nodded.

"That's a bunch of horse shit, Sheriff."

"Maybe you should return to the warmth of that farmhouse," the Sheriff suggested. "We can show ourselves to the barn."

Angus scowled. There was no way he'd let them walk around in that barn alone.

Sam realized there would be no unaccompanied perusal of the farmhouse, at least today. But a glance at the lintel over the door showed the edge of a thin metal line, barely a half-inch curve. It was the place the old man had kept a spare key, back when Sam was young. Some things hadn't changed, Sam thought.

The Sheriff turned back to Diane. "I don't think Steve's going to take long writing this one, Diane. Isn't that right, Steve?"

"It shouldn't take that long."

"We'll have to release it to everyone, but perhaps we can first give it a kind of soft release and call you with a heads up. A day's heads up sounds like it'll work. Won't it, Steve?"

"Sure," Svegman agreed.

Moon led them to the barn, clearly angry about Svegman's posse, but knowing they needed the DNR's blessing. Svegman followed Angus across the narrow, unplowed walk, for now taking the lead. The Sheriff stepped in behind Svegman. Sam and Diane followed.

"So give us the details," the Sheriff said.

"I been feeding Williston's calves since the accident. Wolves came in last night." He turned and glanced at the Sheriff. "Killed 'em. Had a feed." He paused in front of the sliding barn door. "I don't know nothin' about Colorado. But here the packs are growing plenty," Angus said. "They're takin' dogs off porches."

So the woodsman knew about Colorado. Either he'd noticed the plates, or more likely Gunderson told him. Word travels fast.

"Most pet predations happen out in the woods, not on porches," Sam clarified, for the record.

Angus stared at him.

Sam stared back, recognizing that old familiar meanness. It was unpredictability with a sense that just about anything was possible. But Angus was an aging wolverine. Or maybe a weasel, Sam thought, feeling pleasant tension in his solar plexus.

Angus flung the sliding barn door open, then said, "If wolves don't go into barns, then what the hell is this?"

The first thing Sam noticed was the odor. It was like a frozen meat locker, only a little more fetid, with entrails and terminal ooze covering the killing room floor.

"My God," Diane said.

Sam peered across the threshold and examined the floor. "When did you say this happened?"

Angus turned. "Last night."

The first thing Sam Rivers noticed was the state of the carcasses. They appeared to be at least 24 hours old, which meant this couldn't have happened any earlier than the night before last. Interesting, given Moon's assertion. Particularly when Sam could see no good reason to lie.

"This how they came in?" Sam asked. He didn't question the timing, but he remembered the words from the middle of that storm, night before last. Grebs and Gunderson had been somewhere, and there were others who were heading back to Angus's place. But from where?

"This door was unlatched," Angus said. "Must have nosed it open."

"Smart wolves," Sam commented. He peered along the frame, found tufts of gray and black hair. "Steve," he called to the conservation officer, who was behind him. "What do you have in the bag?"

"Digital camera. Evidence kit," he managed, a little shaken by the view and smell.

"Got any baggies?"

Svegman opened the shoulder bag, happy for the diversion. He rummaged through its contents and pulled out a small sheaf of baggies with a rubber band around them.

"Can I have one of those?" Sam asked.

Svegman pulled off his mittens and extracted a baggy, handing it to Sam.

"How about a forceps?"

Svegman returned to the bag and extracted the bright silver tool.

"Is this normal?" Diane asked.

Sam leaned down close to the edge of the door. The others were standing just outside the barn, watching him work. He clamped down on the largest clump of hair, shaking it loose into the baggie. He found two or three more samples and dropped them into separate bags. When he handed the bags to Svegman he said, "nothing normal about it."

Angus appeared to dislike seeing Sam bag hair. Interesting. "Wolf hair is pretty specific. I'm sure this is it, but it's standard with most wolf investigations. You always want a little physical evidence," Sam lied.

"Got plenty of that," Angus growled.

Sam had taken a sample because he wanted to check it. But he was also interested in Angus's reaction. The woodsman's irritation confirmed his decision to ship the sample to the USFW lab in Ashland. As soon as they returned to town, Sam would FedEx it. They'd determine definitively what kind of wolves they were. It looked like the real thing. Sam just wanted to be certain. And if the Sheriff and the Minnesota DNR and Agriculture wanted the final report delayed, giving them time to prepare for the fallout, waiting for the DNA analysis would provide some cover.

Clearly the woodsman was unnerved.

Svegman nodded in agreement, though he wouldn't have bagged the hair.

Diane watched.

The Sheriff was pleased Sam Rivers was along.

Moon finally reached over and flicked on the overhead light, providing a little more illumination of the scene. The smell and shadowed glimpses were bad enough, but under the dull barn light the five onlookers were shocked by the carnage. Everyone but Moon and Sam Rivers.

"My God," Diane repeated.

One glance was enough, not likely something any of them would soon forget. Svegman looked at it and thought *Jesus H. Christ.*

"Doesn't look good," the Sheriff agreed, though he was cool, Sam noticed. He had probably seen plenty worse, involving people, not livestock.

For Sam it was ugly and unusual but not unnerving. He stepped forward. "Got a flashlight, Steve?"

Svegman reached into his bag and extracted a flashlight. Sam flicked it on and carefully stepped to the largest animal, or what was left of it. Then he turned and said, "There should probably be just the two of us in here, stepping around these animals. Or what's left of them."

The Sheriff understood. Crime scene. And it was a chance to get into the house. "Angus, mind if we wait in the house?"

Angus didn't like it. Particularly Clayton Winthrop nosing around the barn uninvited and without an escort. He didn't like it one damn bit. But he couldn't see Clayton, Sam, whatever the hell he called himself, would find anything contrary to what happened. Wolves come in and killed them. "Be quick," he finally said.

Rivers ignored the woodsmen, knowing he'd take however much time his investigation needed. He was fascinated by the kill.

Sam didn't turn to watch them go. His beam flashed over the closest kill. Its head and neck had been partially eaten. Most of the rest of it was stripped, entrails cascading from its belly onto the floor. The upward haunch was almost completely devoured. Sam turned the beam on what was left of the nose. "Got that camera?" he asked.

Svegman stepped closer, ashen. Sam watched him reach into his pack and pull out a portable digital camera with a built-in flash.

"Focus, Steve," Sam advised. "Just focus on what I tell you. You think you can take some pictures?"

Svegman nodded. "I've never seen a kill like this."

"Neither have I. But for the time being let's keep that between ourselves. Can you just shoot where I point the beam?" Sam aimed the beam on the center of the calf's nose, what was left of it. There were teeth marks around the snout.

Svegman sucked it up, pointed, focused and clicked. The camera flashed like a lightning strike. In the same manner they spent the next ten minutes working around the calves, which were all badly eviscerated.

Twice more Sam reached down and placed fur clumps into baggies. There were a couple of clear footprints in the barn floor where the wolves stepped in blood and paced over the cement. Sam had Svegman photograph them; wide angle lens, macro shots. They were big. Svegman didn't have a rule, but Sam could tell they were oversized for gray wolves. He placed the toe of his snow boot beside two of the bloody paw prints, measuring the distance. Svegman took the picture with Sam's boot in the frame, next to the paw print. Later he could use it for a more precise measurement. But he already saw something about them he didn't like. Not only were they oversized, but two pairs of prints had a wider stance than a typical wolf.

"There must have been a bunch of them," Svegman said, the carnage and subsequent feeding so extreme.

"Looks like five," Sam agreed.

Svegman was surprised. "Only five?"

"Wolves can eat almost one quarter their weight in a single sitting," Sam said, still examining the scene. "They gorge, then they sleep it off. Then they'll usually starve a few days before they kill again. Or return to feed off what they've already killed."

"Feast and famine," Svegman said.

"That's it."

On the way back to the house, Angus ruminated about leaving Sam Rivers alone. He was an unwelcome development. And Hank had been right. He wasn't a kid anymore. But it was damn cold. And there was nothing to be done about it. They needed Svegman to authorize the kill. And there was plenty of evidence, even for Sam Rivers.

The Sheriff let Diane walk in front of him and they stepped quickly through the cold to the front door. At first the Sheriff had been disappointed in Sam Rivers. He'd invited a reporter to a crime scene. And that was a clear violation of protocol, though Sheriff Goddard wasn't sure how they did things in the USFW. Maybe it was different if you were investigating animals, not people. But something about Sam Rivers told the lawman there was more to Diane's invitation than friendly courtesy. He appreciated her for the same reason. Because now he might be able to nose around a little himself, inside the house, while the coarse Angus Moon was distracted by his inquisitive guest.

Once inside, the Sheriff glanced around the spare front room. "Might be good to look around," he suggested. "Just get a picture of what's here, in case anyone tries to take advantage of Williston's passing."

Angus eyed the Sheriff with suspicion, but couldn't find the harm. He shrugged and said, "Not much to take, I guess."

"Better to be safe," he said. "You like some water or something, Diane?"

Diane nodded to the offer of water and Angus turned into the small farm kitchen to help her.

The Sheriff stepped down the hallway to the basement door, then down the creaking stairs into the dark cellar. It smelled dank, musty, earthen. There was a workbench under a couple of spare bulbs. There was equipment for making ammo, and the necessary supplies. A peg board with plenty of hooks and tools hung in front of the bench. There was an old furnace at the other end of the room. While he stood next to it he heard the old fuel oil ignition spit and light, the heat firing on.

The Sheriff stepped over to the bench, reviewing it for drawers or some other place Winthrop might have hidden a disk, or any records of Pine Grove Estates. He stepped over to an opened box and reached in. A pile of empty shotgun shells. He took one out and examined it.

"Damn big charge," he said.

He remembered it was for the weapon that removed Williston's head, or most of it. He returned the empty cartridge to the box, had another look, and muttered, "OK," turning back toward the stairs.

In the same manner he examined the rest of the house.

After fetching water for Diane, Angus joined him. The place was typical, the Sheriff thought, of Range farmhouses. Rickety and in need of repair. Other than an old CB in a back room, the place was bare.

"Radio still work?" the Sheriff asked. He hadn't seen a CB rig in quite a while.

"I guess," Angus shrugged, then switched off the room light. A little too quickly, the Sheriff thought.

In Williston's office there was no PC. No computer equipment anywhere. A few file drawers that might contain something, but when he opened them they were largely empty.

"What you looking for?" Angus asked.

"Just trying to get a sense of what's in the place."

"Nothin' but paper in those drawers."

And so it was. Other than rifling through the old man's dresser drawers the Sheriff didn't see anyplace Williston might have stowed a flash drive, CD, DVD or any other client files. He couldn't be certain, but he was beginning to think everything might have turned to ash with the rest of the old man's law office. With regard to the digital video, one could hope. With regard to the incriminating files, the Sheriff knew Jeff Dunlap would be disappointed.

By the time they returned to the front room, Svegman and Sam were coming out of the barn.

"I guess we're done," the Sheriff commented.

Angus watched Sam and Svegman approach. Sam was talking to Svegman, as though tutoring the young CO on some of the finer points of investigating wolf kills. Svegman listened attentively.

He wasn't a kid, Angus thought about Sam Rivers. The new Clayton pissed him off.

Sam came up to the house and into the front door, stamping his feet. Svegman followed and did the same.

Angus was ready to get out to the cabin. He could use a little remedy. Or a lot. And Williston and the others would be interested in his update.

"Damn cold out there," Sam said, shaking it off. "I guess I forgot just how cold it could get up here," he smiled at the Sheriff.

"We're in some kind of snap, for sure," Sheriff Goddard remarked. "The Bank said twelve below."

"What about the wolf kill?" Angus asked, blunt, ready to be done with business.

Sam glanced over at the CO. He pulled off his mittens and blew into his hands, trying to warm them. "What about it?" he asked, turning to Angus.

"Wolves done it," Angus affirmed. It wasn't a question.

Sam looked at him. "Seems so," he said. "But it's peculiar. They killed all three animals and left plenty of food behind. That, and it happened in a barn. I can't quite figure it."

"What's to figure?" Angus asked.

Sam stared at Angus. He remembered this front room. It was spare, with an old sofa next to the wall. The sofa was new, at least that much had changed. There was an easy chair to the right of the front window. Behind Angus was the walkway into the small kitchen, the room he had stumbled out of 20 years earlier, bruised, bloodied and barely alive. Back down the hallway was the rear door, and to the right of the rear door the old man's infamous office, a forbidden place. Along the hallway wall hung several different frames depicting the Winthrop family heritage. He had made enough surreptitious visits to that office to have found the old man's secret hiding place. He wondered about it now. He ignored Angus Moon, blew on his hands and finally said, "plenty."

There was a flight of stairs beyond the old man's office, up to the second floor bedrooms, one of them his. Along the wall he was surprised to see the Winthrops' pictorial history restored. There was the news account of his great grandfather's death from wolves, and beyond it, photo after family photo of slaughtered wolves, some containing entire packs. Before he left, Sam had shattered every frame.

"Plenty what?"

Standing in the old house and seeing the wall and old photos made Sam remember plenty. Seeing the barn was interesting, too. He had spent many boyhood hours in the place, including assembling a pack with winter survival gear, at least enough to escape into the northern wilderness. It was all so long ago, but his visit left him feeling more curious about the place and he knew he'd have to return. Ghosts, he thought. A lot of spirits with whom he needed to converse.

"Damn odd they nosed their way into a barn," Sam repeated, returning to consider Angus.

"I told you the door was cracked."

"I believe you said 'unlatched,' Angus," Sam corrected.

Angus didn't appreciate the clarification. "Fuckin' open," he said, low and even.

Sam grinned. "It's still curious."

"They were followin' their noses," Angus explained. "Pushed the goddamn door open to get at 'em. You ever been hungry?"

"Sure. Not enough to push open a barn door with my nose and kill three feeder calves. But I've been plenty hungry."

Diane was pissed and the Sheriff tired, but Sam thought they both grinned.

"I'm just saying it's a little bizarre. One for the books."

"I don't know about no goddamn books," Angus said.

True enough, Sam knew.

"What about the money?" Angus asked, turning his attention to Svegman. Steve Svegman withered in front of the woodsman's gaze.

"Full reimbursement," Svegman answered. "I don't think we saw anything to presume it was something other than wolves. Did we, Sam?"

Sam paused. He liked having some kind of say in an occurrence that might benefit Angus Moon. "For now, no," he said. "But if you could keep the place untouched, Angus. That'd be helpful."

"This is no goddamn business of yours."

Sam remembered the old hunter's way. Angus liked to raise his voice. A flash of his temper was usually enough to dissuade others.

The Sheriff interceded. "Like I said, Angus. The State can solicit whatever assistance it needs from capable experts, especially the USFW, and particularly in matters of wolf kills, given their sensitive nature." He turned to Sam. "Seen anything, Sam, to prevent Steve here from working up the reimbursement forms?"

"Nope," he said. "But it would be good to keep it open because others in the USFW and DNR will be interested, might want to have another look. And Steve will need to set some traps. What's left of those calves might make good bait."

"I'll complete the paperwork as soon as I get back to the office," Svegman offered.

"I can set my own traps," Angus said. "Or shoot 'em if they come back."

Sam considered it. He knew Angus was equal to trapping the animals, if they returned; had probably already done it in the wild, illegally. "I suspect Steve can issue you a shoot on site permit, if that's what you want."

"Damn right."

"Steve can include it with the reimbursement form."

The accommodation seemed to settle Moon, which disappointed Sam Rivers. He would have preferred him riled before asking his next question.

"Just one more thing. You said the wolves came in last night?"

"Yeah," Angus said.

"From the looks of it those calves have been dead for more than 24 hours."

Angus Moon's face flushed, at least as much as could be seen beneath his grizzled countenance. His dark eyes flashed at Svegman, then the Sheriff.

"Might have been the other night," he shrugged.

"The night of that big storm?" Sam asked.

Angus flashed again, uneasy. "Thas' right."

"So you haven't been out here for 48 hours? You haven't tended to these calves in two days?"

"Snow was too high," he said, irritated. "Goddamn couldn't get nowhere!"

"So you were stuck at your place?" Sam asked.

"Yeah," he said.

"And I've got a bad memory. How far away from here do you live?"

Angus waved off the question. "What the hell difference it make? Everyone knows that storm was the worst in these parts. I live close enough," he finally answered. "But not close enough to make it over in a storm like that one."

"How far is it, Angus, exactly?" This time is was the Sheriff asking. "I don't think I've ever been out to your place?"

"Five, six mile," he said. "Far enough."

"And yesterday," Sam said, "after the plows started clearing the roads, you still didn't come check on these animals?"

"I was busy," Angus said.

Busy doing whatever he was doing the night of the storm. When he wasn't at home. And Sam knew it.

"So they've gone untended for two days?" Sam asked, wanting to be sure.

"That's right. Two fuckin' days. Not that it makes any difference."

"I think he's just trying to understand what happened," the Sheriff said. "We all just want to know what happened here and when."

"Goddamn wolves what happened!" Angus said.

The Sheriff flashed a look at Sam Rivers that told him they'd pushed the man enough. He turned back to Svegman. "Steve'll get you those forms, won't you Steve?"

"Sure."

Angus Moon didn't answer, just nodded.

The Woodsman was pissed, Sam thought, a state of being Sam appreciated. Sam sensed Moon didn't want to see any of them again, if he could manage it.

"Then I guess we'll be heading out," the Sheriff offered, turning toward the door.

Sam took his time getting into his mittens. "If you get lucky and catch something, keep the carcass for us, will you Angus?"

Angus only scowled and nodded with a short jerk of his head.

Sam finished getting into his coat, then stepped into the cold, preferring it to the tight interior of the house. Diane stepped out behind him. Then Svegman and the Sheriff. At his jeep Sam and Diane turned to look back toward the house. Angus was standing in the front window, watching.

The farmhouse and the immediate area surrounding it was a communications black hole. No cell phone reception. Poor media signals, Sam remembered. The poor TV reception from his childhood jump-started his reading. He'd read all of Jack London and everything he could find on wolves. Until he moved out, books were his only recreation. He appreciated outdoor adventures, westerns, survival stories, anything having to do with woods or wilderness.

Diane was staring straight ahead, mute. It made Sam remember Maggie in a similar state, which became more numerous toward the end. She'd wanted to discuss whatever issue pissed her off, but he preferred dodging the issue. He never chose to open the door. Not even a crack.

"What is it?" he asked. Maybe he'd try something different.

"I'm wondering why the hell you invited me out here?"

"I thought you'd be interested."

"But you moved to restrict my story when you could have kept quiet."

"Look, Diane. There are two things going on here. First, I needed to do that kill review without Moon observing our methods. And second, until we know for certain that it was a wolf kill you shouldn't write anything about it."

"What the hell else could it be?!"

"I don't know what it was. Something. There was plenty of evidence of wolves, but wolves wouldn't do this."

They drove a little longer in silence. After a while they reached blacktop and Sam's cell phone went off.

"Rivers," he answered.

"Dean Goddard," the Sheriff said.

"Sheriff."

"I guess you know Angus Moon is still a son of a bitch."

"I noticed."

"And I guess you noticed I don't give a rat's ass what he thinks. If I had more men I'd have him tailed."

"I kind of figured, Sheriff."

"I'm willing to back you up on this delay in cleanup. But if Angus starts making calls to the Cattleman's Association, or one of those ranching outfits, we could be in for a little heat. Up here we have a pretty active organization. And Agriculture still has plenty of power."

"I appreciate it, Sheriff. And for the record, I agree. This just bears a little more investigation. I'm going to FedEx some hair samples to the USFW Forensics Lab in Ashland, Oregon. If I call in a favor I should be able to get the results by tomorrow afternoon."

"What results?"

"DNA analysis. We're stockpiling a database of wolf DNA samples. I'm not expecting anything other than Great Plains gray wolf DNA, but it's worth double checking."

"Great Plains wolf? I thought they were timber wolves?"

"Timber wolves are in Canada and Alaska. What we have here in the Midwest are Great Plains gray wolves. But I have to tell you I saw some anomalies that made me wonder what they were, exactly. Judging from those prints and the remains, some of those animals looked damn big. I'm just curious, and it doesn't hurt to add the data to our files."

"I appreciate it, but I don't think we should sit on this mess any longer than 24 hours. Ranchers get wind of this and there'll be a feeding frenzy in St. Paul. And the last thing we need is one of the local papers running a photo of that slaughter. Right now it appears to be pretty well contained. I'd like to keep it that way. And one other thing," Goddard added, pausing so it would register.

Sam noted the change in tone.

"Next time don't bring the press."

"Fair enough."

"I don't know you well enough to know if there was some other reason for her presence. But we're straight shooters up here, Rivers. So in the future before you pull a stunt like that you better let me in on it, before I'm hip deep in wolf shit."

"Point taken, Sheriff." Diane was still staring out the window, pissed. "I owe you."

The Sheriff agreed. "How's she taking it?"

She was listening, but Sam guessed she could only hear his side of the conversation. "About as well as can be expected."

"That bad, huh?"

"Uh huh."

"We can't keep this out of the press forever. But if Diane runs it first and we can manage the photo that runs with her story, it would be a whole lot better than the alternative."

"Makes sense."

"Good. Now what did you make of the change in Moon's story, about when it happened?"

Sam thought about it. If he told the Sheriff about knowing Angus Moon was out in that storm, he'd have to tell him how he knew, which would make his own story about when he arrived in Defiance a lie. "Not sure why he lied about it. Other than he was shirking his responsibilities. Or maybe he let them alone for two days and couldn't tell they'd been dead for 48 hours. But that doesn't make sense either, because a woodsman like Angus Moon can read carcass as well as any Indian from the last century."

"OK."

"Along with everything else, a little odd."

Up ahead, as they cruised down the blacktop toward town, a small clutch of ravens were pecking at a deer carcass. And that's when Sam remembered. Something else had bothered him about the kill, but he hadn't been able to pinpoint it.

"One other thing," he said. "There were no ravens."

"Ravens?"

"Ravens and wolves have been symbiotic for thousands of years. Not always, but usually. Ravens follow the packs, some speculate to clean up after the wolves have finished gorging. Native Americans believed ravens led the packs to wounded or sickened animals. Wherever you see wolves, you usually find ravens."

The Sheriff thought about it. "No way ravens would get into that barn."

"True enough, Sheriff. But I didn't see any roosting on the roof or in the nearby trees. And I didn't see any sign of them. If they'd been following the pack at least some would hang around a kill that size."

They discussed the next 24 hours, when Sam might return to the house to have another look in the barn. Right now Sam didn't know if he would return, at least with Sheriff Dean Goddard. It was good just knowing he had the option. And the carnage was excellent bait, if the animals grew hungry. They agreed that by tomorrow at this time they'd let Angus clean it up, maybe visit for one more examination of the scene.

Sam drove the remaining miles in silence. At the edge of Defiance he glanced at his watch. It was after 4:00 p.m.

"I think I'm heading back to the hotel. I need to bag it for a couple hours, because after dinner I'm heading back out to the old man's place. Take a closer look. Not in the barn. In the house. And it won't be burglary, since I don't plan on stealing anything. And technically not breaking and entering, since I'll have a key. If we got caught, the most they could get us for is trespassing."

"A key?"

"There was a key on the lintel above the front door. I could just make out the edge of the metal. It's where the old man used to keep a spare."

Diane turned, curious. He had her attention. "And what about Angus Moon?"

"There's an old logging road that comes up through the trees across from the farm. I'll take that to within a quarter mile of the place. Then I can approach it in the dark; see if he's still around. But I don't think he'll be there. Angus seemed in a hurry to get rid of us. And I don't think it was just me. I think he was going somewhere. The man never took off his boots or his coat."

"I noticed," Diane said. She'd also felt curious about the place. When Angus Moon had gone into the kitchen to fetch her water, he kept one ear cocked in Dean Goddard's direction, jumpy about the Sheriff's perambulation through the rest of the farmhouse. As soon as he'd given her a glass of water, without so much as a courteous glance in her direction, Angus was off to find the Sheriff. It was interesting.

"Why would you be going back out to the farmhouse?" she asked.

He considered the comment. He didn't want to mention ghosts. But another pair of eyes might be useful, keeping watch while he searched through the old rooms. "It's been a while and I have a hunch nosing through that old place might be . . .," he paused, thinking about it. "Might turn up something. Just a hunch."

"You weren't there, but Angus wasn't exactly comfortable having Sheriff Goddard take another spin through those rooms."

"Where did Goddard go?"

"While Angus was getting me water the Sheriff checked out the place, top to bottom. Most of the time Angus was with him."

Sam wondered about it.

"Angus is a prick," Diane said. "I assume he doesn't like people nosing through his stuff," she added, poignantly, since they both knew he was in line, with the other members of the Club, to own the place. "But it looked like maybe there was more to it than that."

"Only one way to find out," Sam said. "Any interest in joining me?"

Truth was, she still felt a little pissed about Sam Rivers's attitude. She'd been set up.

"It's supposed to be 20 below tonight," she finally said.

"Perfect cover for a little trespass."

Diane didn't like being used, even if she had sort of been in on it. She was within her rights to use the cocky investigator however she damn well pleased. Miriam's son or no Miriam's son. Her friend was gone and Sam Rivers was clearly his own man. And frankly, she thought, it'd been a damn long while since she'd had a man in her bed.

"Why don't you crash on my couch again? It'll save you a trip."

"That makes sense. So you're joining me?"

"Sure. Beats sitting by the fire with a book. Besides, I haven't ever done any trespass . . . with a lawman."

CHAPTER TWENTY-FOUR

JANUARY 31ST, DUSK—THE CLUB'S CABIN IN SKINWALKER'S BOG

The southern boundary of Skinwalker's Bog was bordered by an old logging road. The road ran thirty miles in a straight line to remote Libby Lake. Since there was nothing at either end but wilderness, and no bars in between, few snowmobilers used it. Bill Grebs hauled his Arctic Cat to a small parking area at one end of the trail. Since the storm, the lot had been used once. Now, at dusk, it was empty. Grebs parked his truck behind a line of black spruce. Then he revved the Cat, backed it off the sled, and headed down the remote trail toward the even-more secluded Libby Lake, a destination he had no intention of reaching.

He'd come in from the opposite side of Skinwalker's Bog, knowing Angus would come later, taking the northern, more familiar approach. Given the terrain and rugged path, Grebs's snowmobile ride and hike to the cabin would take just under an hour, which was fine by him. Bill Grebs needed time to think.

In the growing dark his snowmobile's headlight wobbled over the narrow track. He went three miles before recognizing the cave lane, a place where overhead boughs formed a tight canopy. The ground under the trees was icy and barren. Most riders skirted the trees, but Grebs steered straight into them. Halfway down he appeared to turn into a wall of spruce boughs and disappeared. He was through them in less than a second, the thick branches slapping back behind him. He steered the Cat onto a small side trail leading away from the trees. Fifty more yards of ice-covered ruts brought him to a frozen creek bed. He dropped into the ditch and cut the engine.

Against the left bank a spring torrent had caused a large spruce to buckle and tip halfway over, its flat, broad root structure creating a small enclosure. Grebs pushed the Cat into the hold until nothing but its taillights showed under the wattle of tree roots and debris. He pulled his snowshoes off the back, fitted them on, slogged his way down twenty more feet of solid creek flow, and climbed the bank to the start of a path, indiscernible unless you knew where to look and where you were going. It was a damn cold night, but he wasn't thinking about the freeze.

Before he'd left his office the phone rang. It was 4:45 p.m., and he'd hesitated, not wanting to pick up the receiver. He was running late and anxious to get out to the cabin and enjoy Williston's wake. But official quitting time was still fifteen minutes away, so he finally decided to answer. "Police."

"This Defiance?" drawled a woman's voice.

"This is the Defiance Police."

"This is Clement Beauregard," she said, a little gravelly.

"May I help you?"

"My brother was due in Winnipeg last Wednesday night," she drawled. "S'posed to be on the 11:25 Greyhound. But he never showed," she said, emphasizing the last word.

"Your brother's from Winnipeg?"

"I'm in Winnipeg," she blurted, short. "My brother's s'posed to be somewhere down there. Farm outside Defiance, I think he said."

And suddenly Grebs recognized the name, and accent. James T. "Jimbo" Beauregard. When Grebs first found him he said he had a sister, somewhere in Canada, and that he was on his way to see her. It was the only time Grebs heard Jimbo's last name, and it took a second to register.

"Yeah?" Grebs asked, wondering how in the hell she'd figured out to call Defiance. "And he was supposed to be in Winnipeg on Wednesday?" Grebs feigned interest, buying time.

"Thas' right. Wednesday night."

"Where did you say he was?"

"Last I heard from him, some farm outside your town. He called me las' Monday mornin'. From a farm."

"What's his name?" Last Monday the only place he could have called from was Williston's.

"James Beauregard. Folks call him Jim, or Jimbo."

"Jimbo?"

"Thas' right. Uh-huh. Jimbo. Jimbo Beauregard."

"Can't say I've seen him. He from around here?"

"Course not. We're Cajun. Bayou. Down Louisiana," she said, the 's' like a lazy z. Like teeth on a saw blade.

"But you're in Winnipeg? Manitoba?"

"Thas' right. My cousin Emil started a Cajun Café and I told Jimbo we could use a little help. He was s'posed to be here Wednesday," she repeated.

"Did you say he was taking the Greyhound?"

"Thas' right."

"We don't have a Greyhound bus that comes through Defiance."

"Bemijji," Clement answered, without a beat. "He was takin' it from a place called Bemijji."

"But he said he was in Defiance?"

"Uh-huh," she affirmed. "Stayin' at a farm."

"Did he give you any names?" Grebs tried to ask the question normally, but was buzzing inside.

"Huh-uh," she answered.

He breathed. "Did he say how he was getting to Bemidji?"

"Huh-uh," she said. "A ride, I s'pect."

"We had quite a storm the middle of the week. Maybe he got caught up in it?"

"Maybe," she guessed. "I jus' thought I'd hear from him by now. It's not like Jimbo."

"What's he look like?" Grebs asked.

"He has a mark on his face. Birthmark. Reddish."

Grebs remembered well, listened as Clement Beauregard described her brother in more detail.

She finished by saying, "he's had run-ins. With the law, I mean. He never done nothin' bad. Just a little liftin', time and agin."

"We haven't arrested anyone recently, Ms. Beauregard."

"Glad to hear it." When he called Jimbo'd told her he'd won the money for a bus ticket played cards, fair and square. She'd been worried about the money. She was happy to hear he wasn't in jail, at least in Defiance. She made a note to call the county sheriff's office. "But I'm worried," she added. "Jimbo was a lot a' things, some of them trouble. But if he said he was goin' to be somewhere at a certain time, he shown. I never known him to be late like this, without word," she wondered aloud.

"You sure it was Defiance?" Grebs asked.

"I remember. Hard to forget a name like that."

"I guess," Grebs said, thinking. Hard to know what else to do but play along. He took down the information and assured Ms. Beauregard he'd look into it, let her know what he found. He enquired again after the farm, if she could tell him anything else about it, since the country around Defiance was settled with many farms. But she couldn't. Grebs eased a little.

"We'll keep an eye out," he assured, friendly as he could manage, concerned. "I'll put out a missing person report on him." He took down her number and told her he'd call her Sunday evening, or Monday the latest. It was the weekend and he was heading out himself.

"If you see him, tell him his sister's askin' after him, and please call."

"We sure will, Ms. Beauregard," Grebs said, and rang off.

Grebs approached the cabin quietly, snowshoes swishing through deep powder. He thought about the conversation, worried over it, wondering how and when Jimbo called his sister. Jimbo had been planning to leave. That was a goddamn surprise. The Greyhound out of Bemidji. They were fuckin' lucky he neglected to mention the farm's name, or the rancher who owned it. Mentioning Defiance was bad enough. And it was good she'd phoned Grebs. Let's just hope she stopped there.

The cabin lay 20 yards ahead through the trees. Grebs slowed.

And then in the dark, from his right, a metallic ping silenced his reverie.

Grebs turned, startled, to see Williston holding his .45 automatic. He gripped the slide with his gloved right hand and pulled it back to reset the trigger. If there had been a shell it would have ejected. Instead, he clicked a second time and the firing pin ratcheted down on another empty chamber, making another hollow ping.

"You're dead," Winthrop said. "Sounded like a goddamn moose through those trees."

"That's a good way to get *yourself* dead, Williston."

"Not if I get you first," he said, stepping forward, reaching and slapping the startled Grebs on the back. "Besides, I'm already dead." They chuckled in the dark. "Did you bring those Cohibas?"

With everything else that had happened, Grebs had forgotten Williston's cigars. "Goddamnit. I forgot. I was preoccupied."

"You know how I get when I run out of smokes."

Grebs nodded, knowing once Williston heard why he'd forgotten the cigars, he'd understand. "I know."

"Promise me you won't forget tomorrow."

"You'll have your cigars, Williston. Right now we got bigger things to worry about."

"What's that?"

"Let me get in out of this cold and I'll tell you about it."

Outside the cabin he took off his snowshoes and stuck them in a drift beside the door. Williston went in before him and announced, "The law finally arrived!"

Young and Gunderson were at the table, playing cards and sipping whiskey. They looked up at the cold entry, grinning. "Told ya' I heard him," Williston said.

"Looks like you could use a drink," Gunderson said.

"I'll pour him one, man as deserving as *the law*," Young laughed, getting up and crossing the room.

Once they settled down and Grebs had a drink, he turned to them and said, "guess who called, just before I left?"

"The DNR," Williston said.

Grebs shook his head.

"Ag?" he guessed.

"They won't call, Williston," Gunderson said. "They'll just write the check." He turned to Grebs. "The insurance company?" Hank guessed.

"Clement Beauregard."

No response. None of them knew a *Clement*, but a look of surprise spread over Williston's face. "Christ," he hissed. "One of Jimbo's relatives?"

"A sister," Grebs said. "Remember him saying he was heading up to Canada?"

Williston nodded. The others waited for Grebs's story.

"She wondered about Jimbo," Grebs explained. "Wondered where he was."

"How'd she know where to call?" Williston asked.

"I guess Jimbo made a call. He was planning to leave your place Wednesday. All he told her was he was staying at a farm outside Defiance. Somehow he was going to get to Bemidji and take the Greyhound up to Winnipeg. He was supposed to arrive last Wednesday night. I double-checked the schedules. A bus leaves Bemidji at 2:50, gets into Winnipeg at 11:25."

Now they were all tracking, and worried.

"Ol' Jimbo made a call," Williston finally breathed. "Wonder if he used my phone?" That wouldn't be good. Calls could be traced. The number could be on Clement's bill and his own, if they decided to enquire at the phone company. He had to think about it.

"Not sure where else he could have called from," Grebs said. "After I picked him up at the old rail depot I took him straight to your place. And he never left, far as I know. She said it was Monday morning. He was at your place, wasn't he?"

"He was out there by himself a couple times. That was one of them. He could have used the phone to call when I was out."

"Maybe he had a cell?" Young wondered.

"Jimbo?" Gunderson laughed, no humor in it. "Didn't have a pot to piss in."

They all considered the news, wondering what could be done.

"Goddamnit," Williston repeated, unsettled. He took a long swallow of remedy. It seemed to help, but he felt tension winding tight as a trigger spring. "All she's got is a number, maybe. And given she's calling Grebs, we got it contained. And she hasn't yet figured out anything, about the phone. Hell, maybe the Canadian phone company doesn't keep a record of phone numbers."

He knew it was wishful thinking, but he was trying to ease everyone's worry. There was no goddamn sense getting worked up over something out of your control. But that didn't prevent him from trying to figure out ways to manage it.

"Even if she figured it out, got my number from the fuckin' phone company, so what?" Williston said, trying to reason through it. "I'm dead, and Jimbo's gone. Nothin' to say I wasn't helping out a vagrant. Or maybe he broke into my place?" Though Williston knew that was doubtful, given the remote location of the farm and no easy way to get there.

"Even if he called from my place there's nothing to say he didn't light out after my accident. Could make them wonder if this vagrant might have pulled the trigger."

The others chewed on it. A pall began to settle over their celebration.

Then Bill Grebs remembered more bad news. "And someone broke into the Defiance house."

Williston's eyes darkened, a bad sign.

"Hold on, hold on," Grebs said. "Far as I could tell the only thing missing was some preserves."

The observation didn't lighten Williston's countenance. "When?"

"I found it this morning. I think they got in the night of the storm."

"How long's the kid been here?"

"Checked in at the Hotel yesterday morning, after the storm."

Williston had little doubt it was Clayton who broke into the house. He just wondered what he managed to steal.

"The timing's off for Clayton to have done it," Grebs argued.

Suddenly Williston's glass flew across the room and shattered against a timber. The splintered glass brought an even deeper pall to the cabin. "Who the fuck do you think it was?! It was the goddamn kid for sure. And I bet he got a whole hell of a lot more than preserves."

No one in the room commented on Williston's guess. There were a few long moments during which the unease in the room was as palpable as a winter storm blast. Hal Young finally pushed out his chair and stood. He walked to a corner and picked up a broom and dust pan. Hank looked back at the table. Grebs kept an eye on the dead man.

Williston worried about it all. The damn call and now Clayton, who had very likely recovered 179,000 dollars and who knew what else. "The minute you get a chance," Williston ordered Grebs, "you pull over that little son of a bitch and search his car, his room, every other place he's been."

"That's my intention."

"The woman's place too," Gunderson added.

"Her place too," Grebs agreed.

Angus Moon came through the door with a blast of icy air.

"Shut the goddamn door!" Williston said.

Everyone was startled by his entry, testament to their preoccupation with Grebs's news.

Angus turned and slammed the cabin door.

"Where the hell have you been?" Williston started.

"Gettin' thirsty," Angus answered. "And tendin' to business. Settin' traps for my dogs." He pulled off his woolen ski mask and flung it onto a bench beside the front door.

Williston and the others considered the point. When Williston finally eased a little, congratulating Angus on his efforts, the irritability in the room diminished. For the moment the squall passed.

Bill Grebs handed Angus whiskey in a plastic glass. He drank it off in two long swallows, exhaling deeply when it was done. "It's damn cold out there," he said.

"Well it's fine and tight in here," Winthrop managed, recovering some of his equilibrium. "See any more sign?"

Angus shook his head. "Not exactly. I suspect it'll be the middle of tonight, more likely tomorrow night."

"What makes you so sure they'll return?" Gunderson asked.

"They're hungry and cold," Angus said. "They can probably stand it another night, might even get lucky and catch some mice or a hare. But they'll be back. I know my dogs."

"Guess who called?" Williston said.

Angus looked up. He turned and began to pour himself more whiskey. "Clayton."

"We know all about the prodigal son."

"He's a goddamn pain in the ass, Williston."

"Clement Beauregard," Williston said. They'd get to Clayton.

The name didn't register.

"Jimbo's sister," he explained, before Angus had time to think.

His eyes turned. "What'd she want?"

"Wondered where ol' Jimbo was. Supposed to be in Winnipeg by eleven o'clock Wednesday."

"Winnipeg?" Angus wondered. He reached into his side pocket, extracted a round tin of Timber Wolf chewing tobacco, carefully opened it and placed a pinch inside his lower lip.

"Apparently a cousin has a Cajun Café up there. It's where Jimbo was headed to work."

"I remember a sister, but not Winnipeg," Hal Young added.

"He never said," Williston remarked. "Canada, was all."

They thought about the sister. "Call Grebs?" Angus asked.

"The Defiance police," Williston nodded. "Said James T. Beauregard was staying on some farm outside Defiance. Didn't know where."

"And didn't mention any names," Grebs added. "She didn't have any, except Defiance."

"What're we gonna do?" Angus asked.

Williston considered. "Nothing. Grebs will sit on it. Hope she doesn't call anywhere else. Grebs can call her back tomorrow or the next day, and let her know the Defiance Police have come up empty. Maybe it'll end there."

"Unless she calls the Sheriff," Grebs said.

"Not even sure that's bad. Nobody else knows. Just call her sometime Sunday or Monday. Tell her you put out a BOLO, but no one reported anything."

"I told her I was going to."

BOLO was a 'Be on the Lookout for' report. If he completed one, it'd have to go through the Sheriff's office, which worried Grebs, but he nodded. He liked the idea for the same reason; might throw her off the scent.

They were silent for a few minutes, ruminating. Gunderson and Grebs poured themselves more remedy. Hal Young finished sweeping up the glass.

Angus positioned the chew, tucked it back in his mouth, took another long sip of whiskey. "I seen Clayton," he said.

They turned to him.

"Sam Rivers," Angus said. "And Hank's right. He ain't no kid anymore. Asked a damn lot of questions about the kill. Seems to know somethin' 'bout wolves."

"He was at the house?" Winthrop asked, appearing unperturbed but surprised. This surprise he knew he could handle, might even be a good thing, if it surfaced his missing $179,000.

"At the house and lookin'," Angus answered. "Some kind of expert on wolf kills."

"I'll be damned," Williston smiled. "I knew he worked for the USFW. He always liked the animals." Williston wondered about it. They'd have to keep an eye on the boy. "Anything in particular we need to worry about?"

Angus thought on it, poured himself more whiskey. "He said it was damn strange, never seen anything like it, wolves gettin' into a barn and killin' everything."

"What about Svegman? The DNR weigh-in?"

"Svegman was there. But he followed Clayton's lead." Angus picked up a second plastic cup and spit.

"What about the forms?" Williston asked.

Angus nodded. "Svegman agreed. Clayton didn't stop 'im. We'll be gettin' paid."

The favorable news rippled through the room. They needed some. Gunderson, over by the potbellied stove, raised a plastic glass and clicked it against Hal Young's drink, winking and nodding.

"Now that's what I was hoping to hear," Williston said, pleased. "Let 'em ask questions. If they're fillin' out the forms we're gettin' paid." Then he thought of something, a corroborating issue. "They wouldn't dare not pay. Every rancher in the region would make a stink that'd smell all the way down to the Cities." He'd done work for the local cattleman's association. He knew them.

"Must have accepted it," Gunderson agreed.

"Hell," Winthrop added, "anything would kill in this kind of weather. And the wolves are getting more plentiful every year. It was only a matter of time before some of them got into a barn."

"That's what has the DNR worried," Angus agreed. "That it's genuine. Reporter from the local paper was there. That bright-eyed bitch. She wanted to run with it, but Goddard kept her from it. And Clayton agreed with the Sheriff, far as I could figure."

"The Sheriff was there, too?"

"And the reporter," Angus added, with a glance in Hank's direction.

"What about the remains?" Williston asked.

"What about 'em?"

"Clean it up?"

"Sam Rivers wanted to leave it." The woodsman said Sam's name with derision. "Said he wanted to 'mull' on it," Angus took another sip of the whiskey, starting to feel the burn. "Said it'd be good bait, case they returned."

"He's right."

"Yeah," Angus agreed, reluctantly.

"Don't let Clayton get under your skin, Angus. We can deal with the boy."

Angus looked up from his glass. "He ain't actin' like your boy, Williston."

"Why did he want to mull over the kill?" Grebs asked.

Angus looked at him. "I guess it don't smell right."

Williston could feel their concern. Hal Young and Hank Gunderson stood beside the pot-bellied stove, warming themselves, listening. "Fuck 'em," Williston blurted. "We're gettin' paid and that's all that matters. What about the insurance check?" he growled, turning to Hal Young.

"No questions," Young said, shaking his head. "At least not yet. I don't expect we'll get any. They're getting the Coroner's report, which will clearly state it was a hunting accident."

"Damn right," Winthrop smiled. He walked across the room to where several liquor bottles were stacked on a shelf. He took down a bottle of Crown Royal. "Time I had a proper drink. Don't forget, boys," he said, turning around the room, raising the bottle. "It's my wake!"

Grebs smiled. Gunderson came over to the table with an empty glass. Hal Young grinned. Angus Moon seemed to require more convincing.

"The DNR thought it was unusual," Williston said, talking to him. "So what? If they were that suspicious why are they completing the forms?" It was rhetorical, and Williston didn't wait for anyone to respond. He dismissed the notion with a wave of his hand, pouring whiskey over large square cubes. The liquid sputtered and cracked. "Take them off our trail," he added. "They just don't want it to get out. That's all. Let's have another drink."

As he poured, a distant howl sounded through the cabin wall.

"Quiet," Angus said. The others hadn't heard it.

They paused, listening. Angus had a keen ear and was behind them on the libation count. Winthrop was about to continue pouring when they all heard the howl, faint and far off.

"Wolf," Angus said.

"Christ," Winthrop started laughing. "Forgot to tell you," he said to the others. "We heard them yesterday. They've finally made it to the Bog. What'd I tell ya'?" he said, pouring. "They're breeding like rats. Pretty soon they'll be settling on the outskirts of Defiance."

There was another howl, this time from a different set of jaws.

"There's two," Angus observed. The sound of wolves, particularly in this kind of cold, conveyed an absolute wildness Angus Moon had always appreciated.

"There can be a whole pack for all I care," Winthrop said.

"Any chance they'll check us out?" Hal Young asked.

"Fuck no," Angus spit.

"Wolves?" Winthrop laughed. "Goddamn fools if they do. We'll bag 'em and tag 'em and they know it. Besides, you heard the DNR boys. Wolves don't like the smell of man. Let's cut a deck and deal."

Angus paused long enough to hear three more howls. There was something familiar about them, but they couldn't be his dogs. For starters, his dogs rarely howled. He'd wondered about it when they were growing up. He'd tried to get them to howl, but they seldom opened their mouths, except to whine. Too much dog, he'd guessed.

And Skinwalker's Bog was fifteen miles from Winthrop's farm, as the raven flew. Probably much farther, if the wolves came cross country. His dogs wouldn't travel that far, not away from all that food. They could handle the cold, but they weren't used to starvation. He'd catch them in his traps. Hell, he thought, he bet he'd have trapped some in the morning.

He turned to join the others.

As they sat down to play there was one last long chorus of hungry howls, this time more than three and a little closer. But the men were no longer listening.

CHAPTER TWENTY-FIVE

JANUARY 31ST, LATE EVENING — WILLISTON WINTHROP'S FARM

Sam tried to sleep through the early evening, with limited success. He was preoccupied with the long day, the wolf kill, seeing Angus Moon, meeting the Sheriff, and all the rest of the last couple of days. Then his cell phone went off.

He picked it up from the end table next to Diane's couch. Kay Magdalen. It rang a second time and he hesitated. It was Friday night. He guessed it was important, but he didn't want to hear about Salazar and he had no new feelings about the job. His Colorado life was more than 1,000 miles away. But maybe there was something she could do for him?

"Rivers," he answered.

"Sam," Kay's voice smiled. "So glad you picked up."

"Isn't it Friday night?"

"Clarence and I are sitting here watching the *Gladiator*," she ignored his comment. "Ever seen it?"

She also sounded . . . different. Maybe a little drunk. "Yeah, I saw it. Good movie."

"Russell Crowe kind of reminds me of you."

"Too bulky," Sam said, ignoring her unusual attempt at flattery. "What's going on, Kay? You've never called me on a Friday night. Someone die?"

"Not exactly. You'll never guess who called me this afternoon."

"The Governor?"

"Bigger. The Commissioner," she said.

He waited. He guessed Kay's hunch about forwarding her office phone on weekends to field one of the Commissioner's calls had paid off.

"Seems he's got a burr on his butt about this Interagency Task Force. He was asking about progress. He thinks we need to move on it sooner, rather than later."

She paused, but Sam didn't take the bait.

"Wanted to know the candidates," she finally added.

"So what did you tell him?"

"You and Salazar, for Special Agent."

"Did you tell him Salazar's sleeping with my wife?"

"Ex-wife. I left that part out because it's nobody's business. That's what ex means."

She was right, but he didn't have to like it or admit it.

"He doesn't know anything about Salazar," she continued. "Except that he has an accounting background, which made him snort. You know what it means when the Commissioner snorts?"

"No idea."

"He doesn't like something. Thinks it smells."

There was another pause, before she finally continued. "He thought the position called for a field agent, not a bean counter. And here's the good part. He remembers that article about you in the *Denver Post*. The one about the Key deer. He thought you were probably the better candidate. So you've got a leg up."

If he wanted the job, Sam thought. He still hadn't decided. "Is that it?" he finally asked.

She hesitated. "He thinks there could be a little extra money in it for you. Some kind of promotion. Only thing is, he wants us to decide sooner, rather than later. Like Monday. Tuesday, the latest."

"Did you tell him I was out of town?"

"I did. Know what he said?"

"What?"

"Find him. Tell him. Light a fire under his ass. We need to move on this thing while the funding's still there."

Sam waited. It was dark outside. Even in the comfort of Diane's small living room he could feel the intense cold, like a low-pressure ridge. "OK," he finally said.

"OK what?" Kay pushed.

"OK I'll let you know. Tuesday, the latest."

There was a long pause during which he could hear her heavy exhale. "Just don't push your luck, Rivers," she said, gravelly.

"I appreciate all you're doing, Kay." He thought that sounded a little better, though he knew her efforts wouldn't have much to do with his final decision. "Maybe you can do me a favor?"

"Quid pro quo?" she asked, looking for an angle.

"It's not that big a favor. I'm wondering, since you seem to be working late on a Friday, if you could call Ashland? The Minnesota DNR FedExed a wolf hair sample to forensics with my name on it, and I need them to look at it as soon as they get it."

Sam could call, but he thought they might be more responsive to Kay. And besides, he might need another favor from Forensics and he didn't want to waste the one he had, if he could help it.

"I thought you were on vacation?"

"I am."

"So what are you doing FedExing hair samples on your vacation? Can't it wait?"

"Professional curiosity," he said. "I've got a hunch a wolf kill isn't a wolf kill, but I need Forensics to weigh-in."

"This personal?"

"Isn't it always?"

"That's why you belong on the team," she said.

Sam didn't respond.

"So let me get this straight," she said. "You're using Service resources for your own investigation?"

"I'm helping out the Minnesota DNR on an unusual wolf kill," he clarified. "It's a goodwill thing. If you need a personal angle, consider it an Interagency thing."

Kay snorted. She must have learned that from the Commissioner, Sam thought.

"I'll call," she finally said. "Saturday morning, first thing. You'll get your results in record time. But consider it a big goddamn favor," she said, and then hung up.

Sam chuckled in the dark. Just like her, he thought. She'd help him, but was pissed about it because she knew it wouldn't affect his decision one way or another. He liked Kay Magdalen.

He went into Diane's bathroom and washed up. Her toothbrush, hair brush and a few other items were spread across the narrow tiled counter top. Women's things. It'd been a while. He felt a flash of domesticity and thought he missed it. Then he put it out of his mind. It was after 10:00, time to roll. On his way back to her kitchen he knocked on her door.

"Come on in," she answered.

Sam hesitated, then opened the door. She was sitting in bed next to a desk lamp, propped up on pillows, a book opened in front of her. She wore a black sweatshirt with, Sam guessed, nothing underneath, judging from the way it moved when she leaned to set down her book on the table next to her bed. The bed looked comfortable and so did she.

"You ready?"

"Of course." She stared at him, her long hair mane-like over her shoulders. "Any chance we'll see those wolves?"

"They could return. But it would probably be later. Probably the middle of the night, given what I saw of that barn and the natural distaste they have for anything civilized."

"I'd better put on something more appropriate."

Her tone left no room for interpretation, but it was an interesting choice of words.

Before he could think what to say she added, "how's your car battery? It's going to be pretty damn cold. I don't want to get stuck out there."

"Practically brand new."

"I'll be ready in 5 minutes," she said.

He turned out of her room and shut the door.

They drove to the farmhouse, talking about Williston Winthrop, the wolves, County politics, Denver and wherever else the conversation led them. It was a comfortable ride. It was around twenty below and they were dressed in enough layers to make them a little stiff and moving awkward. But it kept the cold at bay. They passed one or two cars on the highway outside of town, and then nothing for the next eleven miles. Sam drove until he reached a place almost parallel with the old man's farmhouse. They were about a quarter mile south of the house. Between them and the farm a large spread of black spruce and poplar topped a brief rise. A rutted, snow-covered logging road climbed into the trees. Its surface was pristine.

"Nobody's been here," Sam observed, pulling the jeep to the side of its snow-choked entrance.

"Where the hell is here?" Diane asked.

"Close to the farm. Up over that rise through the trees you can come to a place, if I remember right, where you can look down the path and glimpse the farmhouse through the woods. We should be able to see most of the farm, at least enough to see if Angus is still there."

"Or those wolves," Diane added. "I'd rather not run into either."

"Might be a little fun," Sam disagreed. "But we'll have to be careful. Angus is definitely the type to shoot first and ask questions after the smoke clears. If he's still around, we'll head back the way we came. But this afternoon I got the sense he was leaving as soon as we did."

"Me too," she agreed. "Would the wolves bother us?"

"No. If we were lucky enough to sneak up on them they'd turn the minute they saw us. Or should."

They got out of the jeep, fitted their snowshoes, and started up the trail into the trees. The snow was heavy but the evening was still and cold and it felt good to be hiking on the old road, generating a little warmth against the sub-zero weather. Their breath rose in clouds that mingled over the path. They reached the point in the woods Sam remembered. From the seclusion of an abandoned logging trail they could barely make out the farmhouse, less than a quarter mile distant. They watched for any sign of movement, of light, or anyone awake or stirring, but it was quiet in the dark. And Angus Moon's truck was gone.

"Let's go," Sam whispered.

"Wait a minute. What if he parked in the garage?"

"Probably did, if he's still around. It'd be stupid to leave your truck in this kind of cold, unless you had a plug-in." Sam kept staring at the farmhouse. Nothing. "But there's only one way to know for sure." He started moving again along the overgrown trail, descending through the trees to the road and farm.

The partial moon was high, and the house, garage and barn were bathed in pale light, giving everything a ghostly hue. They waited and watched, but the house was frozen still and quiet. They wore ski masks that covered everything but their eyes and mouths. The only movement was their breath, the only sound an occasional grind of dry powder as they steadied themselves or shoed across the snow.

"Looks dead enough," Diane said.

"Feels to me like we're the only living things on the planet," Sam agreed. He tried to figure the best approach to the old farm. "Let's check the garage first."

Diane looked at Sam, then back at the farmhouse. "OK," she said, a little nervous. "You sure you saw a key?"

"Just a glimpse. But there's only one way to be certain," Sam said, and started across the road. "If Angus's truck is in that garage, we'll leave. Quiet, like we came," Sam whispered.

"And what if he returns while we're in there?"

"If he's not there now he won't be back. At least not tonight. Too late. And too damn cold."

She hoped he was right.

The two figures took off their snowshoes and were careful to walk down the driveway's frozen tire ruts. They approached the garage and Sam walked around to the side window. There were two pines growing beside the outside garage wall and he pushed in behind their boughs. When he peered through the glass he saw the pale gleam of a four-door sedan, probably the old man's. Moon's truck was gone.

He returned and said, "Ready?"

"No truck?"

"Just the old man's car. Angus must have gone back to his place. And why not, considering there's no more livestock. And the old man's ghost is still walking around."

"I hope Williston doesn't mind us poking around his place."

"I hope he does."

They came around the front of the house, stepping along the worn path where their footsteps blended with others. Sam turned toward the front door. "We'll knock," he said. "Just to be sure."

"Sure," Diane said. "We'll just knock."

The farmhouse was locked. Sam peered through the dark window, but it was opaque with frost. He knocked, heavy and loud. The percussive sound echoed across the road and into the trees.

"Jesus. You trying to wake the dead?"

"I guess I am," he agreed. Then, "the closest place is Angus's trailer, but as I recall it's six miles through woods. Nothing but trees will hear that knock, no matter how loud I can make it. And if someone's still in the place, I want to know about it. "

Diane looked at him. His eyes peered out of his ski mask, dark and intense. This wasn't exactly breaking and entering, but close enough to give her a rush high up in the center of her chest. She noticed Sam smile and answered with a smile of her own.

Finally, Sam took off his right-hand mitten, reached up in the dark, and felt along the lintel. The key was where he remembered it. The sharp freeze bit his hand. "And here it is," he said, ignoring the cold, inserting it into the lock.

They opened the door and went in. The smell of the house was familiar, with a little more stale and age thrown in. The old man had been 62, still young by Winthrop standards. Sam pulled off his ski mask and stuffed it into a coat pocket. Diane did the same, her long hair falling across her shoulders.

"Leave the lights off," Sam said.

He fished into the belly panel of his coat and brought out the steel handled flashlight, its beam cutting the dark like a blade. Diane reached into her coat pocket and brought out a small handheld flashlight. They examined the contents of the living room, then walked into the kitchen. The table and chairs were unchanged. There was a gas range and a newer refrigerator next to the stove. Sam remembered the day he'd almost shot the old man, the way Williston, drunk, pulled the empty shotgun out of his hands and watched him retch. It was the last time Sam had been in this kitchen.

Truth was, he was thirsty. His mouth felt dry. He walked over to the sink, opened the cupboard and found the glasses were still there, pretty much unchanged. He reached in, took one down, turned on the faucet.

"You think that's a good idea?" Diane asked.

"I need a drink," he said. Something that was often enough said in this kitchen.

His back was turned. He filled the glass and raised it to his lips, recalling the mineral rich taste of it. Like liquid iron. It practically rattled on its way down.

"One thing I do need to take out of here," Sam said, remembering.

"I thought you said we were just looking around."

He opened the cupboard below the sink and found a dish towel hanging on metal tongs. Still there. He pulled it out and wiped down the glass, then returned it to the cupboard. He replaced the dish towel below the sink. "I need more shells for my shotgun. It's an odd gauge and if I'm not mistaken the old man kept shells for it in the basement."

"Why take them?" Diane asked. "Why risk it? Why don't you just go buy some?"

"These were specially made shotguns," Sam said. "They take an unusual load. Besides, no one's going to miss them. They'll just stay down in that dank basement collecting dust."

"It's your show," Diane said.

Sam turned out of the kitchen and started down the hallway.

"Just a minute," Diane said. She'd paused in front of the start of the Winthrop glory wall. "I noticed this when I was here before." She was curious.

"Here's where it begins," Sam said, pointing his light onto the first clipping. He was too far away to read, but he started reciting.

FEARED EATEN BY WOLVES
Searchers Discouraged in Hunt for W. H. "Gray" Winthrop

January 28, 1905, Defiance, Minnesota—The search for W. H. Gray Winthrop, Defiance attorney, avid fisherman and hunter, has been abandoned. Winthrop was last seen entering the remote wilderness at mile marker 76 on the Iron Line, where he was hunting wolves. For two weeks nine men and a half dozen hounds have been scouring the country. They recovered his shotgun and the torn remnants of one snowshoe, both identified as Gray's, and both scarred by fang marks.

Doc Dunlap, who headed the search party, returned yesterday with news that the country for miles around has been thoroughly covered. Other than the shotgun and snowshoe, searchers' efforts have been in vain. Wolves in that vicinity are plentiful and chances are the man's body was entirely devoured.

When he was finished, Diane turned. "When was the last time you read that?"

"Twenty years. Some things you just don't forget."

"Guess not. That was verbatim. You must have a pretty good memory."

"Average," he said. "Just one of the old man's games. He made me memorize it. You'd be surprised how much you can remember when the punishment for getting a word wrong is a smack upside the head that rattles your teeth."

"Oh," she said. But as bad as she knew that sounded she was still interested in what the other pictures portrayed. She cast her small cone of light on the next picture along the wall. In the old photo two men stood over five wolves laid out in front of them on the snow. The next photo showed even more wolves, some of them hanging from a game pole, others laid out in front of the five hoisted wolves.

"I'll leave you to it," he said. "I'm going to get those shells."

"OK," Diane said, absorbed in the pictorial legacy of the Winthrop family clan.

In the basement Sam's beam flashed on two full boxes of 10 gauge shells. He was surprised to find the fresh makings for more shells on the workbench, as though the old man had been in the middle of stocking up before his accident. It supported those who believed the old man hadn't pulled the trigger on purpose.

He placed the two boxes of shells into the back belly panel of his coat. They were heavy behind him, but their awkward weight felt familiar, reassuring. There was something that felt good about taking ammo from the old man's basement, particularly ammo Williston Winthrop would never be able to use.

By the time he emerged from the basement Diane was at the end of the wall.

"That's a lot of wolves," she said.

"I counted them once. Four hundred and seventeen. After my grandfather and the old man cleaned out this area, they began hunting further afield. Went up into Canada, even Alaska."

"Incredible."

"More like a demented obsession. But that was the old man's way."

On the main floor, at the end of the hallway, was the office Sam was never supposed to enter. He remembered it, the smell of cigar smoke still thick in the tight interior of the room. When he was very young his father told him the room was off limits. Innocent and compliant, he obliged. But for Sam Rivers the forbidden, at least in this context, pricked his curiosity like a bug itch. The door was usually closed, but whenever he heard the old man working at his study desk, Sam would pass by the room slowly, listening. Sometimes, when the old man was away, Sam opened the door and peered inside. When he realized he could open and peer without being discovered, at least when he was certain the old man was gone, he lingered at the opening. His curiosity grew. He was surreptitious in his efforts. He was careful—knowing the old man—to leave plenty of time between explorations.

Not long before he fled, Sam had been in the kitchen when he heard a clattering from the nearby office. Standing in front of the sink, he swore he felt the floor vibrate along the floorboards. At the time he wondered about it. Then on one of his perusals of the sacred chamber, he carefully examined the floor. Under a corner of a corded throw rug, he found a section of the boards with slightly larger gaps between the slats. He inserted the edge of a paperclip into one side of the narrow gap. He pried and a foot-square section of floorboards lifted to reveal a deep hollow. Nothing much in it. Papers, a couple of folders, a small metal box.

He'd just turned 17. The papers didn't interest him. Knowing about it was enough. There were coins in the metal box. They were old and tarnished with age.

Now Sam re-entered the old office. He smiled to remember the trepidation that first accompanied his perusal of this room; the way his heart was hammering in his chest, his fear the old man would catch him nosing around his private stuff. Now he was simply curious again, hoping the old man had left something interesting in his secret space.

Diane watched him cross the room, raise the corner of a rug (this one different, but used for the same purpose). Sam left the rug turned over, moved to the old man's desk, found a large paper clip and used it to pry up the edge of the floorboard. Just like when he was a boy.

"A secret stash?"

Clearly she was interested. "I guess. Some place the old man thought was secret. He never let me come into this room. Said his study was off-limits, which in the end only made me curious."

Diane grinned. She could relate.

Sam flipped up the foot-square piece of floorboard, revealing a small cavernous opening. He reached in and pulled out a yellow plastic CD case containing a disk. He flipped it open, turned it over, and noticed the recording grooves near the center hole. "Not much," he said, observing the width of the recording. "But I suspect whatever this contains should be interesting, if the old man was hiding it here." Beneath the jewel case were several files. He pulled them out of the hole. "Pine Grove Estates?" he wondered, reading the tabs. "Ever heard of it?"

Diane shook her head. "Never. Maybe the disk has something. Did your dad have a computer?"

"I haven't seen one." The metal box was gone. The rest of the hold was empty. "We'll just keep these," he said, returning the wooden covering to the floor. "Maybe they contain something worthwhile."

Diane made a note of the folder's subject. She'd never heard of Pine Grove Estates, but she knew she'd be searching for it as soon as she returned home.

"We can check out those disk files at my place."

Sam looked at her. He recognized her reporter's interest. He thought he'd better have a look at the disk before she put it on the pages of the *Gazette*. "Let's check upstairs," he said.

They climbed to the second floor and continued nosing around the old house. In 20 years Sam was surprised to know nothing much had changed. When he opened his old bedroom door he found everything the same. The bed sat in the corner. The overhead light was exactly as it had been. There was a small desk in the corner with a dresser beside it. On top of the dresser was a piece of macramé his Mother made for him when he was a boy, a foot-square black rose. Above his bed, hanging on the wall, was the gun rack he'd made in eighth grade shop, empty.

It was all carefully preserved, clean, the bed still made as though his return was expected. He was surprised to feel nostalgic for his boyhood room, where so much had been wrong for so long.

He walked over to the mattress and sat down. Same give, same resistance, even the same bedspread. He wondered if anyone had slept here since he'd left.

"It's all the same," he said, surprised.

Diane came over and sat beside him.

"It's weird," he added.

"What's so weird about it? What did you expect?"

"I don't know. Guess I hadn't thought about it. I suppose I expected to see storage, or a study or something."

"He has a basement," Diane reminded him.

"Had," Sam corrected. "I know. I just didn't expect it to be exactly the same. I thought maybe there might be something here. It's a little eerie, like visiting a grave and feeling a presence."

"Your dad had a scary feel to him, the few times I met him."

"He had an interesting perspective about women."

"I wouldn't call it interesting," Diane said, remembering. The Range could be a tough place for single women, where some men had a perverse sense of sex roles. "More like, if we didn't fuck there'd be a bounty on us."

The harsh comment made Sam grin. "That's about it," he agreed.

They were quiet for a moment, sitting on the bed.

"Is that what you would say?"

The way she asked felt suddenly different. But it had been a very long time since he had tried to parse a woman's interests, so he hesitated.

"We are born naked and alone, and we die naked and alone. I think we should feel damn fortunate when in between we can be naked and alone together."

It was Diane's turn to chuckle. But what she was thinking was: How did a man as awful as Williston Winthrop have a son like Sam Rivers? She knew Miriam deserved some of the praise. But Miriam had her faults. Miriam was sweet without the willingness or ability to make difficult choices, like divorcing Will Winthrop, for starters.

"What happened to you?" Diane finally asked. "I know Williston beat you up pretty bad. But what finally made you leave for good?"

Sam had never told anyone. "I tried to kill my father."

Diane paused. "I suspect you had motive."

"You didn't see me when I left. I had a black eye, a bruised cheek, three broken ribs. But I didn't find that out until after I thought it was taking too long to heal."

"Where were you?"

"Sisseton, South Dakota, just across the border. I didn't run very far at first, because I wasn't sure about leaving. I wasn't sure where I was going. I wasn't sure about anything."

Diane thought about it. "That was the middle of winter, wasn't it? I remember your mom being pretty upset. But she didn't talk about it much."

"Yeah. It was winter."

It had been twenty years, but remembering it like this Sam could still feel a vestige of the tension he'd felt as a boy. He took the next few minutes relating the story to Diane, including the part about almost killing the old man and then the old man's departure. Now, two decades later, it all sounded surreal, like a very bad dream.

Diane was quiet. Sam guessed she wasn't sure how to take it—the beating that started in this room. Unexpectedly her hand moved to his thigh. While he was wondering how to take it—just consolation?—it squeezed.

Maybe not just consolation, he thought. But while he was wondering how to take *that,* she turned her head, just so. Then he reached up and placed his right hand along Diane's neck, threading his index finger under her ear. She came into his kiss and opened her mouth. Sam raised his left hand to the other side of her head. She reached up to press his hand more firmly against her, affirming it. And after a few long moments with their lips fastened together, neither of them wanting to stop, she pulled his left hand away from the side of her head and moved it to her breast.

CHAPTER TWENTY-SIX

JANUARY 31ST, LATE EVENING—WILLISTON WINTHROP'S FARM

Suddenly a piercing, lonely howl came into the room.

"Christ," Sam said, as if out of a dream. "Did you hear that?"

He was holding her breast and it was having the desired effect. For both of them. He could feel her bra under her sweater. Her breast felt full. She didn't want him to take his hand away, unless it was to reach up under her clothing and . . .

Then another howl.

Reluctantly, Sam got up off the bed and turned to the window.

"Goddamn it," Diane said.

Sam smiled in the dark. He thought about turning back to her, but another howl changed his mind. "Ditto," he said, turning toward the window. "Let's just hold that thought."

"Hold something," she murmured.

It'd been too long. Probably for both of them, Sam guessed. But the wolves had returned and they would have to wait. Given the circumstances, a little tension could be a good thing.

Another howl.

"The wolves are back?"

"Yeah," Sam said. "Sounds like right at the edge of the woods."

Just inside the woods a wolf raised its head and howled a second time. There was a small clearing in the trees. Pale moonlight shown down through the trees and the wolf looked up, parting the air with his belly cry of hunger. The sound reached through the night air into the farmhouse bedroom. Wolves at night, particularly in cold like this, can make a wail that resonates through the frozen dark, as though the wolf was inside the house instead of a quarter mile behind it.

Diane tensed. "That was incredible," she whispered. She'd heard wolf howls, but never this close. It was a thrilling, wild, frightening sound, one that made you happy there was a wall between you and whatever animal made it. She was disappointed by the interruption, but a wolf howl was genuinely distracting.

"Gotta' be the pack that went into the barn."

"You think so?"

The next low chorus of howls made Diane grow more tense. Sam waited by the window, watching the tree line. He heard another wolf call, closer than the last. There was a large expanse of white where the rear field disappeared over a small rise to the woods, but it was empty.

"Do you think they'll come near the house?" Diane wondered. She moved a little closer.

Sam sensed her shuffle. Touching her breast triggered the recollection of one or two fantasies he'd played out in this room that had featured the much younger Diane. He could still feel the fullness beneath his hand. Unexpected, but compelling.

Another howl snapped his reverie. "Wolves hate anything human. They'll give us a wide berth. If it's them, they're back to feed."

They saw movement at the edge of trees, though it was too dim to see clearly. One hundred yards across the field, first one, then another, then all five stepped out of the trees, making the pale moonlight come alive. The first one to come out of the woods raised its head and howled.

"They're so close," Diane said.

"Any closer and . . . "

Sam could hear her breathe beside the opposite stretch of window. He'd noticed this before, how the close proximity of wolves (or any predators, for that matter) made him hyper attentive. Then again, maybe it was the kiss. He listened to his heart beating in the old bedroom. And then the wolves again.

"What?"

"We could see their yellow eyes," which made him think.

They watched them approach, tentative with each step. After a few yards they paused and sent their call into the night sky. Sam had observed wolves often enough to notice their clear shapes and markings even in the moonlight. These wolves were big. Unnaturally large. He couldn't be certain. Their coloring wasn't clear in the dark. But their shapes were more the size of timber wolves or arctic wolves than Great Plains. If they were Great Plains wolves they were the largest he'd ever seen. What he thought was, he needed a closer look.

All those years ago it was wolves that awakened him. Since then he had observed countless packs and examined plenty of individuals up close. And in all that time the thrill of seeing a pack in the wild never abated.

"Why howl and alert everyone to their presence?" Diane wondered.

"It's a warning. Mostly to other wolves. They're making sure everyone in the neighborhood knows it's their kill. Would you go near a howl like that?"

They watched the wolves approach, more emboldened than a normal pack. There was something familiar and unusual about them. They moved as a pack, paused to howl, but kept driving toward the barn, where the rest of their kill remained. The last animal came cowering, taking up the rear. It appeared the least wolf. Its legs were a little too thick. Its coat a little dark. Its tail, ears, snout, all of its proportions a little skewed.

"Goddamn," he said. "Got to be a hybrid." It made him wonder about the others.

As the wolves came closer they began to move with cowering, tentative steps, testing the air. It was an unusual gait. Wild wolves only cowered before other wolves, or other members of the pack, if they were bested, or if their pack position ordained it. These wolves lowered their heads and smelled the air with suspicion. It was unusual movement for a pack.

"Let's just watch, see what they do," he said.

One wolf was out in front, leading. The others followed from a comfortable distance. It took them less than five minutes to approach the house and barn.

They paused, their noses in the wind. When they felt certain nothing in the yard stirred, they came on more quickly.

Sam and Diane were hypnotized by the way the pack moved together, one wolf in the lead, the others following: a web of tooth and claw that could be focused, Sam knew, in an instant.

They visited like ghosts. And while it was the middle of the night, the right time for wolves to approach, a normal pack would have been more reticent. A normal pack would be approaching from behind the barn, from the safety of trees and bush that hugged outlying buildings.

The lead wolf neared the cracked door. He paused, sniffing the night air. His nose bent to the ground. In the moonlight he peered around the door. Sam thought he saw something. Probably Angus Moon's traps. Setting wolf traps in snow was almost impossible. Any fraction of displaced powder, any crease or depression in the snow's surface, and the animals sensed something awry, gave it a wide berth.

But the smell of food was compelling. The lead wolf stepped carefully through the snow toward the cracked barn door. He placed his muzzle through the opening, which was just wide enough to permit its entry. And then he disappeared inside.

"Incredible," Sam said. "No wolf would do that," he whispered. "These animals have some familiarity with buildings." Hybrids, he guessed.

The other wolves followed the same zigzag path toward the door, stepping carefully over the snow, avoiding the delicate surface anomalies where Sam guessed Angus Moon had set foothold traps. And then they were through the opening and gone.

Diane turned to look at him. "What now?" she asked.

He actually considered pulling her back to bed. But now they had to deal with the wolves.

"We trap 'em."

"How in the hell are we going to trap them?"

Sam peered at the barn door. He wondered why Moon left it partially opened. It wouldn't have been normal, but Moon was a born trapper. He was baiting them.

From this distance the black rectangular opening was large enough to permit a wolf to squeeze through it. Sam could barely discern the shadowy opening against the grayer exterior of the barn, the color of weathered wood in moon shade. Trying to get a fix on the door's details from the bedroom window was impossible. "We can go out there and shut them in that barn."

"You want to go out there while they're feeding?"

"You have a better idea?"

"Yes. Sneak back the way we came. Give them the widest possible berth and hope they don't hear us."

"And lose this opportunity to catch them alive, study them?"

"And avoid the opportunity to be attacked, killed," Diane corrected.

"They're busy feeding. We can sneak out and slam that door shut before they hear anything."

"Supposing you can't get the door shut?"

"There's only one way to find out," he said.

"But they're wolves?"

"This may be our best chance to trap them, have a closer look. If I'm right about these animals, we'll need one to corroborate what I suspect will be the results from the DNA analysis."

"They'll hear you coming."

"In this powder we can be quiet."

"We?"

"You wouldn't have me going out there alone, would you?"

"This is crazy."

Sam smiled. "It is crazy," he agreed. "Normal wolves would scatter. But a normal pack wouldn't have entered a barn to feed, let alone kill. They would have fed on their capture someplace safe, eating it in a thicket. I don't know what these wolves would do if they were cornered, but I'm not passing up a chance to trap them in that barn. If I'm right it could explain plenty."

"And what are we going to do with them?"

"Leave them here. Go back to the car. And in the morning alert Svegman so he can get out here and secure them."

"And then?"

"Examine them," Sam said. "We need to understand this pack, this kind of carnage. If they are wild it's a whole new level of wolf behavior. It's a whole new breed of wolf."

"And if someone comes back, like Angus, and happens to open the barn?"

"He'll see the tracks. He'll notice they only go one way."

"And he'll know someone was here, to shut the door?"

"Not that I care. He won't know who was here."

They had two options: leave the house and return to their jeep without disturbing the animals and their middle of the night meal. Or try and trap them. Twenty years ago Sam fled. Today he didn't think twice.

"Let's go."

Diane wanted no part of it, but didn't feel like she had a choice. Eventually she'd have to head back to the jeep. If the wolves were trapped where they couldn't follow, that would be a good thing.

They bundled up for the cold. Then they moved to the front door, opening it without a sound, stepping carefully into the cold.

Their earlier work had worn a path to the barn's entrance. They stepped onto it and, slowly, carefully, approached the barn in silence. Sam stopped ten yards short of the door. He examined its exterior. Normally the door could be slid shut and fastened. Now that he could see it more clearly, Sam recounted the way he'd done it before, absent about the process, automatic. He looked up at the handle, and then along the top sliding door runner. A small pile of snow drifted across the entrance. It had been partially tamped down by the wolves, enough to prevent the door from closing completely.

Diane stood behind him. He turned and pointed to the snow-choked entrance. He made a clearing motion with his hand, pointing again to the bottom of the door. Diane understood and nodded. She took off her mitten, placing it in her front parka pocket. She wore a small cotton glove beneath it, one that would allow the unencumbered positioning of her finger inside the trigger guard of the door handle.

Sam stepped carefully toward the entrance. He could see where the wolves had skirted Angus's foothold traps. He could barely discern where he thought the traps were set, but wasn't certain. Angus had done an excellent job concealing them, knowing wolves had a preternatural sense for anything awry. Now Sam kept to their paw prints, glad they'd forged a path for him.

He concentrated on slowing his movement. The rectangular opening was a deep black gap. He tried to listen in the cold, but could not hear into the barn. He assumed the wolves were feeding. He knew their preoccupation with food would be a good thing, though it could cut both ways. If they were feeding well-away from the door, they might only rise to snarl a warning. But if they were close, or if they felt their feeding was threatened, they could attack.

The wolf tracks moved to the right of the trail, entering the barn door from the side. He followed their tracks, stepping to the right of the barn's entrance, careful his shadow didn't cross the threshold. The powder enveloped his feet, as though he were stepping into fine dry sand.

To shut the door he would have to be directly in front of the threshold. He would stay to the side so as not to forewarn them. He imagined it, stepping over the doorway, one foot into the barn as the other kicked the snow free. Then he'd pivot and pull the slab of wood across its runner.

It would have to be done in one fluid motion. Wolf jaws could exert over 1,000 pounds of pressure. If they were lucky enough to reach him they could snap his forearm like a matchstick.

Adrenaline heightened his senses. He could feel his muscles tighten. Over the door handle there was a latch. He imagined driving it into its metal catch. He imagined the sound it made as it fell into place.

And then he sprang.

Sam took hold of the door handle and began kicking snow across the threshold. He looked up and saw a spray of snow enter the barn. Ten feet away a startled wolf leaped from its feeding, cowering low. It started to growl, crouching, ready to spring. But it paused, rumbling a low growl. Sam pivoted, jerking the door shut. But there was still too much snow in the narrow gap. He held the door handle with both hands, peering through the crack. The wolf was still recoiled ten feet from the opening, watching him, waiting for his next move.

"Come here!"

Diane stepped forward. "What now?"

"We need to clear out this snow. When I tell you, open the door about a foot. I'll try to clear it again and then we can both slam it shut."

She nodded.

"Ready?" he whispered.

Diane stood behind Sam, gripping the handle.

"Now!"

She pulled the door open a foot. Sam grabbed the sliding handle to steady himself, kicking at the snow.

The wolf stayed in its low crouch, ready to spring.

"Shut it!" Sam said, and they pulled hard on the handle. It swung into its slot with a solid thwack and Sam flipped the latch.

They leaned against the door, breathing heavily in the cold night air, their collective pulses rocketing through their veins. After a few moments they eased. Sam stepped away, turned and started back toward the farmhouse.

"Watch those traps," he said, pointing to the ground, stepping carefully to avoid them.

"What now?"

"We'll call Svegman when we get back to town, leave him a message."

These wolves'll keep. I'd guess Angus Moon is sipping on his inheritance, not that he ever needed an excuse," he said, turning to wait for her. "I doubt he'll be out before noon."

Once they were beyond Angus Moon's traps, Diane hurried up behind him.

Sam checked his watch. "1:30."

"That gives us some time. I could use a drink."

The moment wasn't right. Or rather, he didn't know her well enough to say it, but what he thought was, *I could use you.*

"Me too," he finally said.

Part IV

We have the wolf by the ears, and we can neither hold him, nor safely let him go. Justice is in one scale, and self-preservation in the other.

THOMAS JEFFERSON

CHAPTER TWENTY-SEVEN

In the early morning light Angus turned into the drive. He'd been up before dawn, awakened with the others by Williston who had stood in the front room and bellowed, "Get up, you miserable peckerwoods! Our work isn't done! Get up!" A chorus of groans assured him his troops were on the rise.

"Not even light," Grebs commented, from the comfort of his narrow cabin bunk.

"That's right," Williston agreed. "Dark's the best time for our kind of work. It'll get you at the farm by daybreak. See if we've had any luck with those dogs. If Angus is right he'll need help with those sorry animals."

Angus didn't move. Williston finally walked into the small cabin bedroom and pulled down the covers on Moon's bed. The room was cold and the woodsmen cussed. "Christ, Williston. I went to bed two and a half hours ago."

"There'll be plenty of time for sleep after you get those dogs and the check. And today yours truly finally gets buried. We'll have a fitting cele-bration tonight. Last night was just a rehearsal. And if I'm right about those dogs you can take care of them and sleep in tomorrow. Get the fuck up!"

Two hours later Angus turned into the farmhouse drive. He was the first to notice something awry and he didn't like what he saw. There were more tracks around the barn's entrance, ones he hadn't made. He could see they came out of the woods. But the door was closed and latched shut. Angus left it cracked for a reason.

"Shit," he hissed.

Bill Grebs and Hank Gunderson followed Moon's rusting truck down the drive. The cages jostled beneath the old bed's tarp. Angus pulled into the yard, backing around so the taillights faced the closed door. He got out of the cab as the others parked in front of the garage and stepped into the early morning cold.

Sunlight was breaking off the horizon. They'd made good time. The frosty three-mile snowshoe was like a draught of strong coffee.

"What do you think?" Grebs asked.

Angus was walking toward the barn door, studying everything with a tracker's eye. He could see animal prints coming out of the woods. He watched them approach the barn. He saw other trails cross over the path, step to the side and approach the barn door. He could see another pair of tracks approach, their kicking brush marks in the snow, the closed door and fastened latch. And not a goddamn trap triggered. Wolves and men, they'd both been observant.

"I'll be goddamned," he said.

"What?" Grebs asked.

"Looks like my dogs'er back. And they had company," he said, pointing to the tracks.

Grebs approached. Then Gunderson.

"Walk here," Angus said, pointing to the zigzag tracks left by Sam and Diane. "Les' you want to get caught in a trap."

The three of them approached carefully and stood in front of the fastened door. "What's this?" Gunderson asked

Angus listened for movement inside. "Somebody's been here. Since last night. And it looks like my dogs come back to feed."

"They in there?" Gunderson asked, concerned.

Angus nodded. "Looks like."

"Who in the hell was here?" Grebs asked.

"Can't tell," Angus said, looking down, trying to follow the boot tracks. "The snow's trampled and dry. Didn't make any good prints. But whoever was here avoided the traps, just like my dogs," he said, pointing to where the hybrid tracks came down out of the woods, breaking the glistening white plane.

"When did you leave?" Grebs asked.

"Soon as everybody else did. I set the traps, careful about it. Then I waited awhile, maybe another half hour. Took off right around sunset."

"So it was getting dark when you left?" Grebs asked.

"Just about. I wanted to make the edge of the Woods right before dark, so I could see to unlock the chain."

Grebs thought about it. "Clayton," he guessed. He looked back toward the house and saw their tracks come away from the back door. "If it was him he tried to get inside."

Angus peered down at the trail leading toward the barn. "There were at least two of 'em," he said. "And judging by what I can see of the track, I'd say one was a woman."

"Diane Talbott," Grebs guessed. He looked toward the barn. "Just what we fuckin' needed."

Angus turned closer to the door, listening.

"You sure they're in there?" Gunderson asked.

Angus heard movement the other side of the door. "Only one way to know for sure."

"What in the hell are we supposed to do now?" Gunderson asked.

"Get 'em," Angus said. "Teach 'em a goddamn lesson." He turned to the door, worked the latch out of its frozen lock, and slid the door open, only inches. A bar of sunlight fell into the barn, just enough for Angus to see a hybrid's paw. There was a low growl, like distant thunder. And then the paw vanished. "Yeah," he said. "They're in there. Couple nights in the woods 'n they got attitude."

"Sounded wild to me," Hank said, a little worried.

"We need to think about this," Grebs commented. He paused for a minute, looking back to the house. "This could work. Somebody came out to the farm. Found wolves in the barn. Locked 'em in."

"Probably Clayton," Angus guessed.

"Probably," Grebs agreed. "Which is even better. Whoever was here saw wolves. You said so yourself, Angus. Nothing different about them. They're wolves."

"Look like it, anyway," he agreed.

"Damn right. More evidence. When we came out to help clean up the mess," he considered, still thinking . . . "Is there another entrance to this barn?"

"Old grain chute, back side," Angus said.

"Perfect. We came out to help clean up the mess, saw they'd been here. But this time they busted out the old grain chute."

Gunderson saw the reasoning, thought it was a good idea. "Went back to the woods, where wolves would go," he added. "And whoever came out was trespassin'!"

"Whoever came out better have one hell of a good reason, or they'll keep their mouths shut. That'd be something in our favor. The refusal of someone to come forward."

Angus turned back to the door, getting ready to open it. Grebs held him back. "Goddamn it, Angus. Would you wait a minute?"

"Wait for them to come back and get my dogs? We need to get 'em outta there."

"Nobody's gonna' get 'em, because they're wolves," Grebs said. "You're right about working fast. But caging them isn't the thing." He thought for a moment, rubbing his chin. "At least we got lucky in one respect. It's early. If they think the wolves are caught we probably got a little time."

Gunderson and Angus watched Grebs examine the snow.

He turned and said, "open it up a bit and let's see how they're doing."

Angus reached over to pull the door open.

"Careful, Angus. They've been out in the woods awhile. They might not be ready for your kind of affection."

"They'll mind," he said.

He slid the door open a few inches. From inside the barn he heard rustling, then another growl.

"Nothin' a hard hand won't cure," Angus commented.

Grebs looked down at the snow. Tracks were heaviest between the house and the barn's entrance. The rest of the barn was surrounded by an unbroken plain of white. "Looks like they didn't know about the chute. If they did, they didn't check it out. You sure that grain chute is big enough for wolves to get through?"

Angus nodded. "They could get through it."

"Then we open it enough to let them run."

"What?" Angus didn't like the idea of letting his dogs run wild a second time. He didn't think they'd return. "We let 'em go again they could be gone for good."

"Good 'n gone's what we want, now that I think of it. What if someone came while we were cagin 'em, or they even see those cages in the back of your truck, or those pens behind your place?"

"They're my dogs," Angus protested, not wanting to free them. It had taken a lot of hard work to build his breeding stock.

"Think about your share," Grebs reminded him, sensing Moon's disappointment. "Share like that be plenty to get you started with whole new stock. Hell, redo your whole outfit."

Angus considered it. Grebs was right. But he didn't like it, giving up the dogs he'd bred since birth, all of them a damn good mix of dog and wolf, mostly wolf.

"Seems to me they're just about wild enough already," Hank observed.

"Grain chute opens from the inside," Angus remembered.

Grebs looked at Gunderson. That meant one of them would have to enter the barn and open it. "Shit," he finally growled, rubbing his chin. He looked over at Angus. "Got any ideas?"

"Go in and open it," Angus said.

"You think those dogs'll let you?"

Angus stared back at Grebs. "They'll let me," he said.

"Maybe you forgot recent history," Gunderson commented. "You just starved them and then sent them killing on their own."

Angus paused, looking at the barn wall in front of him. "I admit they got a taste for it. But they try anything they'll get a steel toed boot, somethin' they already know."

"I hope to hell they haven't forgotten."

"They're dogs," Angus reassured.

The three men looked at each other.

"Then let's get it done," Grebs finally said. "Before anyone comes and finds us, or sees those cages in the back of your truck. Set 'em free and get the hell out." He looked up over the road but it was still early and the morning was quiet as a graveyard.

Angus started for the door, matter of fact, as though entering it was without risk.

Gunderson stepped back.

Grebs called out behind Moon, "Keep in mind those dogs been runnin' for the last two days, after two days starving. And they did a damn good job killin'. Be careful how you open that door."

Angus turned. "Hell, I made 'em, didn't I?"

Angus opened the door wide enough to sandwich through a narrow gap. He pulled it shut behind him, leaving a narrow crack to let in light, and then stepped to one side. His eyes gradually grew accustomed to the dark. A narrow swath of sunlight bisected the barn. In the partial illumination Angus saw carcasses and bloodied humps. From his right there was movement, and then a flash across the light beam, like a shadow flicker in candlelight. Deeper in darkness he heard rustling and then another low growl.

"What's that?" he said, belligerent. He had a cruel, familiar way of handling dogs. He never let them forget he was their unchallenged alpha. Always had been. Always would be. But they had never all been out of their cages at the same time, on their own.

One of the animals answered with another low growl, slightly more pronounced.

"That you, Arctic?" Angus knew him. He was the black haired one and the biggest. "You'd best be smart and stay out of my way."

There was an eerie stillness in the barn, as though the dogs were considering his offer. He could feel their eyes. Angus had been a predator his entire life. The top of the food chain, the unchallenged king of the wild and everything in it. Now from darkness he sensed the yellow wolf eyes staring at him, watching carefully for weakness, measuring him.

Suddenly there was rustling from one of the calf stalls, followed with a low whine. Angus peered into the darkness. He thought he saw one or two animals shift among the carnage. The barn still reeked of it. He could see their shadows in the barn's darkest reaches, positioning, considering.

"Keep away!"

He spit a long brown spasm of tobacco juice onto the floor. He knew they'd smell it . . . remember what it meant. There was quiet again, and then a long, rumbling growl picked up by another growl. Two of them were defiant.

"Alright," Angus growled himself. "You had a little taste of wild and you want to keep it! And for now I'm going to give it to you."

He peered ahead, unable to see more than a few feet beyond the doorway's ambient light. He shuffled his boots forward, feeling his way across the floor's carnage. He entered the darkness, progressing slowly toward the grain chute. Twice he felt heavy objects and stepped to avoid them. There was more growling from the back of the barn, higher pitched and coming from two other positions, as though they were surrounding him. He could feel their intensity, their keen observation.

In the decade he'd been working with hybrids he had only been attacked once. He'd had a good bitch he'd used for four years. He'd taken her ice fishing, thinking she could use the exercise and the fish, providing he got lucky. Dragging his sled and supplies across the ice, he'd slipped and fallen flat. The bitch didn't miss the opportunity. She pounced on the fallen alpha, her wolf instinct returning, her natural inclination for dominance seeing opportunity. She opened her jaws and enveloped Angus Moon's head. Wolf jaws are powerful enough to snap a moose's thighbone and suck out the marrow. In this case, the act was dominance. Angus was part of her pack. She wasn't going to kill him, just let him know she saw weakness and was vying for dominance. He rolled, fought her off, and then beat her until she cowered like the dog Moon reminded her she was.

In the dark interior of the barn he remembered the slip and fall. He would have to be careful.

"You bastards keep outta my way!" he yelled. He didn't care for the growling, but it was the two he wasn't hearing that worried him most.

"For Christ's sake," Grebs called from the other side of the door. "Who in the hell are you talking to? Just get it open, Angus. We got to get those dogs out, clean up this fuckin' mess and get the hell out of here!"

"Blacker than pitch in here!" He thought he heard movement to his right.

"Hug the wall and feel your way over," Grebs suggested. "Hank's on the other side. He can help from the outside when you get close."

Angus thought about telling Grebs to go fuck himself, but his attention was interrupted by another sound from his right, more growling behind it. He was disoriented in the dark. He wasn't certain the dog had moved, but it sounded closer. Maybe it was just louder. He turned to listen and said, "here now!" taking a step without feeling.

His foot came up against something solid and he lost his balance, started falling. He put his hand out and it slid across gristle and bone, bringing the center of his diaphragm down hard. Air rushed out of him like a bellows. His disorientation was brief but long enough. The animal was on top of him. He raised his arm to protect himself, kicked and rolled to his right, feeling a carcass in the small of his back. The animal grabbed hold of his arm, trying to pull him, shaking its massive jaws, growling in the dark. Angus brought his free hand in front of him, striking hard at its head. He struck three more times before it finally let go and retreated. But it wouldn't go far. Angus was still in the dark on the floor. He had to get up in a hurry.

"What was that?" Grebs yelled.

Angus was on his feet, breathing hard. "Get the fuck out of my way!" he roared. "Goddamnit!" he spit, stricken. He made his way along the wall, struggling to catch his breath. He slid and managed to step over another carcass and found himself at the chute's door. "You fuckin' bastards!"

"What?!" Grebs yelled from outside, but Angus wasn't listening.

"Angus," Gunderson said, just the other side of the wall. "The door's right here," he said, banging on it. Angus reached up, felt for the familiar latch, pulled on it and the square fell open. Sunlight streamed into the barn. Angus squinted in the light and behind him the animals cowered back into the barn's shadows.

"Christ," Gunderson said, looking down at him. Moon's arm was torn and ragged, blood starting to ooze around the holes in his sleeve. "What the hell happened?"

CHAPTER TWENTY-EIGHT

FEBRUARY 1ST, MORNING—DEFIANCE AND DIANE TALBOTT'S CABIN

By the time Sam Rivers stirred it was well after daybreak. He was still half asleep and disoriented. He wasn't in Yellow Rock. There was a feeling of pressure, atmospheric, a dense cold pushing from everywhere but this warm bed, like being inside the shell of an egg. The room was lightly shaded. His eyes fluttered, and there was faint illumination, like the kind along north-facing windows toward the end of the day. Shallow half-light without warmth.

They'd been at the farmhouse, he and Diane. They watched the shadowy creatures come out of the woods, noses in the wind, surreptitious about their return. They howled in the middle of the night, reclaiming their kill. Gradually he began to recollect it, including the message left for Svegman by the time they re-entered cell phone range. But Svegman hadn't returned his call, had he?

And there was the smell. Witch hazel. Ripe. Like autumn woods with an underlying sweetness. The akvavit they drank when they returned hadn't dulled his senses. He remembered every naked inch of the woman beside him. Now he lay perfectly still, thinking about what part of her he wanted to touch first.

Sam Rivers smiled. On the long drive from Yellow Rock he'd had plenty of thinking time. He was 37 and single again, still smarting from the long bad last year of his marriage. It had taken him six months and the ritualistic burial of his wedding ring to help him start feeling better.

Kay Magdalen told him the time it takes to get over a divorce is equal to the half-life of the marriage. All things considered it sounded like a reasonable formula. That would mean three years, for Sam. Five, if you counted the four years they were together before they married. At first, five years sounded like a prison sentence. But on his way over from Yellow Rock he reconsidered it. From 37 to 42, if Kay's formula was right, could be the best goddamn five years of his life. If he abided by the formula, that would mean he would run away from any chance of marriage, at least for the next five years, no matter how attracted he was to a woman. Was that possible? Moreover, if he was candid about his refusal to marry and his need to experiment by 'dating around,' would any woman even bother to date him more than once? For now, it was too much to think about. So he decided to leave it at *this could be the best goddamn five years of my life.*

His evening with Diane was about as unexpected as a January thaw. In his childhood bedroom, she'd felt good. Better than good. Later, during small talk on the return to her place, he wished he would have finished it, because he *thought* he knew where this was headed, but was still so surprised by that sudden kiss he wasn't sure. Carpe Diem. It should be Carpe Momento (seize the moment), because he wished he would have seized Diane. Back there. When the moment was hot.

But then they returned and each had three glasses of akvavit while they sat on the couch, continuing to unwind. Until Diane stood up, reached out her hand, and led him to her bedroom.

"Diane," he started, following her.

"Don't talk."

Jesus, he thought, remembering what happened when they came into her bedroom. Rushed, more like it. Shedding and pulling off clothes on their way to her bed. Pulling at each other and themselves. If their limbs had been tinder they would have set fire to the place. Hell, their limbs were tinder.

He had to get up. He was remembering too much and it was too goddamn visceral and he was starting to think about waking her up. But now there was too goddamn much to do. They would have time to revisit this bed.

She was heavy beside him, weighted in deep sleep, if he was any judge of her breathing. He turned out of bed, carefully so as not to awaken her, and picked up his clothes on his way out of the room.

Diane's bathroom was at the end of the hall. He paced into it, meditative, took a toothbrush out of his kit, added toothpaste and stuck it into his tired mouth, starting to brush. He sat down and pissed, still brushing. The seat was cold. He finished, stood up to look at himself. The Iron Range was starting to have an effect on him. Black whiskers covered his face, disheveled coal black hair creased his head with a greasy sheen, and there was what appeared to be more salt at his temples. Truth is he looked like one of those movie star bad boys. Felt like it, too. His eyes were intense, he thought. If the Range had sullied his features, it had done something else entirely to his perspective. For the first time in a long while he was starting to feel good again.

He walked out of the bathroom, passing Diane's door. He had the sudden urge to re-enter. He remembered her lips and the contour of her face in the moonlight. She was a damn fine-looking woman. Clearly they'd been appreciative of each other.

He returned to the couch and made the call. First to Svegman, but got his voicemail a second time. When he pressed zero it rolled over to an assistant's voicemail. He finally redialed and left another message for Svegman.

Then he dialed the Sheriff. The on-duty deputy patched him over.

"Dean Goddard."

"Sam Rivers, Sheriff. You work every Saturday?"

"Every Saturday. Beats Belinda's church services," he said. "She's gone at the crack of dawn and doesn't come home until after supper."

"Saturday and Sunday? That's one hell of a long weekend."

"Just the half of it. What's up?"

"We went back to the farm last night. Diane and me."

There was a pause. "Thought you might. Wished you hadn't."

"I had a hunch those wolves would return."

"I assume Angus was gone?"

"Yeah."

"You didn't break in, did you?"

"No. I wouldn't have broken into the house." True enough. "I was pretty sure those wolves would return and I wanted to see them."

"Did they?"

"Yup. Got hungry and came back to feed. I thought with all the trampling and Angus setting traps no wolf would come near the place."

"Any get trapped?"

"Not in Angus's footholds. We watched them go into the barn, avoiding those traps like they had a map of the place. Stepped around every one of them. Incredible."

"Smart animals."

"After they entered the barn we gave them a few minutes to settle in, then snuck over and shut and latched the barn door. They're still there. Trapped."

"Did you call Svegman?"

"I did. Early this morning we left him a message. But he hasn't gotten back to me. Any idea where to find him?"

"I'll give him a call. Steve's from Vermilion Falls, but he should be able to get out there by noon. I could go out with him." Dean Goddard might like to have one more look at the house, though he didn't think what he wanted was there.

"That'd be great."

"And for the record," the Sheriff added. "No more visits without the law. I called you for your wolf expertise. If Angus finds you out there again all hell's likely to break loose."

"OK."

"I'll talk to Steve. For the time being, just to keep things simple, I'll make sure Svegman doesn't say anything about your late night trip."

"I'd appreciate that."

"What did you have in mind . . . about the wolves?"

"Ideally I'd like them captured alive. I know they can't stay in that barn, but I'd like to see them, watch them for a while."

"I'll see if he can get some others to assist."

"That'd be good. Thanks."

"We'll be in touch."

They said goodbye and hung up.

That went about as well as Sam figured it could. The Sheriff didn't like their visit, but at least he was following up on the wolves.

Diane Talbott's bedroom door opened.

"Morning," she managed, on her way to the kitchen.

"Morning."

She wore a threadbare pair of aqua sweatpants and a long sleeved blank sweatshirt and unless Sam was mistaken, nothing underneath. Her big hair still fell like a young woman's. A pillow seam lined her left cheek. She was still waking up. "Sleep well?"

"Well enough."

He decided to let her get some coffee, wake up, come to her own terms with the previous evening. "Can I borrow your computer?"

He'd seen it last night in her bedroom, where it had served as a hanger for some of the clothes they'd flung across the room.

"Have at it," she said. "I need coffee."

He fetched the disk, went into the bedroom and closed the door.

The bed looked warm and comfortable. Next to one side rested a nightstand and a reading lamp with six or seven books beneath it. Sam recognized a pocket dictionary, a crossword, and three or four novels, *Storm Prey* one of them. But he didn't recognize the others. The other side of the narrow room had a small table with her computer.

With the largest room in the house given over to her study, there wasn't much space for anything else. You had to walk around the end of the bed to use it. And there was only enough room for one person to sit in front of the screen, but Sam wasn't complaining.

He turned on the PC and waited. It took a minute for the screen to come up, and the hard disk to *phit-phit-phit* through its machinations. After the icons appeared he inserted the disk into the CD drive and waited. It whirred, looking for an application. A small Windows Media Player video window opened on the screen. Sam moved the mouse and clicked play.

Two bodies, and judging from their naked embrace and their horizontal position and rhythm, they were having a good time. Then Sam noticed the Sheriff's clothes tossed over a nearby chair. The Sheriff's gun hung in its holster over the back of a chair. The date appeared in the lower right corner of the video screen. *January 5.* Less than a month earlier. It sure as hell looked like the Sheriff. Sam had never met his wife, but he guessed the woman on the screen wasn't Belinda Goddard. When he played it a second time and examined the room, he recognized a simple dresser, a counter with a TV, a chair with a table, and a door to a bathroom. A motel room. There was a smaller set of clothes laid over the chair next to the sheriff's. One of the items appeared to be some kind of medical smock.

"I'll be goddamned," he muttered.

It was not what he had expected to find in the old man's cache. And it could mean a whole lot more than he wanted to know. Where was Dean Goddard the night Williston Winthrop was killed? If the old man was trying to blackmail the Sheriff, the Sheriff had motive to get rid of him. But Sam had spent enough time tracking predators to get a feel for their personalities. The Sheriff didn't measure up to murder. But you never knew. Ted Bundy was notorious for being thoughtful, articulate and charming. He demonstrated what psychologists describe as a *mask of sanity*. But if the Sheriff was a murderer, Sam Rivers was a rodeo clown. The man was grounded as dirt and balanced as the Gaia theory. On the other hand, there was no accounting for what some people were capable of, when pushed.

Earlier he'd examined the folder's contents, finding corporate charters, stock certificates, assumed name filings, and a few bank statements documenting a lot of money. But it wasn't until he noticed Miriam Samuelson's signature on a corporate charter for Iron County Care that he began to take note. His mom had been a generous woman, but on more than one occasion she'd shaken her head and grumbled about her husband's legal work. And when he was a kid he remembered rumors and comments from the other Club members, about how Williston was capable of turning the law whatever way he wanted.

Sam was no lawyer, but it was easy enough to guess the old man's folder business was outside the law, and appeared to be profitable and larcenous. He suspected Jeff Dunlap would be interested in its contents.

But what about the CD? And what about the Sheriff? And who was the woman?

Sam Rivers set the folder on the bed and closed it. He stood up, wondered about it, and then backed around the bed to the bedroom door and opened it. He could hear Diane in the kitchen.

He came around the corner. She was cleaning some dishes, her hands hovering over the sink.

When she noticed him she said, "How about some coffee?"

He came up beside her and placed a hand on the middle of her back, rubbing a little. She relaxed, a good response.

"That'd be good."

An empty cup sat by the pot. She started to fill it. "So what did you find out?"

"Not sure," he said. "I think I need another opinion, but I'm not sure about that, either."

She handed him the cup. "It's hard to string together an intelligent sentence before my first cup, let alone have a conversation."

Sam took it. "Thanks. The same." But it wasn't too early to notice the plump contour of her lips.

"Black?"

Sam nodded. The coffee was the color of tar. Perfect.

"So what was it?"

"First I need to know if you can keep a secret?"

"Oh?"

"I want you to identify someone in a video. But I'm not sure it should go beyond this room. And you may never be able to tell anyone, or write about it, at least not until we're sure what it's about. But maybe never."

"Never is a long time. What if it's a murder?"

"It's not murder, but it is important. I need to know what I'm seeing, who it is. I suspect you may know . . . her. But if you don't think you can stay quiet about it, so be it. I won't bring you into it."

Diane appeared serious, wondering if she could agree.

And that was a good thing, Sam knew.

"Now that's the most interesting offer I've had since . . ." she said, taking another sip of coffee. "Last night." She grinned and walked into the living room, sat on the couch. Sam followed her. The woman had a backside.

"If I see anyone breaking the law or being violent, I can't make any promises."

Sam thought about it. "Isn't Minnesota a no-fault divorce state?"

"I don't know."

"I believe it is, so technically the person isn't breaking the law. Unless you considered it from a biblical perspective."

"Oh," she said. Then, "I'd better have a look."

Sam led her to the bedroom. Her PC showed the usual assortment of icons with the small black video player overlaying the square center of the screen.

"Have a seat," Sam said.

Diane sat down, staring at the computer, still sipping coffee.

"Click the play button."

She did and the scratchy video played.

Through the entire 49 seconds Diane Talbott just stared. Sam could tell she was absorbing the video's impact. When it was over she said, "I'll be damned." She didn't need to see it again. She stood up from the chair and without looking at Sam walked out of the room.

He followed.

Diane was shaking her head. "I don't believe it." She went into the kitchen and refilled her cup.

"Who's the woman?" Sam asked.

Once they were in the living room Diane sat on the couch. She wasn't shaken. She was chagrined, perplexed. "I just wouldn't have . . . guessed it," she muttered.

"So who's the woman?"

"That's the local doctor. She's also our new Coroner, at least since last year, when old Doc Chauncey retired. Her name's Susan Wallace."

"Married?"

"Nope. Works all the time. I thought she didn't have time to think about a relationship. Looks like they've been working pretty close," Diane said, looking up at Sam to consider it. "I just," she added, surprised, "I guess I'm surprised, but not surprised."

"What do you mean?"

"Belinda, Dean's wife."

"What about her?"

"She turned fundamental. Couple years back, from what I've heard. You pick things up at the paper. Couldn't have children, turned to the bottle, then got Christ and got sober."

"Nothing wrong with that. And sure no reason for her husband to step out," Sam observed, for the moment disappointed with the Sheriff, though he knew first-hand that love could be an intoxicating cocktail.

"Gossip has it, part of Belinda's vows involve no sex."

"What kind of Christian heritage is that?"

"The Iron Orthodox Gospel Church," Diane said. "Their perspective. Or at least the perspective of Bishop Rose, I guess."

"Who the hell is Bishop Rose?"

"The self-appointed Bishop of the Iron Orthodox Gospel Church. There's only one. He's minister, priest, bishop and pope."

"Absolute power."

"Absolutely."

"So what in the hell was the old man doing with the video?"

"No idea," Diane said. "And how in the hell did he get it?"

"You think he was using it? Blackmailing the Sheriff about something?"

Diane looked up. "I can't imagine Williston Winthrop having this and not using it. Though it was recent enough, maybe he hadn't had a chance. Before you go accusing Dean Goddard of anything," she paused, "too god-awful, you might reconsider. I've known the guy a long time. I suspect his," she paused again, "lapse in judgment, however understandable, is tearing the guy up." And now she was staring at Sam Rivers. "But Dean Goddard isn't capable of murder."

"But the old man must have been thinking about using it. If you don't know about their relationship," he said, thinking out loud, "probably no one does."

"If I know Dean Goddard, he'd do plenty to keep this quiet. Not because he's a bad man. But he definitely likes his job. But he wouldn't kill over it. He'd face the rain. If he was being blackmailed he'd out it and then arrest Will Winthrop for extortion. Whatever this is, it has nothing to do with murder." Then she grew thoughtful. "And he has the perfect alibi," she added.

"What?"

"The night Will Winthrop died the Sheriff and just about all other town and county notables were in Vermilion Falls, at the VFW for their annual volunteer firefighters fund drive."

"You saw him?"

"I danced with him."

"How long was he there?"

"From before dinner to around 10. He was one of the hosts. He set it up."

"So he has an alibi. And I haven't seen anything to suggest Dean is anything but a reasonable guy," Sam agreed. "I just wonder how far he would go to keep this quiet, to avoid a little bad press?"

"A *little* bad press? You've been away too long. Press like this in a place like Vermilion County would bury the Sheriff. Could cost him his job."

Sam shook his head. "I appreciate that, but would the Sheriff step over the line to save his job?"

"I think just about anyone is capable of anything, given the right time and place. But I'm not saying Dean Goddard did anything."

"Did you recognize the room?" Sam asked, coming back to the video.

"Pretty sure it's the Vermilion Falls Motel."

"What are those files?" she asked, remembering the folder.

"Looks like some kind of scam Williston was into."

"You think the scam is related to the video? You think the Sheriff knew about it but was keeping his mouth shut, because of that movie?"

"No idea," Sam said. "Could be. Maybe we should ask him."

Sam wondered about a next step. He owed the Sheriff a favor. But he had to know what the Sheriff did, if anything, to keep his relationship quiet.

"That'd be direct."

"I'd like to give him the benefit of the doubt." He thought for a minute. "And there's the problem of these files," he added.

"What problem?"

"They should be shared with someone in a position to do something about them, if I'm reading them right."

"I don't get it."

"I'd bet Jeff Dunlap would give his left nut to get his hands on these files."

"So give them to him?"

"Can't. Technically, they're evidence. They should come from the investigating officer. Otherwise they might be inadmissible, given how we acquired them."

"So what if the Sheriff gave them to him?"

"That's what I had in mind, providing the Sheriff would play along," Sam said.

"I guess there's only one way to find out."

CHAPTER TWENTY-NINE

The Deputy staffing the front office turned around and yelled back to the Sheriff through his opened door. "Lady from Canada on line 1. Something about a missing brother."

Dean had been working on some paper. He picked up his phone and pushed 1. "This is Sheriff Goddard," he started.

"Sheriff, Clement Beauregard."

An older woman, judging from the gravelly tone. She didn't sound Canadian. Was that what his Deputy said? Canadian?

"From Manitoba," she added.

"Ma'am?" Dean asked.

"Ah've got a brotha' down there. At least wuz. Outside Defiance, Minnesota?" She had a thick southern drawl.

He didn't know if it was a question. "Yes?"

"His name's James T. Beauregard," she said, hesitating. "People call him Jimbo." She waited. "Or Jim."

"Yeah?" Dean said.

"He was stayin' on some farm outside a town. Said he'd be here by Wensday, but din't show."

"He's missing, ma'am?"

"Ah guess. Yeah. You know Defiance?"

"Small town west of us," Dean explained. "Not that far. When was he in Defiance?"

"Not in town, Sheriff," she drawled. "Said he wuz on some farm outside a' town."

"There are a lot of farms all over the area, Ma'am. Did he give you a name? Address?"

"No sah," she said, cordial.

"And you're looking for him?"

"Uh-huh," she answered. "He was s'posed to be in Manitoba las' Wensday."

"Driving?" Dean asked.

"Catchin' the Greyhound outta Bemijji. Said it wuz all lined up."

"What was his business," the Sheriff caught himself, "*outside* Defiance?"

"Jimbo didn't have no biz'ness. Jimbo was comin' here to lend a hand. My cousin Emil opened the Cajun Café. We needed help with the place and I knew Jimbo could'a used the work."

"Was he visiting someone?"

"Said he got a job on some farm."

"How did he get to Defiance?" Dean asked. He didn't think Defiance had any bus service.

"Thumb, mos' likely," she said. "Or the rails."

Goddard's eyes rolled up toward the ceiling. A vagrant. Chances are he could be anywhere. Maybe he didn't really like working, but didn't want to tell his sister, Dean thought. "I can ask the cop in Defiance," he said.

"Officer Grebs?" she asked.

Apparently she'd done her homework. "Yeah," Dean said. "Have you spoken with him?"

"Ah have. Said he'd look into it. I jus' thought somethin' might have happened somewhere else. Jimbo said he'd be here on the 11:25 Greyhound outta Bemijji. He ain't perticular 'bout much, but he's always punctual. Has been, anyway."

"Are there any other, ah, reasons he might be late, Ma'am?" Dean asked. He needed to know if the man was a schizophrenic or used alcohol or drugs. And Clement Beauregard sounded like the type who wouldn't whitewash a brother's bad habits.

"Whaddya' mean?" she asked.

"Does your brother have any mental issues, ma'am. Is he on any medication? Does he drink? Does he use drugs?"

"Jimbo? Lord no. Take some nips now and again, but not reglar. He's had bad luck, most his life. Has a mark on his face. A big red birth mark. People have always thought it strange, but we know it's where God touched him."

Another bizarre stroke from God's hand, Dean thought. Goddard noted the time the man was due in Manitoba, reminded himself to call Greyhound and ask about it, if he got a spare moment. He took down the rest of the information on Jimbo. Nothing much. A big guy, overweight. Prominent birthmark on his left cheek. Maybe Grebs would know something.

When the Sheriff mentioned the Defiance town cop, Clement Beauregard told him Grebs was running a missing persons on him. That would be a BOLO Report. If so, it'd have to come through the Sheriff's office, and he hadn't seen anything yet. He'd have to get an update from Grebs, soon as he got a chance.

Dean promised Ms. Beauregard he'd get back to her no later than tomorrow afternoon, then rang off. He was back at his paperwork less than five minutes before the phone rang again.

"Line 1," the deputy called through his door. "Dunlap."

Goddard picked it up. "Shouldn't you be tending to family matters?"

"I knew you'd be in. Goddamn it, Dean, get a life."

"Jeff," Dean heard Dunlap's wife in the background. "Watch your tongue."

"Yeah, Dad," agreed Dunlap's seven year old son.

"Yeah," then his daughter.

They were out doing something as a family, Dean guessed. There was something about the imagined scene that made the Sheriff nostalgic, longing for what he suspected he would never have.

"Sorry," Jeff said to the others in his car. Then back to the Sheriff. "Taking Katie to catechism. Just trying to keep abreast of the important stuff. Like Pine Grove."

"Watch your goddamn mouth," Dean admonished. "God's gonna wash it out with soap. And for you he's got an extra-big bar."

"Better him than Marlys," he said, referring to his wife. "Guess what happened at the Winthrop's farmhouse?"

"What?"

"Wolves returned."

"Really?"

"Really. Meeting Steve Svegman from the DNR out there around noon."

"Angus trap them?"

"Nope. Your friend Sam Rivers was out there last night. Said he had a hunch they might return."

"So he was right."

"Yep. But if Angus Moon knew Sam Rivers had gone out there in the middle of the night and trapped those wolves he'd have an aneurysm."

"And then he'd kill something. What about Pine Grove?"

"Nothing new. I didn't find anything at the farm. Nosed around a little, but there aren't a lot of places in that old house to hide case files."

"Wouldn't take more than a crack."

"A pretty wide crack, I'd guess, if we assume he's been bilking them awhile. And taking notes."

"Maybe. What about the house in Defiance?"

"I went over to the house. Someone got in before me."

"Broke in?"

"Uh-huh. A window well in the back. Went in through the basement." Dean had a strong suspicion Sam Rivers felt nostalgic and made a visit, but the timing wasn't right. "Whoever it was didn't take much, far as I could tell. Some preserves."

"Preserves?" Jeff asked, surprised. "You mean, like, jam?"

"Yeah."

"You sure they didn't walk off with any files?"

"When I nosed around the place I couldn't find anywhere files would be kept. Dimes to donuts it went up in that office fire."

"I spoke with Walt," Dunlap said, referring to the Fire Marshall. "Says all signs point to an electrical fire. Another accident."

"When it rains it goddamn pours," Dean observed. There was plenty gone wrong with that man and his aftermath. A little too plenty, the Sheriff thought.

"Whoops. We're here," Jeff said, referring to church. "I'll catch you later, maybe at the office."

"Later."

The Sheriff hung up. He didn't wait long.

"Line 1," the deputy called through his door. "Sam Rivers."

"Morning. Didn't we just talk?"

"Diane and I have to come over to Vermilion Falls. Any chance you could join us for a cup of coffee?"

Dean wondered about it. "Sure. I'm about ready for a coffee break. I'm heading out to meet Svegman at noon. What time can you be here?"

"We're practically on our way. We'll meet you at the Rangers Café. If you get there before us, get a booth."

"Business, or pleasure?" Dean enquired.

Sam hesitated. "Both."

CHAPTER THIRTY

FEBRUARY 1ST, BEFORE NOON—THE VERMILION FALLS STRIP, ON THE EDGE OF TOWN

Lindy's Tap was a well-known Vermilion Falls establishment. For most Minnesota bars it was illegal to sell off-sale liquor, unless you had a special license, which Lindy's didn't. But it was an illegality Lindy considered more of a guideline than a rule, especially when it came to Bill Grebs. When Bill Grebs walked through the door, Lindy Lewis nodded and said, "William. Coffee?"

"That'd be nice," answered Grebs. It had been a long morning.

"Hair of the dog?" Lindy asked.

Grebs let his eyes grow accustomed to the dark. Apart from two overweight beer drinkers swilling suds instead of coffee, the place was empty. The tipplers were focused on a fishing show broadcasting on the behind the bar TV. "Why not?" Grebs grinned.

Lindy poured the coffee into a large cup, leaving a good inch at the top. He lowered the cup behind the bar and surreptitiously topped off the coffee with an inch of whiskey. Technically, Grebs wasn't on duty. But appearances were important, he knew. Particularly on the Range.

"Obliged," he said, taking the cup in hand.

"What's new in Defiance?"

"Been nothin' but chaos since Williston's accident."

"I read about the fire," Lindy said.

They had agreed not to broadcast the wolf kill. Too much unnecessary press might interest the wrong people. The last thing the Club wanted were treehuggers from that Wolf Center nosing around. Clayton Winthrop was bad enough. But a little gossip in the right corners might cloud things up. "Did you hear about the wolves?" Grebs asked.

"Wolves?"

"Wolves got into Williston's barn and killed his feeder calves."

"No shit? I didn't read that in the paper."

"Killed all three of them and ate their fill. The DNR's being quiet about it. I guess they don't want the bad publicity," Grebs said. In places like Lindy's Tap, the DNR was an unpopular governmental entity. If Iron Range residents thought the DNR was covering up, it would only add to the outrage.

"Jesus H. Christ. Never heard *anything* like that."

"You know how plentiful they're getting."

Lindy nodded. "Had Buck Withers in here the other day. He said he had to kill a pair that dug a den on the rear acreage of his farm. They were harassing his livestock."

"That's what I mean."

"Said he didn't say anything to the DNR. Just shot 'em and dragged 'em into the woods. Buried 'em."

"That's a logical course of action, unless you need to get reimbursed."

"I'd do it," Lindy said. "Do it in a second, if my livestock were threatened."

"And damn well better do it before any more are taken."

"The fuckin' DNR. And we're payin' for 'em."

"Just ain't right," Grebs agreed.

There was a long pause as the two men considered what was wrong with government. Then Lindy said, "It's a shame about Williston." Lindy knew Grebs and Williston had been close. Sometimes the two men would come into his Vermilion Falls bar, or buy spirits. Lindy passed along his wholesale price to his friends.

"A definite loss for the Range," Grebs said, sincere enough.

"That man had a string of bad luck," Lindy said.

"Not that it'll bother him now," Grebs said.

"Yup. That's a fact."

They talked briefly while Grebs finished his coffee. It tasted excellent, an hour before noon. Just the thing Grebs needed to put the unpleasantness of his early morning behind him.

"Gonna need a few items," Grebs said.

When Grebs was buying in bulk, or something special, he always turned to Lindy, who gave him better prices than anyplace else on the Range. Given the Club's recent heavy partying, he needed to replenish, particularly in light of this evening's celebration.

"A couple bottles of Crown Royal. A bottle of Stoli. Give me that Reserva Del Senor Tequila, the brown stuff. And one bottle of Glenlivet," he said.

"Jesus," he said. "You're gettin' ready to party."

Grebs just grinned and nodded.

Lindy glanced down at the bar's only other patrons. Their glasses were still half full. They were watching a fisherman stand at the edge of his boat, fighting to reel in his catch. Lindy nodded and disappeared in the back. Grebs drained his cup while Lindy filled a large grocery bag. He came out with two double-bagged sacks, the Crown Royal boxes in one of them.

"Williston's drink," he said, remembering.

Grebs hadn't thought about it. "Yup," he said. "Me and the boys are toasting Williston tonight, after his burial. We thought the best way to do it would be with his Canadian Whiskey. Not very partial to it myself. But Williston would have liked the gesture."

"That man had expensive tastes."

"That was Williston."

Lindy took Grebs's money and the town cop said goodbye. He had a couple more errands to run. He had to go to the hardware store and pick up some ammo and supplies. He had to go to the grocery store. And he needed a carton of Old Golds. Williston's Cohibas, too, he reminded himself. He placed the liquor into his truck's back seat, pulled out of the parking lot, and turned toward Walling's Hardware.

Across the street Sam and Diane stared out the tinted windows of the Rangers Café. They were waiting for the Sheriff, who was taking longer than he expected. They watched Bill Grebs head into town.

"What do you suppose the Defiance town cop's up to?" Sam asked.

"Having a drink and buying some liquor, I suspect." Lindy's place wasn't a big secret. If serious drinkers didn't know about his lax observance of liquor laws, they had their suspicions. Lindy was careful. He never sold to anyone he hadn't known since birth. He had plenty of customers.

"The funeral's at 3:00 p.m.," Sam observed.

"I suspect he's stocking up."

"A little post-burial fling?"

"Why not? They can afford whatever they want now, can't they?"

"Guess I'd do the same thing."

"You're not going to the party?"

"Wasn't invited," Sam said.

"Imagine that? Doesn't seem neighborly."

"Not that I won't have a celebratory drink," he added.

Sheriff Dean Goddard appeared not long after Grebs wheeled out of Lindy's. When he came in, Sam moved over to sit near Diane.

"Sheriff," they nodded. Sam picked up the coffee pot and topped off his cup. Diane's too. "Coffee?" he asked Dean.

"Sure."

When Sam reached over to fill his cup Dean noticed Sam's wrist scab. "What happened to your wrist?"

"Cut it on some glass."

The Sheriff thought he knew how. Which meant Sam Rivers had been lying about when he arrived in town. "Healing OK?"

"Seems to be."

"That's good," Dean said. Then he pulled his own coat sleeve down and examined his laceration. "Me, too."

"What happened?" Sam asked.

"Cut it on some broken window glass."

He looked at Sam, but the USFW special agent gave no inclination he understood the Sheriff's inquisitive eyes.

"Sorry to hear it."

"Shit happens," the Sheriff said, shrugging.

They talked briefly. The Sheriff dropped his enquiry about the wrist cut, which reaffirmed Sam's sense of him. Though he didn't react to it, he recognized the look, thought it told him the Sheriff knew how Sam had cut himself. And why wouldn't Sam be interested in visiting the old house? If all he took, far as the Sheriff knew, were some preserves, no harm, no foul. The Sheriff, Sam thought, was reasonable, friendly, professional. He hadn't seen or felt anything to change his mind. Jeff Dunlap said he was an excellent lawman. Diane agreed. And he was no friend of Bill Grebs. That was four votes in the man's favor.

Sam finally reached down beside him and pulled up a brown legal folder with expandable sections and an overhanging flap. He reached into the folder and pulled out the CD. He set it on the table and slid it over to Dean.

"What's this?" This time it was his turn to play dumb.

"I told you I was out at the farmhouse?"

Dean nodded.

"When I mentioned it before I left out the part about finding the old man's spare key and going into the house. And I lied about not finding anything. I just didn't know what it was."

The Sheriff glanced at Diane. She held his eyes long enough to tell him they both knew.

"The old man had a special place," Sam explained. "A recess in his study floor. Nobody knew about it. When I was a kid it had mostly old coins. I wanted to see if he still used it. The coins were gone, but we found something we thought we might pass along to you." The Sheriff hadn't lost his matter-of-fact demeanor, but Sam could sense his concern.

"Ordinarily I wouldn't have touched a thing," Sam added. "Not coins, anyway. There's nothing of the old man's I need or want. I cut those strings a long time ago. I don't need any reminders of him."

"So what is it?" the Sheriff asked, just to be certain.

"A video."

The Sheriff looked away. His index finger started tapping the table. Finally he reached over and picked up the disk. He turned it over, but there were no markings on it. "And I'm in it?"

"Yeah," Sam affirmed.

"I see," he said, and looked away again. Truth was, Sheriff Dean Goddard felt entirely different than he thought he would, now that others knew his secret.

"I wasn't sure if you could tell who was on it. I mean," he paused, "the woman."

"Can't really tell," Diane offered, blushing a little, "except by the clothes hanging over a chair."

The Sheriff sat back, thinking. He wasn't sure where to go with it, but the truth was he felt a lot better about one thing; knowing he no longer had to keep entirely silent about something that was slowly eating at his core. It was odd. He felt embarrassed, like a boy caught in a lie. And he didn't know if he even needed to say anything about what Williston Winthrop wanted, though he would. Because Dean Goddard had told Williston Winthrop almost nothing. But for a lawman that prided himself on his stellar record, the affair and the resulting compromise, small as it was, burned in his consciousness like a scarlet letter.

First he turned to Diane. "You know Belinda," he said.

"Not really, but," Diane paused, "I heard there was some struggle."

"First alcohol, after she lost the baby and found out there wouldn't be another opportunity. Then this church," he said, feeling more comfortable than he'd imagined, telling it. "I'm not making excuses. There's no excuse for what I've done. But you marry one person and one day you wake up to find an entirely different person. And by then you have separate bedrooms and talk maybe once or twice a week." He paused, looking away. "And then you meet someone. Someone who helps you remember what it is you thought you could live without."

"Sheriff, we're not here to judge you. What you do with your personal life is your own business," Sam said. "What I really want to know is why the old man had that disk in his file?"

That's it, then, Dean Goddard thought. He wasn't surprised. Sam Rivers didn't give a rat's ass about his moral struggles, probably wouldn't have cared less if the affair had come to light in some other public way. It was the location of the evidence. The Sheriff understood Sam Rivers's perspective, because it would have been his own.

"Your old man," he began, slowly, shaking his head. "Williston Winthrop was a crook and we all knew it. At least Jeff Dunlap and I knew it. Jeff turned him in once before on an ethics violation, but the St. Paul Ethics Board just slapped his goddamn wrist. Williston knew people. Jeff didn't like him and didn't trust him and he thought he was up to no good." The Sheriff looked away, thought for a minute. Then continued. "And then Susan . . . Dr. Wallace got a call from an assisted living facility out of Eveleth. Gertie Wendell needed some treatment. Normally it was handled by a physician out of Eveleth, but he was in South America. The place was nice enough, but Gertie was its only patient, and it was small, and something about it didn't seem right. Susan told me about it and I shared it with Jeff. I went over to have a look, but it was legitimate. Just to be sure Jeff started looking into it."

"Pine Grove Estates?" Sam asked.

Dean looked at him. He glanced at the folder in front of him, thick enough to contain plenty of information. Probably the whole file on Pine Grove. "That's right," Dean said. "It took Jeff Dunlap six months to get to the bottom of it. And by the time he did, guess what he found?"

"The old man," Sam said.

"That's right. Williston Winthrop was behind everything. He'd been bilking spinsters out of their fortunes for more than a decade."

Sam only nodded, still waiting for the reason Williston had the disk.

"Couple Sundays back Williston Winthrop called me over to his office. That afternoon he showed me the video. He told me all he wanted to know was what a person could find out overhearing a conversation in Opel's Café. He wanted to know what Jeff Dunlap knew."

"About Pine Grove?" Sam asked.

"Yeah, though he didn't mention it by name."

"So you told him?"

"Nope. I almost reached across the desk and throttled him. I was too angry to talk. If I'd had a match and some gas I would have set the place on fire. Burned down the Winthrop building with Williston in it."

"Maybe someone beat you to it?" Sam asked.

"Maybe. And I wondered. God knows your father had plenty of enemies. But Walt Gibbons says it was an electrical fire."

It was damn convenient, Sam thought.

"I didn't set it, but I was happy to see it burn," Dean said.

"That much coincidence is hard to let go."

Dean shrugged. "But you can imagine how fortunate I felt, at the time. I was hoping that was the end of it."

"So did you tell him anything?"

"He threatened to give copies of the disk to Diane, and the bishop of my wife's church. Maybe pass some others around." It was an excuse, but it sounded as lame to the Sheriff as it had every time he'd repeated it to himself. "Here's the deal," he said. "I called Williston that night. Called him from a friend's cabin. I gave him five names, including Miriam Samuelson and Iron County Care."

Those were names in the folder. Iron County Care was one of the umbrella corporations of Pine Grove Estates. It would have been enough.

"Then you told him what he needed to know."

"Williston was a crook, a thief, and a son of a bitch. But he was smart. I told him enough so he knew Jeff Dunlap was onto him."

The Sheriff knew his career in law enforcement was over. He was already trying to think how he could break the news to his friend, Jeff Dunlap. He wondered how far Jeff would pursue the prosecution. Probably hand it over to someone else in the office. Dean Goddard felt relieved, ready to face it. He was glad Belinda had the church; she'd need it.

"That's it?" Sam asked.

"It's enough."

Sam nodded. Then looked away.

"Who knows?" the Sheriff wondered.

"Me and Diane," Sam said.

Dean Goddard looked away.

"Sheriff, from what Diane tells me and what I know of your situation and your perspective about law enforcement I'm a little surprised. But that's not to say I wouldn't have done the same thing, given a similar situation. Far as I know this is the only record of it," he said, glancing down at the disk. "And from our perspectives," he looked at Diane, "this conversation is as far as it goes."

"I divulged information that compromised an investigation by the county attorney's office."

"You did. And you committed adultery, if you want to put a fine point on it. But the old man is dead and as far as I can tell there's not a goddamn thing to be gained by releasing what he had on you. The old man was a son of a bitch and you weren't the first or only person he tried to swindle or ruin."

The Sheriff stared at him. Then he looked at Diane.

"I agree," she said.

"What about the *Gazette*? What about a story?"

Diane looked away. "I have to admit it's one of the juicier stories to come my way. But if I shared it with anyone Williston Winthrop would smile from his grave. And I couldn't abide by that." She paused. "The paper's not gonna find out about it from me."

"Or me," Sam affirmed.

Dean Goddard paused and looked away. "Then that's it?" he asked, turning back to both of them.

"This is dead," Sam affirmed. "It's not the kind of news that helps anyone with anything."

For the first time the Sheriff looked a little wistful. "What I've got to do is set things right with my wife," he said. "Belinda and I don't belong married anymore, regardless how the public will take it."

"She deserves to know," Diane agreed.

"This is the twenty-first century," Sam offered. "About as many people get divorced as stay married."

"You don't know the Range," the Sheriff offered. "But there's no other way."

"That's right, Sheriff," Diane said. "I may not agree with your wife's religious perspective, but she needs to know."

"Yes," Dean said, resigned.

"There *is* something you could help me with," Sam added.

"Name it."

"I think this folder contains everything Jeff Dunlap needs to prosecute his case against the old man."

"That'd be good."

Sam picked up the folder. "But in order for the records to be admissible, it's probably best they come from the investigating officer." He slid the folder over to Dean.

Dean reached over and picked it up. "I'll drop it off with Jeff after I get back from the farm."

Sam told him where to find the secret floor cubby. The Sheriff could check it out and tell Jeff Dunlap about its location.

After Sam and Diane left the Café they went into town. They parked along the street, walking the sidewalk to the grocery. They passed Bill Grebs's truck and Sam peered into the cab. In the narrow back seat he saw two sacks and five bottles. Judging from the looks of it the Defiance town cop had just broken Minnesota's liquor laws. He paused to be sure. There were three bottles in a far sack and up close, two dark blue boxes— Crown Royal. "The good stuff," the old man was fond of saying.

They kept walking down the block. When they crossed in front of Webster's Tobacco they caught a glimpse of Bill Grebs. He was turned away from them. In front of him, on the countertop, rested a carton of Old Golds, and three boxes of Cohibas.

Sam didn't want to run into Grebs, at least not until the cemetery, later today. He'd say hello to the officer over the old man's grave.

They were well down the street when Sam remembered the Cohibas. They were the old man's smokes. Williston had always liked the Cuban knock-offs. Especially with a glass of Canadian whiskey.

CHAPTER THIRTY-ONE

FEBRUARY 1ST, AFTERNOON—WILLISTON WINTHROP'S BURIAL

On their return to Diane's cabin, Sam's cell phone went off. He pulled it out and glanced at the display. Kay Magdalen.

He flipped open his phone. "Kay?"

"Yeah. Me again. This is getting to be a bad habit."

"What?"

"Working on the weekends, making business calls. I need a life."

"Clarence must be an understanding guy."

She ignored the comment. "McCollum didn't have your cell phone number. And now he's off. Want to know what he found out?"

"What?"

"They're hybrids. All but one. An Arctic wolf."

Sam's jeep veered a little. "No shit?"

"Do I stutter?"

He paused, trying to absorb what that meant. "That's interesting."

"I thought so. The hybrids were part Arctic, part Malamute."

"A breeder," Sam said.

"Probably."

"Someone's breeding Arctics?"

"An Arctic," she said, reminding him there was only one.

Sam knew they'd been big. Where in the hell did they find an Arctic wolf? In the Lower 48 it was an uncommon subspecies. But in Alaska and northern Canada they were abundant and, in many jurisdictions, fair game. Anyone could have obtained one and bred it.

"No Arctic wolf could get into the Lower 48 without a customs declaration," Sam remembered.

"If they brought it in legally."

"Breeding hybrids is legal in Minnesota. The state doesn't even maintain a registry for hybrid breeders. But there would have to be something in customs, at least a destination address."

"If they brought it in legally," Kay repeated.

"Can you have someone in audit check the declarations? Say, over the last five years?"

"It's Saturday, Rivers. I can check on Monday."

"Call Gibson. Call him at home. He owes me a favor. And this is important."

There was a long pause.

"Could you? Please." A plea from Sam Rivers came off stilted.

"Rivers, when was the last time I called anyone about work on a weekend?"

"Friday night counts as the start of the weekend."

"Before that."

She was irritated.

"It will put you in my good graces." That was going to piss her off.

"Maybe I should call Salazar. He's kind of anxious to please, these days."

Sam figured he deserved that. He let the comment pass.

"Call Gibson. I'd call him but I don't have the directory. He owes me. Gibson'll do it right away. And if I know him he's home in front of ESPN, nursing a beer."

"I'll call him," she finally said, short. "I'll give him your cell and you can talk with him."

"Thanks, Kay."

"You made any decisions?"

"Monday," he said. "Tuesday, latest. We'll talk then."

"Hybrids?" Diane asked, after he'd hung up. She'd heard that much and was curious.

"The animals in the barn. They were half Malamute, half Arctic wolf. Except for one full Arctic wolf."

"What's that mean? Were they wild?"

"Probably bred."

"So someone raised them?"

"There's a good market for wolf-dog hybrids, mostly by people who think the animal will make a kick-ass pet. But hybrids aren't like regular dogs. And they're not the greatest pets."

"People want to buy them?"

"Some people do. People who usually don't know any better. And unscrupulous breeders will give them what they want. As long as they get paid."

By the time they reached Diane's, the afternoon was squeezing out of the day. He had an hour until the funeral. They rested on Diane's couch.

"Do you think a lot of people will attend the funeral?" Diane asked.

"Probably not. The Club," Sam answered. "The old man wasn't popular. He had enemies, not friends. He had clients, but from what I've heard his rates were about as high as you can legally charge. Whatever legal judgments he won for clients, much of it was taken up in attorney's fees and expenses. Even his winning clients were disappointed, according to Jeff Dunlap."

"I didn't really know him. I saw him around town, but not often. Miriam shared plenty that was," she paused, "pretty awful. What makes someone into a man like Williston Winthrop?"

"Greed," Sam answered. He thought for a minute and added, "I think the seven deadly sins sum it up pretty well. And being raised with the belief that you own the wild and everything in it, that it is part of your rightful claim and heritage, and in the case of Winthrops, duty. "

"But why?"

"I don't remember much about my grandfather. I know he killed more wolves than any other man on the Range. He was an über-hunter. An alpha, just like the old man. They both reveled in exacting Winthrop family revenge. At least until passage of the Endangered Species Act."

"What about you? Why didn't you grow up wanting to 'exact Winthrop family revenge'?"

Sam thought about it. He'd spent plenty of time wondering why he hadn't become more like the old man. But unlike his grandfather or Williston he'd never felt the need to conquer the wild, to own it. Wild places were his sanctuary, though he had no illusions about wilderness and the animals inhabiting it.

He guessed the old man had Sam figured out. He had 'his mother in his blood.'

"Miriam Samuelson," Sam finally said, remembering how much his mother enjoyed a clear glass lake at sunset with loons crooning in the distance.

"She was a wonderful woman."

They were quiet for a while, sitting together on the couch, remembering Sam's mother, their thoughts drifting. And then Diane closed

the space between them and kissed Sam's cheek, which caused him to
recollect her swollen lips and the previous night.

"You're a sweet man, Sam Rivers."

Diane started to pick up their coffee cups from the morning. Sam
Rivers grabbed her back pocket and pulled her down. She was startled,
but her eyes reflected his own sudden interest. They came together quickly, hurriedly. It took only moments for the breathing to pick up, their
pulses hammering. Sam slid his hand inside her sweatshirt, cupped her
right breast, found the top of her bra and pulled it down when suddenly
the phone rang.

Saved by the goddamn bell, he thought.

"Could be Goddard."

She looked at him, her dark eyes narrow, focused and glazed. Her
eyes confirmed it; 'screw the phone.'

But it rang again.

"And I've got to go. But I'll be back."

Diane got up to answer. It was Steve Svegman, looking for Sam.

"They got away," Svegman said. He sounded irritated.

"What?" Sam Rivers was looking forward to examining those hybrids.

"Angus was there and he wasn't happy. He wanted to know who in
the hell trespassed?"

"The Sheriff with you?"

"He came later. Told Angus he'd been there last night, just to checkup on the place."

"What happened to the animals?"

"We could see their tracks come down out of the woods. But we
could also see them return, from around back."

"Around back of the barn?"

"Yeah. A grain chute door. Must have been unlatched. When they ate
their fill they took off."

"Shit," Sam said. He remembered the chute. Also remembered they
hadn't checked it.

"Yeah," Svegman said. "I was out there for almost three hours. The
Sheriff and I helped Moon clean up what was left. Not a pleasant task."

"You didn't want to leave it? Those animals might return."

"Angus wanted it cleaned up. Said the animals were too damn smart, missing his traps like they did. Said he couldn't abide the mess for another night."

"At least it was frozen," Sam said.

"It stunk."

Sam knew it did. "One thing about those animals. They're not wolves. Not exactly."

"What are they?"

Sam Rivers explained about the results from Ashland Forensics.

"What's it mean?"

"I suspect they were bred. But until I have more information we'd better keep it to ourselves. For now, anyway."

"Sheriff know?"

"I just found out myself. I'll call him."

He thanked the conservation officer and hung up.

Diane had taken their coffee cups to the kitchen. When she returned the smolder was out of her eyes.

"I don't have to go just yet."

"We need some time," she said.

"Yes," he finally said. "Later."

He reached up and gave her long thick hair a playful tug. Then he left, while he still had the will.

In his jeep, on the way over, his cell phone went off. It was a 303 number. Gibson. He flipped it open.

"Rivers."

"Sam?"

"Gibbs. What are you watching?"

"Nothing, now. I *was* watching Tiger Woods make a late round charge on day three of the U.S. Open. Then I got a call from Kay Magdalen. It's Saturday, isn't it?"

"She's giving me a hand."

"I guess that means *I'm* giving you a hand."

"It's my lucky day."

"It is your lucky day. Because I found it on the first search."

"What?"

"I could only find one Arctic wolf delivered to Northern Minnesota, to Snow Bank kennels, four years ago. Came in from Manitoba."

"Got an address?"

"That's all I got. The customs declaration and license were all legit. It's a rural route. But I can't read the signature. Got a pen?"

Sam pulled to the highway's icy shoulder and rummaged through his console. He found a black felt-tipped pen and a square of white post-it notes. He took down the address: Snow Bank Kennels, Rural Route 8, Defiance, MN 55054. He also jotted down the license number.

"What in the hell you doing in Northern Minnesota on February 1? Cold enough for you?"

"About 20 below."

"It's Minnesota. What did you expect?"

"Did I ever tell you I was born and raised here?"

"Never. But it figures. Know what Kay Magdalen told me?"

"What?"

"She told me to tell you, 'Don't be an idiot. Take the job.'"

"Glad to know she's minding my privacy rights."

"You're the right guy for the job, Sam."

Gibson knew his situation. He knew he'd taken a job with local investigations to try and save his marriage. He also knew the divorce was final and the marriage over. If Gibbs knew, everyone knew. Including Salazar. And Maggie. "I'll take it under advisement." But it wouldn't really affect his decision.

"Consider us even. And no more Saturday calls."

"Not today," Sam said. "I promise."

Before pulling back onto the road he called the Sheriff.

"Sheriff Goddard."

"Sheriff. Sam Rivers."

"Did you hear how we spent our afternoon?"

"I heard. Thanks for covering for me."

"The least I could do."

Sam explained about Ashland's finding and the hybrids. The Sheriff wondered if they could be wild and Sam told him it was unlikely.

"What's it mean?"

"I don't know. But while we're thinking about it can you look up an address?"

Sam gave him the Snow Bank Kennels address.

"I don't have to look it up. Took it down this afternoon. That's Angus Moon's address. He gave it to Svegman when he filled out those reimbursement forms. Everything but the Snow Bank Kennels."

It was like a lost puzzle piece suddenly found. "Sheriff," he said. "I think we need to pay Angus Moon a visit."

"Exactly what I was thinking."

Sam told him where he was headed.

"Don't say anything to Angus Moon. After it's over, meet me at the office. We'll give Angus Moon time to get home, and then pay him a visit together."

The remainder of his trip to the cemetery gave him a little time to contemplate current events. Ever since he'd found out about the old man's death he'd looked forward to the burial. He wanted to greet all of them, what was left of the old man's Club, the remnants of Williston's avarice and greed. He wanted to look them in the eye, unable to do so when he was a child. But since his arrival, events had taken on a life of their own. For starters, he was no closer to the identity of canislupustruth@yahoo.com than he had been back in Yellow Rock. It could have been anyone. And he was no clearer about the reason for the messages. If he was being summoned, who had done it, and for what purpose?

He looked forward to watching the four members stand beside the grave. He suspected they'd be surprised, though by now they all knew he'd returned. They'd object, of course, but they would keep their objections to themselves. Because there wasn't a goddamn thing they could do about it.

As he covered the distance Sam became preoccupied by more than the identity of canislupustruth and his emails. Or *her* emails, if it was a woman. He had questions. The old man knew he was being investigated. And if the Sheriff and Jeff Dunlap were correct, the investigation into Pine Grove Estates could put the man away for the rest of his life. Did that prompt Williston Winthrop, a man as tough as boot leather, or Italian leather, given his expensive tastes, to kill himself? The idea was unimaginable, Sam knew.

And hybrids had entered the barn. If Angus owned the hybrids did they stage the kill? Was the Club just trying to get rid of the calves because they didn't want to care for them? Then get the state to pay for it? It would be like Bill Grebs and Angus Moon, he guessed. And probably Young and Gunderson, too. In one well-planned moment they could rid themselves of the need to care for the calves and ship and sell them. And news of the kill would be proof wolves were getting out of hand. The ranchers' outrage over this kill would be heard much further than St. Paul. Every rancher in the nation would be pointing to it as evidence wolves needed to be contained and killed. And definitely taken off the Endangered Species List. Except the Club hadn't anticipated Sam Rivers's return or his particular expertise. It seemed unthinkable they'd risk staging the kill, but Sam didn't believe the animals had busted loose, made their way six miles through woods to Winthrop's farm, entered the barn and went on a rampage.

There were plenty of questions. He was looking forward to posing a few to Angus Moon, after the burial, out at Moon's place.

The drive was helped. He had time think, to mull, and to let recent events percolate through the cold.

On the way through town he passed the gutted Winthrop building. It was a frozen black hulk. It was an eerie presence in the middle of town. Like a charred skeleton, Sam thought.

As he thought, other questions arose, but the answers seemed to swim at the periphery of his awareness.

He approached the outskirts of Defiance. There was a turnoff for the cemetery. He could see through the gate to the maintenance shed near the front opening. There was a man leaning over the blade end of a backhoe, chipping away frozen clods. Sam glanced at him. Beneath the dangling Nordic earflaps he recognized Ben Saunders, a kid he knew in school. He'd been a heavy drinker. As Sam passed, Ben kept his attention on the backhoe.

The main cemetery road was a long drive bisecting two graveyard knolls. At the base of the knoll a few vehicles were already parked: a police car, Hank Gunderson's blue pickup, Angus Moon's junker, a Honda CR-V and a nondescript Chrysler. Sam assumed the CR-V was Hal Young's. Sam guessed the Chrysler was a clergy car, owned by whomever the Club had paid to say a few words over the grave. Sam pulled up and parked behind the CR-V. He checked his watch and saw it was a quarter to 4:00. The service must have been brief, shorter than expected. That made sense. And Sam preferred it this way, making his entrance with the rest of the Club standing over the grave.

Atop one knoll Williston Winthrop's grave was still open. Behind it the wilderness bush was an impenetrable weave. The other knoll was opened to an arctic wind that had started to come on when the sun was still off the horizon. It was a fitting backdrop for the old man's burial.

A plowed path wound through the tombstones that knifed above the snow. At the top of the hill the five figures gathered around his father's grave. Approaching the site he couldn't see a casket. Everyone stood around the open grave. Even the hearse had departed.

The old man's already in the ground. But not covered. Not yet.

The western horizon was fiery red. The wind whipped out of the northwest and in spite of a promontory planted to cut off the breeze, the icy gusts blew small drifts of snow over the frozen crusted surface, like sand over desert dunes.

At the top of the hill the figures bent and tightened against the cold. They looked up to watch Clayton Winthrop make his way there.

When Sam reached the top he came to stand beside them. The old man's simple wooden casket lay in the bottom of an eight-by-four-by-five-foot rectangular hole. The earth had been chiseled out of the ground. Even burying the son of a bitch was difficult, Sam thought. As it should be.

Grebs, Angus and Gunderson stared at him. Young looked at him and jerked away, as if the winter had blown something into his face, forcing him to squint and turn aside. Then Gunderson focused his attention toward the grave. The pastor nodded to Sam, a question in his eyes.

Grebs and Angus didn't turn away. They stood with fixed gazes. Sam held them, then stepped within earshot of the pastor and said, "I'm his son."

The pastor's eyes squinted his acknowledgment. "Would you like to say anything?" the pastor wondered, thinking it was odd Sam hadn't attended the service, which had been brief and at which no one spoke.

Sam shook his head no.

Then the pastor started speaking. Sam couldn't hear everything, but it was bits and pieces of words spoken by a pastor who clearly didn't know the old man.

"Good man . . . God-fearing . . . Kingdom of Heaven . . . Hell . . .," The wind tore the words out of his mouth. Sam guessed it was the preacher's standard homily, spoken over a man, who as far as Sam knew, had never seen the inside of a church.

Finally, the pastor hurried through the Lord's Prayer and it was over. He bent to the frozen pile of dirt, starting to pick up a mitten full of earth when Sam interrupted.

It was all moving too fast. Sam didn't know what he'd expected, but he was finally at the edge of the old man's grave, and within minutes the ceremony, the ritual, such as it was, would come to a close. It was the cold whipping across the cemetery rise. It was seeing them all here. He wanted to walk over to Angus and tell him he knew about his hybrids. Somehow he felt cheated.

The others watched Clayton Winthrop move to the head of the grave. The frozen clods dropped from the pastor's hand.

Then Sam scraped up a pile of frozen earth and held it, thinking over the casket. He wished the old man was alive. Sam wished he had returned while the old man was among them, and given the son of a bitch a taste of the anger he'd known as a boy. But it would have been hollow. It would have made no goddamn difference to Williston Winthrop. He would have laughed at the gesture.

Sam let go the earth and clods fell across the top of the casket like rattling clumps of ice. "May you sleep more contented in death than you ever were in life," Sam whispered. He tried to summon some small vestige of hope for the old man's soul. He tried to summon something like forgiveness, but he couldn't forget everything the old man had done to him. He felt sorry for the bitterness of the old man's life. That much he'd worked out. People wanted forgiveness. People believed you needed to forgive in order to move on. Forgive and forget. But could a person really forget that kind of pain?

Sam knew he'd moved on. He'd made a life for himself. His life. And though it hadn't turned out exactly the way he'd wanted, it was his, just the way it was.

About all he could summon for the old man was the faintest particle of pity. And not a whole lot of that.

The others watched Sam's lips move but could not hear him.

Then a powerful blast of icy air broke them up like bowling pins.

Young was the first to peel off and go. He struck down the path, hunched against the wind. Gunderson followed him, bent and angled toward his truck. Both of them left without a glance in Sam's direction. The pastor turned to leave and then Angus Moon shot an angry glance at Sam, turned and started down the path. Grebs was the only one who decided to have a word. In spite of the cold he stepped a few paces to where Sam was standing at the head of the grave.

"Clayton," he said, nodding. "Heard you was in town."

"It's Sam. Sam Rivers."

"Yeah," Grebs said, looking away. "I heard something like that." Another icy blast brought his breath up short. Then, "I know there was no love lost between you and Williston."

Sam remained quiet, holding the law man's squint.

"Tell you the truth, I'm a little surprised to see you."

"Say what you will about the old man, he was still my father."

"When was the last time you saw him?"

"It's been twenty years."

"You be stayin' on long?"

"Haven't decided." Sam wondered if Grebs knew why he had left. If he had, Sam knew, Grebs would probably use it to pressure him to move on. But Grebs only stared at Sam *as if* he knew, which Sam remembered was one of his interrogation tactics; feigned knowledge of some kind of transgression until the person grew uneasy and confessed.

"We had a little trouble over at your Mom's place," he said, staring at Sam.

"Trouble?"

"Someone broke in the other night. Probably the night of that big storm."

The night Grebs was up to some bedlam of his own, Sam thought, remembering the conversation he'd overheard hunkered down in the roadside ditch. It was an age ago. "From what I remember Mom didn't have much worth stealing."

"That's the peculiar part," Grebs said. "Just took some of her preserves, far as I can tell." He was peering at Sam, trying to figure him.

"She put up some mean preserves. Whoever did it had taste, I'll say that for them."

"Do you remember where you were that night?"

"On my way here," Sam said. "I came in the day after the storm. Come to think of it I stopped for gas in Brainerd early that morning, if you need someone to vouch for me. What were you up to that night?"

A shadow passed over the policeman's face. He looked away. Then he recovered, turned and grinned. "Any business in town?"

"Yup," Sam said. "But it's private." The town cop was starting to annoy him.

"No reason to get your hair up, son. I still have some responsibilities here. People still pay me to know other people's business."

"But I'm not one of them."

"It's the jurisdiction. Doesn't matter if you live here or not. If you come into Defiance, I worry about you."

"What are you worried about?"

Grebs paused. "That some people don't forget the past. Don't let it go."

Sam didn't smile. He kept his pulse even. "Some things are hard to let go."

Grebs sighed and looked away. "I suppose," he said. "No harm in remembering, as long as it doesn't lead anywhere."

"Not sure where it'll lead. Still trying to figure it out." Grebs didn't like that answer, which was just fine with Sam Rivers.

The town cop looked at him and managed another steely grin. "Godspeed, then," he said, and turned and started down the hill. After taking a few steps he looked back and said, "any problems me looking into the back boot of that jeep?"

Sam returned the look, unsmiling but calm. "Got a warrant?"

Grebs's eyes narrowed. "Don't stretch your welcome, Clayton," he said, then turned and kept walking down the narrow path through the graves. On the way down he stopped and peered into Sam's jeep.

No law against that, Sam thought. At the bottom of the hill Bill Grebs was the last to get into his car.

After everyone left, Sam turned and followed the icy trail to his jeep. When he was finally inside, he turned the key and the engine ground once, then gave out a small wheeze and stopped. He pumped the gas and tried a second time and the engine turned over, like an insolent child not wanting to wake up. He thought he'd better wait a minute, let it warm up.

He looked down at the gravedigger's truck. Ben Saunders had gotten into his cab to warm himself. Now that he was warm, Sam guessed he would finish the job. Then he watched Ben step out of his truck. The man paused with his door still open. He looked up at the grave, as if in consideration, and then cast a glance toward Sam's jeep.

Sam watched him through the frosted windshield.

There were so many things that were still unclear.

The mystery of canislupustruth.

The old man's accident.

People age, Sam knew. They age and change. And Williston had been 62.

His jeep's heater was blaring and the inside of the cab was starting to warm. He pulled off his mittens, reached over and picked up the post-it pad and the black felt-tipped pen. He searched through his center console for another pen. He didn't like felt tips. He was left-handed. When his hand moved left to right over his fresh writing, the ink from felt tips rubbed off on the heel of his hand, leaving a black smear. But there were no other pens.

He hadn't made a list since the night he'd buried Charlie. He could hardly remember it now. Though the pure memory of Charlie made him smile.

Canislupustruth, he wrote. Then underlined it.

The Iron County Gun Club, he wrote beneath it. Then he added (Bill Grebs, Hank Gunderson, Angus Moon, Hal Young).

Storm, he wrote. Hybrids, he added.

He glanced up. In the distance Sam watched Ben's hand reach into the cab and pull something out. The jeep's defroster was beginning to clear his windshield. Sam watched the man raise a pint bottle to his lips and drain its trace of amber liquid. There was only a swallow. The gravedigger's desultory toss of the bottle punctuated his thirst. He guessed Ben Saunders still had a problem.

Crown Royal, he thought, before he wrote it.

Then he pulled the post-it off the pad and placed it in the center of his steering wheel. There were more questions. He reconsidered the list.

He glanced up again and saw Ben look to the horizon, perhaps calculating the remaining daylight. The western edge of sky was starting to turn crimson. Then the gravedigger got into his truck, started it, turned around, and steered out of the cemetery.

Ben was returning to town to fetch a pint, something to help him through the labor of filling in the grave, Sam guessed. He watched the gravedigger's truck lights disappear around the cemetery road curve.

Sam stared at the tire tracks in front of him. He noticed Hal Young's CR-V tracks as they pulled away from the road's shoulder and blended with the rest of the road. Then Sam reached out with his pen and wrote Cohibas after Crown Royal. The old man's favorites. He examined the list.

He had seen those tire tracks before. He remembered the night of the storm, crossing Hal Young's place on his way up Beacon Street to break into his mother's house. Hal Young had been home that night, he remembered. He'd thought it was Hal Young's wife, but he remembered hearing Young's wife had died about a year ago. So it must have been Hal that night, returning to his office home. So who in the hell was out with Angus Moon, attending to the hybrids?

And then it occurred to him, like a jolt from a frayed wire. He reached into his coat pocket, dialed the Sheriff.

"Sheriff Goddard."

"Dean. Sam Rivers."

"You already finished?"

"Just about."

"Come on over."

"In a bit. Just one question. Did you get a copy of the Coroner's report?"

"Came in yesterday, I think." He could hear the Sheriff moving papers around his desk. "What about it?" he asked.

"Just out of curiosity, how was the old man identified?"

"I don't need the Coroner's report to tell you that. We all recognized him."

"How?"

"Well," Dean thought, trying to remember. "I'd seen him just a few days prior. He had his camo coveralls. Boots. Socks. The same damn outfit he was wearing the night of the accident. Even the back half of his orange hunting cap was there, what was left of it," Dean added. "And his wallet. And there was that cannon of a shotgun."

"That's it?"

"We all knew him," the Sheriff explained. "It only took a glance from all of us. Smith Garnes and Susan. That Club. It was Williston."

"So it was identification by physical appearance?"

"What other kind is there?"

"DNA. Fingerprints."

Dean chuckled. "This is Vermilion Falls, not Denver. If we know something for certain we don't spend extra dollars we don't have to verify what we already know. It was Williston."

"Yeah," Sam said, thoughtful about it. "Thanks. I'll be over in a bit," he added.

"See you when you get here," the Sheriff said, and rang off.

Sam placed the post-it pad and the black pen into his coat pocket. Then he pulled on his mittens, opened the car door and started running up the path toward the grave.

At the gravesite he glanced back to the cemetery gates. He was alone, and would be, for a few more minutes. Then he took one careful step from the frozen dirt edge, and dropped into the old man's grave.

He scrambled to the casket's side and wasted little time swinging open the lid. He wasn't prepared for the heavy mound of gauze covering the old man's head, making him look like some kind of space alien. He hadn't thought about the head being covered. He tried to focus on examining the rest of him.

He needed something from the old man. He tried to understand it, the massive lump lying in front of him, exposed to the winter cold. His body had changed, grown larger, Sam guessed because of age. But the Sheriff said he'd clearly recognized him. He peered at it.

The hands were folded over the lower chest. They were pale and large, similar to what he remembered about the old man, but something not quite right. Maybe it was puffiness from the way he died, Sam thought. Maybe it was over four days with the life gone out of them. It had been 20 years. Sam could see the old man's belly. There were several more inches to it, what could be expected, given 20 years of indulgence. The belly looked a lot like the rest of him. Puffy.

But these didn't look like the hands with which Sam had been painfully familiar.

He reached into his pocket, pulled out the pen, and levered it under the frozen hands, trying to lift them. They were stuck together, unyielding. He applied more pressure, and a thumb pried slowly into the air, pulled away from the other thumb, as though it was some kind of malleable metal.

The thumbs were thick and wide. They didn't look like the old man's hands. Could be. It had been a long time, Sam thought again. A lot changes in two decades. People get old, gain weight.

He bent down over the corpse and tried to pry up the hands, to have a better look. He pulled off his mittens. He needed the dexterity as long as he could maintain it in this cold. As soon as he touched the corpse's hands their clammy foreignness made him shudder. He held onto them, trying to pry them up. His own hands were biting with the cold. He lost his grip and the hands snapped back into their frozen position, centered over the old man's chest.

He reached down again, gripping the icy appendages as though they were stumps of frozen meat. He lifted with his back, putting his entire body into it. The hands rose begrudgingly from the chest. The left hand came away slowly, starting to rise from the body. He could feel its frigid meatiness raise a few inches and then hold there. It was like bending lead. He loosened his grip and the hand stayed in the air, poised as though it were starting to extend itself in permanent greeting.

Sam glanced up over the lip of the grave. He was still alone. Then he looked back at the hand.

With the same painful lifting he managed to hoist the right arm into the air. It hung aloft. Now both hands were lifting up to the sky. When Sam bent the right arm up, the corpse's shirt sleeve slid down the raised wrist. It was turned so Sam could barely see its white underside. He remembered the wrist. He recalled the ragged scar where the skin was now clear.

He examined it closely, to be sure. No scar. Then he reached down, took his felt tipped pen, and began scrolling its tip over the dead man's right thumb, then his left. He took the post-it pack and used it to press against one thumb, then the other. He examined the tablet. Two good clear prints. The Sheriff could run them for him. Sam didn't know who it was, but he didn't think it was Williston Winthrop.

And then he heard the far off drone of a truck, slowing before its turn from the highway through the cemetery gates.

Sam stood up. His own exposed hands were numbing. Christ, he thought, carefully putting the post-it notes in his coat's breast pocket, with the pen, struggling to get into his mittens. Then he slammed the lid and hurried out of the grave, glancing back long enough to make sure there was nothing amiss. He lurched down the hillside, his two partially covered hands frozen in the biting cold. They were beginning to ache, but he barely noticed, remembering the corpse's hands raised in a kind of greeting, a shy wave, a dead reckoning.

CHAPTER THIRTY-TWO

FEBRUARY 1ST, EVENING—VERMILION COUNTY SHERIFF'S OFFICE

The Sheriff let him in.

The drive from the cemetery had partially warmed Sam, but his hands were only just starting to thaw. Ever since touching the corpse he'd wanted to wash them.

He excused himself and walked across the hall to the restroom. He used plenty of soap and water. The warm water made his fists ache. He pulled a paper towel from the dispenser and looked up. His beard formed a dark shadow across his cheeks and down the front of his neck. His face appeared leaner than he'd seen it in awhile. But his eyes, he thought . . . He looked like a bum, but his eyes were filled with clear intensity.

"Don't get too comfortable," the Sheriff said when Sam came into his office.

Sam glanced over and nodded to Smith Garnes, working the night desk. Garnes nodded back.

"To tell you the truth, Sheriff, I'm not sure Angus Moon went back to his place." Sam had thought about it. He thought he had an idea where Moon might have gone. And the others.

"What makes you say that?"

"Just a hunch, really." He opened his coat, unzipped the small inside breast pocket and carefully extracted the two post-it notes with thumbprints.

"What's that?"

"I'm wondering if you can do me a favor?"

The Sheriff glanced down at the small squares of paper. He could see they were prints.

"What did you have in mind?"

"I'm wondering if we can run these two prints?"

He could feel Smith Garnes look up from his paperwork.

"Where in the hell did they come from?"

Sam paused. "I'd rather not say, just yet. I'm just wondering if we can run them. I think they're important."

Judging from the recognition in the Sheriff's eyes, Sam thought he suspected their origin.

"It'll take a while to get results," the Sheriff warned.

"Not from Ashland. Saturday nights they have a skeleton crew that's always working leftovers. You give them something live and they're on it like a pack of jackals."

"Just so I understand," the Sheriff said. "You want to copy these prints, fax them into Ashland and have those guys run them?"

"First I think we should try and enlarge them. Can your copier enlarge?"

The Sheriff knew it made sense, might work. "Smith," he said, glancing over to his deputy. "Fire up the copier." Dean Goddard picked up one of the post-its and considered it. "It'll take us a minute to copy and enlarge it. You have their fax?" he asked.

"I'll call them."

The mechanics of getting the prints ready for faxing took a little time. "Needs to warm up," Smith said, standing over the corner machine.

Sam used the couple minutes to phone Ashland and tell them what was coming. As he suspected, they appreciated the idea of working on something fresh. After the copier warmed up Sam placed one of the notes on the clean plate of glass. He used the copier's console to increase the size 100 percent. Then he pushed *copy* and the bright scan made three passes.

"It's slow, but has excellent resolution," Dean said.

And so it did. When the sheet came out it displayed a very clear print. Sam copied the other print, took the two sheets out of the copier, and walked over to the office fax. It, too, was a little old, took some time to warm up. The Ashland office was waiting for the prints. He fed in the pages and heard the fax dial, then the tone pickup, and twenty seconds later the verification page printed out.

They sat and waited. Sam told the Sheriff about seeing Bill Grebs buy liquor at Lindy's Tap.

"It happens," the Sheriff said, shaking his head. "Harder than hell to catch something like that. And I'm not sure it's the best use of our resources."

"I'm not filing a complaint. But he bought about five bottles, including the two bottles of Canadian whiskey, the old man's favorite."

The Sheriff wondered about it, but only shrugged.

"I think they were going to party tonight. Did I ever tell you, Sheriff, how that Club built a cabin in the middle of Skinwalker's Bog?"

"Skinwalker's Bog?" he asked, doubtfully. "Nobody goes into Skinwalker's."

"Think it's haunted?"

"Hardly. A mosquito-infested swamp, more like it. Takes twenty minutes to hike twenty feet. I suppose," Dean said, looking at Sam Rivers, "they first turn into weasels, so they get in through game trails?"

There was a snicker from Smith Garnes over at his desk.

"They figured out a couple entrances down off two logging roads that border the place," Sam said.

"So you think they're partying out there tonight?"

"I think so."

"And you know how to get there?"

"I don't. But I think Diane Talbott might."

"How in the hell would she know?"

"I told her about it the other night and she said she'd been down one of those roads, looking for some rare bog flowers. Not exactly flowers, but orchids."

"Orchids?" The Sheriff thought the story was getting more bizarre.

"There are some rare orchids out there, Chief," Smith Garnes chimed in.

"Don't tell me you're an orchid hunter, Smith?"

Smith looked thoughtful for a minute. "Not Skinwalker's. Like you said, it's too damn dense. But I'll go over to the SNA bog near Pine Mountain," he said. "Different times of the year."

"Imagine that," the Sheriff said.

"They're somethin' to see," Smith Garnes said, defending himself.

"They are," Sam agreed. "Beautiful, exotic plants. Right here in Minnesota."

"So Talbott found the cabin?"

"Not the cabin. Just quite a ways down the overgrown logging road she found a place where it looked like some cars had parked, more than a couple times. And beyond it, the other side of some bushes, there was the start of a narrow trail."

"And you think that's the trail to the Club's cabin?"

"One of them."

"Why in the hell would they go all the way out there when they could just drive to one of their houses?"

Before Sam could answer, the phone rang. The Sheriff picked up. "Sheriff Dean Goddard."

He was sitting at his desk, listening to the voice on the other end of the line. "Yessir," Goddard said. "He's right here." He glanced over at Sam.

Sam stood, ready to take the phone. But the Sheriff kept listening.

"Uh-huh," the Sheriff said. He looked across his desk for a clean sheet of paper. He found a pad and picked up a pen. His brow turned quizzical. "Uh-huh," the Sheriff said. "Just a minute." He tucked the phone under his chin, holding it against his shoulder. He readied himself for writing.

"James T. Beauregard," he said. "Biloxi?"

He wrote them on the notepad. Underlined them. He recognized the name. "You know, that's damn curious," he said.

Sam Rivers and Smith Garnes watched him. If that was the person in the grave Sam Rivers had never heard of him. They watched the Sheriff look across the papers on the desk. He shuffled through several, looking for the paper he'd jotted notes on just that morning. When he found it he read the paper and said into the phone, "I had a call about that guy just this morning."

The person on the other end said something. Dean thanked him, told him Sam Rivers appreciated his efforts, and hung up.

"Who?" Sam asked.

"James T. Beauregard. From Biloxi, Mississippi. He stole a car few years back, got him printed. Served some time. Not much. Want to tell me where you got these prints?"

"I think we need to speak with the Coroner." Sam was careful not to say her name, letting him know it was official.

When he shared the reason why, Dean Goddard said, "I was afraid you were going to say that." From the side desk, Smith Garnes took it in fast, knew what it meant.

Then the Sheriff made the call. "Susan," he said. "Can you come down here?"

By 9:00 p.m. Dr. Susan Wallace, Smith Garnes and Sam Rivers were assembled in Dean's office. Dr. Wallace verified there was nothing but circumstantial evidence that had confirmed the identification of Williston Winthrop. Because of its location, clothes, the victim's wallet, and other identifying characteristics, and because they all knew Williston Winthrop, and knew the body before them was clearly that man, the Coroner decided further identification—like a print or DNA analysis—was a waste of time and money. Now if they wanted to find out for certain, they'd have to exhume it.

The Sheriff's legal pad contained a brief description of James T. "Jimbo" Beauregard, one he'd jotted down from the morning's conversation with Clement. It bore similarities to Williston Winthrop, except for a prominent birthmark on the face. But he hadn't been that particular taking down more details. They'd have to call Clement. But when they tried they only received her voicemail. The Sheriff left his number and asked her to call him. So it sounded like Clement's brother was probably dead. Which meant Williston could still be alive. And they knew where they might find him.

The Sheriff liked Sam Rivers's idea of surprise, which is why he asked two more deputies and Steve Svegman to join him at his office. He told them all to bring their weapons and to dress for a hike through frozen woods. One of the deputies was out on patrol. The Sheriff radioed him and told him to come in.

Sam Rivers called Diane and brought her up on current events. He suggested she might want to come along, and the Sheriff didn't protest. This would be good press for Sheriff Dean Goddard and he knew he'd need all the good press he could get, soon enough.

Sam asked Diane to bring over the duffle with his gun and night hunting garb, absent the money. When Diane arrived she brought it into the Sheriff's office. Sam extracted the ten gauge pieces from the bag.

"Where in the hell did you get that?" the Sheriff asked, recognizing the gun.

"It was a present."

"That's the same gun that killed whoever the hell's in that grave."

"Just like it," Sam said. "This one was promised to me when I was a kid. Then the old man changed his mind, so I took it and hid it before I left."

Dean thought of Miriam Samuelson's place. "In your mother's house?"

"That's right."

The Sheriff smiled. "I remember Williston mentioning there was another one of those. That it had been stolen and he was going to get it back."

"Not stolen," Sam asserted. "Just hidden someplace safe and reclaimed." Sam took the gun stock in hand. The solid walnut was heavy and large. He affixed it to the barrel. He screwed down the other pieces and raised the shotgun to his shoulder, aiming down the blackened double barrel. He was surprised by its heft, less substantial than he remembered. He'd added a few years since he'd held the gun. It had been a lifetime. If Sam Rivers's childhood had trained him for anything, it was to hunt predators, whether in Skinwalker's Bog, the Jakarta pet market or the Florida Keys. Sam Rivers was made for this role. He'd have to tell Kay Magdalen.

He didn't know what they might walk into, but he knew he had to be armed when they did. Besides, there were wolves in those woods, and hybrids, at least one or more raised by Angus Moon, if he was right. He wasn't sure what they might do when confronted. In almost all known instances, normal wolves would turn at the sight of man and disappear into woods. But hybrids who had lived with men, who had endured a man like Angus and then ran wild, would be different. Sam couldn't imagine them turning and running. They might feel what he did and have a hunger to set things right. It wasn't revenge, exactly, just a sense of how things should be and the power to make things right.

He put on his camouflaged, insulated fatigues. When Diane came into the room, bundled up tight as a mummy, she looked at Sam and smiled.

"You look like special ops."

"Special Agent, USFW."

By the time Svegman arrived they were prepared for their expedition. It was going to be a ride and hike, the Sheriff informed them. Probably at least a couple miles. Dr. Susan Wallace would stay behind and provide radio support from the Sheriff's office, in case they needed help. They were headed into Skinwalker's Bog.

CHAPTER THIRTY-THREE

FEBRUARY 2ND, JUST AFTER MIDNIGHT—THE CABIN IN SKINWALKER'S BOG

The five men sat at the cabin table. The blistered pine lay covered with red, white and blue poker chips, cards, a couple of ashtrays and glasses. Bill Grebs's Old Gold cigarette sent a slender trail into the thick cabin air. In the other ashtray Williston had parked one of his Cohibas. Since the evening started he'd had one of the long cigars almost perpetually stuck into the corner of his smiling mouth.

After the burial, all of the Club members made their way to Skinwalker's Bog. They forged their own trails and had all arrived within an hour of each other, around dinnertime. And Williston had been ready. He'd fired thick fillets over the grill. He'd baked potatoes, cut a small hole in the center of three large Vidalia onions and filled them with Worcestershire sauce, topping them off with thick pads of butter. Then he wrapped them in foil and baked them with the potatoes. It had been a feast, washed down with plenty of libation. Now, just after midnight, the five men were practically giddy with good humor.

"I'll call you and raise you," Gunderson said, tossing his chips onto the considerable pile.

Winthrop, Grebs and Gunderson were the only three left playing the hand.

Williston loved the game. He turned to Hank and smiled. "I'll call ya'," he answered, adding the necessary chips to the centered mound.

They turned to Grebs. He was a careful player. But they'd been drinking long enough, and it was, after all, a celebration. As the Club members figured, they were all millionaires, give or take a few thousand. Before Svegman had left the farmhouse he told Angus he'd get the check to them on Monday. Angus figured he'd be sleeping in. He told Svegman to leave it in the farmhouse mailbox.

Grebs had two pair, sixes and sevens. He peered at the remaining players and smiled. What the hell? It was liberating to know money was no longer an issue. Not a real issue. Now they simply had to figure out how to spend it. And paying attention to whatever other opportunities came their way. "I'll call," he said, tossing in his chips.

Gunderson laid down his cards. He did it slowly, with flourish, one card at a time.

"A six," he said, setting it down. "And a three." He peered at the two men, smiling. The rest of the men knew Hank. This was his technique for showing three of a kind. And sure enough. He laid them all down at once, beaming. "Three aces," he said, like a schoolboy, poised to rake in the cash.

Grebs cursed and threw down his hand. Williston reached over and grabbed Gunderson's arm. "Wait a minute, goddamn it." The others stopped. You never knew about Williston. He looked Hank Gunderson in the eye and said, laying down his cards. "A flush."

Gunderson swore, but his curse was drowned out by a howl of laughter that would have awakened the phantoms in Skinwalker's Bog.

"I'm out of remedy," Williston finally chuckled, rising to fetch what was left of his Canadian whiskey, parked in a snowdrift outside the front door.

Nearly two hours earlier three cars approached the chained entrance to the overgrown logging road. Tire tracks confirmed the entryway to the boundary of Skinwalker's Bog. Diane remembered, then spotted the road as Sam's jeep passed in front of the chain.

"That's the place," she said.

Sam drove beyond it and pulled to the side of the road. A patrol car followed behind, then Steve Svegman's DNR vehicle. Sam got out to examine the entrance. The Sheriff opened his patrol car door and stood up in the cold.

Sam Rivers approached. "Looks like a couple of big vehicles, maybe a truck and an SUV, entered that logging road, judging from the tracks. Recently."

Dean leaned down into the nearby patrol car and said, "Smith, can you fetch those bolt cutters from the trunk and take that chain down?"

"No problem."

Diane wore a heavy down parka that hung above her knees. She had a pair of nylon ski pants over two sets of long underwear. Her breath clouded out of her ski mask.

The Sheriff turned and started walking toward the chain. "Can we drive into it?"

"Not with our patrol cars."

"We can climb into Svegman's DNR vehicle and my jeep," Sam suggested. "We should be able to make it."

"That'll work."

Smith's bolt cutters made an easy snap on one side of the chain. Then he dragged the cut end across the opening.

The group piled into the two vehicles. Then both vehicles turned carefully into the bush-covered lane, following the tire tracks. After a half hour they came up a small rise and saw the tracks turn off the old logging road to the left. Sam Rivers got out of his jeep and followed them another fifty yards until he came up behind Bill Grebs's pickup and Hal Young's CR-V.

The others cut their engines and waited for Sam's return. When he came out of the trees he raised one mittened hand and twirled it in a rapid circle. Car doors opened, quietly, and the group got out of their vehicles. After taking out their snowshoes the Sheriff closed the jeep door without a sound. Once his snowshoes were affixed he followed Sam up the trail. He came around the sides of both parked cars and pushed his way out in front. There was a small opening in the trees along the path where a shallow pool of moonlight fell down around him. He motioned for the others to approach and in a moment they all stood in the pool, listening.

From the other side of the woods they heard wolves, faint and far off but distinct.

"They're a few miles," Sam whispered. "Sounds like they're waking up."

"Probably going to hunt," Svegman whispered.

"Cold like this would make anything howl," the Sheriff added.

"The cold doesn't bother them," Sam said. "They're marking territory. These woods are theirs. Those calls are to let others know they shouldn't come near."

"Let's hope they make an exception for law enforcement," the Sheriff said.

"The only way we'd get in trouble is if we happened on a fresh kill while they were just starting to eat. Even then you could probably scare them off. Wolves don't like us much, seem to know we're trouble."

There was another chorus of howls from deep in Skinwalker's Bog.

"Problem is, you just never know about hybrids," Sam added. "Which is why it's a good thing we're all armed."

The Sheriff pointed to the tracks disappearing through a pair of black spruce boughs. "Looks like we have an easy enough path to follow."

"They may have blazed it for us," Sam said. "But if what I've heard about this place is true, I suspect it isn't easy."

"If Bill Grebs can walk it, so can we," the Sheriff observed.

Sam turned and snowshoed four paces before pushing into a wall of black spruce. The others fell in behind him in single file.

On occasion, the woods were so thick Sam had to switch on his flashlight. He covered over the front of the flashlight with his hand, muffling its brightness. When he was certain it was safe he shined the light on the ground behind him so the others could approach in safety. They made slow progress through the trees.

The evening wore on. They did not hear the wolves again. Sam knew that could mean anything.

The air was particularly cold, but Sam no longer noticed it. His camo coverings added a layer of insulation and his head, like the others', was covered with a ski mask. Tracking carefully along the trail was absorbing work. After more than an hour they came to a small rise that climbed upward a few feet. When they walked onto it, Sam could see the path continue at this level. The swamp thicket changed to old-growth woods. The trail was still very dark but partial moonlight filtered through the trees, enough to see where others had passed before him.

Sam turned off his light and walked in the faint glow. The others followed carefully through the trees.

They walked less than a hundred yards, winding through the island of woods, when Sam stopped. The others stopped behind him. Sam peered ahead. Through the trees, falling down on the path, he noticed a faint change in the intensity of the light. He motioned ahead to the others, but raised his finger to his lips. Then he went forward fifteen paces, rounded the corner of a large fir tree, and saw the lights of a cabin through the trees.

He carefully retraced his steps. He knew they'd been fortunate to come after a big snow, when the trail was easy to follow and covered with powder.

"It's around the corner," he whispered. The Sheriff nodded, turned around and passed the word down the line. They all stiffened at the news.

Sam turned and started forward along the trail. They all followed to the corner tree. Fifty yards ahead the cabin lights were barely visible. Sam moved forward another twenty yards, where the path bent through some Norway pines.

Now they were close enough to see through the windows. Not close enough to see details, but they could see occasional movement from within the cabin, what appeared to be figures sitting at a table. The windows were frosted over and the shapes were blurry.

The cabin looked large enough for a few rooms. One large front room and two or three rear bedrooms, Sam guessed. It was a typical cabin layout. He suspected there was a rear door that went back into the woods to an outhouse. Ideally one of them should work their way around the back through the woods and cover the rear. But it would be difficult to move through the heavy bush without a trail and not make noise.

It was important they maintain surprise. Everyone was armed. Sam wasn't worried the Club members would have time to move for their weapons, largely deer rifles, he guessed. Surprise gave them a formidable advantage. And he suspected by this hour their senses would be dulled by plenty of remedy.

Sam retreated to where Sheriff Goddard waited in the trees.

"I'll get around back. I suspect there's a back door and we should cover it before we move in."

The Sheriff agreed.

Sam snowshoed soundless through the crystalline glaze. He walked without raising his feet more than a couple inches above the powder. He could feel it shift beneath his boot, pack down under the pressure, then fill in behind him as he moved forward. In a long few minutes he'd cut the distance to the cabin in half. He was almost close enough to get a good look when he heard the Club members erupt. He'd heard it before. Poker. And unless he was mistaken someone had just won a big hand. Sam peered through the front window and saw someone pass in front of the opaque pane. It had been twenty years and he couldn't be certain, but it looked like the old man.

His heartbeat rocketed. He squinted through the frosted glass. He remained still, his snowshoes planted in the narrow path.

Behind him, the others watched Sam freeze.

With what appeared to be Williston so close to the front door and window, Sam knew moving might betray his position, so he waited and watched.

Then suddenly the front door opened and the old man stepped out and bent over to the right of the door. He leaned out far enough to fetch a bottle from a snowdrift, where the natural deep freeze was keeping the liquor cold.

The old man glanced to his right, found the bottle he was after, straightened up and saw Sam standing in the outer rim of cabin light, like an apparition.

For a moment the unexpected body scared hell out of him. And though Sam was covered head to heel in camo, carrying the big weapon in front of him, the old man focused on Sam's eyes. Then he glanced behind Sam, to where the others waited in the trees.

Then Sam watched recognition bloom across the old man's face like a bad fever flush. Williston quickly turned, closed the door, and slid a bold lock into place. There was a shout from inside the cabin, followed by chaos.

Goddard, Garnes and Svegman rushed forward. Sam turned onto the perimeter path and struggled to hurry around the cabin corner. Diane waited in the trees with the two remaining deputies, who were falling in behind the others.

Deputy Garnes and the Sheriff came to either side of the front door. Sam disappeared around the corner. Svegman joined Garnes to the side and Goddard yelled, "It's Sheriff Goddard! Open the door!"

The only thing Sam heard were his own movements rushing through the snow. Then when he turned the corner a loud bang made him duck. He realized the bang was a back door snapping shut, and he jumped forward along the pitch-black cabin wall. He fought his way through branches, sounding like a goddamn hippo breaking through the trees.

Back at the front door the Sheriff didn't wait long before the bolt lock slid open and Bill Grebs opened the door.

"Sheriff," Bill Grebs said, trying to act normal. "What in the hell are you doing in the middle of Skinwalker's Bog?"

In back of the cabin the well-worn path made a straight line fifty feet to an outhouse. To the right of the outhouse black spruce boughs wavered where someone had just whipped through them.

Sam ran down the path and hesitated in front of the structure. If Williston was armed, he'd use the gun. He peered around the corner of the house and noticed freshly broken snow disappear around the spreading spruce boughs. The old man was on the run.

Williston Winthrop knew these woods. He could be waiting fifty yards up ahead with the barrel of his rifle aimed at whoever had guts enough to follow. On the other hand, Sam reasoned, he'd probably seen they had force. Sam guessed it would keep him running. And Sam had come too far not to follow. He only hoped Williston Winthrop hadn't had time to pick up a weapon. He turned onto the old man's trail and began to follow.

Williston's face had been gray, unshaven, and he was heavier, his square shoulders gone round. He'd aged, but he was still formidable. And Sam thought he saw something he had never seen break across the old man's face: surprise, followed quickly by fear.

Sam moved forward slowly, following the old man's tracks through the snow. The length of the stride was long, but as he tracked, moving through the trees, the seconds growing into minutes; he watched the stride shorten, the steps contract. The cabin light quickly receded until he was surrounded by dark woods and silence. The tracks continued through the trees. The woods were thick but on occasion islands of larger pines rose into the dark sky.

Sam trailed for several more minutes. He paused, listening for the old man's footsteps, but heard nothing. He carried the 10 gauge and was ready to use it. He followed the broken trail through the snow, cautiously moving forward. The adrenalin left his senses keen and hyper aware. Concentrated fascination.

For over an hour he tracked. He wondered how long the old man could maintain it. He wondered where he was going. The old man couldn't have left with much. His tracks showed he was in boots, in places struggling through deep snow. Sam turned around a thick pine bough and came out into a thirty-foot opening in the trees.

And across the clear expanse of white waited Williston Winthrop. Sam could hear his labored breathing, watched it clouding in front of him as he tried to recover. He was winded, tired and waiting.

"Thought it was you," his father managed, a little wheezy. "Clayton," the old man added, as though speaking his name might soften the boy.

"Rivers. Sam Rivers."

The old man's breathing quieted enough to chuckle. The chuckle led to a brief coughing fit. After it passed he said, "Is it, now? And why the name change, son? Unhappy with your heritage?" There was familiar derision in the old man's voice. It reminded him of his childhood, of being Williston Winthrop's son. It blew the ash off a coal Sam could feel fester, turn scarlet.

"Just needed a change."

"Just a change," the old man wheezed. "Well isn't that sweet. Do you think a different name is going to do it? Still Miriam Samuelson's boy, I 'spect."

Sam considered raising the 10 gauge and firing. The idea was spontaneous, powerful, not easily resisted. Blow a hole in the old man's chest, vaporize his heart. At least what passed for one. His finger inched forward to the trigger guard.

"Take it easy, son," Williston said. "We're just having a family discussion here. Remember. I think you should give the old Decimator a rest, put it down."

Sam thought about it, about shooting him.

"Maybe you should just give me the gun, Clayton. Here I am out in these woods, unarmed. It's certain I won't be heading back to that cabin. Give a man a fighting chance."

When Sam didn't move, the old man made one step forward.

Sam raised the gun from his waist to point it dead center at the old man's chest. Then he pulled back the firing hammer. "This time it's loaded."

The 62-year-old peered at the narrow black holes, noticed their deadly trajectory. He stopped and raised his hands. "Hold on, son. I'm stepping back," he said, returning to his original position. "No sense in getting trigger happy. You've handled yourself well to this point."

"I'm about to come into a fair amount of money. That is, if I stay dead. Providing none of your other friends out there saw me. Right now the most that can happen is fraud over that wolf kill. But truth is, that would be hard to prove, without those wolves."

Williston was getting warmed up. Sam remembered the monologues, which could go on for hours.

"Just think about it, is all I'm asking," Williston continued, stepping again to his former position.

Sam's barrel rose a few more degrees, enough to remove the old man's head.

"OK, OK. I'm stepping back. Let's just talk about this. It's business, son. Business. You could share in this, if you played it smart. You could have half my share, which is considerable. I'll even let you keep that 179,000," he added.

So he knew about the money. "That was my mother's gift," Sam said. "Like the house."

"That was my money, son."

It was good to see the old man hadn't lost his love for the green.

"Never was. Never will be."

"I knew you'd come back. I knew she hid it somewhere. Why do you think I sent you all those messages? I don't know how you found out about my accident, but for two years I tried getting you back," Williston said. "And this is the treatment I get?"

Canislupustruth@yahoo.com. The old man sent him every email, tried to lure him back because he'd wanted his money, and guessed Sam Rivers might be able to recover it.

"That 179,000 I'm willing to let go," Williston said, even again, the calm returning to his voice. "Call it the first installment of plenty more where that came from," he said.

Twenty years was a long time, Sam thought. He'd struggled, found his way, made a place for himself, and begun to thrive, at least until Maggie. But even Maggie had been a move toward his heart, not away from it. In all that time Williston Winthrop had continued the natural course of being himself. And it was different now, standing in front of him, remembering the towering presence of his youth, the one who badgered, bullied and abused. Now the old man looked like an aging, tired crook, standing at the edge of a clearing in the middle of deep woods. And the wilderness he had so long dominated was taking its toll.

"You want this gun?"

Williston was surprised, nodded. "Well . . . Yeah. I mean, sure, son. I could set you up real nice . . . give you plenty, once everything comes in, gets settled."

Sam flipped open the shotgun's chambers. He pulled the shells from its double barrel. He gave them a good hard fling into the dark, where they disappeared into the cold.

There was a large granite stone at the edge of the swamp, directly behind him, its surface as smooth as a dinosaur's egg. Sam turned the shotgun around, picked up the barrel end of the Decimator, bent and put his arms into the swing, driving the gun's stock onto the rock hard surface. It was an axe blow. The Decimator's walnut stock splintered.

Behind him the old man gasped. "Wait."

Sam moved one step forward and swung again, slamming the trigger mechanism onto the stone, swinging in three clear, heavy hammer strikes before pausing long enough to bring the battered barrel up to examine it. The fragile metal trigger had broken and flown off into deep snow. The hollow mechanism was caved in and flattened. The Decimator would never fire again.

Then he flung what was left of the shotgun across the frozen swamp. It landed at the old man's feet.

He watched the old man step forward, like someone either on the edge of outburst, or nearly broken. Williston slowly retrieved what was left of the heirloom. He brushed off the barrel, looked across the swamp to his son.

Sam thought he might charge. The gun's destruction was the kind of violation that he once would have answered with some rage-filled destruction of his own. But maybe he finally understood his situation, the new situation with his son.

They were finished. Sam watched the man, who was still breathing hard. Part of Sam hoped he might charge.

Then Williston Winthrop turned and disappeared into the trees.

"Run," Sam said, in a tone he knew the departed Williston wouldn't hear. Not that it mattered now. The old man's tracks would be easy enough to follow, if he survived what was left of the dark and cold.

CHAPTER THIRTY-FOUR

FEBRUARY 2ND, EARLY MORNING—VERMILION FALLS

Back in Vermilion Falls, Grebs, Gunderson and Moon sat in three separate holding cells, each positioned so they could not hear or speak to one another. Hal Young had been moved to a small basement utility room, a single bare bulb hanging over his head. Large patches of paint peeled over the makeshift interrogation room's cement walls. The floor was the color of tarnished gray metal. In the spare light the insurance agent looked grim.

Sheriff Dean Goddard sat alone with him, talking matter-of-factly and without abatement.

"I know in time you're going to tell me what happened, Hal. We've known each other a long time. We already have the physical evidence of the alleged wolf kill. We can press that charge and it'll stick. It's the other matters you were involved with that should scare you, Hal. Murder isn't a hanging crime in this state. But people are put away for life. I suspect, Hal, you've never seen the inside of a state penitentiary." He said the word 'penitentiary' carefully, like a dull knife blade. It was having an effect.

"Prison is a nasty place," the Sheriff continued. "If I were you I'd do whatever I could to mitigate my sentence."

The Sheriff leaned over conspiratorially and softened his tone. "The plain and simple truth, Hal, is that I don't believe you were the ringleader of this little adventure. And I don't believe you were a wholly willing participant. I think the Club needed your insurance angle and you were pressured until you went along. Don't get me wrong. That's not a ticket to innocence. You'll have to pay. But if you cooperate you're likely to receive a lesser punishment than the other members of your Club." Sheriff Goddard had his attention. "We think they were using you. And I know you, Hal. I just don't see you surviving very long in a state penitentiary." The Sheriff's eyes were calm, concerned.

The Sheriff continued in this vein for a while longer. Hal Young's face remained ashen. Unless the Sheriff was a very bad judge of character, Hal Young would soon chatter like a songbird at dawn.

In the intense light of Rangers Café, Sam, Diane, Svegman and one of the deputies sat at a pre-dawn table drinking coffee and waiting for first light. Diane had her tablet out and was asking questions, trying to nail down the facts for the story she was still hoping to submit to the *Star Tribune* down in the Cities before the morning copy deadline. Dawn was still an hour away.

The group had long since worked through the details of what they knew. Sam told the others about his father. Everyone who heard the story had the same question: if Williston Winthrop was loose in Skinwalker's Bog, who was buried in his grave? The Sheriff told them about James T. Beauregard and Sam remembered the Defiance Hotel proprietor mentioning Grebs picking up the vagrant. It had a sickening way of adding up, much as none of them wanted to admit it.

At dawn they were going to pick up Williston Winthrop's trail. No one expected Winthrop to return to the cabin, but just in case, Smith Garnes and a deputy remained at the hideout. And they had the CB. The reception was terrible but they'd been able to make their words known. Winthrop had not returned.

In another hour it would start getting light. The others finished their coffee and began getting ready.

"Do you think he survived the cold?" Diane asked. She started donning a thick down coat.

"He's lived in these woods his whole life," Sam said. "He's probably alive. I'm more worried he found some way to get out."

"Not likely," Svegman said. "We've got conservation officers patrolling those rural maintenance roads and we've already picked up the other vehicles. If he gets out he'll have to walk a week to do it."

Sam knew the old man was tough enough to last until dawn. But he also knew he'd been forced from the cabin so quickly he'd run without getting properly equipped. "We'll pick up his trail. I suspect we'll find him before noon."

The others readied for their return to the woods and cold.

CHAPTER THIRTY-FIVE

The hybrids cornered the deer in a thicket. While the rest of the wolf-dogs faced the wavering antlers, the Arctic came up behind the animal and fastened his widening jaws onto its hindquarters. The lead wolf thought the buck would fall, but one powerful hoof kick sent him through the air with his mouth full of deer hair and a piece of torn hide. Then the buck crashed through the brush and was ahead of them. The Arctic managed to rise and in a few minutes assumed the lead again.

The wolves pounded through thick woods and the leader sensed the deer's tiredness. The snow was deep and the buck's hooves, unlike the wolf webbed paws, was unable to skitter across the white surface. Its torn hindquarter was a ragged flesh wound, bleeding as it ran. The predators couldn't see the blood, which froze as soon as it fell and was covered over by dry powder. But it left a scent trail through the dark night air that intensified the wolves' yearning.

The Arctic raced at a steady sprint. The hybrids followed close behind. They moved through the trees as one tight pack of hunger and purpose.

In the darkness Williston Winthrop struggled through the snow, trying to keep his balance. His chest felt raspy and it was difficult to catch his breath. In the abject darkness spots floated across his vision and he did not know where to turn. For the last few hours he had been hiking at a good, steady rate, sometimes crawling to get through a wall of black spruce or alder, then stopping long enough to recover, then starting again, until he felt the oncoming need to lie down and sleep.

But not here, he told himself, knowing the desire to sleep was the first sign of hypothermia. He was still cogent enough to know if he lay down he would never rise. He continued through the dark, stumbling, reckoning his direction by the stars, heading north. He didn't have any matches. He couldn't return to their cabin. He had to keep moving as far from the cabin and Skinwalker's Bog as possible. His only hope was to find some remote cabin that he could break into, get himself thawed, maybe find some food and something to drink and figure out a way to get across the border.

If he had any hope of reaching the border he would have to keep pushing. Finally, he stopped long enough to listen in the dark. There was nothing behind him. He found a large fir tree and managed to crawl in beneath the lower boughs to where the falling snow had not penetrated. There was a small cave and he sat for a while catching his breath, listening. He set the shotgun's barrel beside him in the dark, careful to keep his full attention focused on the sound. It was then he began noticing the cold and his considerable weariness.

But I cannot stop, he suddenly thought, in an increasingly rare lucid moment. It was the only coherent thought he could manage as he gasped to take in more air.

He clawed at his chest. Under the considerable layers of clothes he thought he felt warm enough to perspire. He had never traveled through woods like this, hell-bent on escape, with fear driving him like a wild animal. He had been blind, walking in the dark. His face was raw where branches had cut it. But there was no other option, run into the woods, north to Canada. A long ways, a Herculean marathon, but not impossible, providing he could find some remote cabin, break in, warm himself, rest and get together the necessary supplies. Was it even possible?

He laughed, but the exhalation of air made him bend over in a fit of coughing. After it subsided he reached up and again tried to take in more air. He was exhausted but knew he had to move.

He crawled out from under the tree boughs and was immediately struck by a sense of warming air. It was getting warmer, wasn't it? He thought maybe it was a southern warm front coming in. Unseasonable, but lucky. He'd been lucky.

He stomped forward not more than fifty paces before realizing he'd forgotten the shotgun, what was left of it, now only the gnarled steel barrel. But what was left of it could still be a formidable weapon in the hands of someone who knew how to use it.

He retraced his steps, stumbling back over them. But they didn't return him to the place he had just been. Was he disoriented? It was still dark in the woods. In places he had trouble following the tracks. Twice he came to trees he thought might be the one, but both times their understory cave was empty. He started laughing. The laughing brought on another fit of coughing and he doubled over in the cold.

He bent over, coughing into the snow, tasting blood and wondering if the stream of spittle hanging from his mouth was red.

He stepped forward, wearily entering the dark. He guessed the posse would not follow in the night. Few were man enough to follow Williston Winthrop through Skinwalker's Bog. Angus Moon could do it. Bill Grebs, maybe. But Winthrop hadn't known many men his caliber. He stumbled ahead in the dark and knew the abominable cold and deep snow and complete darkness were his friends. They were trying to set him free and he was going to let them.

A sharp pain cut across his chest and he reached up to claw at it. He paused long enough for the pain to subside. He tried to listen in the dark but heard nothing. He hit the side of his head wondering if he were losing his sense of hearing along with his sight, because he heard a vague high-pitched whine.

After a moment he felt strong enough to continue and took a few more steps through the deep snow.

The Arctic was the first to reach the deer. The large buck was cornered in another thicket, no place to turn. The wolves crept up slowly, watching the deer's breath cloud the frozen air. Its antlered head was bent forward, ready to fend off a frontal assault. Instinctively the hybrids moved around the animal. They kept it corralled but were careful to keep out of the reach of its horns. Twice the animal bucked forward looking for a way to break through the menacing gray line. Twice the hybrids came together like a wall.

Finally, the big Arctic worked in behind the animal's kicking hindquarters. He saw his opportunity and leaped forward with purpose, jaws open. He fastened himself near the place where he'd earlier torn flesh. He could smell the bloody wound, taste the small measure of it. He clamped down hard and let his full body weight hang heavy on the deer's backside.

This time, coincident with the leader's leap, two pack members crouched forward on either side of the wavering horns. The deer hunched down with the big wolf on its hindquarters, too tired to kick. It shifted its horns to the left and right, heaving in the snow.

Then the fourth hybrid lunged unexpectedly and fastened itself on the back of the deer's heavily muscled neck. The deer arched, hoping to catch the hybrid with a thrust of horns. The wolf-dog felt the horns cut into the gray fur and it was forced off the animal, but the action of arching left the underside of the deer's throat exposed and another wolf-dog moved in.

Under the weight of three wolves the exhausted animal toppled in the snow. The hybrid on the front clamped down on the deer's windpipe until the animal ceased to breathe and lay still.

The big wolf licked the blood from the hindquarter wound. He whined. The others whined and worried over the dead animal. They had felled deer before, knowing how to quarry and kill. But until Angus gave the OK they had never been allowed to feed. Now they worried and their tails wagged over their kill. The Arctic moved in and began to feed.

Williston Winthrop stumbled forward. Ahead, he thought he heard whining. He was exhausted, his breathing short and ragged. His tongue was parched, scratchy. Each breath rasped at his chest, the frozen air taken with difficulty, but he continued stumbling forward.

He thought he heard whining. Or was it the sound of small children? He heard them in the dark. The woods were thick and he moved toward the sound. Where there were children there would be shelter. And with shelter, warmth. The prospect compelled him and he pushed through tree branches, lurching ahead.

The lead wolf was the first to hear something breaking through the thicket. There was almost no wind, so they didn't smell or notice the approach. Now the Arctic could sense the familiar, complete stink of him.

The man moved forward as though he were blind. The Arctic watched him through intense yellow eyes. The man stumbled five paces until he was almost upon them. The lead wolf sensed weakness but the other wolf-dogs skirted around to the opposite side of the deer, moving away from where they'd begun to feed. They were hungry and had their first independent taste of blood, but the man frightened them. The Arctic did not move. He lowered his head, watched and waited.

"Dogs," the man managed, without authority, barely audible.

The leader cowered before the word. But it was a weak sound uttered from a weakened animal. And now the big Arctic leaned into the sound, creeping forward in the dark.

The man wavered, practically walking into the deer. In one easy motion the Arctic struck the man full force, knocking him back in the snow. The man fell over and lay on his back struggling for breath, clearly exhausted, his arms thrashing. The wolf recognized opportunity and with instinctual precision moved in and took it.

EPILOGUE

FEBRUARY 3ᴿᴰ, MID-MORNING—VERMILION COUNTY SHERIFF'S OFFICE
AND ANGUS MOON'S CABIN

By late Monday morning three deputies, led by Smith Garnes, stumbled onto Williston Winthrop's body. They found the nearby remnants of the deer carcass and plenty of blood and tracks. But the wolves were gone. All except Williston Winthrop, who was a frozen, bloodless hump in the arctic cold.

Smith Garnes climbed to a copse of rock rising out of Skinwalker's Bog, not far from Williston Winthrop's body. Garnes was able to send out a crackling message. They'd found the man. He'd been killed by wolves. Word spread quickly. Sam was with Dean Goddard when the call came in. Sam wanted to know about it, and Smith told him everything he could. Sam Rivers felt certain it was the hybrids. It would be extraordinary behavior for wild wolves. But given that Williston Winthrop may have stumbled onto a fresh kill and he was in the middle of deep wilderness, it was possible, Sam guessed. He asked Smith Garnes to obtain whatever hair samples he could find.

The Sheriff's prediction with regard to Hal Young had been spot on. Around dawn the quiet insurance agent began telling them everything. At least everything he knew. Grebs discovered James Beauregard trying to warm himself in the abandoned Iron Rail depot near the edge of Defiance. He mistook him for Williston, thinking it was some kind of prank. When he realized the man was a vagrant, Bill Grebs saw what could be done. Hal Young confessed about the plan to kill Jimbo. He told them about Angus and Williston's evening walk toward the tracks, and the insurance angle. Hal Young didn't know anything about Pine Grove Estates or that Williston had been swindling Range spinsters for more than a decade.

The insurance man also explained about the hybrids. Angus Moon had a breeding area behind his cabin, back in the woods. Before unleashing them on the calves he'd nailed each of them into their dilapidated quarters and gave them nothing but water for two days. The Club believed the controversy would cover their tracks and provide actual evidence wolves were getting more plentiful and dangerous. Williston Winthrop wanted a return to the days of wolf bounties, or at the very least to have the vermin removed from the Endangered Species List.

Hal Young didn't know everything, but he knew plenty. After sharing all the details with Dean Goddard and Smith Garnes he appeared sallow-eyed and gray-faced. He was beginning to realize he was looking at serious time.

Hank Gunderson was the next to fall.

Bill Grebs refused to answer any of their questions and had requested a lawyer. Angus Moon was belligerent and threatening and would have likely killed someone, or something, if given the chance.

On Monday morning Sam received a call from Sheriff Goddard.

"Enjoying our warm spell?" the Sheriff asked.

The Canadian cold front had retreated and it was a balmy 25 degrees Fahrenheit, swimsuit weather by Defiance standards.

"Feels like Colorado."

"Where are you?" the Sheriff asked.

"Ranger's Café, having a little breakfast, plotting my future."

Sam was up to his usual habits, compiling a list of advantages and disadvantages. The college ruled notebook lay open in front of him, next to the cup of coffee the waitress kept filling. There were several items listed on both sides of the ledger. A few crossed out. A few had lines indicating order changes, while others had been rephrased. He was trying to determine if he should move forward with the national field agent job and the Interagency Task Force. It was Monday and Sam Rivers owed Kay Magdalen a call. But he wasn't ready to make it. Not yet. After considering his list he noticed Diane's name wasn't on it. That was interesting. It led him to remember the previous evening, in which they both spent a good long while with the sex, making up for lost time. This morning, too.

Sam appreciated Diane. The sex was . . . well . . . the sex caused him to remember what had been missing from his life. Diane made him remember a person's skin was the body's largest organ, though she brought all of him alive. Still, the reason she wasn't on his list was because she wasn't part of his long-term equation. She was part of something, but Sam wasn't sure what. And he knew this decision he had to make alone.

Dean knew all about Sam's employment opportunity with the USFW. "Take the job," he advised. "You're a natural."

"Uh-huh." He appreciated the comment, though it wouldn't impact his decision.

"I wonder if you can do me a favor?" Dean asked.

"Name it."

"Can you go out to Angus Moon's cabin? I need some physical evidence of those kennels and his work breeding hybrids. And we need some samples we can tie to those hybrids and the calf kill."

"No problem, Sheriff. I'll head out now. I don't seem to be making much headway here."

The Sheriff gave him directions. It was at least a half hour drive involving plenty of remote turns. Sam Rivers looked forward to cruising through the Northern Minnesota woods. It would give him time to think.

Angus Moon's place was set so far back into a stand of Norway pines it was invisible from the road. The entrance was marked by a lone, rusted mailbox with "R.R. 8" scrawled on its side. If you'd been moving down the road with any speed you would have passed it. The driveway turned up through the trees and disappeared.

Sam turned up the drive, genuinely interested in what he was going to find. He couldn't imagine Angus Moon's place. Or rather, none of what he imagined was pleasant.

After a couple hundred feet his jeep topped a tree-covered hill. At the bottom of the hill rested the dilapidated double-wide. There was a small clearing with two rusted-out cars almost completely covered with snow. There was a small path to some steps that climbed to a scarred white metal door. An antenna stuck out like a skeletal hand above the trailer's faded brown trim. Sam followed the driveway down to a closed garage. To the right of the garage there was another snow-covered vehicle, sitting like an old carcass. The fresh snow made it all appear clean and preternaturally white. But Sam could easily imagine the scene in deep summer, dirty and unkempt.

None of what he found at Angus Moon's surprised him. It was a northwoods hideout more than a cabin. The rusting hulks, the battered, faded double-wide, even the small antenna reaching out of its roof reminded Sam of the desultory woodsman's life. He was a wild, dangerous man and if a woman had ever seen this place she would have turned and run screaming through the trees.

As soon as Sam got out of his jeep he could smell the pungent odor of the kennel. Judging from the absence of a single whine or rustle the kennels were empty, or their inhabitants dead. He pulled a few baggies off the front seat, stuffed them into his coat pocket and walked up through the snow to examine the trailer's front door. The aluminum doorknob was locked. He peered through the front door window, but the frosted glass was opaque. He knocked, though knew no one would answer. While he waited, just to be sure, he took a closer look at the door. If he wanted, he could easily enter the place. A simple shoulder in the top center would break it open. But he didn't have a warrant, and he didn't want to jeopardize any evidence, and besides, the breeding operation was up in the woods behind the trailer. Dean Goddard asked him to check out the kennel, not the man's living space, though Sam was curious.

The trail into the woods was easy to find. He climbed up the icy path through the trees. Fifty yards back he saw the small shelters and three or four fenced-in outdoor pens. As he approached, even in the cold, the fetid reek of the hybrids' confinement was strong. It was feces, wolf urine, with maybe a subtext of glandular fear, if such a thing was possible; it became more overpowering the closer he came to the dilapidated compound.

Earlier, when he'd heard how Angus Moon had nailed each hybrid into a small house, he'd been outraged. He couldn't imagine the hybrids' lives, or the Arctic or Malamute who bred them. Or rather, he guessed it was similar to his own childhood, only worse. The thought of it made him hunger for a swifter and more exacting revenge than the slow wheels of the criminal justice system. But he would settle for prison, recognizing a cage would be the best punishment for a man like Angus Moon.

Still, to bring a living animal into this world, in these environs, and to know nothing but Angus Moon's ugly perspective on the world, would be a living hell. Sam Rivers knew life was difficult enough without being handicapped by a man like Moon. He had to remind himself he was here to help put the man away forever, and try and be appeased, if not entirely satisfied with the effort.

He approached the nearest house and saw the plane of snow where it covered a plywood board. Probably the covering Angus nailed over the nearest house, Sam thought. He moved to the front of the house and saw hair along the scarred wooden edge. He bent down and started pulling a sample from the ragged wood.

Something stirred inside.

Sam jumped back. He thought maybe a wild creature had moved into the house to get out of the cold. But what kind of creature would dare venture into a wolf den, when the smell was overpowering and where it would be almost certain to be killed and eaten? Some snow shook loose across the threshold, surfacing a heavy chain, angled down over the worn wooden lip of the entrance.

There was another move from inside the house, though not hurried.

Sam stepped back a little further, peering inside. And then he saw the weak, small head turn and peer out of the dark opening. One of its eyes was cobalt blue. The other wolf yellow. Its head was in the shape of a wolf. Something between a wolf pup and a youngster, maybe just 4 months old? Weighted down by a chain, its head hung low as it peered suspiciously into the bright morning.

"Hey," Sam said.

The chain hung from a makeshift rope collar. The animal peered up, but didn't react to his voice. Its face was gaunt and its forward limb, at least what Sam could see, was thin and spindly. But its paw was big. If it was a pup, it was going to be a big hybrid, providing it survived the day.

"Come on out here," Sam said, softly.

Something like a glint of recognition came into its tired eyes. Something like hope, though Sam couldn't see for sure. Sam looked around, wondering if the animal had water, wondering when it was last fed. He would have to get it some water and find out where Moon kept the dog food. He remembered the shed beside the garage and was about ready to retreat and get this creature some food when it moved forward, just a little. Its gaunt, large head came forward and peered out of the house opening. It eyed Sam with suspicion, clearly in a weakened state. But it came forward, one step out of the house with its head poised over its paw. Then it grew tired and lay down, unable to continue. Its chain pulled against the rope collar, but it could only lay in submission.

Sam came forward, cautious but feeling pity. He would have to determine if the dog could be saved. It appeared to have a gentle demeanor, which would have been incredible given its life until now. But the only way to tell for sure was to get it healthy and spend some time with the animal. Sam found the nearby water bowl turned over and covered with a dusting of snow. He kneeled down in front of the young dog. When he did, the dog managed to lift its head. From back in the house Sam heard a tail lift and drop, lift and drop. Then it was still.

Sam squinted to the back of the house and saw another dog's body, unmoving, clearly dead.

"Let's get you out of here. But first let me get you some water and food."

On the way back to the trailer he banged the ice out of the bottom of the water bowl. It shattered against a tree. He retreated down the icy path, retracing his steps to the trailer's front door. He didn't know where Angus Moon kept fresh water, but he was certain he could find some in the double-wide. He did not pause on the front step, setting his shoulder into door's top center. The latch shattered and the cheap metal entrance swung open.

It was a simple, surprisingly clean cabin, but he did not pause to consider it. He glanced to his right, found the small kitchen, walked across the threadbare carpet and started the sink spigot. He filled the bowl, returned up the path, and laid it in front of the young dog. As soon as it smelled water it raised its head and came out far enough to bend and drink. At first it was tentative and weak. But once it tasted the water its tongue seemed to strengthen from the refreshment. Its head bent in earnest and it lapped and lapped.

"Take it easy. You're going to get sick."

But the dog didn't listen.

Sam retreated down the icy path to the shed. He opened the door and found three large bags of kibble, one of them opened. The shed was filled with an assortment of odds and ends, including several foothold traps hanging from nails in the sidewall. Sam found a scoop in the opened bag. There was a small stack of bowls. He took one and filled it with kibble. On his way out he grabbed a pair of bolt cutters. He wasn't sure where that chain went, but he knew he was going to free the pup.

Back at the dog house the pup looked energized by the water. As soon as it got a whiff of the kibble it started whining. Sam set the bowl down in front of it and the dog took a lunging bite of the food, wolfing it down. Then another.

The chain impaired its ability to eat. Sam took the bolt cutters to where the last link disappeared into the house. He affixed the tip of the cutters into the link, closed the two handles and the link snapped, the chain freed. As if in answer the pup's head came all the way up, but it didn't hesitate or alter its focus. It returned to the bowl, hurriedly wolfing down mouthfuls of kibble.

Sam watched the dog eat. It was going to be a big dog, if it survived. He'd never seen such a scruffy animal. And its coat was matted and thick, dirty from being inside the filthy house. He watched it turn around the bowl, no longer impeded or held back by the chain. Sam leaned down and looked into the house and saw what appeared to be a pure bred Malamute. Probably the female Angus Moon used to breed the hybrids. This one's mother, Sam guessed. It was dead, frozen in the house. The poor, hungry pup in front of him had been chained into the house beside his dying, then dead, mother.

It sickened Sam Rivers. It reminded him why he was here. He took out the baggies and while the pup finished the kibble Sam turned to the other houses and gathered more hair samples. If he hadn't needed the samples and the evidence he would have returned to the shed, found some gasoline and torched the stinking houses.

When the pup finished the kibble it moved back to the bowl of water and finished it, too. Sam waited to see if he'd keep it down. It was a male and it peered at him with the most beautiful pair of mixed-colored eyes. If Sam was any judge of dogs this one's demeanor conveyed cooperation. He considered it, and realized it was probably an offspring from a recent litter, but, he guessed Angus Moon had been unable to sell it since it appeared to be more Malamute than wolf and had heterochromia, two different-colored eyes, a relatively rare occurrence.

"Come here," he said, bending a little and beckoning with his hand.

The dog came forward, shy, its head lowered, tail between its legs, wagging a little, uncertain.

Sam did not have to tell the pup to follow him. After gathering and marking the fur samples, Sam returned to the shed. The pup trailed a cautious distance behind him. Sam found some brushes in the shed. The dog was remarkably sweet for a hybrid. Perhaps he hadn't yet come into his wolf heritage. Or maybe he had simply gotten more of his mother than his Arctic father. Whatever, Sam spent a half hour brushing the puppy, who seemed to know Sam meant no harm. He enjoyed being groomed. Unusually, he did not whine or turn away, but sat stoically while Sam brushed out the clumps, the matted fur, the pieces of god-knew-what, mixed in with hay and wood chips.

"You're going to need a bath, for starters," Sam said. "And a checkup."

The dog's tail wagged when Sam spoke. Sam smiled. "Your one eye is a lot like Charlie's," Sam said, a little wistful, remembering his friend. The dog's tail wagged.

Back on the road the dog sat beside him on the passenger seat. Sam rolled down the two rear windows to provide ventilation. He had the heater blasting in the front. The dog sat still, happy to be in the jeep. Sam guessed it was the first time the pup had ever been in a car, had probably never been away from the compound. It was remarkably calm, had a kind of natural regal demeanor, watching the snowy world go by. It was gaunt but alert now, since it had eaten and drank.

Near town Sam phoned Diane.

"Sam," she said.

"Finished with that article?"

"Finished the first one by noon. The editor's damn happy about it. Now I'm working on some background pieces, for tomorrow and the day after. People are going to want to know about this. It's a huge story and I have the exclusive. You couldn't make up a story like this," she said, happily.

"Can you do me a favor?"

"Haven't I proved that already?"

Sam smiled. "Do you know any vets in the area?"

"Sure. People tell me Dave O'Connor's a good one. His office is on the edge of Vermilion Falls."

"Can you get me a number?"

"Sure."

He waited while she looked it up. When she found it he pulled over and wrote it down.

"Why do you want a vet?"

"Found a pup out at Moon's place, needs some tending."

"You coming now?"

"Figured I would. Then I need to go over to the Sheriff's office."

"What are you doing later?"

"Later?"

"After the Sheriff. I still owe you a drink and a meal. Maybe you should come over and I'll fix you some dinner and we can celebrate?"

"I can do that." He imagined her lips.

"Pick up some akvavit, would you?"

There was a pause. It'd been a long time since he'd had the pleasure of a woman's intimate company. "That's a dangerous mixture."

"I wasn't going to mix anything with it. Just going to have it straight up."

He thought she smiled, over the phone. "I'll pick it up."

On the way to the vet's office he finally phoned Kay Magdalen.

"Magdalen," she answered, gravelly, her voice short.

"Kay. Sam Rivers."

"Of course it's Sam Rivers. I've already got them putting your name-plate on your new office. Don't disappoint me."

Sam smiled. "I want a raise and I need some special allowances."

"Rivers," she said, a little miffed. "Anyone ever told you you're a pain in the ass and high maintenance?"

He could tell she was pleased. "Only you."

"The raise is already in the works. That's a given. What allowances?"

"I'm thinking the office needs a mascot. How do you think the Service would feel about me having a dog?"

"At the office?"

"Yeah. At the office? Like in Europe. And didn't the Service once look at using dogs in the field?"

"This is Denver. Not Denmark. And I don't remember the Service ever using dogs in the field."

"I may need the allowance," he said, matter of fact. So she would know he was serious.

There was a long pause. Finally, she said, "OK, Rivers. We'll look into it. Just get your ass back here."

"The Sheriff needs me to stay and clear up a few details. I suspect I'll have to be here at least through next weekend."

There was another pause. This time he could hear Kay's exasperation over the phone.

"Consider it community-law enforcement relations," Sam added, but he was thinking about Diane.

"Goddamnit, Rivers." There was another pause. "Did you plan on doing any work when you returned?"

"Whatever you need, Kay."

"Damn right," came her gravelly reply.

Sam Rivers smiled.

ABOUT THE AUTHOR

Cary J. Griffith is the author of two nonfiction books, *Lost in the Wild* (2006) and *Opening Goliath* (2009). In 2010 *Opening Goliath* was the recipient of a Minnesota Book Award. This is his first published novel.

ALSO BY CARY J. GRIFFITH
Lost in the Wild
Opening Goliath (winner of a 2010 Minnesota Book Award)